won him the Roald Dahl Funny Prize, is author of numerous books including these award-winning Eddie Dickens adventures, which have been translated into over 30 languages. He wrote BBC Radio's first truly interactive radio drama, collaborated with Sir Paul McCartney on his first children's book and is a 'regularly irregular' reviewer of children's books for the *Guardian*. Married with a son, he lives in Tunbridge Wells, where he cultivates his impressive beard.

Philip Ardagh

The Further Adventures of Eddie Dickens

Illustrated by David Roberts

FABER & FABER

This edition first published in 2014
by Faber and Faber Limited
Bloomsbury House, 74–77 Great Russell Street
London WC1B 3DA

Typeset by Faber and Faber Limited
Printed and bound by CPI Group (UK) Ltd, Croydon, CR0 4YY

Philip Ardagh is hereby identified as author of this work in accordance
with Section 77 of the Copyright, Designs and Patents Act 1988

'McMuffin' is a registered trademark of the McDonald's Corporation

A CIP record for this book
is available from the British Library

ISBN 978-0571-31053-1

FSC
www.fsc.org
MIX
Paper from
responsible sources
FSC® C101712

2 4 6 8 10 9 7 5 3 1

Foreword

In which the author blathers on about this and that whilst you skip the page

It's hard for me to remember a time without Eddie Dickens. I wrote the very first Eddie Dickens adventure in the late 1990s as a series of letters to my nephew, Ben; it was published as *Awful End* in 2000; and the final Further Adventure was published in 2006. But it didn't end there. Eddie ended up being published in over thirty languages – each foreign-language edition using David Roberts's fantastic illustrations – and I still get to travel the globe today because of that one boy, his crazy relatives and six adventures. So, yup, Eddie Dickens really did change my life.

And, over these years, I've often been asked who's my favourite character and I've always skirted around the issue, pussyfooted about, and mixed my metaphors. Here's the truth: I love Even Madder Aunt Maud and her stuffed stoat Malcolm, which is why what happens in these Further Adventures is all the more shocking . . . Now read on!

PHILIP ARDAGH
England, 2014

Contents

Dubious Deeds

Book One of the Further Adventures of
Eddie Dickens Trilogy

*This one's for
Scottish Lassie, Tessa MacGregor,
and for Aussie Sheila, Louise Sherwin-Stark.
A big professional 'thank you' to you both.*

A Message from the Author

Who's glad to be back

Eddie Dickens is back and this time he's angry! Well, that's not strictly true, but it'd be a good line to have running along the bottom of the poster if this were a movie.

Eddie's adventures didn't end with the Eddie Dickens Trilogy. Life had a lot more in store for him, and here's the first of his Further Adventures. *Dubious Deeds* finds Eddie where I am right now, in the heathery Highlands of Scotland. He may be away from the familiar surroundings of Awful End but you can be sure that his family are very much in mind.

So raise your stuffed stoats in the air and let the story commence . . .

PHILIP ARDAGH
Scotland, 2003

Contents

Episode 1

The Tartan Tiger

In which Eddie sets foot in a strange country and in warm horse manure

Scotland was nothing like Eddie Dickens had imagined because Eddie Dickens had never imagined Scotland. All things Scottish were all the rage when Eddie arrived in the heathery Highlands, but no one could accuse the Dickens family of being swayed by fashion. Eddie was there on business. One of Scotland's biggest fans in those days was Queen Victoria, who was on the throne at the time, except for when she nipped to the loo or made public appearances, thus giving her subjects the opportunity to try to assassinate her (which was also a popular pastime in those days). Victoria (whose first name was really Alexandrina) had a castle in Scotland and once had a Scottish ghillie as her favourite. If you're wondering whether a ghillie is fish, fowl or geological feature, I should tell you that the answer is 'none of the above'. A ghillie is a Scottish servant, and Queen Victoria's Scottish servant was a rather tall, hairy chap called John Brown who is one of the few Scottish characters in this book whose name doesn't begin with 'Mac' or 'Mc'.

The Scotsman who greeted Eddie at the tiny railway station was also very hairy but was very, very small indeed.

'I'm McFeeeeeeee,' he said, lifting Eddie's carpetbag down from the railway carriage which, if you're an American, you'd probably call a 'railroad car', but it's the same difference. Either way, it was pulled by that famous London-to-Scotland locomotive, the *Tartan Tiger*.

The way the little ginger-haired man said 'McFeeeeeeee' made Eddie suspect that it was spelled with seven 'e's, but he was wrong. There were eight and, if you don't believe me, you can count them. See?

Eddie used to travel with a large trunk but – ever since a nasty incident where Even Madder Aunt Maud (who was really his *great*-aunt) had stowed away on board a ship inside it he now liked to travel with luggage that was smaller than his smallest relative, thus ensuring none of them could be hiding inside.

'A pleasure to meet you, Mr McFeeeeeeee,' said Eddie.

'That should be eight "e"s,' said Mr McFeeeeeeee.

'I beg your pardon?' said Eddie, stepping on to the platform, closing the door of the railway carriage behind him.

'You said my name as though it were spelled with only seven "e"s, Master Edmund, and there are eight,' Angus McFeeeeeeee explained. He spoke with a very broad Scottish accent. Actually, he spoke with his mouth, but the words that came out were in broad Scots.

'I beg your pardon,' Eddie repeated, but as an apology this time rather than meaning 'what-do-you-mean?' . . . if you see what *I* mean?

'I forgive you,' said McFeeeeeeee, 'what with you being a wee Sassenach and all.'

'A wee whaty-what?' Eddie asked politely. He had discovered early on in life that, if you don't understand something or know what's going on, it's best to ask . . . or who knew where it might lead?

'A Sassenach is someone not from the Highlands,' explained McFeeeeeeee. 'A foreigner.'

'I've never been a foreigner before,' Eddie confessed. He didn't feel any different, which, the truth be told, made him feel a little disappointed.

'You've always been a wee foreigner to me,' the man pointed out.

'I suppose I must have been,' said Eddie. 'Funny to think that I've always been a foreigner to some people, without really thinking about it.'

Back in VR's day – VR being short for *Victoria Regina* which was Latin for 'Queen Victoria' but using up more letters of the alphabet *and* italics – the English thought that everyone else in their right minds would want to be English too, so being a foreigner was being second best. And shifty. And untrustworthy.

And here was McFeeeeeeee not only calling him a foreigner, but a wee one. Eddie knew what 'wee' meant – apart from *that*, of course. It meant 'small' and he thought it was a bit of a cheek to be

10

called a 'wee' anything by a fully grown man who was actually smaller than he was *and* who, with that tartan tam-o'-shanter on his head, resembled nothing more than a hairy mushroom!

A tam-o'-shanter is a type of hat. (Have a look at the picture of McFeeeeeeee, which should be around here somewhere if I remembered to ask the illustrator to draw one.) Tartan – a checked pattern – requires a little more explanation but, have no fear, one of the characters will do that later, thus saving me the bother of having to do so now. (I have plants to water and cats to feed.)

Mr Angus McFeeeeeeee was the Dickens family lawyer in Scotland. Like the Queen, the Dickens family – or, to be more precise, Mad Uncle Jack and Even Madder Aunt Maud – had property in Scotland but, unlike Her Majesty, they very rarely went there. They preferred to stay in their treehouse and hollow cow, respectively, back in the garden of Awful End (where Eddie now lived with his parents).

Back in the days when Even Madder Aunt Maud was no one's mad aunt, let alone an even madder *great*-aunt, she was just plain Mad Mrs Jack Dickens. You may think that 'Jack' was an odd name for a woman, especially one called Maud, but married women were referred to by their husbands' first as well as last names. (It's true,

I tell you!) If you were married to a Bill Bloggs, you were called Mrs Bill Bloggs. Before Maud had married, though, her maiden – unmarried – name had been MacMuckle so, until she and Jack Dickens tied the knot, she was plain Mad Maud MacMuckle.

('Tying the knot' is another way of saying 'getting married', by the way, and probably dates back to some strange knot-tying ritual but I've no idea what, and the thought of knot-tying doesn't excite me enough to go and look it up. If, however, string is your thing, then perhaps you could investigate this one for yourself, string and knots being so closely associated. But please leave me out of it. I don't want to get involved. Don't write and tell me the answer. *Please*. I mean it. If I really wanted to know that badly, I could always visit the Rope Museum at Mickleham Priory and see if anyone there knows. After all, rope is really very fat string, isn't it? But 'very fat string' sounds stupid, so someone came up with another name for it. And, anyway, perhaps it was a *hanky* which had a knot tied in it in this marriage ritual and not string – fat or otherwise – at all.)

Meanwhile, back in the adventure: according to Even Madder Aunt Maud, the MacMuckle family had once owned huge swathes of Scotland (not that Eddie knew what a swathe was) and a number of very fine Scottish properties. Now, however, all that was left in family hands was Tall Hall by the MacMuckle Falls, which Maud had inherited and, therefore, by law now belonged to her husband. (In other words, if a woman was lucky enough to get married back then, all she ended up with was her husband's names and all he ended up with was everything she owned: property, money, everything! Unless, of course, your name was Queen Victoria, then the rules were conveniently different.)

Apparently, Tall Hall by the MacMuckle Falls was more than just a manor house but less than a castle. The clue is in the name. The MacMuckles had started to build it with a castle in mind, and had got as far as erecting some very fine, tall walls but then the money had run out, so they put an ordinary roof on it. There were no exciting battlements or turrets. Hence Tall Hall. The MacMuckle Falls that Tall Hall was next to was rather a grand name for a rather unimpressive waterfall.

'It was more like a burst pipe than one of Nature's wonders,' Even Madder Aunt Maud had told Eddie before his departure. Soon he'd find out for himself, because Tall Hall by the MacMuckle Falls was Eddie's destination but, for impatient readers, here's a picture of both the house and the falls in the meantime:

Hasn't that nice illustrator David Roberts done a lovely job, as always? He should think about taking up drawing professionally.

Those of you who've read the Eddie Dickens Trilogy – hi there, I thought I recognised you – will be aware that, more often than not, Eddie never reaches his destination or takes a very, very long time getting there, so you may be pleasantly surprised to learn that Eddie will reach Tall Hall by the MacMuckle Falls near the beginning of Episode 3. Author's honour. Which is the same as 'scout's honour', except from an author who was never in the scouts. Perhaps I should have said 'on my honour', which is nice and old-fashioned and fits in with the feel of this 'Further Adventure'.

'When will we reach Tall Hall, Mr McFeeeeeeee?' Eddie asked the Scottish lawyer as he followed him out of the tiny country station and into a lane, where a pony and trap was waiting for them.

'You're to spend the night in my house and tomorrow I shall take you there,' said Mr McFeeeeeeee. 'And that was nine "e"s you used just then to say my name, Master Edmund. Don't you go overdoing it now, laddie.'

'It's an unusual name, Mr McFeeeeeeee,' said Eddie, being extremely careful to get it right this time. (Angus McFeeeeeeee obviously had a very keen ear when it came to the pronunciation of his name.)

The lawyer shook his head. 'Not in these parts it ain't, laddie, though the spelling is. There's many a McFee and MacFee – with an "m-*a*-c" – in the Highlands, but ours is the only branch of the clan with quite so many "e"s.' Eddie could hear the pride in the little man's voice.

McFeeeeeeee put Eddie's carpetbag in the back of the trap and climbed into the driver's seat. Eddie jumped up behind him. With a flick of the reins, they were off.

'What exactly is a clan?' asked Eddie.

'A tribe. A family,' Angus McFeeeeeeee explained. 'My particular branch of the family were fearsome fighters. Back in the days when we were openly at war with you English, my ancestors used to be famous for jumping out of trees on to unsuspecting English soldiers riding beneath them . . . and strangling them with their bare hands.'

'H-H-How interesting,' said Eddie, politely. He looked at the tiny, mushroom-like man at the reins of the pony and trap and couldn't imagine him coming from fearsome fighter stock.

'My ancestors wanted their victims to know which clan had defeated them before they gasped their last breath,' Angus McFeeeeeeee continued. 'So, as they jumped from their treeeeeeees, they shouted McFeeeeeeee!'

'And their battle-cry became your unique branch of the family name? Amazing,' said Eddie. 'What about the MacMuckles? Did they go around killing the English too?'

The lawyer frowned, his eyebrows – like two furry ginger caterpillars – forming a 'v' above his eyes. 'There are those who claim that the MacMuckles *were* English,' he said, as though the word 'English' was something unpleasant, like dog poo. 'There're some historians who argue that they began life as the Mac-less Muckle family and that the "Mac" was added at a later date. Many a true Scot wouldnae have anything to do with them.'

Eddie thought about Even Madder Aunt Maud. She certainly didn't sound Scottish. 'Do people get on with the MacMuckles nowadays?' asked Eddie.

The trap went over a bump as the horse left the lane and set off down a rutted track. Both Angus McFeeeeeeee and Eddieeeeeeee – oops, sorry, that should, of course, be Eddie. I was wondering how long it would be before I got confused – bounced up and down on the wooden bench seat.

'Short cut,' the lawyer explained.

'The MacMuckles,' Eddie repeated. 'Do they get on with their neighbours nowadays?'

'There are no MacMuckles,' said the Scotsman. 'Well, that's not strictly true, of course. I should say that your great-aunt is the last of the MacMuckles; though, technically, she is now a Dickens.'

'The whole family – the whole clan – has died out?' asked Eddie, obviously amazed. 'I'm amazed,' he added, which he needn't have done. (I said it was *obvious* that he was, didn't I?)

'Well, they couldn't keep marrying each other and the other clans wouldnae have anything to do with them, so they eventually began to die out until only your great-aunt was left,' said the lawyer.

'Wow!' mused Eddie. 'So Even Madder Aunt

17

Maud is the Last of the MacMuckles of Tall Hall by the MacMuckle Falls!'

'Errrr,' said Angus McFeeeeeeee, with some embarrassment.

'What is it?' asked Eddie.

'Well . . . er . . . whilst the MacMuckles were still alive and living at Tall Hall, it was called the MacMuckle Falls but, once they'd gone, the locals renamed it.'

'So what's the waterfall called now?' Eddie asked.

'Gudger's Dump.'

'Why Gudger's Dump?' asked Eddie.

'Gudger McCloud was a poacher who made the MacMuckles' lives a misery,' confessed the lawyer, somewhat sheepishly. 'I suspect it's simply that the clans wanted to wipe out all memory of the MacMuckle name and called their so-called waterfall after Gudger to add insult in injury.'

'I get the feeling that Even Madder Aunt Maud's family weren't too popular around here,' Eddie commented.

'About as popular as a conger eel slipped down the end of a bagpipe,' agreed McFeeeeeeee.

Eddie imagined that that must be very unpopular indeed.

They reached a five-bar gate, recently painted white.

'Jump down and open that, would you, laddie?'

asked the lawyer, 'whoaing' the horse.

Eddie stepped out of the trap straight on to a pile of horse manure. It was still warm.

'That's supposed to be good luck, in these parts,' Mr McFeeeeeeee reassured him, but Eddie was pretty sure that he was trying not to laugh.

Episode 2

A Mixed Clan

*In which Eddie meets more McFeeeeeeees
and other local wildlife*

Angus McFeeeeeeee's house seemed very small compared to Awful End and even to the house Eddie had been born in and lived in with his parents before that. (Unlike Awful End, the house Eddie was born in doesn't exist any more. This probably has something to do with the fact that it was burnt to the ground and never rebuilt. Where it once stood is now part of a business park which is probably best known for being the UK headquarters of the company owned by the man who invented those spiky pyjamas which stop the wearer from snoring.) By local standards, however, McFeeeeeeee's house seemed large. The only other dwellings Eddie had laid eyes on during their short pony-and-trap journey were what the lawyer described as 'crofters' cottages': they were small, often round, and usually roughly thatched; the cottages, that is, not the crofters.

'What do crofters do?' Eddie had asked his travelling companion.

'Eat, sleep, drink –' began McFeeeeeeee.

'Crofting?' Eddie'd interrupted. 'What's crofting?'

'Farming,' the lawyer told him.

Mrs McFeeeeeeee was there on the doorstep to greet Master Edmund Dickens all the way from England. She was a McMuffin by birth – no relation to Dr Muffin, who'd caused that fire at the Dickens house I just mentioned, nor of the delicious breakfast products from the McDonald's chain of fast-food restaurants (for whom 'McMuffin', I have no doubt whatsoever, is a registered trademark). Unlike her husband, Mrs McFeeeeeeee was very welcoming indeed.

'How nice to have you here in the Highlands, Master Edmund,' she beamed. 'And how are your dear mad great-uncle and even madder great-aunt?'

'They're very well, thank you, Mrs McFeeeeeeeee –'

'Just the eight "e"s, remember,' Mr McFeeeeeeee interrupted him.

'Sorry,' said Eddie (having lost count). 'They send their regards, Mrs McFeeeeeeee.'

'How kind,' said the jolly woman, ushering Eddie into the house. 'Are they as nutty as ever?'

'As nutty as a fruitcake,' Eddie reassured her and, mark my words, fruitcakes were even nuttier in those days. You could hardly move for nuts. In fact, for a short period during Queen Victoria's reign, they might just as accurately have been called 'nutcakes' as 'fruitcakes'.

Speaking of which, the lawyer's wife now offered Eddie some refreshment. 'You must be hungry after your long journey,' she said.

'Thank you. I am a little,' Eddie confessed, 'though I did eat on the train.' His mother had made him a packed lunch comprised mainly of broad-bean sandwiches, which are, gentle readers, I promise you, as unpleasant as they sound; overcooked broad beans, in their leathery wrinkled skins, between slices of Mrs Dickens's home-made bread.

For the Victorian poor, bread was usually the main part of their diet – in other words, mostly what they ate – and there was lots of skulduggery going on in the making of bread back then to 'bulk it out' so that the bakers could make the maximum amount of money out of the minimum amount of flour. A common trick was to add sawdust and other floor-sweepings. The well-off, however, had their own cooks and servants to make their bread for them, so could usually avoid such nasties. Eddie's mother actually liked to bake her own bread. The problem was that she also liked to add her own special ingredients, which included:

1. ground acorns
2. squirrel droppings (but only from red squirrels, not grey)
4. powdered deer's antler (stolen from one of the many mounted deer's heads on the walls of Awful End)
5. wallpaper paste (a real favourite)
6. watch springs.

Back in the days before watches were battery-powered and quartz-controlled, they had a mechanical clockwork mechanism of many moving parts, and springs were an all-important component of these works. One day, Mrs Dickens had come upon a whole drawer full of such springs and immediately put them to good use, adding a pinch of them to her bread mix every time she baked thereafter. The result? A Mrs Dickens loaf of bread was probably more of a threat to your health than one sold by an unscrupulous baker; the difference being that Eddie's mother *liked* it that way. Eddie, of course, had no choice. The bread of his home-made broad-bean sandwiches was crunchy, to say the least.

Before we get back to Mrs McFeeeeeeee (formerly Miss McMuffin), I thought you might be interested to know that the sandwich was named after the person who's said to have invented the idea of putting a tasty filling between two handy-to-hold slices of bread. You would, therefore, expect that person to have been called Sandwich. It makes sense, doesn't it? If a sandwich is named after the person who invented it, then logic dictates that his name must have been Sandwich? Funnily enough, though, his name was Montagu (without an 'e' on the end). So the sandwich is named after a man called Montagu. Clear? I thought not. Perhaps I should add that he was the *Earl* of Sandwich, which is the name of a place. In fact, there's a place called Sandwich not a million miles from where I live, and there's a place called Ham near by, too. The arm of the signpost pointing in their direction used to read:

**HAM
SANDWICH**

but it was stolen so many times – by people who thought it was funny, I imagine – that it was finally replaced with one that read:

**SANDWICH
HAM**

which isn't nearly as amusing but which still makes you think.

Mrs McFeeeeeeee gave Eddie a large slice of cold game pie and some cold potatoes. 'A wee something to keep you going until supper time,' she said, handing him a large fork, before Mr McFeeeeeeee's man, McDuff, had even had time to bring in Eddie's carpetbag.

25

'Thank you,' said Eddie. He sat on a high-backed chair in the parlour and ate. The meal was delicious.

When Eddie had finished, Mrs McFeeeeeeee asked if he'd like to have a nap, but he said that he'd like to explore. He could really do with stretching his legs after being cooped up in that train for all that time. The countryside was breathtaking, which is another way of saying that it took his breath away, which is another way of saying it made him gasp. It was so dramatic.

Although there are many different parts of Scotland with many different towns, cities and villages, it can be roughly divided into two sections: the Highlands and the Lowlands. One is much hillier and more full of mountains than the other. No prizes for guessing which is which. The Dickens house (formerly the MacMuckle house) in Scotland was, as I've already mentioned, very much in the Highlands, and so was their lawyer's home. From every window, Eddie could see moorlands covered in heather, and blue mountains cutting into the skyline on the horizon (except for from the loo window, which was made of some kind of frosted glass, which meant that Eddie couldn't see anything out of it but the failing daylight).

'Stick to the paths and you cannae go wrong,' Mrs McFeeeeeeee reassured him. 'Apart from the road, the only way from here is up, so, wherever you wander, you won't lose sight of the house down below, and you'll be able to head back towards it. It also means that you'll have a nice downhill walk on your way back.'

Having once been lost on the misty moors back home, Eddie was glad that he'd be able to keep the house in sight. He set off with interest and, after about an hour, sat down on a rocky outcrop by a clump of trees and looked back down into the valley. Smoke was coming from the house's chimney.

'McFeeeeeeeeeeeeeeeeeeeeeeeeeee!' cried a high-pitched voice and someone fell out of the branches of a tree almost directly above Eddie. There was a nasty 'THUD' and a mini-version of Angus McFeeeeeeee leapt to his feet, awkwardly brushing bits of heather and dirt off his clothes.

'Were you planning to try to strangle me with your bare hands?' asked Eddie. He didn't look particularly worried for three reasons:

1. he was used to being around strange people (*aka* 'his family')
2. this boy's hands didn't look big enough to put around Eddie's neck to strangle him, bare or otherwise
3. his uncle lived in a treehouse and had fallen out of it in front of Eddie on more than one occasion, so narrowly avoiding being hit by people falling from trees could be described as a familiar occurrence in Eddie's life.

''Course not,' said the mini-McFeeeeeeee, looking a little shame-faced. He'd probably been hoping to land on Eddie, or frighten him at the very least. 'So you're the English boy, aye?'

'Yes,' said Eddie. 'Is Angus McFeeeeeeee your father? You certainly look like him.'

'Angus McFeeeeeeee is no father of mine,' snapped the boy. 'He works for *English* clients.'

'He works for my great-uncle, if that's what you mean, but I imagine that he must have plenty of Scottish clients too,' Eddie pointed out.

'If I were a lawyer, I wouldnae work for no Englishman,' said the boy. He even spoke just like a high-pitched version of Angus McFeeeeeeee. 'Were you not a wee bit surprised by my sudden appearance from above?'

'Oh, a little,' Eddie lied, politely, just to cheer up the boy. He put out his hand. 'I'm Eddie Dickens,' he said. 'Though I suspect that you already know that.'

'Magnus,' said the boy, though not shaking the offered hand.

'McFeeeeeeee?' asked Eddie. The boy nodded. 'You're not a great fan of us English then?'

'Why should we be ruled by an English queen?' squeaked Magnus defiantly.

'I think she rules most of the world,' Eddie reminded him, which wasn't far from the truth. In those days, the British Empire was spread across much of the world (except Europe) and was shown on maps and globes in pink, as though all these foreign countries were blushing with pride at being ruled over by Her Majesty Queen Victoria.

'It isnae right, I tell you,' Magnus muttered.

'Because she's a woman?' asked Eddie. 'Or because she's English?'

'English, of course!' said little Magnus McFeeeeeeee. 'Bertie is just as bad.' Bertie was Prince Edward, Prince of Wales, which has little to do with being a prince *in* Wales. It was simply the title given to the Queen's eldest son, who was, by birthright, first in line to throne. 'I know a riddle about him,' sniggered Magnus. 'What's the difference between the Prince of Wales, an orphan, a bald-headed man, and a gorilla?'

Eddie was shocked. He suspected that it was rather disrespectful even to try to guess the answers to riddles which included a gorilla and a member of the royal family in the same sentence. 'I've no idea,' he said. 'I think I'd better be heading back down now.' He began his descent of the sloping moorside.

Magnus McFeeeeeeee ran alongside him. 'Do you give up, English?' he demanded.

'I suppose,' said Eddie, secretly intrigued by what the answer might be.

'The Prince of Wales is the heir apparent, an

orphan has ne'er a parent, a bald-headed man has no hair apparent, and the gorilla has a hairy parent.' Magnus grinned, then gave a high-pitched snort, like an excited (Scottish) piglet.

Try as hard as he might, Eddie couldn't hide his smile. Any joke with the phrase 'a hairy parent' in it was quite funny as far as he was concerned. The truth be told, it was quite a good joke for those days, and isn't too bad today, as long as you know that 'heir apparent' means 'next-in-line-to-the-throne' and that 'ne'er' means 'never'.

'Did you make that up yourself, Magnus?' Eddie asked with a sneaking admiration, trudging through the purple heather.

'I didnae,' said the mini-McFeeeeeeee, with a shake of his head. 'But here's one I did: Why will the Queen of England come in handy if you need to measure up for a pair of curtains?'

'I don't know,' said Eddie a little guiltily. 'Why will Queen Victoria come in handy if I need to measure up for a pair of curtains?'

'Because she's a ruler, stupid!' With that, Magnus McFeeeeeeee ran charging ahead of Eddie down the hill. 'McFeeeeeeeeeeeeeeeeeeeeee!' he yelled. If Magnus had been in charge of the original McFeeeeeeee battlecry, Eddie wondered how many 'e's that branch of the clan would have ended up with in their name.

31

By the way, I should explain that the Victorians loved a good pun. Any joke involving a play on words was seen as very clever and a bundle of laughs. By today's standards, some of them are so laboured and complicated that laughing at them is the last thing you want to do. Running away screaming, 'Enough! No more!' is the more likely reaction. Don't believe me? Then here are just three that were popular in the late 1880s (from my copy of *Old Roxbee's Appalling Puns of the 1880s*). I can only apologise in advance to anyone trying to translate these into another language – or trying to come up with equally appalling puns from the 1880s in their particular mother/father tongue – and would like to remind all concerned that I didn't make these up myself.

Q: What is the difference between a cat and a comma?
A: A cat has its claws at the end of its paws but a comma its pauses at the end of its clauses.

Groan!

Q: What fashionable game do frogs play?
A: Croaky (croquet)

Aaaargh!

> **Q:** *Is it true that a leopard can't change his spots?*
> **A:** *No, because when he becomes tired of one spot he can simply move to another.*

Please stop, Mr Ardagh! Please! We'll be good, we promise! Just make the nasty jokes go away.

Okay, we'll end this episode here and begin the next one with Eddic Dickens about to head off for Tall Hall by the MacMuckle Falls/Gudger's Dump. (I did promise you we would, didn't I?)

A Surprise for All Concerned

In which the reason for Eddie's trip
to Scotland is revealed

After a sleepless night in what he suspected was the lumpiest bed in the Highlands, if not Scotland or the entire British Empire, Eddie was up bright and early. It was the sky that was bright, I hasten to add. Not Eddie. After a night of not sleeping, his brain was particularly sluggish and, if asked what – for example – was seven plus eleven, he'd probably have replied, 'Oslo,' which is, in fact, the answer to an entirely different question altogether.

Fortunately, the only question he was asked first thing was by Mrs McFeeeeeeee (formerly Miss McMuffin) and that was: 'What would you be liking for your breakfast, m'dear?' to which he replied 'Boots and shoes' (which was actually the answer to the question: 'What is one of the main manufacturing industries in the town of Northampton?').

If Eddie's mother had been the one asking the question, then there's every possibility that Eddie would have ended up being served with boots and shoes, if she'd had the ingredients readily to hand. Fortunately for Eddie, though, Mrs McFeeeeeeee realised that he'd just spent his first night in a foreign land (if you didn't count his time at sea, which was more foreign *water*, or on a small sandy hummock mainly inhabited by turtles), so made allowances for him.

She served up some biscuits which she called bannocks and some potato cakes, all to be washed down with a big steaming mug of tea. Angus McFeeeeeeee sat at the head of the table, drinking tea from an even bigger mug, which had the effect of making him look even smaller. Mrs McFeeeeeeee sat at the other, and their son Magnus (who'd said that Angus was no father of his because he had English clients) sat opposite Eddie, giving him a glassy stare.

Living in a household where a stuffed stoat was

considered by some as an honorary member of the family, Eddie was as used to glassy stares as he was to people falling out of trees, so was equally unimpressed by Magnus's latest tactic.

'Is it true ya have a tail, English?' asked Magnus, before stuffing a forkful of potato cake into his mouth and chewing furiously.

'Magnus!' said his mother sternly.

Mr McFeeeeeeee, who was busy reading that morning's edition of the *Highlands Gazette*, either didn't hear what his son had said or pretended not to notice.

'What do you mean – ?' asked Eddie.

'Ignore the boy,' Mrs McFeeeeeeee pleaded. 'He has no manners.'

Instead, Magnus ignored her. 'I read in a book once that all you poor English have tails,' he went on. 'Like monkeys,' he smirked.

Mrs McFeeeeeeee leapt to her feet and hit Magnus with a ladle (a big spoon) which she had readily to hand. (Perhaps she often used it for this purpose.) 'Master Edmund is a guest in this house and his family are respected clients of your father,' she said. 'You're not to talk to him in this manner.'

Magnus rubbed the back of his head. 'Will ye no' keep doin' that, Ma,' he grumbled. (Aha! I was right.) 'Anyhow, English here knows I was only joking.'

'Of course you were,' said Eddie, for a quiet life. He found being called 'English' effectively annoying, but he wasn't about to admit it. He concentrated on his breakfast instead, which tasted delicious. It was often his favourite meal back home, too, because Dawkins (his father's gentleman's gentleman) was excellent at rustling up what he called 'eggy snacks'.

Mr McFeeeeeeee folded his paper in half and laid it on the breakfast table. 'Is there any more mash in the pot?' he asked. For some reason best known to himself, he called tea 'mash', so don't you go thinking there were potatoes in there too.

'You've had the last of it, Angus,' said his wife.

'Then I'll have McDuff bring round the pony and trap so as I can be takin' the boy to Tall Hall,' he said.

His wife stood up and busied herself clearing the table. Breakfast was the one meal she liked to prepare and clear away herself. Her one maid wasn't live-in and didn't usually arrive at the house until after Angus McFee had left for his office in town.

No sooner had Angus left the room than the mini-version of him, Magnus, had snatched the paper from his place at the table. Magnus flipped through the pages until he apparently came to a story which caught his eye.

'Oh! It says in this here article that there's now conclusive proof that the Scots are more intelligent than the English,' he said. 'They did a series of scientific tests with a Scotsman, an Englishman, a monkey and a parrot and . . .' he pretended to read on, '. . . apparently, the Englishman came last in all of them. No surprises there, then!' Magnus grinned.

'Very funny,' sighed Eddie.

Not ten minutes later, he was in the trap with Angus McFeeeeeeee at the reins of the pony once more. When he got out to open the freshly painted white gate, Eddie was careful to be on the lookout for horse manure – steaming or otherwise – but noticed that it had already been cleared away from the night before. McFeeeeeeee rode the pony and trap through, and Eddie closed the gate, then jumped up behind the lawyer again.

The ride to Tall Hall was uneventful, but the scenery was even more dramatic than Eddie'd seen on the way to the McFeeeeeeees' house. They passed a few more crofters' cottages and saw one or two people, but for much of the time their only audience was some very shaggy-looking red-coloured cattle, with long fringes over their eyes and very large pairs of horns on their heads, and some equally shaggy-looking goats with equally impressive sets of horns. Once Eddie even thought he'd caught sight of a large-antlered deer.

Then Tall Hall came into view; the Scottish seat of the last of the MacMuckles by birth, the woman Eddie knew as Even Madder Aunt Maud. Eddie felt proud that this huge house now belonged to the Dickens family. It certainly was a strange sight with its very high walls and small windows, but with its very ordinary roof plonked down on top of it.

'Where's Gudger's Dump – I mean the MacMuckle Falls?' asked Eddie as the trap clattered up the uneven and very stony track leading to the hall. It had obviously once been a cobbled driveway, but the cobbles had been robbed out – pinched/nicked/purloined/stolen/half-inched/removed – to build other things elsewhere, and the few remaining lay like a smattering of stones found naturally in the soil.

'There,' the lawyer pointed.

It took Eddie some time to realise what McFeeeeeeee was pointing at. Today, we live in a world where Do-It-Yourself 'water features' are everywhere. Nowadays, around my neck of the woods, it's unusual to find a garden that *doesn't* have an artificial plastic-lined pond or an imitation Greek urn with water bubbling out of it, or a glass wall with a thin veil of water cascading down it, or a human-made stream flowing down steps of pebbles, all powered by an electric water pump. Back then there were really only two types of water feature: those made by Mother Nature and those made for very rich people by landscape gardeners who did things on a big scale.

Mother Nature nearly always did a good job, on a variety of scales ranging from intimate sources of springs bubbling out of the earth to dramatic, pounding waterfalls with thousands of gallons of water pouring from staggering heights. Professional gardeners created huge formal ponds, stone-statued fountains of writhing mermaids or characters from ancient Greek mythology, with jets of water spraying here, there and everywhere.

The name Gudger's Dump certainly suited what Eddie saw before him far better than the grandly entitled MacMuckle Falls. It looked like a dribbling bog; an accident . . . a puddle left by a passing herd of elephants. It was also slimy, black and horrible.

Reaching the front of the house, Angus McFeeeeeeee pulled the horse to a halt, jumped down from his seat, adjusted his tam-o'-shanter to a more jaunty angle on his head, and produced a large key from his pocket. He handed it to Eddie, who had jumped down beside him on the gravel. 'Would ya like to do the honours?' he asked. Eddie took the key. 'Thank you,' he said. They strode together across the driveway. Eddie's Scottish mission was a clear one. He was to visit Tall Hall and take a look around to see what state everything was in. He was to check that the furniture wasn't rotten and the roof fallen in, for example, and to see which – if any – items were worth boxing and sending down to Awful End. They were planning to sell the last of the MacMuckle property.

'A house in Scotland's no use to me,' Even Madder Aunt Maud had told Eddie before his departure. 'I have all I need here. My Malcolm. My Jack. My shiny things and, of course, my Marjorie.' She patted a wall. 'What more could a woman need?' She picked up a large glass eye from a bowl of assorted shiny things and popped it in her mouth, sucking it like a gobstopper.

The Malcolm she was referring to was her stuffed stoat who went with her just about everywhere. 'Her Jack' was her husband, Mad Uncle Jack. Her shiny things were . . . shiny things. She liked shiny things. She begged, borrowed and even (sometimes) stole them. And Marjorie? She was the large hollow wooden cow she lived in and that she and Eddie were sitting inside at the time. Her walls were papered with what looked to Eddie suspiciously like shredded American one-thousand-dollar bills, but that couldn't be right. Could it? Eddie's great-uncle had been equally dismissive about Tall Hall. 'I have no need of a home all the way up there,' he said. '*It* might be different if it had a lake full of fish, of course. One can never have too much fish . . . but, as far as I can recall from my single visit, many years before you were born, Melony –'

'Eddie,' Eddie corrected him. Melony was the name of a girl who came every other month to oil the hinge on Mr Dickens's pocket knife.

'– and there was no lake and no fish. No fish I say!'

It wasn't that Mad Uncle Jack enjoyed fishing –

I'm not sure whether he went fishing in his entire life – it's just that (with the exception of the dried swordfish he now carried about with him in his jacket pocket, as a back-scratcher and ear cleaner) he used dried fish as a method of payment. Please don't ask. I have no idea why.

Eddie's father, Mr Dickens, had also seemed to think that getting rid of Tall Hall was a good idea. 'Any nice pieces of furniture can be brought back to Awful End and the rest sold with the house,' he said. 'Some of the money made from the sale can go towards my buying new materials.'

These 'new materials' were for his latest hobby: sculpting. Having painted the ceiling of the hall at Awful End, he had recently turned his attention to this different art form. The general consensus is that his painting abilities were worse than awful. Unfortunately, his sculpting abilities were worse still. (Mad Uncle Jack did a little and was a whole lot better.)

Mr Dickens had started on a small scale, carving the corks from wine bottles into Great Characters From History. In his eagerness to carve, he'd opened a great many bottles of wine from the

43

Awful End cellars and, not wanting to waste their contents, often drank them before letting carving commence.

Mr Dickens's cork-carvings were bad enough when he was sober. Imagine what they were like after he'd had too much to drink. A few of them survive today (in the archives of the Society of Amateur Sculptors, Bricklayers and Dramatists, in Manchester), and I for one find it extremely difficult to tell which way up they should be. Julius Caesar's feet, for instance, look remarkably similar to his head.

Another problem with Mr Dickens carving whilst under the influence of alcohol was that he was forever cutting himself. He now had bandages on most fingers. But that hadn't stopped him starting work on a whole new scale. He'd gone from carving corks to carving logs and had even had one of the ex-soldiers who often helped out at Awful End chop down an oak tree in the grounds. Although the falling tree had destroyed the orangery – a very fancy greenhouse – the old gardener's cottage (though, fortunately, there was no old gardener in it at the time) and part of the stable block, no one seemed to mind and Mr Dickens had plenty of wood to work with.

His greatest triumph up to that time was carved from the main trunk of the tree. It was, according to him, a statue of his son, Eddie, on the back of a turtle. Although it was finally used as firewood in the great winter of '98, there is in existence a photograph of it taken by the world-famous photographer Wolfe Tablet. The picture is dark and grainy but you can still clearly see that the sculpture looks like a badly carved liver sausage on the back of a huge – equally badly carved – bowler hat.

As for Eddie's mother's opinion about what should be done with Tall Hall, she didn't have one. When Eddie'd asked her about it, she'd been far too busy trying to wash the dirt out of a piece of coal.

'I just can't get this black off,' she'd said, scrubbing it with a nailbrush.

So there it was: all four members of Eddie's immediate family happy to sell off Tall Hall. Having heard from Angus McFeeeeeeee what the locals had thought of the MacMuckles, and having seen what young Magnus's attitude was towards the English in general, Eddie didn't think there'd be any tears shed if the house were put up for sale . . . as long as, of course, a Scot bought it.

Eddie mounted the two stone steps to the front door and put the key in the lock.

'McFeeeeeeee!' cried a voice, and Eddie turned in time to see a huge horse thundering across the open ground straight towards them, steam rising from its flared nostrils. It appeared to be being ridden by . . . by a headless horseman!

A Clash of Wills

*In which Eddie waves a temporary bye-bye to his
lawyer and meets some strange fruit-eaters*

Angus McFeeeeeeee's reaction to the headless
apparition was rather different to Eddie's.
Whereas Eddie recoiled in horror, not quite
believing his eyes, the lawyer simply strode
purposefully across the grass towards the oncoming
horse.

'What is it, man?' he demanded in his broad
Scottish accent.

'McFeeeeeeee!' the voice repeated, and it
suddenly occurred to Eddie that headless horsemen

wouldn't have mouths (on account of having no heads) so were unlikely to be able to shout 'McFeeeeeeee', especially with exactly the right number of 'e's. This last point led Eddie to further deduce that it was likely that McFeeeeeeee was known to the horseman and that, by McFeeeeeeee's behaviour, the horseman, in turn, was known to McFeeeeeeee.

The rider dismounted and landed on the springy turf with quite a thud. Now that he was at Eddie's eye level, all became clear. The newcomer was a small man but with a very high collar and large neckerchief (which is a cross between a scarf and a tie, and unlike a handkerchief – which is for the hand or, maybe, the nose – was for the *neck*). Having such a short neck, the man's head was almost completely obscured by his monstrous collar!

'What's the matter, McCrumb?' McFeeeeeeee asked.

'It's Mary MacHine,' said McCrumb. 'A piano's fallen on her. It doesnae look like she'll survive.'

'I'm a lawyer, not a priest,' said McFeeeeeeee, which Eddie thought was rather unsympathetic. If he were ever squashed by a piano, he hoped that the news would, at least, merit an 'I'm sorry to hear that'.

'It's not spiritual help she's after, man: she wants you to change the will!' said McCrumb. 'You must hurry.'

The lawyer still seemed a little reluctant to leave Eddie. 'She only wrote her new will at the end of last month. Why would she want to change it now?'

'She wants to write Mungo McDougal out of it. She doesnae want the man to get a single brass farthing!'

(A farthing, brass or otherwise, was the coin with the lowest value of all coins or notes/bills in Britain; it was a quarter of one penny, or half a halfpenny, which was called a ha'penny. And don't you go thinking that there were a hundred pennies to the pound. Oh, no. That would be faaaaaaaar too simple. There were twelve pennies to a shilling and twenty shillings to the pound, which means – if this calculator's still working properly – that there were 240 pennies to the pound back then. And not only back then, come to think of it. There were

240 pennies to the pound when I was growing up, and I'm not that old. There aren't *that* many white hairs in this beard of mine, yet.)

A look of surprise crossed McFeeeeeeee's face, and got lost somewhere in those bushy eyebrows of his. 'But Mungo McDougal's forever buying Mary MacHine presents. I thought she liked the man.'

'It was he who bought her the piano . . .' McCrumb explained. 'It was riddled with woodworm.'

'Hence its collapse?' asked McFeeeeeeee.

'Hence its collapse,' McCrumb confirmed.

'Oh,' said Angus McFeeeeeeee.

Eddie came to a quick decision. 'If you must go to Mrs MacHine, Mr McFeeeeeeee, then go you must. I'll be fine here, going through the house on my own.'

'I'll ride with Mr McCrumb on his horse and leave you the pony and trap –' suggested the lawyer.

'No, don't worry, sir,' said Eddie. 'You can come back for me later when your work is done.' The truth be told, Eddie preferred the idea of going through Tall Hall his own. That way he could spend as much or as little time in a room as he wanted. He could explore exactly how *he* wanted to explore.

'If you're sure,' said Angus McFeeeeeeee doubtfully.

'The boy's sure!' said McCrumb, placing his foot in his stirrup and swinging himself back on to his mount. Up on his horse, his head looked invisible to Eddie once again. 'Now hurry, McFeeeeeeee. It's a *grand* piano and Mrs MacHine may soon breathe her last!'

Angus McFeeeeeeee, one hand on his tam-o'-shanter to keep it in place, ran back down the driveway and into the pony and trap. With a flick of the reins he was rattling after McCrumb across the grass.

Eddie climbed back up the two stone steps, which looked like they were sagging in the middle where they'd been worn by hundreds of years of treading feet, and turned the key in the lock. The huge oak door swung open with a creak that would have delighted the sound-effects department of a film crew making a horror movie.

*

Whatever Eddie expected to find inside, it wasn't a room with people in it. The front door opened straight into a great hall with a high hammer-beamed ceiling and a huge table in the centre which was probably long enough to seat about sixty people. As it was, there were six people seated around it at one end, and that was enough of a shock.

'Who are you?' asked a very puzzled and surprised Eddie.

A woman seated near the head of the table got to her feet and glided across the stone-flagged floor towards him. 'I think you'll find the question should be who are *you*, laddie?' She prodded Eddie with the tip of the long fingernail of her index finger.

'Me . . . I'm – er –' Eddie had been wrong-footed but quickly regained his composure. 'No, I think the question's still who are *you*?' He looked back at the others, still seated around the table.

They appeared to be eating a meal consisting entirely of fruit and nuts.

Eddie put his hand in his pocket and pulled out a fob watch on a chain. This was in the days before wristwatches, remember; though, by a quirk of fate, when he'd been aboard a ship named the *Pompous Pig*, Eddie had met the man who would later invent the steam wristwatch. (For those storing information for future use, the inventor's name was Tobias Belch.) On the back of this particular fob watch were the words:

TO MAUD
HAPPY 2ND BIRTHDAY
JACK

because it had been lent to Eddie by his great-aunt, Mad Uncle Jack having given it to her for her twenty-first birthday (ignore the '2nd' part!). Back in the days when she was still known as plain Mad Aunt Maud – before she'd become even madder – this self-same watch had indirectly led to Eddie being locked up in St Horrid's Home for Grateful Orphans.

Life can be strange like that. It's to do with something called either 'cause and effect' or 'the Chaos Theory'. Both work on the principle that someone picking his or her nose in South Africa can have an effect on politics in China, if the wind's blowing in the right direction ... or something like that. I wasn't giving the subject my undivided attention when it was being discussed on the radio the other day.

Eddie checked the time. It was just gone eleven o'clock, so he couldn't tell whether these people, whoever they were, were having a late breakfast, an early lunch or something in between. They came in all shapes and sizes but, apart from the fruit-eating, all had one thing in common. They were all wearing tartan – checked – clothing. But none of it matched.

For example, the woman who'd come over and prodded Eddie was wearing a black dress with a tartan shawl that was predominantly (mainly) green and black squares. The two women at the table (whom Eddie was later to discover were mother and daughter) were both wearing mainly red tartans, but the mother – who was almost as wide as she was tall – was wearing a much stripier tartan than her daughter's (which was more 'boxy'). As you can gather, tartans aren't the easiest things to describe. The three men at the table, all of whom had enormous beards, were wearing predominantly orange, blue and black tartans. The overall effect was of a television with the colour-balance turned up too high and everyone looking over-bright and zingy (although, with television not having been invented yet, this would have been a meaningless comparison to Eddie).

The tall woman in the black dress still hadn't answered Eddie's question, so Eddie tried a different approach. 'My name is Edmund Dickens,' he said. 'I am the great-nephew of the very last of the MacMuckles, the owners of Tall Hall and I was – er – wondering what you're all doing here.'

The bearded man at the head of the table stood up, the legs of his enormous carved chair scraping across the stone flagging, causing a sound with an effect not dissimilar to someone scratching their fingernails down a blackboard, and setting Eddie's teeth on edge. The man strode over to the woman's side and glared down at Eddie. He looked like an angry mountain, if there are such things. Volcanoes, perhaps?

'The last of the MacMuckles?' he said, sounding very indignant indeed. 'The *last* of the MacMuckles? I think not.'

There were murmurs of agreement from those still at the table, like when Members of Parliament say, 'Hear! Hear!' when they agree with whoever's speaking at the time.

'Young man,' said the mountain of a man, leaning so far forward that the wispy end of his thick black beard tickled Eddie's forehead, 'we, the assembled company, are the last of the MacMuckles.'

Many a MacMuckle . . .

*In which Eddie is given a local history
lesson and a punch on the nose*

To say that Eddie 'was surprised' by the man's statement would be like saying that if someone tied your hands and feet together, filled each and every one of your pockets with rocks, chained you to a block of concrete and then threw you in a flooded mine shaft that you'd 'get a little wet'.

In modern parlance, Eddie was jaw-droppingly gobsmacked. He was stunned. His mind was boggled. He could hardly believe what he was hearing but, his mother having cleaned out both of his ears with a broad bean soaked in alcohol (attached to the end of a crochet needle), just two nights previously, he accepted that his ears were operating at 100 per cent efficiency.

'You're a MacMuckle?' he gasped.

'We all are!' said the other five, in chorus. All of them spoke with broad Scottish accents.

'This is Alexander MacMuckle, Clan Chief of the MacMuckles,' said the woman, nodding in the direction of the fierce-looking bearded man towering above Eddie.

'What's all this nonsense about your great-aunt being the last MacMuckle?' he demanded.

'I – er – Before she was married she was called Mad Maud MacMuckle,' Eddie explained.

A look passed between the woman and Alexander MacMuckle.

'Mad Maud MacMuckle?' asked Alexander Muckle.

'Well, I suppose she's Mrs Jack Dickens now,' said Eddie. 'But we all call her Even Madder Aunt Maud ... except for Mad Uncle Jack – Mad Mr Jack Dickens – that is. He calls her love pumpkin and my little couchy-coo and suchlike.' As he spoke, Eddie realised that if *anyone* was going to get confused about being last in the line of MacMuckles when there were actually other MacMuckles still out there, it'd be Even Madder Aunt Maud. Even Mad Uncle Jack had been rather vague about the whole thing. When, back at Awful End and up in his treehouse, Eddie had asked him about the MacMuckles, MUJ had started drawing a family tree but, when it began to look a bit like a scarecrow with straw hair and twigs-for-fingers, that's what he turned it into a picture of ... and then coloured it in ... and *then* put it up in his study next to a drawing of a frog which had once started out as a map showing Eddie how to get to somewhere (though he could no longer remember where).

'I – I see,' said the woman, who clearly didn't.

'Who was Maud MacMuckle's father?' asked Alexander MacMuckle, looking less stern and more confused.

'That would be Mad Fraser MacMuckle,' said Eddie. 'I think he'd have been my great-great-uncle, but he died a long, long time ago.'

'Well,' said Alexander MacMuckle, 'any relative of a MacMuckle is welcome in Tall Hall –'

'– by the MacMuckle Falls,' chanted the others.

Eddie wondered if these MacMuckles knew that it'd been renamed 'Gudger's Dump', and what they'd have to say about it.

'This is my sister Martha MacMuckle,' Alexander MacMuckle said, putting his arm around the tall woman in the black dress. 'Won't you come and sit with us, Master Dickens?'

His head still reeling at what all this might mean, Eddie followed them over to the table where an extra place was hastily laid for him.

The very wide woman introduced herself as Nelly MacMuckle and the blushing girl next to her as her daughter Roberta. She proffered Eddie a bowl of fruit. He chose an apple.

'Thank you,' he said.

'We're vegetarians you see, dear,' she said.

'But this is a fruit, not a vegetable,' Eddie responded. Vegetarians were much rarer in Britain then than they are now.

'What Nelly means is that we don't eat meat,' explained another of the bearded men, who said that his name was 'Iain with two 'i's, unlike that Englishman Lord Nelson who only had one.' I warned you that puns were popular back then. (It helps if you know that Lord Nelson was a one-eyed admiral.) Although Iain probably made the same joke every time he said his name, he laughed heartily.

Soon all six of them had introduced themselves as: Alexander, Martha, Nelly, Iain, Hamish and Roberta MacMuckle.

'I thought everyone in the same clan wore the same tartan,' said Eddie, between bites of his apple. It was delicious.

Martha MacMuckle snorted. 'And that all the men wore kilts, I suppose?'

'Let me tell you a wee bit about clan tartans,' boomed Alexander MacMuckle, cutting into a pear with a small bone-handled knife. 'Have ye heard of a fella by the name of Sir Walter Scott?'

Eddie shook his head. 'But with a name like that he certainly sounds Scottish,' he said.

'Well, not that long ago' (if you must know, dear readers, the year was 1822) 'Sir Walter was put in charge of organising an event where the Clan Chiefs – the heads of the various families – would be presented to King George IV . . .' At the mention of the previous monarch's name, there was much mumbling under the assembled company's breath. Eddie got the distinct impression that the British royal family weren't the most popular people in Tall Hall. 'The event was intended to be dramatic and romantic and full of pageantry –'

'You English like pageantry,' said Nelly with a

61

stern look on her face which would have said (if looks could speak), 'And we all know that pageantry is not a good thing.'

'So Sir Walter laid down a few ground rules. He decided that each clan should have its own special tartan and the particular patterns were decided then and there,' said Alexander.

'Many of them were made up on the spot!' said Martha.

'But I thought they were traditional designs going back hundreds of years!' said Eddie.

'So do most people,' said Nelly. 'There's been *breacan* – tartan – around Scotland for centuries, but nothing as organised and regimented until recent times, laddie, with particular setts for particular clans.'

'Setts?' asked Eddie, surprising himself by remembering that this was the proper name for badgers' burrows.

'Patterns,' growled Alexander MacMuckle.

'And many of them have only recently been made up?' Eddie gasped.

The MacMuckles nodded as one. And how right they were. The belief that this fairly modern idea is steeped in ancient Celtic history is how, in the twenty-first century, there comes to be a whole Scottish industry grown up around people who believe they have Scottish ancestry buying rugs, shawls, tam-o'-shanters, kilts and so on in particular tartans closest to their names. 'Smith?' the helpful Scottish shop assistant, grins. 'Oh, that's a well-known corruption of the Scottish name MacSplurge, and entitles you to wear the clan tartan. We have a very fine range of items in the tartan, including this superb machine-made imitation-leather keyring for just one hundred and thirty-five dollars,' which is a fine thing for the Scottish economy.

'What about kilts?' asked Eddie, thinking about the pleated tartan skirt he'd seen his great-great-uncle Mad Fraser MacMuckle wearing in the oil painting Even Madder Aunt Maud had hanging upside down at the head of her bed inside Marjorie.

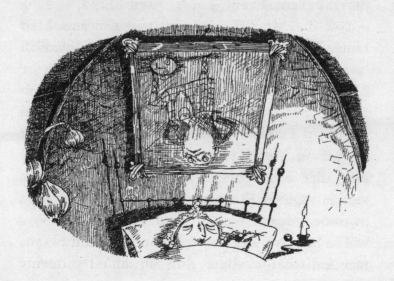

'A genuinely ancient form of Scottish dress?' asked Martha MacMuckle with a look of contempt.

'Invented by an Englishman named Thomas Rawlinson in 1768,' said her brother. 'We Scots only started making a point of wearing them when you English banned them, thus makin' it a matter of honour!'

There was a cheer from the others around the table, resulting in some of those who were still eating showering the others with half-chewed bits of fruit and nut. The spitees (if there is such a word) swore at the spitters in colourful Scots.

Eddie wondered what Mr McFeeeeeeee would make of these MacMuckles. There he was thinking that his client, Even Madder Aunt Maud, was the last of the MacMuckles and that she and Mad Uncle Jack were the rightful owners of Tall Hall . . . yet here was a whole different branch of the MacMuckle family, including one who claimed to be the Clan Chief. Not only that, McFeeeeeeee had suggested that the MacMuckles had been either English or supporters of the English, but *these* particular MacMuckles seemed as pro-Scottish and anti-Queen Victoria as Angus McFeeeeeeee's own son Magnus!

The history lesson over, Eddie thought it best to mention what was worrying him about suddenly discovering that he had a whole bunch of distant relatives whom, less than an hour before, he hadn't even known existed. 'Er, Mr MacMuckle –' he began.

'Yes?' replied Alexander, Iain and Hamish, three pairs of eyes on him at once.

'I meant *you*, sir,' he said, addressing himself to Alexander, him having been introduced as the Clan Chief and being therefore, Eddie supposed, the most important person in the room.

'Yes, laddie, what is it? What's prayin' on your mind?'

Eddie knew that this next part would be awkward but, having once ended up being arrested and (wrongly) put in an orphanage, rather than break a promise and, therefore, bring possible shame to the Dickens family, he knew that he must stake the Dickens claim. 'I'm afraid you can't – er – stay here . . . any of you. I came to Tall Hall in advance of my great-aunt and great-uncle putting it up for sale.'

There was a loud clatter as Hamish MacMuckle, by far the smallest of the MacMuckles but with the biggest, reddest beard Eddie had ever seen (and would ever see), dropped the pewter platter he was holding to the stone floor. Walnuts shattered and skidded across the huge flagstones.

Alexander MacMuckle was back on his feet

at the head of the table. He glared at Eddie so effectively that it makes one wonder whether he'd been practising in the mirror or taking special night classes. 'Tall Hall is not for Mad Fraser MacMuckle's daughter to sell!' he shouted – yes, shouted. 'This place is MINE, I tell you. It belongs to ME.'

Eddie knew that it would be very silly of him to argue.

Martha MacMuckle put a calming hand on Alexander's shoulder and he sank back into his seat – rather like a throne – shaking with anger.

'Forgive my brother,' she said, 'but surely you can understand his upset?'

Little Hamish stomped over to Eddie and, to everyone's amazement, punched him on the nose. More surprised than hurt, Eddie staggered backwards and landed on his bottom with a jarring bump. Hamish stomped back to his place.

Moments later, Roberta MacMuckle was helping up Eddie. She handed him a lacy hanky she'd had tucked up the left sleeve of her blouse. 'Your nose is bleeding, Master Eddie,' she said.

He took the hanky and pressed it to his nose. It smelt of heather. 'Thank you, Miss Roberta,' he said.

'My friends call me Robbie,' she said.

'Thank you, Robbie,' said Eddie.

Roberta smiled. Eddie smiled. He thought she was rather pretty.

Just then, Angus McFeeeeeeee came charging through the front door. He stopped dead in his tracks (which may be a cliché but describes exactly what happened). 'What the devil's going on here?' he demanded.

Disputed Deeds

*In which Eddie gets a guided tour and a
right royal surprise*

'Y ou didnae waste your time in throwin' a party,
Master Edmund!' said Angus McFeeeeeeee
in obvious amazement. 'Are you not going to
introduce me to your friends?'

'These are no friends of mine, Mr McFeeeeeeee,'
began Eddie, then, realising that this sounded
rather ruder than he'd intended, quickly added:
'What I meant to say was that they were here when
I arrived.'

The lawyer raised one of his caterpillar-like

eyebrows into a quizzical arch. 'Were they indeed? We appear to have a clear-cut case of breaking and entering. Well,' he said, now confronting the assembled MacMuckles. 'What do you have to say for yourselves?'

'What I have to say,' said Alexander, 'is that a wee chap like you should be extremely careful who you go accusin' of breakin' and entering!'

Something changed in Angus McFeeecccee and Eddie could suddenly picture him falling from a tree with the cry of 'McFeeeeeeee!' on his lips and his bare hands around the neck of his enemy. 'I may appear small to you, sir!' he breathed heavily. 'But I have the might of the Law on my side!'

Nelly MacMuckle stepped between the two feuding men, filling the space quite nicely.

'Gentlemen, gentlemen!' she said. 'There's no need for this. Alexander, you must simply explain the situation to Mr –'

'This is Mr Angus McFeeeeeeee, my family's lawyer,' said Eddie.

'– to Mr McFeeeeeeee. He can't know the facts until you give them to him now, can he? Fruit?' Nelly thrust the bowl right under McFeeeeeeee's nose.

He seemed disarmed. 'What? Er – no, thank you.' It was hard to be angry when fruit was on offer. A nice apple can sometimes have a calming effect on even the most angry of people.

'You see, Mr McFeeeee –' began Eddie.

'McFeeeeeeee,' McFeeeeeeee corrected him.

'This is Mr Alexander MacMuckle, Clan Chief of the MacMuckles. He claims that Tall Hall isn't Mad Uncle Jack's and Even Madder Aunt Maud's to sell. He says it belongs to him.'

The lawyer's eyes narrowed. 'And I suppose you have papers to prove it, sir? And I am using the term *sir* loosely!'

'To prove what exactly, Mr McFeeeeeeee?'

'That you're a MacMuckle. That you're the Clan Chief and that you have a right to this property. I hold the deeds to this house and lands on behalf of Mad Mrs Jack Dickens, formerly Mad Maud MacMuckle ... and possession is nine-tenths of the law. Where's your documentation, Mr MacMuckle?'

'I usually find that in any dispute *this* puts across my point of view most effectively,' said the now red-faced Alexander MacMuckle, waving his huge fist in the lawyer's face.

Little Hamish wandered over and was about to bop McFeeeeeeee on the nose, in the same way that he had Eddie, when Martha MacMuckle grabbed his wrist with her long, slender fingers (including the one with which she had so successfully prodded Eddie on his arrival).

'Stop acting like children, the lot of you!' she pleaded. 'We cannae go on like this!'

This had the desired effect and, over the next half an hour or so, Eddie and McFeeeeeeee sat with the six MacMuckles or, if the lawyer's suspicions were correct, the six people *claiming* to be MacMuckles, and each side heard the other's explanation as to the state of affairs: Eddie and McFeeeeeeee were under the impression that Even Madder Aunt Maud was the last of the MacMuckles and, as her husband, Mad Uncle Jack was therefore the rightful owner of the hall, its contents and lands, and could do with them as he pleased; Alexander claimed that he and the others were all MacMuckles and, as Clan Chief, the hall was rightfully his and couldn't therefore be sold.

Eddie was simply relieved that there was no more nose-punching or fist-waving. Nutty though his family undoubtedly was, the most aggressive any of them ever got was when Even Madder Aunt Maud hit or prodded people with her stuffed stoat Malcolm.

Though once a leader-of-men in the army (and some of them were still hanging around following him all these years later), Mad Uncle Jack had claimed never to have fired a shot in anger, which was probably true because my research has uncovered the fact that he could never load his rifle properly and that the man who was supposed to do it for him – a Welshman named Private Evan Topping – used to fill it with wads of blotting paper (which he kept hidden in his kitbag for this specific purpose) because, his commanding officer or not, he didn't trust Mad Major Dickens with a loaded weapon. It is, I suspect, thanks to Private Topping that more people didn't die in Mad Uncle Jack's regiment.

True, Eddie's father, Mr Dickens, had once blown up his bedroom, but that had been as a result of lighting an early-morning cigar when the gas from a lamp had been left on.

True, Eddie's mother, Mrs Dickens, had killed Private Gorey (retired) in the sunken garden at Awful End when she'd thrown a mortar shell over a wall, but that had been an accident.

As for being on the receiving end of violence, Even Madder Aunt Maud had once been hit by a hot-air balloon (which she rather enjoyed) and chased by peelers (policemen) with dogs through a hawthorn hedge. (As you can see, there's a picture of this below. It first appeared in another one of my books, in which I described the incident, but I liked it so much I wanted to give those of you who've never seen it before a chance to have a look at it, and those of you who *have*, a chance to enjoy it for a second time. I'm kind-hearted like that.)

Back to the receiving end of violence. Mad Uncle Jack had been stabbed in the bottom with a toasting fork and regularly fell out of his treehouse, and both of Eddie's parents had been victims of the two explosions already outlined, and Eddie himself had been kidnapped by escaped convicts once and locked up in that orphanage and a police cell or two . . .

. . . but, otherwise, he and his family had never really been touched by violence. Eddie suspected that this was not the case with the MacMuckles, who seemed almost eager to get involved in fisticuffs, as his nose attested. Well, the male MacMuckles, anyway. He looked across the table at Miss Roberta – Robbie – and caught her looking at him. She looked down at her lap, blushing.

Angus McFeeeeeeee was very keen that the MacMuckles 'or whoever they are' leave Tall Hall whilst the matter was being resolved. As far as he was concerned, it was down to them to prove their right to the property and not the other way around, the house having been in the Dickenses' hands for many years without anyone contesting their right, and with the deeds in his safe at his office in town.

'If we let them stay, they may refuse to leave. They may steal property rightfully belonging to your family. They may –'

'And how do you intend to get them out?' Eddie interrupted the lawyer. They were whispering in a dusty corner of the great hall, below one of the many stags' heads mounted on the wall; one of the hundreds of victims of MacMuckle hunts over the years. 'Will you bring in the police? We could end up with a full-scale battle on our hands, Mr McFeeeeeeee! I know that you're a lawyer and I'm just a boy but I'm here representing my family, and . . . and I think it'd be best if we let the MacMuckles stay here while everything gets sorted out. The house'd be empty otherwise, anyway.'

'Very well,' said Angus McFeeeeeeee, somewhat reluctantly, 'but I'll have to write to your great-uncle for further instructions.'

With the news that the Dickenses' lawyer wasn't about to try to have them thrown out, the MacMuckles became civil once more; almost friendly, some of them.

'I'd like to stay and look around Tall Hall, whoever it rightfully belongs to,' said Eddie.

'Can I show him?' asked Robbie.

Nelly, the girl's mother, shook her head. 'No, let Hamish,' she said, 'by way of an apology for what he did to ya, laddie.'

Eddie would far rather have had the guided tour from the heather-smelling Miss Roberta than the hairy nose-puncher. (By putting a hyphen between the words 'nose' and 'puncher', I'm making it clear that it's the nose-puncher who was hairy and not the noses he punched. If he were a non-hairy puncher of hairy noses, I would have written either 'hairy nose puncher' without any hyphens or 'hairy-nose puncher' like this. If he were a hairy puncher of hairy noses, I would probably have given up altogether. As for describing Robbie/Roberta as 'heather-smelling', there's a problem in English that 'smelling' can mean to smell something (as in 'he smells the cheese') or to smell of something (as in 'he smells *of* cheese') which is why this old joke works:

MAUD: My Malcolm has no nose.
EDDIE: How does he smell?
MAUD: Stoaty.

In this instance, I mean that Robbie smelt of heather (as did her hanky) because she was wearing toilet water, which may sound like something that needs mopping up but was, in this case, water with crushed heather in it, making a kind of weak smelling-of-heather perfume. She may, of course, have gone out of her way to run through the wild heather, rubbing her hands against the flowers to release their scent and sniff it in, but that's not what I meant.

Phew! I'm pleased to have clarified that.)

*

It didn't take Eddie long to realise who little Hamish MacMuckle reminded him of. Why, it was young Magnus McFeeeeeeee, of course: the lawyer's son. Admittedly, Magnus didn't have a great big red beard covering most of his face and hadn't (yet) punched Eddie on the nose, but Eddie suspected that he'd very much like to, what with Eddie being English and all that! Both Hamish and Magnus reminded Eddie of coiled springs – not unlike the ones in his mother's home-made sandwiches – full of energy and waiting to 'BOING!'.

Hamish's guided tour of Tall Hall was certainly fast and consisted more of grunts and single words rather than fully formed sentences, all spoken in broad Scots: '. . . another bathroom . . . bedroom . . . bedroom . . . damp patch . . . wardrobe . . .' Although Eddie was probably taller than him, he found it difficult to keep up with the little nose-bopping Scotsman.

'How long have you been staying here?' asked Eddie as they hurried down yet another flight of servants' stairs at the back of the house (far more cramped than the grand, ornately carved wooden staircase which the owners would usually have used).

'Wuz born here,' said Hamish, charging through an open doorway into a large kitchen.

77

'But I thought this place had been empty for years.'

'Has been,' said Hamish, marching them past a long kitchen table on which lay apple cores, skins, nutshells and the peel of a wide variety of vegetables, from potatoes to turnips and parsnips. 'We only moved back in t'other day.'

Hamish led him past an open door to a small room with a tiny window. It looked to Eddie like a prison cell.

'What's that?' he asked.

'Game larder,' said Hamish.

'A what?'

'Where they used to hang the poor wee dead animals and birds killed in the hunt,' said the Scot, clenching his fist.

Eddie was half-expecting another punch on the

78

nose, but for being a meat-eater this time. 'Are all your branch of the MacMuckle family tree vegetarians?' he asked.

'Each and every one of us,' said Hamish, with obvious pride.

They were now in a wide passageway. 'What's in there?' asked Eddie, nodding in the direction of an impressive door, studded with black nails.

'Cellar,' said Hamish without stopping.

'Can we take a look?' asked Eddie, thinking back to the cellar at Awful End and all the wine bottles his father had opened and drunk, just so that he could carve the corks. Eddie wasn't a great fan of his father's artistic endeavours – the truth be told, he thought his father was a dreadful painter and an appalling sculptor – but he admired his dedication.

'Can't go down there,' said Hamish.

'Why not?' Eddie asked.

'We havenae found the key yet.'

'Oh,' said Eddie, a little disappointed.

The tour continued.

Eddie had to admit, to himself at least, that he was in two minds about the strange predicament he'd found himself in. On the one hand, he thought it was a shame that this extraordinary house, in such beautiful surroundings, might not actually belong to his family, and that some of the wonderful pieces of furniture and bits-and-bobs/ knick-knacks might not be theirs to keep. On the other hand, the plan was for the Dickenses to sell the house anyway, which meant that it would be lived in by strangers. And, if these MacMuckles had a genuine claim to Tall Hall, wouldn't it be nice that it stayed in Even Madder Aunt Maud's family for its rightful heirs to enjoy?

In other words, he wasn't sure whether he wanted Angus McFeeeeeeee to have to hand over the deeds of the property and land to Alexander MacMuckle or not. And he had no idea how long such a thing might take to happen in Scottish Law anyway.

He knew that English Law (also with a capital 'L') could be a very slow process. Once a local schoolteacher had tried to sue when Mad Uncle Jack had grown a particularly ugly hybrid vegetable and named it after him. Some gardeners made it their life's work to grow new varieties of flowers and vegetables, with varying degrees of success. Mad Uncle Jack's cross between a pea and some root vegetable or other had come about accidentally and the result looked like a very large, very hard and very knobbly pea; the kind of evil giant pea that would be discovered pulling levers behind a curtain at the end of a film in which vegetables were rising up against their human masters.

Mad Uncle Jack had decided to give a name to this extraordinary new vegetable, which didn't taste too bad if boiled long enough and was served with plenty of salt, ground black pepper and butter. Eventually, he settled on 'Lance Peevance' because, as he later explained in the local court, 'Peevance incorporates the pea element of my triumphant vegetable-child, and it is also the name of that man there,' he paused to point at the schoolteacher who was also in court that day . because he'd brought the legal action against Eddie's great-uncle, 'who bears more than a passing resemblance to it.'

Lance Peevance – the man not the vegetable – had, by now, had quite enough of Mad Mr Dickens and tried to make a lunge at him, screaming: 'I'll get you yet, Dickens!' which didn't please the judge.

The judge was already on Mad Uncle Jack's side, as it happened. Although schoolteachers were well-respected members of society and seen as 'better' than scullery maids, for example, they still had to *work* for a living. Mad Uncle Jack, on the other hand, was a true gentleman *and* lived up at the big house, which meant that, in the judge's eyes, he should really be allowed to do what he liked and that included calling ugly vegetables after Mr Peevance.

Having said that, both Mad Uncle Jack's and Mr Peevance's lawyers wanted to make as much money from the case as possible, so kept on raising very complicated legal objections on both sides, and sending each other very expensive letters (which their respective clients would, of course, eventually have to pay for).

After three and a half years, judgement was finally passed in Mad Uncle Jack's favour and Lance Peevance was ruined. As a result, he owed his lawyer and the courts so much money that he fled the country disguised as a bag of coal.

On a matter of principle, Mad Uncle Jack paid for WANTED posters to be printed at his own expense. On them was an artist's impression of his own new variety of vegetable, under which were the words:

HAVE YOU SEEN A MISSING SCHOOLTEACHER, WITH MORE THAN A PASSING RESEMBLANCE TO THIS VEGETABLE?

As a direct result of seeing a copy of the poster, a Briton holidaying in France later recognised Lance Peevance and had him arrested. Mad Uncle Jack felt that this was proof, if proof were needed, that calling his vegetable-child 'Lance Peevance' in the first place had been completely and utterly justified.

Amazingly, a few years back, this very trial was turned into a modern (and somewhat avant-garde) opera called *Vegetation Litigation!* for a TV series on one of those arty satellite channels, but the names of the people were changed to ones that were easier to rhyme with 'vegetable patch' and 'court case'.

Back in Tall Hall, however, Eddie's tour was about to be cut short by the sudden arrival of Angus's son Magnus McFeeeeeeee.

'Victoria!' he shouted, bursting into the great hall which Eddie and Hamish were crossing whilst the others were still deep in conversation around one end of the huge table. 'Queen Victoria!' He'd obviously been running and was dripping with sweat. He had a stitch and was clutching his side. He took in great gulps of air, then spoke again. 'She's paying a visit!'

Episode 7

Something in the Air

*In which Eddie gets to confront a suspect
and consume some rather nice cake*

Two days had passed since Magnus MacMuckle
had burst into Tall Hall with his extraordinary
news. At first, everyone had assumed that he'd
meant that Queen Victoria was turning up at the
hall unannounced at any moment. Then it became
clear that he meant that Her Majesty was paying
a visit *to the area*, and not then and there, but the
following week.

Eddie was excited because he'd never laid eyes
on his monarch and was hoping to catch a glimpse

of her at the very least. Perhaps she'd arrive at the same station he had, but on her special royal train (so she could sit on her special lightweight portable travelling throne), and he could be in the crowd waving a small Union Flag – which he had learnt was the correct name for the Union Jack when it was being flown on land.

Angus McFeeeeeeee seemed excited in the same way, making comments such as 'Can ya imagine it? Our own dear queen comin' to these parts?' But Eddie wasn't so sure about the MacMuckles. They seemed to be experiencing a different kind of excitement.

When Eddie was older and recalling the events that happened that year in Scotland, he wrote: 'Looking back on it, it is obvious that their reaction was very different to ours.' Hindsight – looking back on events with the knowledge you could only have after they'd happened – is a very fine thing, but it's true to say that there was certainly something about the MacMuckles' reaction that made him very uneasy.

Another thing which bothered Eddie was young Magnus McFeeeeeeee's reaction on discovering Tall Hall full of strangers. Unlike his father, who'd been surprised, Magnus didn't even ask who anyone was. It was almost as if he knew them already. And now, two days later,

Eddie decided to approach him on that very subject.

Magnus McFeeeeeeee was outside the back door of his home scraping dried mud off a pair of his father's walking boots with an old butter knife.

'You already knew that the MacMuckles had moved into Tall Hall, didn't you?' said Eddie, coming up behind him from the garden and leaning over his shoulder. Magnus jerked back in surprise.

'Ya shouldnae creep up on people, English,' he said. 'Did your mammie no teach ya manners?'

'You haven't answered my question,' said Eddie.

'Is that what that was?' said Magnus, busying himself with the boots.

'You weren't surprised to see them there. The truth be told, I was wondering whether the message about the Queen was more for them than for me and your father,' said Eddie.

'I walk into the house to find me da and half a dozen other folk seated at a table. For all I know they're furniture removers or people come to see the house with a view to buy. There's no mystery.'

'If this were a town, I might believe you,' said Eddie, above the noise of scraping knife on mud and boot, 'but in the countryside everyone knows everyone's business – unless they deliberately want it kept secret. You'd have known if there were furniture movers or prospective buyers around! And then there's the matter of how the MacMuckles got into the hall in the first place.'

Magnus avoided his gaze.

'Aha!' said Eddie triumphantly. 'So I was right! You lent them the key, didn't you? As my family's lawyer, your father holds the key to Tall Hall and you must somehow have "borrowed" it and given it to the MacMuckles.'

'Then how did my father come to have the key in order for ya to open the door yusself, the other day, English? Answer me that.'

Eddie had already thought of that before he'd confronted Magnus, so had an immediate response. 'The MacMuckles must have made a copy. All they had to do was press the original in some melted wax or a cake of soap to make a mould.'

The lawyer's son was clearly impressed. 'You've thought of everything,' he said.

'Do you deny it?' asked Eddie.

'I neither deny nor admit anything, English,' said Magnus. The blade of the butter knife flashed in the weak sunlight. He sounded like a lawyer.

'Didn't you stop to think what this might do to your father?' asked Eddie. 'What if these people had stolen everything from the hall or wrecked the place? Your father would have been held responsible. He's supposed to be looking after it.'

'He's no father of mine,' muttered the boy.

'Magnus?' called Mrs McFeeeeeeee's voice from the parlour. 'Have you not finished your father's boots yet?'

'Nearly, Mother,' Magnus called back. 'But English keeps gettin' in me way.'

'Who?' called his mother.

'Edmund,' replied Magnus, sheepishly, just as Mrs McFeeeeeeee appeared at the back door. 'I said Edmund.'

Magnus's mum was holding her large ladle again. 'Sure you did, son,' she said. 'Now you've got the mud off, perhaps you'd be kind enough to give them a good polish?'

'I'll be sure to, Mother,' said Magnus, deliberately stepping on Eddie's toe as he stomped off around the side of the house.

'Come and sit with me, Master Edmund,' said Mrs McFeeeeeeee. 'We'll have some cake and talk about the Queen's visit. It'll be one of the most exciting things ever to have happened around here.'

The cake was excellent. There was no denying that Eddie enjoyed some of the best food he'd ever eaten whilst staying with the McFeeeeeeees. The conversation was most interesting too. It turned out that Mrs McFeeeeeeee knew someone who knew someone who knew someone who knew Sir James Clark. Now, that's not very interesting unless you know that Sir James – another Scotsman – either was or used to be the Queen's Personal Physician (which is a posh title for the Queen's Own Doctor).

'I'm sure he'd fit in well at Awful End,' said Mrs McFeeeeeeee, who had – as you may have gathered from her earlier comments – had the pleasure (?!) of meeting Mad Uncle Jack and Even Madder Aunt Maud on their one joint trip to Tall Hall, and had no illusions about their sanity. 'Apparently he's quite mad. I have it on good authority that he's little more than a naval doctor but, as a friend of Her Majesty's mother, somehow landed himself this plum job!' She offered Eddie another piece of cake. He couldn't resist.

'Thank you,' said Eddie. A cake without broad beans or springs was a rare treat.

'I also have it on good authority that Sir James is a great believer in fresh air as the cure for all ills but is highly suspicious of foliage. I'm told that he planned to have Buckingham Palace pumped full of air to protect it from the surrounding trees which were, he was convinced, clogging up the atmosphere!'

'Did Her Majesty agree to it?' asked Eddie, his mouth full. Although Eddie's mother, Mrs Dickens, was well known for speaking with her mouth full – whether it was with ice cubes, onions, acorns or even dressing-gown cord tassels — it was not encouraged in the Dickens household, and shows just how delicious Mrs McFeeeeeeee's cake was and just how interested Eddie was in the topic of conversation. Royal gossip was as popular back then as it is now.

'I believe that Her Majesty was on the verge of agreeing to the plan when Sir James brought in another physician, a Dr Arnott, to give additional advice. All was going fine until Dr Arnott confided to the Queen his strong belief that the average person could live for hundreds of years if only he had the maximum amount of fresh air!'

Just in case you're under the impression that Mrs McFeeeeeeee's friend-of-a-friend-of-a-friend (or whoever) was pulling her leg, let me assure you that everything she said was pretty much true. Both Dr Arnott and Sir James Clark were fresh-air freaks. Sir James was also, by all accounts, a pretty rotten doctor. On one occasion he diagnosed Queen Victoria as having a bad attack of indigestion, but it turned out to be typhoid. On another – much more serious – occasion he pronounced one of the Queen Mother's ladies-in-waiting was pregnant when her tummy swelled up. She was unmarried and this caused a terrible scandal and she lost her job, despite her claims that she *couldn't* be pregnant. It later turned out that the poor young woman (whose name was Lady Flora Hastings) wasn't pregnant at all but had cancer of the liver, which was eventually correctly diagnosed by someone else. The good thing was that she had cleared her name. The sad thing was that the cancer killed her soon after.

Mrs McFeeeeeeee talked on, and Eddie listened with rapt attention. Meanwhile, not five miles away, in an abandoned crofter's cottage – yup, you're right, it was the cottage and not the crofter that was abandoned (the crofter having won a lot of sheep in a card game in the local pub had moved to a better cottage nearer the pub) – a very secret meeting was taking place. The three men present all stayed in the shadows and spoke in hushed tones.

'Do ya have the weapon?' asked one.

'I thought *you* had it,' said the second.

'Do nae worry, I have it,' said the third.

'Are you both clear on your duties?' said the first.

'Aye,' said the second.

'Aye,' nodded the third.

'If anything should go wrong with the first shot . . .' said the first.

'It won't,' said the second.

'There'll be no Scottish blood on our hands,' said the third.

There was a noise from outside. The three men froze, then the first tiptoed over to the window. He lifted the edge of a piece of hessian sacking that had been nailed up in front of the window to create a curtain. He looked through the grimy glass into the failing light of evening. A shaggy mountain goat trotted daintily through what had once been the crofter's small garden, sending a pebble skittering across the ground.

'False alarm,' said the first.

'When Victoria comes calling we'll give her a day to remember, all right!' said the second.

'That we will,' grinned the third.

'Careful you don't get the rifle tangled up in your beard, Hamish!' said the second.

'Ssssh!' said the first. 'No names, remember.'

Hamish grinned again. The rifle he was holding was taller than he was.

A Highland Fling

*In which plans are made and
we meet the Q-PUS*

In the days that followed, more news about Queen Victoria's forthcoming visit became known. She'd be staying on the Gloaming estate (just a mile or so to the west of Tall Hall) at Gloaming Castle as a guest of Sir Rumpus Rhome (pronounced 'Room'), who was an absentee landlord. This meant that although he owned hundreds of acres of the surrounding countryside, he actually lived somewhere else completely. In Sir Rumpus's case, this was London, where he also owned large tracts of land. His main residence was Number One Rhome Square, which was always written as Number One with letters, and never with the simple numeral '1'. It was a very beautiful townhouse built in the classical style with stucco pilasters all along the front. (Stucco is plaster meant to look like stone, and pilasters are sort-of fake columns that are for decoration rather than to hold things up.)

Sir Rumpus hated everything about his Scottish estate except for the hunting. He hated the mountains. He hated all that fresh air. And, most of all, he hated the Scots, who 'spoke funny' and, in his opinion, looked at him in a funny way too.

In his opinion – and the only opinion that seemed to matter to Sir Rumpus was his *own* – the Scots were a disrespectful bunch. Sir Rumpus, whom you've probably guessed by now was English, was big on respect. He liked people bowing and scraping before him – and even touching their forelocks if they could find them – and he got plenty of that from people in and around Number One Rhome (pronounced 'Room') Square . . . but these Scottish people seemed much fiercer and more independent. They didn't seem to understand that he was not only English but also a knight – a 'Sir' – which made him doubly superior to them. In fact, he had the worrying suspicion that they did as he instructed only because he was paying them, and they *still* begrudged his presence, which was a sorry state of affairs.

Gloaming Castle still stands today but it's no longer a private house. It's an exclusive Scottish country-house hotel (according to the glossy brochure) and I stayed there for one night when researching the events that you're now reading. I'd like to have stayed longer but the price of half a grapefruit on the breakfast menu was more than I'd normally pay for an entire meal for the two of us, including all the lemonade you can drink.

Number One Rhome Square is no more. Neither is Rhome Square itself, come to that. In the First World War (*aka* World War One, The Great War or The War To End All Wars) the house was blown up by a primitive bomb dropped from a Zeppelin (which was a big airship). During the Second World War (*aka* World War Two, or The War That Followed The War To End All Wars), the square was destroyed by a number of bombs dropped from aeroplanes.

After the war, the square was 'redeveloped' and in its place stands a very fine multistorey car park, one of the largest in the city and much appreciated by businessmen and women who would otherwise find it difficult to find parking spaces in the area. It's called 'Rhome Square Car Park' which is the only reminder of what once stood there. Everyone pronounces it 'Rome Square' rather than 'Room Square' which would really annoy Sir Rumpus if he hadn't died a long time ago.

Sir Rumpus Rhome's love of hunting can't be overstated. He loved killing living things and the bigger the better. If he could have found a way of shipping elephants to his Scottish estate just so that he could shoot them he would have. An elephant with antlers would have been the icing on the cake. Some hunters love the thrill of the chase. Sir Rumpus's dictum, however, was: 'The easier the better.' Sometimes he instructed his gamekeeper to hide behind a bush with, say, a deer, and to release it just as Sir Rumpus was ready to shoot something. This resulted in more than one gamekeeper being shot in error, which meant even more excitement for Sir Rumpus and a small bonus for the injured men.

Queen Victoria and her party – which meant the people who travelled with her, and didn't necessarily involve balloons and loud music – would be spending a weekend at Gloaming and her visit would include watching an afternoon's hunting.

Of course, Her Majesty Queen Victoria would not actually be taking part in the hunt. Oh, no. She had very clear views on women and hunting. Once, when she learnt that one of her granddaughters had been hunting, she sent her a letter saying, 'I was rather shocked to hear of you shooting,' and 'to look on is harmless, but it is not ladylike to kill animals'. Then she used a brilliant phrase: 'It might do you great harm if that were known, as *only fast ladies do such things.*'

Wow! Obviously, getting the reputation as a 'fast lady' was Not A Good Thing. Sir Rumpus and all the male guests would do the hunting. Victoria and the ladies would simply do the looking on. Sir Rumpus was honoured and delighted.

So were Mr and Mrs McFeeeeeeee. They'd received an invitation. The Q-PUS (the Queen's Private Under Secretary) had been sent up a few days in advance and, in addition to all the bigwigs/big cheeses/top dogs/A-list people who always got invited to such events, had been asked to additionally invite 'colourful local characters'.

Queen Victoria was big on colourful local characters. Her security detail – in other words those in charge of her safety – were not. 'Colourful local characters' often turned out to be 'eccentrics' and 'eccentrics' often turned out to be nutters.

Mr McFeeeeeeee was a pretty safe bet. He not only had a suitably funny Scottish name with an interesting story behind it for Her Majesty to find entertaining – ancestors jumping out of trees and strangling people with their bare hands – but he was also a lawyer and could be relied on to behave and not drop his trousers halfway through the proceeding in order to show the Queen a birthmark on his left buttock, as a previous 'colourful local character'/eccentric/

100

nutter had done at a house party in Yorkshire. (There is a strong possibility that the latter was Mad Uncle Jack's brother George, of burning-down-the-Houses-of-Parliament fame, though his diary entry for that day is barely legible, the ink having been smudged by what appears to be liquid paraffin.)

Mrs McFeeeeeeee would be invited to attend the royal festivities simply because she was Mr McFeeeeeeee's wife. Little Magnus McFeeeeeeee was not to be invited. 'I wouldnae come if I was asked,' he'd told Eddie, spitting on the ground, and Eddie hadn't doubted him for a second.

The Q-PUS had also made inquiries (which are like enquiries but spelt with an 'i') about the owner of Tall Hall. 'The MacMuckle family were known to the late King, and Her Majesty is most eager that the present owner, or his representative, attend,' he told Angus McFeeeeeeee who, as well as being an invitee, had been given the job of suggesting other suitable candidates for invitation to the Q-PUS, and for rounding them up.

'I have the great-nephew of the last surviving MacMuckle staying with me as we speak,' he'd proudly told the Queen's man, 'but he's just a child.'

'Excellent!' said the Q-PUS. 'Her Majesty loves children.' This was fortunate because, by the end of her life, she was to have over forty – yes, *forty* – grandchildren. Imagine if, as a granny, she'd been asked to babysit them all on the same night!

'Master Edmund Dickens, for that is the laddie's name, is the self-same wee Edmund who found the stolen Dog's Bone Diamond belonging to the fabulously rich American dog-food tycoon Eli Bowser,' said Angus McFeeeeeeee, rather proudly.

'I'm sure Her Majesty will be most interested to meet him,' said the Q-PUS. 'I seem to remember that a stuffed ferret was somehow involved in the process.' He vaguely recalled having had the newspaper reports of the whole extraordinary affair read to him by the Queen's Private Under Under Secretary (the Q-PUUS) or the Queen's Private Assistant Under Secretary (the Q-PAUS). They looked very similar to each other, so he couldn't remember for sure which it had been.

'Stoat,' said Angus McFeeeeeeee.

'I beg your pardon?' said the Q-PUS.

'It was a stuffed stoat,' explained McFeeeeeeee. 'Not a stuffed ferret.'

'I see.' The Q-PUS nodded, as though this were an important detail. Perhaps it was.

And so plans were made in this way, and the date of the arrival of HM (Her Majesty) drew closer and closer.

A Right Royal Arrival

*In which a jam-filled biscuit and a lone piper
get trodden on by royal feet*

When the day of the Queen's visit finally arrived, the headteacher – well, the truth be told, the *only* teacher – of the local school had not only written a special song for the occasion but had also found time it to teach her pupils to sing when HM Queen Victoria stepped from the royal train on to the green carpet. Yes, of course, it should have been a *red* carpet but, at the dead of night, a group of unidentified anti-royalists had stolen the red carpet, which had been locked in the Station Master's office. By the time Mr McTafferty had discovered the theft, there was no time for him to order a replacement but, making one of those snap decisions that had seen him rise through the ranks of railway company employees, he decided that a green carpet was better than no carpet at all, and had 'borrowed' the stair carpet from Mrs MacHine's cottage who, being in hospital with injuries sustained from being flattened by a woodworm-ridden grand piano, wouldn't notice it had gone. Or so he hoped.

With the aid of a tailor's tape measure and a complicated diagram supplied in advance by the Q-PUS, McTafferty had calculated exactly where the door of the Queen's carriage would come to rest and, therefore, where the carpet should be placed. He had just had enough time to run across with the carpet from Mrs MacHine's cottage and unroll it across the platform in position when a cry from one of the crowd indicated that the royal train was coming into view.

Imagine the scene. Go on, *please* imagine the scene. It saves me having to describe it. Think of people in their (Scottish) Sunday best. Think of bunting and Union Flags strung up everywhere, like paper chains come Christmastime. Think of children with freshly scrubbed faces and hair dampened and flattened. Think of a small – a *very* small – brass band with kilted bandsmen, their gleaming instruments glinting in the sun. Can you do that for me? I'm most grateful. Now throw in a buzz of anticipation and a feeling of great excitement and then we can all move on.

The train came to halt with a loud hissssssssssssssssssssssssssss (much louder than the hiss of escaping gas in Episode 1 of *Dreadful Acts*) and the band struck up a suitably stirring tune for the occasion. It reached a crashing climax as the door to the carriage was opened from the outside by two strapping guardsmen in 'traditional' garb, and a royal leg appeared. Then Miss MacTash (the headteacher) raised her baton, and her three rows of smartly dressed pupils began to sing:

'Welcome Royal Majesty,
Our mighty Queen Victoria,
You are Britain's finest
Which is why we all adore ya!'

There were a few raised eyebrows and mutterings in the crowd at this last line; some from people who certainly didn't adore her, and some from those who did, but thought that *'we all adore ya!'* wasn't appropriate language with which to address Her Majesty. In fact, not fifteen months later, Miss

MacTash was forced to retire from her post at the school a year earlier than she originally planned. This was partly as a result of this song, and partly to do with a playground incident involving one of the youngest – and certainly lightest – children in the school and a golden eagle (one of a local nesting pair).

Queen Victoria, on the other hand, seemed delighted by the welcoming committee and charmed by the small group of singing schoolchildren. She probably wasn't listening to the lyrics, however, because she was distracted by something she'd stepped on which, on closer inspection by the Sergeant-at-Arms who was accompanying her, turned out to be a jam-filled biscuit.

Mrs MacHine was particularly fond of jam-filled biscuits and left them dotted about the house, some deliberately – should the need for a biscuit suddenly come upon her – and some by mistake, when she'd put them down for a moment and forgotten about them, or they'd slipped from the edge of one of her bone-china plates. The offending biscuit, which had to be peeled from the sole of Victoria's boot, was from the latter category. Mrs MacHine must have dropped it on the stairs and, in his hurry to remove her stair carpet, Station Master McTafferty hadn't noticed that it was still attached.

Once removed from the royal boot (her left), the
Sergeant-at-Arms handed the flattened biscuit to
the Q-PUS, who was walking two paces behind
him, who, in turn, handed it to the Q-PUUS, who
was walking two paces behind *him*, who, in turn,
handed it to the Q-PAUS, who was still emerging
from the carriage and, having missed what had
happened, assumed that they'd all been handed
biscuits by way of a welcome, so ate this one with a
beaming smile on his face. That night, he wrote in
his diary that it had tasted 'a little leathery', which
was hardly surprising under the circumstances (or
under the royal boot).

Now Lord Rhome (pronounced 'Room')
stepped forward and bowed deeply. 'Welcome,
Your Majesty,' he said, eyeing the green carpet
with some puzzlement before straightening up
again. 'My coach is at your disposal,' he added,

indicating its whereabouts with a dramatic flourish of the arm. It would have been hard for her to have missed it. The green stair carpet ended at a gate at the edge of the platform, opening on to the road where His Lordship's fine black coach stood, the door held open by a liveried footman. (Liveried has nothing to do with describing Eddie's father's paintings, which usually had a liver-sausagy look about them, but means that the footman was in a special footman's uniform.) As the name suggests, footmen either ran after the coach on foot or jumped up on to special running plates at the back of the coach and stood there (on their feet). Only a coachman actually got to sit on the thing and drive it.

Those not familiar with the area would have assumed that the two liveried – there's that word again – footmen were those usually employed by Lord Rhome at his Gloaming estate, but they'd be wrong. These two men were, in fact, what we'd today call 'undercover policemen'; highly trained to protect the monarch from any surprise attacks. They were from New Scotland Yard in London, the old Scotland Yard (which they'd called plain Scotland Yard, after the palace used by visiting Kings and Queens of Scotland back in the days before Scotland was ruled by the English) having been blown up by Fenians in May 1884, which was somewhat embarrassing for the policemen who worked there because their job was to put a stop to that kind of thing. It's a bit like a fire-prevention officer's office burning down. You feel sorry and all that, and are glad that he managed to save the goldfish in time, but it's funny in a way too. Or, at least, the *idea* of it is. If you're wondering what Fenians (pronounced as though spelt Feenians) are, I don't blame you. You've probably guessed that they were people of some sort, which is a good guess, but I should explain that they were Irish people, and not only Irish people, but also Irish people who generally didn't like the idea of the British monarchy and the British Government – the one with the capital 'G' – ruling Ireland, which made Fenians particularly unpopular with the English authorities, who thought that they had every right to be ruling Ireland because – er – England, Scotland and Wales combined to make a bigger island than Ireland . . . so there! (Or something like that. Who knows?)

Oh, whilst we're on the subject of islands, let me quickly point out something strange which occurred to Eddie when he once saw an actor-manager named Mr Pumblesnook performing a piece from one of Shakespeare's plays, a few years previously. In it was a soliloquy about England which included the words *'this sceptered isle'*, which was a bit odd because it occurred to Eddie that England wasn't an isle – an island – at all. It had land borders with Scotland and Wales. Spain had land borders with just two countries too, and nobody called *it* an island, so what was going on? He'd asked Mr Pumblesnook about it but the actor-manager had muttered something about 'never questioning the mighty bard' and had hurried away to stop his wife, Mrs Pumblesnook, doing whatever it was she liked to do with the blotches of skin she peeled off her face and kept in a special pocket until the time was right.

As Queen Victoria made the short journey along the green stair carpet, the cheers of the crowd mingled with a few cries of 'Go back to England where you belong!' (followed, in each instance, by a muffled thud of the offending shouter being merrily bopped on the head by a smiling policeman in dress uniform) ringing in her ears, a lone piper stepped out at the side of Lord Rhome's coach and horses. He was very tall, and very impressively dressed, and was jumped on by the two liveried footmen before you could say, 'They're really two policemen in disguise.'

The two men, Mr Digg (with two 'g's) and Mr Delve, threw themselves at the Lone Piper, knocking the wind out of him and his set of bagpipes, which whined a like flatulent cat, and if you don't know what 'flatulent' means, I'm not going to be the one to tell you. The Lone Piper – who really was a lone piper – wrestled with his attackers, assuming that they were assassins in disguise, planning to harm Her Majesty, whilst Digg (with two 'g's) and Delve wrestled with *him*, assuming that *he* was the assassin in disguise.

The reasons for this fracas – nice word, huh? It means 'noisy quarrel' or 'brawl' and comes from the French word *fracasser*, 'to shatter' – were a direct result of a last-minute change of plan and a failure to communicate. As those of you who can remember as far back as the first page of Episode 1 will recall, Queen Victoria loved all things Scottish, and a lone piper (*aka* a bloke on his own with a set of bagpipes) was just the sort of thing which added so significantly to her Scottish enjoyment. Unfortunately, however, the lone piper the Q-PUS had had lined up – sorry about the two 'had's in a row, but I didn't invent the language – had – blimey, there's another one – caught a rare kind of flu which you could only catch off a certain breed of pig if you spent too much time with one, so was currently tucked up in bed with a cuddly toy rabbit and a temperature of 104. The cuddly toy rabbit was described as being his mascot, and the temperature of 104 as

111

being dangerous. What the Q-PUS had forgotten to tell those protecting Victoria was that he'd managed to find a last-minute replacement. It was this last-minute replacement whom Mr Digg (with two 'g's) and Mr Delve were now sitting on.

I'd like to be able to tell you what the Lone Piper was saying – and, even with his broad Scottish accent, it was clear enough for the Scotland Yard men to include in their report – but I can't repeat it here because it was t-o-o r-u-d-e. The Lone Piper was very, very, *very* angry. Eddie had witnessed the whole thing from his vantage point at the roadside, where he stood with Mrs McFeeeeeeee on one side and Mr McFeeeeeeee on the other. All three of them were dressed in their almost best, so that they could change into their very best for the main reception.

When Queen Victoria came through the open gate on to the road, she was either so busy acknowledging the crowd with a gentle nod or the very slightest wave of a royal hand or so well trained as not to let such things faze her that she simply stepped on to the Lone Piper, who was struggling on the ground, and into Lord Rhome's coach, the Sergeant-at-Arms doing the same.

When the coach pulled away, heading for Gloaming Castle, the Q-PUS explained to Digg (you must be familiar with the spelling by now)

112

and Delve that the Lone Piper was indeed not only a genuine lone piper but, when he wasn't piping alone, also a retired captain in the British Army. The poor man had been trampled by so many feet that he woke up with some very interesting bruises the following morning. By way of an apology, he was later sent a boxful of figs. They gave him an upset tummy.

Once at Gloaming Castle, Queen Victoria was offered what, according to the itinerary, was 'light refreshment' but, by today's standards, would be better described as 'a pig-out'. There seemed to be course after course, ending with a see-through jelly filled with flower petals. Only the select few were invited to this stage of the proceedings: members of the Rhome family and those making up the shooting party. In other words, after lunch they'd either go out shooting or go out and watch the shooting. The main reception for all the local dignitaries (and Eddie) was scheduled for the evening.

Eddie couldn't wait for the evening to come so, to take his mind off things, he decided to go to Tall Hall to see how things were. Well, 'to see how things were' was the reason that Eddie would have given if he'd been asked why he was going up there again; having been a number of times since he'd first discovered the so-called MacMuckle clan squatting there. I've no doubt that the real reason smelt of heather and had a pretty smile.

Eddie found the front door locked, and no one answered his repeated knocking. Skirting around to the back of the house and down a short flight of stone steps, he found that the door leading into the kitchens wouldn't budge either. But he knew where they hid the key. He ran back up the steps and over to a flowerbed. Lifting a large piece of stone that, by the look of the carvings on it, must once have been part of an older building, he wrestled the rusty old key from a colony of woodlice (or should that be 'woodlouses'?) and let himself in.

The place seemed deserted and, although Eddie had at least as much right as the others to be there, if not more so, it felt a little as though he were trespassing.

'Hello?' he called, his voice echoing 'o', 'o', 'o' through the vast hall. Nothing. After a quick scout around, Eddie was on the verge of giving up and going when he heard some muffled thuds coming from . . . coming from where, exactly?

Not Quite What It Seems

*In which Eddie makes a discovery and the author
writes the longest episode in the book*

The noises finally led Eddie Dickens to the large
studded door; the one which little Hamish
had told him led down to the cellar; the one for
which Hamish had told him they'd been unable to
find the key.

Someone must have found the key, though,
Eddie thought, because noises were most definitely
coming from down there.

He banged on the door. 'Hello!' he shouted. The
muffled thudding continued on the other side.

'Hello!' he shouted once more, then added: 'Are you all right?'

Then he heard the most extraordinary cry . . . or snort . . . or something. He wasn't even quite sure whether it was human or not.

Eddie grabbed a stool and scrambled up on to it, feeling along the top of the door frame to see whether the key had been put there out of view. No luck.

His heart was pounding faster now. He had a terrible sinking feeling. He'd believed that those claiming to be MacMuckles *were* MacMuckles and had even instructed Angus McFeeeeeeee to let them stay here at Tall Hall against the lawyer's advice . . . but what if they were, in truth, a band of villainous impostors involved in some dreadful scheme, and they were using this very cellar as a dungeon, packed with prisoners?

No. Eddie mustn't let his imagination run away with him. How often did one run into villains in real life? Well, in Eddie Dickens's case, quite frequently. He'd encountered the Cruel-Streaks, who were a very nasty family running an orphanage for their own betterment, rather than the poor orphans'; he'd been kidnapped by escaped convicts up on a misty moor; he'd foiled an attempted jewel robbery aboard ship . . . So, seeing as how he seemed to attract trouble like a picnic attracts ants and wasps, no, it *wasn't* beyond the realms of possibility that he was right about being wrong about these so-called MacMuckles.

But what should he do? There was no way that he could get that cellar door open without a key and, until he knew what lay behind it, he wasn't happy about the idea of going around accusing anyone of anything.

What if there were a perfectly good explanation for all that terrible thudding . . . though he was very hard-pressed to think of one. Perhaps he should go and find Mr McFeeeeeeee and see what he thought. The grounds of Tall Hall bordered the Gloaming estate. Tall Hall was the nearest building to Gloaming Castle, where, at that very moment, Queen Victoria and her party were residing.

Then Eddie had another even more worrying thought. What if it were the MacMuckles who were locked in their own cellar? What if anti-royalist intruders had somehow overpowered Alexander, Iain, Hamish, Martha, Nelly and Roberta – sweet Robbie – and locked them all in there, binding and gagging them so that they couldn't cry for help?

Eddie had been bound and gagged once. Admittedly that had been in an open rowing boat rather than a cellar, but he imagined that the experience must be pretty similar: unpleasant.

Eddie pressed his ear flat against the thick wooden door. He didn't know what he was listening to, but he didn't like what he heard.

Eddie was within a cat's whisker's width of deciding that, whatever the consequences and however embarrassed he'd be if there were a perfectly innocent explanation for scuffling and thudding in the locked cellar, he must tell *somebody* when he heard voices. Someone was coming.

There were few places to hide in the corridor but one was all he needed. Eddie crouched down behind an enormous Chinese-looking vase, taller than a man, with the pattern of a blue dragon snaking across the front.

No sooner had he ducked out of sight than, peering around the bulbous middle of the china monstrosity, he saw Nelly and Martha coming into view.

'Don't look so worried,' Martha said to Nelly. 'It'll soon be over and the Queen will be gone.'

'If it goes wrong, we could all end up in the Tower!' said Nelly, sounding as worried as she looked; her face puffy and her eyes red.

'The boys have been over the plans a hundred times,' Martha tried to reassure her. 'And the cause is a good one.'

'But the rifle –'

'It's been especially adapted. It won't fail.'

'It can't fail, or we'll end up with Scottish blood on our hands,' said Nelly.

They disappeared into the larder.

Eddie's heart was pounding in his ears like a jack-hammer. No, hang on: the *sound* of Eddie's heart was pounding in his ears like a jack-hammer. If his heart really had been in his ears he'd have been in an even worse state than he was. Which was pretty bad.

'*If it goes wrong, we could all end up in the Tower!*' Nelly had said. The Tower of London. That's where they used to send traitors before their execution, Eddie thought. And what treason did the so-called MacMuckles have planned? What had Martha said? '*It'll soon be over and the Queen will be gone.*' That was it. Gone? Gone where?

Eddie had a very uneasy feeling about this;

a stomach-churning, sicky-sick feeling. The occupants of Tall Hall were obviously mixed up in some very unsavoury scheme.

When Eddie was satisfied that the two MacMuckles (if that was what they really were) were occupied by whatever it was that they were doing in the larder, he decided that he must make a break for it. Slipping out from behind the vase, he tiptoed past the open larder doorway, knowing that, if either of them were to glance his way, he could be spotted at any moment. With an almost audible sigh of relief, he made it out of the door, up the steps and slipped away through the grounds. He must find the royal shooting party on the Gloaming estate and warn them that someone meant the Queen some serious harm!

*

Lord Rhome stomped across the heather with glee. He was taking part in his two favourite pastimes: hunting deer and showing off his wealth and importance to people who really mattered; and few people mattered to him more than Queen Victoria.

There had been a time when the Queen had pretty much disappeared from public life altogether. This started when her beloved husband, Prince Albert, had died, and it lasted for about twenty-five years. TWENTY-FIVE YEARS? Yup, *at least* twenty-five years. Like Mad Uncle Jack and the Dickens family portraits, Victoria carried a picture of Albert with her wherever she went, after his death (though it probably wasn't stuck to the lining of her coat with a nail or old sticking plasters), and she also went a little – how shall I put it? – odd. That's it: *odd*.

For example, although Albert was dead and buried and not sleeping in his bed, let alone using the chamber pot kept under it, she gave strict instructions that the chamber pot be cleaned every day. And who would dare argue with someone who ruled great big chunks of the world?

Then, in 1887, she'd been on the throne for fifty years – except for when she nipped off it for reasons already outlined – and took part in huge celebrations to mark this 'golden jubilee'. She had such a great time that she decided to get out and about more and have some FUN; which she did, pretty much for the rest of her life, which is how she came to be visiting the Gloaming estate and watching 'Roomy' (as she called Lord Rhome) and the gentlemen guests take part in the shoot.

Because it's all rather relevant to what's about to happen (and I should know what's about to happen because I'm the one who's about to write about it), I think I should give over a few pages to telling you about some of the attempts and so-called attempts that had been made on the Queen's life until then.

In 1840, a chap called Oxford (not to be confused with the *place* called Oxford, which is unlikely because one was a person with the first name of Edward and the other was – and still is, I assume – a city in Oxfordshire, full of dreaming spires and tourists) shot at Victoria and Albert in their open carriage as they were making their way up Constitution Hill. He ended up in a lunatic asylum on the basis, no doubt, that anyone trying to kill the lovely monarch must have been mad.

In 1842, a certain John Francis tried to kill the Queen not once, but twice. One day he shot at Victoria and Albert as they were trundling down the Mall – the long, straight road leading to and from Buckingham Palace – but his pistol didn't fire properly. Because V & A were embarrassed at the idea of anyone wanting to shoot at them, they decided not to tell anybody . . . so the security measures weren't tightened and this meant John Francis could take *another* pot shot at them the next day. This was very considerate of the royal couple and he took advantage of their kindness. The pistol worked this time, but Francis missed and he was caught.

Just over a month later, *another* John tried to shoot the Queen or, at the very least, to get her attention. This was a boy called John William Bean and he'd probably have had better luck if his gun had contained more gunpowder and less tobacco. Nobody said that would-be assassins have to be *smart*.

The next attack wasn't until nearly thirty years later, which wasn't surprising, what with Her Majesty staying at home moping for much of the time, rather than going out and about, making herself an easy target. It was 1872, and a young man named Arthur O'Connor pointed a gun at the Queen as she passed by in her carriage. One of Victoria's many sons, also called Arthur, chased after O'Connor but Victoria's ghillie, John Brown, reached him first and wrestled him to the ground.

Brown – Scottish and hairy despite the lack of a Mac or Mc in front of his name, you will recall – not only got all the public credit and praise from the Queen but also £25 a year for life and a nice big gold medal (just the sort of shiny thing Even Madder Aunt Maud would have loved to have got her hands on). Prince Arthur thought this was jolly unfair because he'd been *just* as brave as Brown and all he got was a measly gold pin and a 'what a good boy you are to your mummy' kind of thank-you. O'Connor's gun turned out not to have been loaded anyway.

Then, in 1882, it was Brown's turn to be pipped to the post in the saving stakes. (That's s-t-a-k-e-s, as opposed to s-t-e-a-k-s. 'Saving steaks' would suggest saving red meat, which would make no sense in this context whatsoever, so why bring it up? What do you mean *I* brought it up, not you? Oh, I see. You have a point there. Sorry. Never let it be said that I don't apologise when I'm wrong.)

Where was I? Aha! March 2nd, 1882. Windsor Railway Station, that's where. The Queen's carriage was waiting outside and a Mc – a Roderick McLean, to be precise – shot at it with real bullets in his gun and everything. John Brown saw this as a chance to be a hero again – and maybe even get another medal – but, unfortunately for him, he wasn't the first to reach McLean and tackle him. No, sir. That honour went to a couple of Eton schoolboys who repeatedly hit Mr McLean with their rolled-up umbrellas until the authorities grabbed a hold of him and dragged him away.

So, with all these attempted assassinations in mind, let us return to the springy heather on the Gloaming estate where rather a lot of people – a number of whom weren't big fans of the English in general and the English monarch in particular – were wandering around carrying BIG RIFLES. It wouldn't be spoiling the action to say that not all of them had shooting deer in mind.

125

The start of the shoot did not go well for Lord Rhome. The deer seemed to be hiding, which wasn't cricket. Of course, the game of cricket has little to do with shooting deer – except that both were enjoyed by the ruling classes – but 'not cricket' is a phrase. It means not playing by the rules. And, as far as Lord Rhome was concerned, the deer should have been darting about in the open where he could shoot at them; not keeping a low profile. Had the deer themselves been familiar with the phrase, perhaps they'd have thought that what wasn't cricket was these nasty men wanting to shoot them!

If steam really could come out of people's ears, like it does in cartoons when people are about to explode with rage, it'd certainly have been coming out of both of Lord Rhome's (in a very impressive fashion). He was very frustrated, but trying to remain the perfect host in front of the most important guest he could ever hope to have on the Gloaming estate.

'*Cooo-Eeee!*' called a voice, and Rhome turned to see two complete strangers stomping purposefully across the heather towards them. Both appeared elderly. One – a man – was ridiculously thin and seemed to have large fern-like leaves sticking out of every pocket. The other – the woman who had '*Cooo-Eeee*'-ed – was clutching what looked like a stuffed ferret or somesuch thing.

'Sorry we're late,' said the man.

'And who, sir, are you?' demanded Rhome.

Mad Uncle Jack (for, yes, it was indeed he and Even Madder Aunt Maud who'd put in a late appearance in this adventure) pushed aside the large leaf protruding from the top pocket of his jacket, which had been partially obscuring his beakiest of beaky noses. 'Didn't recognise me with my camouflage, huh?' he chortled. 'I wanted to blend in with the local scenery.'

'Who the devil are you, sir?' demanded Lord Rhome, which was fair enough considering that

127

the reason he didn't recognise Mad Uncle Jack had less to do with the 'camouflage' and more to do with the fact that, until that moment, the two men had never met in their entire lives.

There was frantic whispering going on between those surrounding Queen Victoria. There had obviously been a serious breach in security if this strange pair had managed to get in stuffed-stoat-throwing distance of Her Majesty.

One of the many famous things about Queen Victoria was that, no matter where she was, she never looked behind her when she sat down. What I mean is, she never had to look behind her to check that there was something to sit *on*. Wherever she was, there was always a servant ready to slip a chair (usually her throne, I'd imagine) beneath the royal behind.

As Even Madder Aunt Maud came striding towards her now, skirt hitched high and shouting, 'Hello there, Queenie!' Victoria sat down with surprise. An even bigger surprise was that she found herself sitting on nothing and then ended up on the ground with quite a thud.

The man who had been holding the chair had abandoned his post in order to keep the frightening woman away from his beloved queen. He was now being prodded with Malcolm's nose for his pains.

128

Talking of pains, how was Her Majesty? Fine. It wasn't the contact between bottom and ground that had shocked her, or even the loss of dignity. It was the fact that for the first time in her entire reign she'd gone to sit down and there hadn't been a chair. It was like the sky suddenly turning green, or water suddenly flowing uphill. Such things just *didn't* happen.

'Quite extraordinary,' she was muttering as she was helped to her feet. 'Quite remarkable.'

'The last of the MacMuckles!' shouted a running man in livery, appearing from the direction in which Mad Uncle Jack and Even Madder Aunt Maud had just appeared.

A startled look crossed the faces of a number of the gun-carriers who were accompanying the royal party on the shoot; including a small, red-bearded chap who looked very keen to punch anybody and everybody on the nose.

The Sergeant-at-Arms stepped forward to confront the running man whilst Mr Digg and Mr Delve, plus the Q-PUS and various others, created a protective ring of people around the Queen.

'This lady and gentleman are the Dickenses,' the man explained. 'Mrs Dickens is the last of the MacMuckles of Tall Hall by the MacMuckle Falls . . . They are late invitees, and wouldn't wait for me to accompany them up here.'

'Aha!' said Lord Rhome at the mention of Tall
Hall. He'd been listening in on the conversation.
Now it all made sense. This beaky man was a
gentleman and a landowner and that made all
the difference. He shook Mad Uncle Jack's hand.
'Welcome,' he said.

'I like your hat,' said Mad Uncle Jack.

'Er, thank you,' responded Lord Rhome, who
wasn't actually wearing one.

Even Madder Aunt Maud, meanwhile, was
trying to speak to Victoria through the legs of those
standing between her and the Queen.

'Ow, come on out, you know you love me!' she
said teasingly.

For those of you shocked by her obvious lack of respect and deference towards Her Majesty, I should make it clear that Even Madder Aunt Maud had mistaken Victoria for someone else. You may find this hard to believe, particularly when she greeted the Queen with a cheery 'Hullo there, Queenie!' but therein lies a clue. When Even Madder Aunt Maud was still plain Mad Aunt Maud, she'd had a friend named Charlotte Hailstrom who bore a striking resemblance to Victoria and had, as a result, earned the nickname 'Queenie'. Unfortunately, this meant that Queen Victoria bore a striking resemblance to Charlotte Hailstrom and, having never met HM before and having not seen Charlotte for many years, Even Madder Aunt Maud simply assumed that she was her old friend Queenie.

Of course, Queen Victoria had no way of knowing this and, on top of still recovering from the shock of sitting down on nothing more than thin air, was hoping beyond hope that someone would make the worrying woman go away!

Now, let me freeze the action as only an author can – or a reader too, if you simply stop reading; that's one of the great things about books – and explain how MUJ and EMAM come to be here right at the end of this first Further Adventure.

It's simple really. Had they been at Tall Hall

when the Q-PUS had sent out the invitations on Angus McFeeeeeeee's recommendations, they'd automatically have been invited but, in their absence, Eddie had been invited to the evening reception in their place. When McFeeeeeeee had written to Mad Uncle Jack about the bunch of people living in Tall Hall, claiming to be not only MacMuckles but also its rightful owners, Mad Uncle Jack had changed his plans and decided to come up to Scotland after all. McFeeeeeeee had then informed the Q-PUS who, in turn, had arranged an invitation for 'Mad Mr Dickens' to attend the shoot and reception with his wife.

What *had* McFeeeeeeee been thinking? He had no excuse. He'd met them before! He *knew* what they were like . . . and, yet, here they were.

'Stag!' went up a cry, bringing us firmly back into the action.

Suddenly, all thoughts of strange latecomers were forgotten. Now, at long last, Lord Rhome might have the chance to shoot some deer.

The beast – large red and antlered – was some way off and appeared to be staring straight at the shooting party with unblinking eyes. It had emerged from behind a rocky outcrop.

The small, red-bearded Scot, whom Eddie had known as Hamish MacMuckle, stepped forward and handed Lord Rhome a rifle.

'Murder!' cried a voice. 'Kidnap!' and Eddie Dickens came into view, being chased by a swarm of policemen.

The stag disappeared behind the rock again, and Lord Rhome fumed once more. 'Piccadilly Circus!' he groaned. 'This is busier than Piccadilly Circus!'

Thwarted Plots!

*In which Eddie is both wrong and right
and Malcolm plays his part*

It was fortunate for Eddie that his great-aunt and great-uncle were on the scene when he arrived. They were able to confirm his identity and to avoid him being wrestled to the ground, or worse, as a possible would-be assassin.

'Her Majesty's life is in terrible danger!' Eddie shouted, trying to escape the police sheep snapping at his ankles.

He – What do you mean, 'What are police sheep?' Oh, good point. Let me clear this one up as quickly as possible so that we can move on. There's something called distemper which is a type of water-based paint, but ignore that. There's something else called distemper which is, according to *Old Roxbee's Book of Doggy Ailments*, 'a highly contagious viral disease involving a high fever and yucky gunky stuff coming from the nose and eyes'. At least, *canine* distemper is, and that's what all the local police dogs were suffering from at the time, so the police had quickly trained up some of the local sheep.

Before you start muttering, 'I don't believe a word of it!' and go off and play with your own stuffed stoat in the corner of your hollow cow or dried-fish treehouse, I should like to point out that it's quite common for people to keep sheep as pets and that, once treated like a dog, they start behaving very much like them too. Constable Jock McGlock, whose job it had been to train the five police sheep, was delighted with how they'd responded, but trying to catch Eddie Dickens had been the first real test.

'The MacMuckles aren't MacMuckles. They've got somebody locked in the cellar and they're planning to shoot the Queen with some special rifle,' shouted Eddie, between gasps for air, as he fell to the heathery ground. That had been one long run from Tall Hall to the shooting party.

'Hello, young Edmund,' said Mad Uncle Jack looking down at his great-nephew. 'Is that a recent haircut?'

Fortunately, Mr Digg and Mr Delve stepped in and asked Eddie to explain himself as soon as possible.

As Eddie spoke, he looked around and his eyes widened. There were Mad Uncle Jack and Even Madder Aunt Maud (with Malcolm), Queen Victoria and her entourage, and various well-to-do men there for the shooting and their well-to-do wives standing around watching . . . and then there were those obviously there to assist, with guns, ammunition, refreshing drinkies and the like. What made them stand out from the others were that they were in Scottish dress and very hairy and . . . and one of them was so-called Hamish.

'Arrest that man!' shouted Eddie. 'He's one of the gang.'

Little Hamish put up a good fight. He managed to bop several people on the nose, including himself, and even managed to bite one of the sheep's legs but, much to the pride of Jock McGlock, the sheep gave as good as it got and bit him back. (The truth be told, Eddie was secretly quite proud of *both* of them; what with neither of them being an actual meat-eater!)

'Wait!' bellowed a voice in the distance, and the

stag reappeared from behind the rocky outcrop. It started ambling down the hillside towards them.

As it got nearer it became obvious that this was no 'monarch of the glen' but more of a deer-coloured pantomime horse with a pair of antlers added.

It stopped and the front part lifted off its head. Inside was the man Eddie knew as Alexander MacMuckle, Clan Chief. Despite his comic bottom half, he still made an imposing figure.

Now the back half of the stag separated from the front and stood up. This was Iain-with-two-'i's-unlike-that-Englishman-Lord-Nelson 'MacMuckle'.

Anyone holding a rifle was now pointing it at the pair of them.

'Will somebody please tell me what's going on?' groaned Lord Rhome, for whom one thing was certain beyond a shadow of a doubt: Queen Victoria would never accept an invitation from him ever again.

'We'll not leave brave wee Hamish to face you on his own,' boomed Alexander. And then explain he did.

The MacMuckles at Tall Hall were not MacMuckles at all. That was true enough, but they weren't out to harm the Queen or anyone else for that matter. Quite the opposite, in fact. Their mission was to prevent harm . . . to the animals.

As a dedicated group of vegetarian animal-lovers, they had pretended to be MacMuckles and rightful heirs to Tall Hall so that they could set up there as part of a plan to save the animals from being shot for sport on the neighbouring Gloaming estate. (At this stage of the telling, Alexander glared at Lord Rhome.) As the English lord wasn't a regular visitor to his Scottish home, they thought they'd have time to develop their plans, until news of the Queen's visit and the shooting party changed everything. They'd already enlisted the help of young Magnus McFeeeeeeee, who was eager to be a party to anything which might upset an English lord, and now he had the added bonus of 'getting one over the English Queen'.

Over the previous few nights they'd been rounding up the deer and wild goats and any other creatures on the Gloaming estate that they feared Lord Rhome and the shooting party might try to kill and had led them all down into the huge cellar under Tall Hall. Although Alexander, Iain, Hamish, Martha, Nelly and Roberta really were vegetarians, much of the fruit and vegetables Eddie had seen being prepared in the kitchens had been to feed the animals.

Once the animals were safe, they'd wanted to find a way to deflect suspicion so that their scheme wouldn't be rumbled even before it had got off the ground. Then they'd found the body of a fine stag in a rocky crevice, which must have somehow lost its footing and fallen to its death. This was when Alexander'd had his brilliant idea: he and Iain would run around dressed as a stag and Lord Rhome would then shoot 'it'. By the time the shooting party reached the spot, though, all they'd find was the body of the already-dead stag.

'You were willing to be shot yourself in place of an animal?' said Mr Digg.

'I don't believe a word of it,' said Mr Delve.

'Then look at Lord Rhome's weapon, man,' said Alexander, indignantly.

This was the hunting rifle little, hairy Hamish had been holding. They soon discovered that it had been adapted to fire nothing more than blanks. So the whole plan had depended on Lord Rhome shooting the pantomime stag with his doctored weapon. If anyone else had fired real ammunition . . .

Eddie thought back to the conversation between Martha and Nelly and their fears that Scottish blood might be spilled. No wonder they'd been worried. This had been a risky plan!

Alexander and the others had obviously been relying on the fact that the only person who could pull rank on His Lordship was the Queen and, as I pointed out before, she never shot at living things herself.

Whilst everyone else had been gripped in fascination as Alexander explained their failed scheme, still dressed as the front end of a stag with the head tucked underneath his arm, Even Madder Aunt Maud had been showing Malcolm the heather. Now she came upon the huge bearded man quite by chance.

'Oh, hello, Alexander,' she said absent-mindedly. 'How's your sister Martha?'

Alexander grunted some form of acknowledgement through his mighty Scottish beard.

'You know these people?' gasped Eddie.

'Of course. He's Alexander McMickle and there's Iain with three feet.'

'Two 'i's,' Iain McMickle corrected her. 'Good afternoon, Mad Miss Maud MacMuckle.'

'Who are they?' demanded Mr Digg and Mr Delve.

'The McMickles? Loyal servants to the MacMuckles for generations,' said Even Madder Aunt Maud, moving on, 'until my father had some argument with them over a missing egg-spoon and had them all banished from the district.' She was now showing Malcolm a passing bumblebee.

'Take them away!' sighed Mr Delve, and the policemen (and sheep) that had swarmed up the hillside after Eddie now went down the hillside with Alexander, Iain and Hamish McMickle in custody.

'What will you charge them with?' Eddie asked Mr Digg, as they watched them go.

'Stealing my animals, trespass and impersonating a stag, if I have anything to do with it!' fumed Lord Rhome.

'I feel so stupid,' said Eddie. 'I thought they were going to try to harm Her Majesty.'

'Better safe than sorry, ay?' said Mr Delve.

But, underneath it all, Eddie couldn't help admiring the McMickles for what they'd tried to do.

★

Nobody could deny that Eddie had been wrong about the so-called MacMuckles, or the McMickles, as they'd turned out to be called – and I should probably point out that 'Many a McMickle does not a MacMuckle make', just to get it out of my system – but I don't want you to go away with the misconception that there wasn't a foiled attempt on Queen Victoria's life that day. There was.

Once the men-dressed-as-deer scam had been revealed, and explained to everyone's satisfaction, no one was quite sure what to do. Lord Rhome was all for having the animals let out of the cellar and shot anyway, but the Queen was appalled at the idea and said so in no uncertain terms. He had been about to suggest that they let loose the police sheep and shoot at them, but decided against it.

'We could dig for truffles,' Even Madder Aunt Maud suggested, thrusting Malcolm into Eddie's arms and throwing herself to the ground, digging in a patch of earth between the clumps of heather. It reminded Eddie of her once digging for a shiny thing in a snowdrift.

Embarrassed as only a child can be by the behaviour of his or her relative, Eddie stood in front of her in the hope that he was blocking her from Queen Victoria's view.

Mad Uncle Jack, meanwhile, was deep in conversation with a man with an impressively twirly moustache. It was a very one-sided conversation, with the man doing little more than grunting and nodding.

This didn't stop MUJ, though, who was thoroughly enjoying himself. He was probably secretly rather pleased that he didn't have to do any actual shooting, being such a dreadful shot. Unfortunately (or not, as we shall see), Mad Uncle Jack suddenly became distracted by a particular clump of heather, the shape of which reminded him of his father's – Dr Malcontent Dickens's – head, at exactly the same time that he was drawing from his jacket pocket the dried swordfish he used as a back-scratcher. Twisting around rather suddenly whilst clutching the fish, he knocked the startled man with the moustache to the ground.

When members of Her Majesty's security detail

– yup, Mr Digg and Mr Delve again – rushed forward to help him up, they noticed that the man's moustache had fallen off, and, being highly trained police officers, they registered that it was unusual for such facial hair to come off in one piece like that, so they were immediately very suspicious. When the man himself noticed his moustache lying on the ground like a very hairy, very dead caterpillar, he tried to make a run for it but the hands which had been helping him to his feet now grabbed him. Mr Digg held his right arm and Mr Delve his left.

It was during this struggle that a pistol fell from one of the man's pockets.

Polite as always, and a little guilty at having accidentally knocked the poor chap to the ground, Mad Uncle Jack bent down and picked the pistol out of the springy heather, with the intention of returning it to the would-be assassin.

'You dropped this, sir,' he announced.

As I've already pointed out more than once, Mad Uncle Jack was not very good with guns and his waving this one around made everyone very nervous.

Particularly Eddie.

'WEAPON!' shouted the Q-PUS when he saw the pistol, causing Mad Uncle Jack to turn towards him to see what all the fuss was about.

144

As his great-uncle began to turn, Eddie feared the worst and, literally, sprang into action.

'I prefer a pocket knife myself,' Mad Uncle Jack was saying, just as he accidentally pulled the trigger.

In the meantime, Eddie was throwing himself bodily between the Queen and the bullet, which was a very brave, or very foolish, thing to do.

He didn't make it in time.

Fortunately for HM Queen Victoria and her adoring (English) subjects, Malcolm did.

Eddie had still been holding Malcolm whilst Even Madder Aunt Maud was digging for truffles in the undergrowth. The stuffed stoat had reached Her Majesty before Eddie had, as this freeze-frame diagram below clearly illustrates.

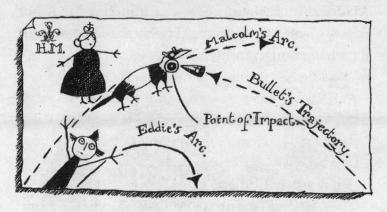

And that is why, six months later, the Dickens family came to be at Buckingham Palace and how

Malcolm the stuffed stoat came to be presented with a medal for bravery by a grateful monarch. Eddie, of course, got nothing. Think back to that incident with John Brown and Prince Arthur. You don't get medals for coming second – well, you do at the Olympics but not when it comes to saving monarchs from potential assassins – and it was Malcolm who took the bullet for her. He didn't seem to mind; Malcolm, that is. Even Madder Aunt Maud had the bullet removed and kept it in a jar on a shelf inside Marjorie. Malcolm, meanwhile, was stitched up and was as good as . . . well . . . certainly not as good as new, but as good as he had been prior to saving the life of the monarch. He didn't get £25 a year for life but, being stuffed, he didn't mind and, being mad, neither did Even Madder Aunt Maud. (She was impressed that her friend Charlotte 'Queenie' Hailstrom lived in such a nice big house, though.)

And what became of the McMickles? The Dickenses were very happy to let them stay in Tall Hall. The McMickle clan had been loyal servants to the MacMuckle clan in the past – I'm not clear what the egg-spoon incident had been which had caused the rift between the two families but it clearly didn't bother Even Madder Aunt Maud – and Mad Uncle Jack and Even Madder Aunt Maud were perfectly willing to give them a (very high) roof over their heads. Eddie was very satisfied that Robbie and her family ended up living there. One of the McMickles' first jobs now that they were legitimately living in Tall Hall was to fence off the grounds so that, once they were released from the cellar, the animals didn't end up straight back on the Gloaming estate where Lord Rhome could take pot shots at them.

Of course, Lord Rhome was furious. After all, they were *his* animals and he had every right to have them back, but the McMickles had a very good lawyer indeed, in the form of Angus McFeeeeeeee, who knew the Scottish Law (with a capital 'S' and a capital 'L') inside out and who kept Lord Rhome's Scottish lawyer (McFeeeeeeee's good friend Marcus MacGoon) busy with endless legal paperwork.

Whenever, on one of his less and less frequent trips to his Scottish estate, Lord Rhome summoned Mr MacGoon, the lawyer kept on reminding him that 'Possession is nine-tenths of the law,' which always threw His Lordship into a terrible rage.

Fighting an English absentee landlord made Angus McFeeeeeeee a hero in his son Magnus's eyes and when, many, many years after this adventure ended, Angus McFeeeeeeee died an old, old man, Magnus McFeeeeeeee gave a very stirring speech in memory of his much-loved dad. Magnus too became a lawyer and campaigned for Scottish independence throughout his life. Today, a McFeeeeeeee sits in the Scottish Parliament. He may be very small but he has a loud voice and strong opinions and makes sure that McFeeeeeeee is spelt with eight 'e's on the order papers.

And that nugget of information almost brings us to the close of this, the first of Eddie's Further Adventures.

Almost.

But not quite.

There's the small matter of the MacMuckle Falls or Gudger's Dump. Take your pick. You may recall that this feeble apology of a waterfall was somewhat black and slimy. Small wonder. One morning, about two years after Eddie's eventful visit, it erupted in a fountain of thick, black liquid. The earth had revealed its secret: beneath the grounds of Tall Hall lay one of the very few, if not the *only*, oil deposits on mainland Scotland.

When the McMickles reported this to Mad Uncle Jack, he ordered it plugged. (He even drew a sketch of what he'd like the plug to look like; with a long chain like the one in his favourite bathroom at Awful End.) What did he want with all that oil or the money it could generate? It would only mean that a rig would have to be built, along with roads and buildings and all sorts of other things that would mess up the peaceful life of the Highlands and upset the animals. He was quite happy to leave things the way they were. It was dried fish he was interested in. Not oil.

If you think he was mad to turn down the opportunity to make money – especially when he'd been planning to sell Tall Hall in the first place in order to make some – I need only remind you what members of his family called him: *Mad* Uncle Jack and – do you know what? – I expect that they loved him all the more for it anyway.

It's adventures that make life really worth living, not money. And Eddie had plenty more of those to come.

THE END
until a further Further Adventure

AUTHOR'S NOTE

Some readers have mentioned that they're not
sure which parts (if any) of my books are made
up and which parts (if any) are true. I know how
they feel.

Horrendous
Habits

Book Two of the Further Adventures of
Eddie Dickens Trilogy

For my son, Frederick.
Hi, Freddie!

A Message from the Author

Who's admiring his new pair of trousers

This book is full of monks. In fact, it's *so* full of monks that my wife Héloïse suggested that I call it 'Monkey Business' but, as you can see, I didn't. It's a very good title though, but please don't tell her I said so. I don't want to encourage her. Where would it end?

In the previous Further Adventure, *Dubious Deeds*, Eddie spent most of his time in Scotland. This time around he's much closer to home but might just as well be in Scotland because he can't remember where he lives.

Confused? Then read on . . .

PHILIP ARDAGH
East Sussex, 2005

Contents

Episode 1

A New Arrival

*In which, somewhat surprisingly,
a baby is found in the bulrushes*

'What is it?' demanded Even Madder Aunt
Maud, stomping towards a patch of
bulrushes, with Malcolm her stuffed stoat (who
looked suspiciously like a stuffed ferret) under one
arm.

'It sounds like a baby,' said Eddie, above the
wailing which had attracted them down to the
water's edge in the first place. (At Even Madder
Aunt Maud's insistence, she and Eddie had been
playing an unusual game of croquet on the lower
lawn at Awful End. Unusual because, instead of

159

croquet balls, they'd been using croquet turnips, or 'rutabagas' as our American friends would say. She'd found a whole sack of them down by the compost heaps and hadn't wanted them to go to waste.)

Eddie ran past Maud to the edge of the ornamental lake. 'Yes!' he cried. 'It's a baby!'

'A baby what?' demanded Even Madder Aunt Maud.

'A baby,' Eddie repeated, wading into the shallows and parting the bulrushes. He didn't think he could put it any more simply than that.

'A baby carrot? A baby carriage? A baby possum?' Even Madder Aunt Maud wanted to know. She'd recently read about the extraordinary wildlife of the continent of Australia in a book entitled *The Extraordinary Wildlife of the Continent of Australia* and was delighted to have the opportunity to introduce the word possum into a conversation quite legitimately. (It's a tree-dwelling animal with a pouch like a kangaroo's and a tail designed for grasping branches, in case you didn't already know.)

'A baby *baby*,' said Eddie, lifting the crying child out of a basket firmly wedged amongst the tall stalks at the water's edge. (That's the tall stalks of the bulrushes, of course, spelled s-t-a-l-k-s. I don't want you to go thinking that the baby in the basket was in the lake wedged between the bird kind of

160

storks, spelled s-t-o-r-k-s. It's important to clear this up right now because, in Eddie's day, children were often told that it was the stork – the bird not the bulrush stems – that delivered new babies to households.) 'It's a human baby.'

Eddie held the crying infant in his arms and waded back on to the lawn. It stopped crying almost immediately.

Even Madder Aunt Maud glared down at the little bundle of joy. 'It's got a very large head,' she announced.

'Babies generally have, Mad Aunt Maud,' said Eddie.

'What was it doing floating around in my lake like . . . like . . .'

'Like Moses in the bulrushes?' Eddie suggested helpfully.

'Who in the what?' asked his great-aunt.

'Moses in the Bible,' said Eddie.

'I thought you said in the bulrushes?' said Even Madder Aunt Maud, narrowing her eyes as though suspecting Eddie of playing some trick on her.

'Moses in the bulrushes in the Bible,' he explained.

Even Madder Aunt Maud seemed to have absolutely no idea what he was talking about, so she hit him over the head with Malcolm. 'Oh do be quiet,' she said.

The moment the very rigid (and very hard) stuffed stoat came into contact with Eddie's head, it was the babe in his arms who cried out and not Eddie. It glared at Even Madder Aunt Maud and let out a particularly plaintive wail.

'That thing just threatened me!' said EMAM in amazement. 'Did you see the look it gave me? Well, did you?'

'It's only a baby, Mad Aunt Maud,' said Eddie. 'I'm sure it meant no harm.'

'Then what was it doing lurking in my cake?'

'You mean lake,' Eddie corrected her, as politely as possible.

'And she said lake,' said Eddie's father, Mr Dickens, appearing at her side. 'The cake thing was a typing error. Mr Ardagh gets sloppy like that sometimes. Some readers even write in to complain.'

Eddie had less than no idea of what his father was talking about.

'Where did you find that child?' Mr Dickens wanted to know.

'It was in a basket in the bulrushes,' said Eddie.

'Like Moses in the Bible,' said Even Madder Aunt Maud, which surprised Eddie more than a little.

'What kind of basket?' asked Mr Dickens.

'Does that matter, Father?' asked Eddie. 'I mean,

shouldn't we get the poor thing inside and make sure it's dry and . . . and suchlike?'

'Matter? Of course it matters. If we are to return this baby to its rightful owners, then the basket might contain a vital clue as to their identity.'

Even Madder Aunt Maud was seized by the idea and when she was seized by an idea she ran with it, mixed metaphors or no mixed metaphors. 'If it's a laundry basket, then the baby's parents could work in a laundry. If it's a snake charmer's basket, its parents could be snake charmers. If it's a picnic basket, its parents could . . . could, er –'

'Like sandwiches?' Mr Dickens suggested, helpfully, one eyebrow – though I'm not sure which – slightly raised.

Eddie carefully handed the baby, who was wrapped in a snow-white blanket, to his father, who accepted him – he'll turn out to be a he – like a man who'd never held a baby in his life. He'd certainly never held Eddie when he was a baby. Victorian fathers didn't generally do such things. Their job as fathers was to look at their offspring over the top of a newspaper once in a while, or demand to see them in their study in their Sunday best.

The baby now safely in Mr Dickens's arms (where he started wailing again the moment Eddie let go of him), Eddie waded back into the shallows of the ornamental lake and dragged out the basket.

He inspected it. It was a very ordinary basketylooking basket and there was no conveniently placed luggage label with a name and address on it, either. In fact, there was no label of any kind, and nothing to offer any obvious clues that Eddie could see. 'It's just a basket,' he said.

'Couldn't we put it back?' suggested Even Madder Aunt Maud, looking down at the baby.

'WAAAAAAAAAAAAAAAAAA!' said the baby (for much longer than space in this book permits).

'The basket or the baby, Even Madder Aunt Maud?' asked a disbelieving Eddie.

'Put it back?' asked Mr Dickens above the din, raising the other eyebrow (whichever one that was). He handed his son the baby, who instantly fell silent again.

'In my youth, I went fishing with my brothers

in the lochs of Scotland,' said Even Madder Aunt Maud. 'If they didn't like the look of a fish they caught, they put it back.'

'Hmmm,' said Mr Dickens. 'An interesting idea, Aunt,' he said, 'but might I suggest that it's rather a short-term solution.'

'But you never had any brothers,' Eddie pointed out as politely as possible.

'And we never went fishing!' Even Madder Aunt Maud added triumphantly, as though this were some sort of game and she'd just scored big points off Eddie.

'I'll take the baby to Mother. She'll know what to do,' said Eddie, though the truth be told, he rather suspected that she might not. In the brief time that Eddie had not been at school or at sea in his early childhood, Eddie had been looked after by Nanny Louche, an onion-seller by profession who'd been given the job of caring for Baby Edmund by default. (Here, 'by default' means 'by mistake', only more so.) Eddie had no memory of her now, but had a nice warm feeling every time he smelt raw unpeeled onions or saw someone wearing a stripy shirt.

He eventually found his mother in the drawing room, unravelling the flowery-patterned cover of one of the armchairs. 'This will make useful string,' she explained, rolling the unpicked thread into a ball. 'Is that your baby, dearest?'

165

'No, Mother. I just found it.'

'Well you can't keep it, I'm afraid, Edmund. They're very demanding and very expensive to maintain. I had one once, you know.'

'Yes I do know, Mother,' said Eddie. 'That was me.'

Mrs Dickens got up off her knees and sat herself down in the chair that she'd been quietly ruining. 'Why so it was!' she laughed. 'Now do explain what's going on.'

Eddie sat on a footstool opposite her, still carefully cradling the baby in his arms. The baby gurgled contentedly, whilst the water in Eddie's shoes squelched noisily. He'd left a trail of muddy wet footprints across the room. 'Even Madder Aunt Maud and I were playing croquet on the lower lawn when we heard a baby crying and I found it in a basket in the bulrushes, like Moses.'

'Like who, dear?'

'Moses –' said Eddie.

'Moses?'

'Never mind, Mother,' said Eddie. 'I was wondering what we should do with it.'

'Do?' asked his mother.

'With the baby,' said Eddie. 'To make sure that it's comfortable and unharmed.'

Mrs Dickens leant forward and unwrapped the

blanket. 'It,' she pronounced, 'is a he, and he looks perfectly happy to me. If he were hungry, unhappy or in pain he'd be crying.'

'That's a relief, mother,' said Eddie, wrapping him up again. 'Shouldn't you take him?'

'Where?'

'Out of my arms.'

'Why?'

That was a good question. 'Because – er – you're a grown-up and a mother and you understand these things.'

Mrs Dickens laughed again. 'Really, Edmund! Where do you get such ideas from? Just because I'm an adult and a mother doesn't mean I can make the slightest sense of this world, or anyone in it!'

'Then what shall I do with him?' asked Eddie, looking down at the baby, who looked back up at him with a pair of big, trusting, clear-blue eyes.

'Name him, of course,' said Eddie's mother. 'You can't go around calling him "it" or "him" all the time.'

Eddie stood up and walked over to one of the huge windows overlooking the lawn, sloping down to the lake in the distance.

'But what about his parents?' said Eddie.

'They can call him what they like,' said Mrs Dickens.

'Shouldn't we try to find them?'

'Perhaps your father could place an advertisement in the local newspaper,' she suggested. '"Found, one baby boy." They're bound to notice he's missing sooner or later.'

'But what if it was his mother or father who put him in the basket in the first place?' Eddie suggested. 'Maybe they couldn't afford to look after him –'

'It's an expensive blanket,' Mrs Dickens commented. She had joined her son by the window and was picking at the corner of the material.

'So it is!' said Eddie, clearly impressed. 'I think I shall call him Ned.' Eddie had recently been reading about the remarkable exploits of Ned Kelly, the Australian outlaw, in a book entitled *The Remarkable Exploits of Ned Kelly, The Australian Outlaw*, and thought the name rather exciting. (In case you were wondering, an Australian cousin on Eddie's mother's side of the family had recently sent over a whole box of books. I've no idea why.)

'Baby Ned,' said Mrs Dickens. 'An excellent choice, Eddie.'

Much to Eddie's amazement, it was Gibbering Jane who took charge of Baby Ned. All Eddie had ever heard her do was gibber – hence the name – but the first thing she said on seeing the baby was, 'Oh, ain't he cute, Master Edmund? Can I 'old 'im?' and, when he passed Ned over, Eddie was delighted to find that the baby didn't start bawling again. It turned out that Jane (a failed chambermaid who spent most of her time in a cupboard under the stairs but, nowadays, did a few light duties about the place too) had been the second eldest of twelve children and had helped to bring up some of the younger ones before she'd ended up in service (which, in her case, meant working for the Dickenses).

In next to no time, she'd found some old napkins to use as nappies and had washed and changed Ned. She took the cutlery drawer out of an empty old kitchen dresser in one of the many unused rooms in the house, and turned it into a cot for him.

'What about food?' asked Eddie. 'What do babies eat?'

'Don't you worry about that,' said Jane.

Eddie was incredibly impressed. He left Ned

cooing happily, and went in search of his father, squelching his way around the house and garden.

Unfortunately, he found Mr Dickens in conversation with Mad Uncle Jack at the foot of his treehouse (in which his great-uncle now lived much of the time). Unfortunately because Eddie knew that, with MUJ around, a straightforward conversation would be out of the question.

'I was wondering how we should go about locating the baby's parents, Father,' said Eddie tentatively.

'What kind of tree am I?' barked Mad Uncle Jack, no pun intended. Tree . . . bark . . . Never mind.

'I'm sorry?' asked Eddie.

'I should have thought that the question was perfectly clear,' said Mad Uncle Jack.

'I – er –'

'Do I speak with a stutter?'

'No –'

'Was I whispering?'

'No, I –'

'Was I speaking Chinese?'

'It's not that, Mad Unc –'

'Then what kind of tree am I?'

'It's a puzzle, my boy,' said Mr Dickens. 'Your great-uncle is asking you a riddle.'

'Oh, I see,' said Eddie, somewhat relieved. 'I don't know, Mad Uncle Jack. What kind of tree are you?'

'Tree?'

'Yes. I give up,' said Eddie. 'What kind of tree are you?'

'TREE?'

'Yes,' said Eddie, a little nervously now. 'W-What kind of tree are you?'

Mad Uncle Jack glared at him and frowned one of his thinnest of thin frowns above his thinnest of thin noses. 'Tree? Don't be so damned impertinent!'

Seeing his son's predicament, Mr Dickens came to Eddie's rescue. 'We'll see if anyone comes to the house asking about the missing child,' he said, 'and, if not, we'll inform the authorities.'

'Good idea,' said Eddie. They had a plan at last.

'I'm an oak!' laughed Mad Uncle Jack. He now had an acorn hanging from either ear, like a pair of nature's earrings.

Episode 2

Disaster Strikes

*In which we learn of a proposed beating,
and end with a 'CRUNCH!'*

The following morning, Eddie didn't get to see Baby Ned before breakfast, which began with his father announcing that – No, hang on, let him tell it:

'Today is the annual beating the bounds!' said Mr Dickens over the top of the bacon piled high on his plate.

'What's that, Father?' asked Eddie politely.

'Questions! Questions!' said his father.

'It means once-a-year,' said his mother from her end of the table.

'I know what annual means, Mother,' said Eddie. 'I was wondering about the beating the bounds part.'

172

'Questions! Questions!' his father repeated.

Eddie reached for the china marmalade pot. It was shaped like an orange, with the leaves on the top acting as the handle to the lid. He lifted it. The pot was empty.

'We appear to have run out of marmalade,' said Eddie.

'Disgraceful!' said Mr Dickens. 'Ring for Daphne.'

Dawkins was Mr Dickens's gentleman's gentleman but, since coming with them to Awful End, now did just about everything around the house . . . but Mr Dickens called him Daphne. He wasn't good at remembering names.

Eddie got up from his seat and yanked the bell pull. Down in the depths of Awful End, a little bell (in a row of little bells) rang. Dawkins looked up from the ironing board on which he was ironing his favourite pieces of tissue paper and, by looking at the label under the jangling bell, which read 'Morning Room', he could see where his services were required. He put down the iron, slipped on the jacket of his suit and began the long trek up the stairs.

Meanwhile, Mr Dickens was explaining 'beating the bounds' to his son.

'The age-old tradition of beating the bounds goes back hundreds of years in this country,

Jonathan.' (See? I told you he was bad with names.) 'Its origins have been lost in the mists of time.'

'Oranges?' asked Mrs Dickens. 'Did you say oranges, dear?'

'Origins,' repeated Mr Dickens.

'I'm sorry,' said his wife. 'I was sure you said oranges.'

Mr Dickens chewed on a piece of bacon and gave his wife a funny look. She didn't seem to know what to do with it, so she gave it straight back. Watching the funny look pass between them – quite a feat when they were at opposite ends of an impressively long breakfast table – Eddie wished his father would hurry up and explain the bounds part and get on to the beating. It sounded painful.

'The bounds in question are boundaries, so if, for example, you're beating the parish bounds it would be the perimeter of the parish.' Mr Dickens pulled a small piece of bacon rind from his mouth, which had been lodged between his teeth.

At that moment, Dawkins entered the breakfast room. He was about to say one of his favourite lines, 'You rang, sir?' (which is one of the first things they teach you to say at gentleman's gentleman school), when Eddie's mother preempted him, which isn't as painful as it sounds. It simply means 'got in there before he did'.

'Oranges,' she said. 'We've run out of oranges.'

'Origins, not oranges,' Mr Dickens corrected her.

'Marmalade,' Eddie corrected them both. 'Could we have some more marmalade, please, Dawkins?'

'Very good, Master Edmund,' said Dawkins, taking the empty pot in his gloved hand and leaving the room. (That 'very good' wasn't a 'very good' as in 'well done' but as in 'yes, I'll do that at once'.)

'Where was I?' asked Mr Dickens. 'I suspect these interruptions add nothing to the plot.'

'You were about to explain the beating part,' his son reminded him.

'Tradition has it that, once a year, people would walk along a boundary, beating the ground with sticks,' Mr Dickens continued. 'This would have two functions: firstly, in order to remind everyone who traipsed after the beater exactly where the boundary was and, secondly, to thrash aside any

175

nettles – for example – which may be obscuring the boundary.'

Mrs Dickens laughed.

'What's funny about that, my love?' asked her husband.

'I wasn't laughing at your explanation,' Eddie's mother explained. 'It's simply that I've made an amusing face out of the food upon my breakfast plate.'

She held up the plate and turned it around for them to see. The sausage nose, rasher-of-bacon mouth and mushroom eyes did, indeed, make an impressive face. The scrambled-egg hair was a stroke of genius. What was equally impressive was the way in which she'd managed to stick everything in place so that it hadn't slid off the plate when she held it up at right angles to the table. She'd used marmalade. Hence the empty pot.

'Enchanting,' said Mr Dickens. He loved most things about his wife, including the way she played with her food. They'd first met as children and, during one of their earliest encounters, she'd been in the middle of a game of hide-and-seek with a bowl of trifle.

She put her plate back down on the linen tablecloth, and Eddie's father went on with his explanation. 'An alternative version of beating the bounds has a boy being beaten at regular intervals along the boundary. If you do this, he isn't going to forget the route in a hurry, now, is he?'

The door opened and Dawkins re-entered the room, the refilled orange-shaped marmalade pot on a silver salver (which is a small round tray). He placed it in front of Eddie. 'Your marmalade, Master Edmund,' he said.

'Thank you very much,' said Eddie.

The gentleman's gentleman nodded and left the room, eager to get back to ironing his tissue paper. He loved tissue paper and his favourite tissue paper was freshly ironed tissue paper, still warm.

Whilst Eddie spread the marmalade on his toast (from which he'd already pulled the watch springs his mother insisted on being added to the flour), and whilst his mother proceeded to pull each item of food off her plate with her fingers, lick the marmalade glue from the back and put it back down again, Mr Dickens proceeded to explain the Awful End approach to beating the bounds.

'It isn't common practice for private estates to have beating the bounds ceremonies, but Mad Uncle Jack says that it's been going on here for as long as he can remember.'

'But if it's an annual event, Father, why haven't I seen it before?' asked Eddie, which was a good question. Eddie and his parents had been living at Awful End for a few years by then.

His father was about to say 'Questions! Questions!' yet *again*, when Mad Uncle Jack burst through the door in person. (Mad Uncle Jack was the person, not the door.)

'Good morning, everybody!' he said, his eyes twinkling with excitement above his beakiest of beaky noses. 'Today's the day!'

'No one could argue with that, Mudge!' said Mrs Dickens, 'mudge' being how one pronounces MUJ unless one says 'em-ew-jay'.

'I want everyone up and out of here and ready to witness the beating of the bounds by ten o'clock,' announced Eddie's great-uncle.

'What about Baby Ned –?' Eddie began.

'We've fine weather for it!' said MUJ. He spun around one-hundred-and-eighty degrees and strode out of the room as fast as his spindly legs would allow.

At that precise moment a horrible thought struck Eddie. The colour drained from his face. (There's no point in looking for the nearest illustration.

They're all in black and white.) His father said that, traditionally, it was a *boy* who was beaten when beating the bounds: a b-o-y.

The last time that he'd checked, he was the only boy at Awful End, apart from Ned, of course, who was more of a baby than a boy. In a *typical* house of that size there would have been numerous servants including, at the very least, a boot boy, but Awful End was far from typical. The house itself was occupied by Eddie and his parents, Dawkins and Gibbering Jane. Mad Uncle Jack lived in the treehouse in the grounds; Even Madder Aunt Maud lived in Marjorie (a giant hollow cow) in the rose garden; and then there was the handful of ex-soldiers on the estate, who'd once served under Mad Uncle Jack in his regiment.

Fortunately for Eddie, it transpired that Mad Uncle Jack and Even Madder Aunt Maud had a slightly different approach to the more traditional beating the bounds. Each year – on the years that they remembered to do it, that is (and no one was in a hurry to remind them) – they now beat one of the ex-soldiers with Maud's stuffed stoat Malcolm (or was it Sally?).

Each year, MUJ asked for a volunteer from their ranks and each year one of their number was pushed forward by the others to act as the unwilling participant.

179

In the year that the events in this Further Adventures unfolded, Mad Uncle Jack's ex-soldiers were spending much of their time working on the vast cast-iron bridge he was having constructed between his treehouse and Marjorie the hollow cow ('So that I can hurry to my love pumpkin with grace and ease' was how he'd put it. The love pumpkin, of course, being his dear wife Even Madder Aunt Maud).

The bridge was designed by that fairly well-known engineer Fandango Jones who – according to him, at least – had once worked alongside the very famous Victorian engineer Isambard Kingdom Brunel. What no one ever dared ask, and Fandango Jones never volunteered, was what kind of work it was, exactly, that he'd done alongside Brunel. Some of the less kind critics of his work have suggested that it was carrying the great man's hat, others that it was selling those little bags of roast chestnuts, but we can't be sure. What we *can* be sure about, though, was that Isambard Kingdom Brunel was a better engineer than Fandango Jones, which is probably why he had three names when Fandango Jones only had two.

According to an anonymous pamphlet praising the life and achievement of Fandango Jones, published a year or so before his death (and probably by Jones himself, with help with the spelling of some of the harder words from his wife Clarissa), Jones's given name was Clement; it being a tradition in his branch of the Jones family that all eldest sons were called 'Clement'. On page three of *Bridging the Gap: Being the Life of that Fairly Well-Known Engineer Fandango Jones*, it reveals that this Clement Jones gained the nickname Fandango from the way in which he would explain his latest design by 'pacing it out upon the floor, with the sure and swift-footedness of one dancing the fandango' but, I assume, without the aid of castanets or a tambourine.

As well as being a little – how shall I put it? – eccentric, Mr Jones was also quite frightening to look at. He was small and squat with a stovepipe hat – made from two stovepipe hats riveted together to give it extra height – and very bushy side-whiskers which his loving wife Clarissa referred to as his 'mutton chops'. What was most unusual, though, was that the small round spectacles he wore at all times contained blue-tinted lenses. Most unfortunate (and this is well recorded, but not in the pamphlet *Bridging the Gap: Being the Life of that Fairly Well-Known Engineer Fandango Jones*) is the fact that he was one of those people who spat when he spoke . . .

. . . which is why, when Eddie and his parents congregated at the front of the house after a

181

marmalade-filled breakfast, Eddie found Even Madder Aunt Maud had her umbrella up and in front of her whilst in conversation with the engineer.

'But why iron?' she was arguing for the umpteenth time. 'Why not wood? A wooden bridge would do.'

'Your husband specifically specified an iron bridge, madam,' said Fandango Jones, spraying EMAM's umbrella as he spoke.

'Or rope? I believe in some parts of the empire, there are some perfectly good rope bridges.'

'The use of iron was at your husband's insistence.'

'Or paper. I have it on good authority that the Japanese build the walls of their houses from paper. How about a nice paper bridge? *Thick* paper mind you.'

'Madam. The choice of material was not mine, but –'

'Or soup. Why not a bridge of soup?'

'Soup?'

'Soup!'

'That's –' Fandango Jones was about to say 'madness' when he stopped himself. Not because he thought it'd be rude to call his current employer's wife mad – with a name such as Even Madder Mrs Dickens it might even be considered appropriate – but because the thought occurred to him that this lady brandishing a stuffed stoat in one hand and an umbrella in the other might have a point. If no one had built a bridge of soup before, and he was to do so, then he could be the first! He could imagine the headline in *Civil Engineers Bi-Monthly*: '**FANDANGO JONES BUILDS FIRST BRIDGE MADE FROM SOUP**'. It was when he was imagining the subheading, '**They Said It Could Not Be Done**', that his face fell. Of course it couldn't be done. It was an impossible idea. It was a ridiculous, silly idea. 'The bridge is to be made of iron, madam, and there's an end to it.'

It was just as Jones spat out the word 'it' that a chimney (shaped like a giant barley sugar, apparently) fell from the roof of Awful End and landed on Eddie's father, Mr Dickens, with a fairly dreadful 'CRUNCH'.

Episode 3

Flat Out

In which fate, in the form of a chimney,
deals a blow to poor Mr Dickens

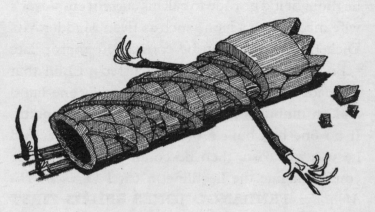

I once wrote a book called *Heir of Mystery* and in it is a picture of a man, named Vern De Vere, lying under a large sign that fell off the wall of an army recruiting office and landed on top of him. You couldn't tell that it was Mr De Vere because all that was sticking out from under the sign were his arms and legs.

As you can see, this would have been very similar to the sight that faced Mr Dickens's relatives as they looked down on the poor man trapped under the chimney stack.

Unlike Mr De Vere, who didn't survive his tragic accident, Mr Dickens was alive and, if not exactly well, at least groaning. Mrs Dickens thought she heard her husband mutter 'I'll get you for this, Ardagh!' but put it down to the ramblings of a seriously injured man. It made no sense at all.

It was Eddie who suggested that they lift the large chunk of stone off his father. The others were busy gawping. With the help of Ex-Private Drabb (who'd been 'volunteered' to be beaten in that year's beating the bounds), Eddie lifted up the chimney and dropped it to one side. It made quite a thud when it hit the driveway.

Ex-Private Drabb looked surprisingly muscular for a man of his age, for he was, to borrow my mother's phrase, 'no spring chicken'. This was misleading. Those weren't really broad shoulders, a large chest and muscles bulging under his clothing; he had various cushions stuffed in there to act as padding. Padding against what? Being beaten with a stuffed stoat at regular intervals, that's what.

I think there's a saying along the lines of 'one man's misfortune is another man's fortune' and if there isn't there should be. Poor old Mr Dickens being flattened by one of Awful End's numerous chimneys may have been rather bad luck for Mr Dickens, but was excellent news for Ex-Private Drabb. Beating the bounds of the Awful End estate would be postponed or, if luck was *really* on his side, maybe even cancelled altogether.

The chimney removed, Mrs Dickens threw herself to the gravelly ground and cradled her husband in her marmalade-stained lap. 'Speak to me!' she pleaded.

'Father!' Eddie cried. 'Are you all right?'

'Damn and confound it!' said Mad Uncle Jack, looking up at the roof. 'More repairs!'

'Get up, lazybones,' said Even Madder Aunt Maud prodding Mr Dickens with the tip of her now-closed umbrella (which made a change from using the tip of Malcolm's nose).

'Father!' Eddie repeated.

'Why can't I be in a book about nice fluffy bunnies where not much happens?' groaned Mr Dickens.

'Mad!' said Even Madder Aunt Maud. 'He's gone quite mad. We'll have to have him shot.'

'*Fwumbblewww,*' said Mrs Dickens, who'd now filled her mouth with gravel to calm her nerves.

'I'll fetch Dawkins,' said Ex-Private Drabb, scuttling off into the house.

'Roof tiles are expensive enough,' muttered MUJ, 'but a whole replacement chimney?'

'Hmmmm,' said Fandango Jones, who'd produced a notebook from his pocket and was writing notes and drawing angles and lines and diagrams with a stubby pencil. 'Most interesting.'

'We must get a stonemason!' said Mad Uncle Jack.

'We must get sandwiches!' said Even Madder Aunt Maud.

'We must get the police!' spat Mr Jones, the engineer, having completed some complicated calculations in his head.

'We must get a DOCTOR!' shouted Eddie.

That shut them all up.

'Yes,' said Mad Uncle Jack, looking down at Eddie's father as though he'd forgotten he was lying there. 'We must send Dawkins to fetch Doctor Humple at once.'

'And have him bring sandwiches!' Even Madder Aunt Maud added. 'And what fillings would my little Malcolm like?' she asked the stuffed stoat. It said nothing, giving her a glassy stare. No surprises there, then.

Nowadays we know that we shouldn't move people when they've been injured, until the professionals arrive. Back in those days, it was thought that you'd be better off lying on a bed or a couch or something more comfortable than a gravel driveway if you'd just been hit by a chimney. In fact, in *Old Roxbee's Book of Common Household Ailments*, under 'Injuries Incurred Upon Being Hit By A Fallen Chimney' it states:

In order to assist the poor unfortunate struck by said chimney, remove him to a comfortable spot and tenderly apply a bread poultice to the affected area, offering gentle words of encouragement throughout the treatment. If the patient's life appears to be in serious danger, do not feel it your duty to inform him, but simply offer a soothing, 'There, there,' whilst patting his hand with your own.

The advice, of course, applied equally well to 'shes' as 'hes', but it was usually only men who got a mention in such books of the time, except in sections particularly devoted to women, dealing with such matters as 'Upon Being Upset by a Fellow Guest at a Ladies' Luncheon Party', 'Upon Having An Attack of the Vapours' and 'Upon Being Confronted by a Particularly Unpleasant Shade of Pink Without Sufficient Warning'.

Fortunately for Eddie's father, there wasn't a copy of *Old Roxbee's Book of Common Household Ailments* to be found in Awful End, or he'd probably have suffered more pain and indignity than being carried to a chaise longue in the withdrawing room, which would, no doubt, have involved covering him from head to toe – because his 'affected area' was just about everywhere – in porridge, it being the closest thing to a poultice they'd have to hand. Having said that, as you'll discover, the Dickenses had their own ideas.

It was whilst Dawkins and Ex-Private Drabb were doing the carrying that there was a nasty clicking sound and Dawkins's back locked in position. His back locking in position meant that Dawkins could no longer stand up straight and certainly was in no position to ride a horse into town to fetch Dr Humple. Which is how Eddie came to volunteer to take the pony and trap . . . and, dear reader, how he came to have a terrible accident of his own.

The pony which was pulling the trap (more than a cart but less than a carriage) that Eddie was sitting in hadn't belonged to the Dickens family for very long. His name was Horsey and he'd been given to Eddie's father by the Thackerys who'd been their nearest neighbours when they'd lived in their previous house (since burnt to the ground). The Thackerys – not to be confused with the Thacker*ays*, of whom the famous author William Makepeace Thackeray was one – were fairly regular visitors to Awful End, though they did their best to stay out of the way of Mad Uncle Jack and Even Madder Aunt Maud. It was Laudanum and Florinda they'd come to see. ('Mr and Mrs Dickens' to you and me. Or 'mother and father' to

Eddie.) Hey! Wait a minute. I think this is the very first time in five books that I've actually told you Eddie's parents' first names. I hope it was worth the wait.

Jonas Thackery and his wife Emily had eight children, the youngest (Joy) being just a few years old and the oldest (Thomas) being older than his mother, for legal reasons. (It had something to do with inheritance and taxes.) The Thackerys loved animals and the children were forever looking after birds with broken wings or rabbits with a slight limp, even if it meant injuring them in the first place.

They were never more happy than when they were nursing a pig back to health or informing a goat that her kid would make a full recovery. They'd gained quite a reputation locally when Mrs Thackery had managed to nurse an injured racehorse named *Forward Motion* (in italics) back to health when the usual prescription was shooting them. The cure had involved the use of a great deal of something called 'rubbing alcohol' and a variety of different herbs. Mrs Thackery was drunk for weeks and her breath stank of ragwort, but the horse made a full recovery.

At the very first race *Forward Motion* (in italics) ran in after his miraculous cure, he was so full of energy that he galloped straight into the stands and trampled several race-goers to death. Fortunately for the Thackerys, the race-goers were from abroad and, not being British, the tragedy didn't merit more than a few lines in the national newspapers. The only Thackery who didn't like animals one tiny bit (except on his plate with at least two vegetables) was David Thackery, who was about Eddie's age. When he grew up, he wanted to be a man of the cloth. Despite what it may sound like, 'a man of the cloth' isn't a window cleaner or even a tailor but another name for a churchman. His ultimate aim was to be an archbishop (or, perhaps, a saint), but he'd be happy starting off as a rector or a vicar or something like that.

David Thackery was always quick to point out that animals didn't have souls and couldn't go to heaven, so wouldn't his parents and siblings be better off caring for less fortunate people rather than wasting their time with silly-old-animals? This would usually cause his mother to burst into tears and to bury her face in the nearest furry patient.

Whenever Mr and Mrs Thackery came to visit the Dickens at Awful End, they always brought one or other of their children with them and at least one animal. On the occasion that they'd brought Horsey as a present, they'd also brought David. Whilst Laudanum and Florinda Dickens and Jonas and Emily Thackery went inside for tea, Eddie and David were instructed to 'take the air'. (They didn't have to take it anywhere except inside their lungs. It was a way of telling them to go outside.)

'Show Edmund what we've brought the family this time, dearest,' Mrs Thackery had instructed her son.

Eddie had been delighted with Horsey, but time spent with David was always a different matter. And now Eddie and Horsey were heading for Dr Humple, and that terrible, terrible accident I already mentioned. The suspense is killing me.

A Crash after the Crunch

In which Eddie Dickens doesn't know he is

Eddie's biggest problem at that precise moment was that he didn't know that he was. Eddie Dickens, that is. All he knew for sure was that he was lying face down in a gorse bush and that his head hurt. Quite a lot of him hurt, in fact. Gorse bushes are renowned for their prickles and a good percentage of prickles from this particular bush were sticking into him. Now Eddie knew what it would feel like to be a hedgehog who'd absent-mindedly put his coat on inside out.

Eddie managed to struggle free of the bush, tearing much of his clothing, and some of his skin, in the process. Upright and dizzy, he looked around. 'Who am I?' he wondered, and only then did he wonder *where* he was.

Eddie's left knee hurt even more than his head and he found it difficult to scramble up the grassy bank to the road but, whoever he might turn out to be, he knew that he couldn't lie around in a gorse bush in a ditch all day.

Eddie didn't know what to expect as he climbed the bank but, one thing's for certain, it wasn't a bright red dragon carrying a basket of fruit. But that's exactly what he did see.

The dragon smiled. 'Apple?' it asked, though I somehow wish it had said 'banana'.

Eddie collapsed to the ground unconscious.

Time passed. Eddie opened his eyes. He was staring up at a ceiling; and what a ceiling.

Where on Earth was he? Lying in the middle of a cathedral or something? How had he got there? He tried to sit up. His head swam. He felt all woo-oo-oo-oozy and he was disoriented, which means the same as 'disorientated' but is shorter.

'*Wozzgowinnon?*' he slurred.

He felt a hand on his shoulder. 'Rest, my child,' said a kindly voice.

'*Hooamma? Wurramma?*' he asked, which may sound a bit like the way some of the Scottish folk spoke in the first book in these Further Adventures, but actually meant 'Who am I? Where am I?', which were both perfectly reasonable questions under the circumstances.

'Rest now, questions later,' said the man – yes it was definitely a man – with the kindly voice.

Eddie looked at him. The man was no oil-painting. He looked quite frightening, in fact; his face half in shadow beneath some kind of hood. He looked sinister. He had a very, *very* large nose which was very, *very* warty, and he had three peg-like teeth overhanging his lower lip. Then there were his clothes. He appeared to be wearing a light brown sack. But the man's voice soothed Eddie. He felt safe, somehow. Eddie groaned and lay back down again. He'd just remembered the bright red dragon.

'I must have been seeing things,' he groaned.

The bright red dragon peered over the man's shoulder. 'How is the boyo?' it asked.

Eddie fainted again. It seemed the most logical thing to do.

★

Now, I'm such a quiet narrator that you've probably forgotten all about me, so I hope that it doesn't come as too much of a shock if I stop the action, introduce myself – Hello, reader dearest, I'm the very lovely Philip Ardagh, remember? – and tell you a little bit about where Eddie-who's-forgotten-that-he-*is*-Eddie had ended up. He was in the vast medieval pile of Lamberley Monastery. The monastery was originally built in the year 1074 by Abbot Grynge ('Abbot' being his job title rather than a first name). Of course, he didn't do any of the actual building himself. He was an abbot, not a stonemason or a general dogsbody/gopher/serf/fetcher-and-carrier. He had other people to do all the hard work for him. He was a distant relative of a guy named Bishop Odo who, in turn, was the half-brother of William the Conqueror. And William the Conqueror (once he'd conquered) became King William I of England. This meant that Odo could do pretty much what he wanted to do – until, that is, William threw him in jail in 1082 for plotting against him – and so, as a member of Odo's family, Abbot Grynge would get a lot of favours, too.

People weren't going to argue with Grynge because he could either say: 'I'm going to get my distant cousin's half-brother's army on to you', or 'I'll get the Pope on to you.' Either way, Abbot Grynge was not a man to be messed with.

According to the *Lamberley Chronicles* (written by monks some two hundred years later), 'he was a man of great humbleness and consideration'. According to a piece of graffiti scratched into the monastery stonework in 1089, Grynge was 'a fatty'. What is known for sure, though, is that Abbot Grynge refused to listen to advice not to build his brand-spanking-new monastery where he did. There are a number of bogs, quagmires, marshes and areas of generally 'soft ground' in the vicinity (see *Dreadful Acts*), and Grynge's monastery was built on one of them. Within twenty years or so of the final tile being placed on the roof, the whole thing began to sink. It started at one end, so the whole building had a slight tilt to it, like a ship listing in heavy seas. The result was that if the monks prayed on their knees on the slippery stone floor of the chapel, they found themselves sliding towards the altar like pucks in an ice hockey game. Within a hundred years, the ground floor had become the basement.

By a strange quirk of fate – or, possibly, because God works in mysterious ways – it was the fact that

Lamberley Monastery was built in such a stupid place and suffered the consequences that led to it still standing (even if at a funny angle and partially underground) in Eddie's time. In 1535, another king (Henry VIII) had fallen out with the Pope and decided to get rid of all the monasteries, taking all the land and riches for himself.

According to local tradition, when King Henry's men turned up at Lamberley and saw the funny tilted building in the squishy ground, they assumed that it was already abandoned so didn't bother to destroy it and throw out the monks (who were probably hiding on the floor with all the lights out), and went on their way. The monks just went on living there.

Monks from different orders follow different rules. Two of the most common monastic orders in England – before Henry VIII kicked them out – were the Franciscans and Benedictines. Franciscan monks followed the way of life as laid down by a chap called St Francis of Assisi and Benedictines followed the rules of St Benedict of Nosin. The monks at Lamberley were of the lesser-known Bertian order, founded by Ethelbert the Funny in about 828 AD. Ethelbert the Funny was brother of Ethelbert the Forked-Beard and Ethelbert the Lazy; though why their parents called them *all* Ethelbert escapes me. Perhaps it was a family tradition – there's no record of their father's name – or perhaps the Ethelberts' parents were completely lacking in imagination.

There is a theory that, because in those days the majority of children died before reaching adulthood, their parents expected at least two Ethelberts to die anyway and for them to be left with just the one. *The Lamberley Chronicles* (which I've already mentioned, I'm sure) state that Ethelbert the Lazy died in adulthood, when he couldn't be bothered to get out of the way of a rampaging sheep (which, in turn, dislodged a human-squashingly-large boulder), and that Ethelbert the Forked-Beard later shaved off his beard and became Ethelbert the Clean-Shaven. But, for obvious reasons, it's Ethelbert the Funny with whom the chronicles are most interested.

This particular Ethelbert was given the nickname 'the Funny' on the basis of one joke which, sad to say, isn't even the remotest bit funny by today's standards. Life can be like that. Once Ethelbert was outside his family hovel picking vegetables from a three-foot square strip of soil – remember that: *three-foot* square – which he'd carefully de-stoned, sieved, composted and weeded, when the local baron's henchman appeared in the lane, leading a large horse. The henchman wandered over to Ethelbert. The horse, which must have been bored and had its mind on other things, stepped on Ethelbert's feet with one of its huge iron-shod hooves.

Pulling the horse off, the baron's henchman was most apologetic. 'Are your feet damaged?' he asked.

Ethelbert looked down at his trampled tiny three-foot vegetable patch, and sighed. 'All three feet,' he said, and the legend of Ethelbert the Funny was born.

Geddit? Not that there's much to get. Anyway, that must have been what passed as great humour in the ninth century because, as well as having broken toes, Bert – oh, go on, let's call him Bert now – got his nickname. But how did he get from being one of three Ethelberts living with his mum and dad in a hovel to founding an order of monks? He had a vision, of course. This was a staunchly Christian country and most people who had visions had Christian ones; the Virgin Mary appearing unto them and that kind of thing.

For Bert, it was a little bit different. One day a vegetable spoke to him and tried to lead him into temptation, but Bert guessed that the vegetable was actually the Devil in disguise and rejected his advances. At least, that's how he told it. People were soon flocking from far and wide to come and meet him, and/or to see the vegetable patch. Soon people sought his opinion on everything from the best time to plant runner beans to complicated theological matters.

On his thirty-third birthday he founded his first Bertian monastery, in Yorkshire. The Bertian monks grew the best vegetables of all the local monasteries and told the funniest jokes (which was a bit of a cheat because some monasteries were silent orders where the monks weren't permitted to speak). The years passed, Bert died, but Bertian monasteries sprang up in various parts of the British Isles, but never mainland Europe.

Abbot Grynge chose to follow the Bertian order and built his monastery in Lamberley because he too enjoyed a good vegetable and a good joke and was of the opinion that other orders took life a bit too seriously.

Over the centuries, efforts were made to shore up Lamberley Monastery, and various buildings were added, knocked down or altered but, whatever its shape or size, the monastery continued its slow descent into the boggy ground.

Life in a typical medieval monastery was hard, with long hours and lots of chanting. Monks got to live in fine stone buildings rather than peasants' hovels and the food and drink was usually pretty good, but it was no easy option. Life for monks of the Bertian order was a bit different. Although there were strict rules about wearing scratchy monks' habits of a particular shade of brown, the wearing of humorous undergarments beneath them was actively encouraged.

Who knows what brightly coloured garments the most recent abbot, Abbot Po, had on under his habit as he dabbed Eddie's face with a wet cloth? Whatever they were, I doubt they could have competed with his extraordinary features. I know

I've already told you that his nose was big and warty . . . but 'big' and 'warty' are relative terms. If you're an ant – and if you really *are* an ant, by the way, congratulations on your reading skills (or on your listening skills if you're having this read to you) – then a stag beetle would seem big, but a stag beetle seems tiny if you're an elephant. (And if you're an elephant, please don't sit on me.) By the same token, if you've never had a wart, you may consider someone with one or two warts as being warty . . . but, when all is said and done, Abbot Po's nose was, by human standards, not only GIGANTIC but also warty beyond the normal terms of the definition. Add his protruding upper peg-like teeth and you will, no doubt, agree that he wasn't conventionally handsome. (If you like warty big-nosed folk with peg teeth, however, you'd probably have found him a real treat to the eye.)

What no one who met Abbot Po ever argued about was that he had a beautiful voice. It was soft and gentle and comforting and reassuring and a whole host of other nice and soothing things besides. It sounded like kindness itself.

'What's your name?' he asked Eddie when the boy's eyelids flickered open. 'Can you tell me your name?'

'I'm . . . I – er – don't remember,' Eddie groaned, craning his neck forward as he tried to sit up.

'It doesn't matter,' said Abbot Po, still dabbing Eddie's forehead with the cloth. 'It'll come back to you. Now lie still.'

'Where am I?' asked Eddie.

'Somewhere where you'll be well looked after,' the monk assured him.

'The dragon?' asked Eddie. 'There really was a dragon, wasn't there?'

'There was and there wasn't,' said Abbot Po. 'You weren't imagining things, if that's what you were wondering. What you saw was Brother Hyams dressed as a dragon.'

'Why . . .?'

'Why was he dressed as a dragon? Because he's Welsh, you see,' said Abbot Po, as though it made sense (which, as you'll discover, it did).

'Ned,' said Eddie.

'Ned?' asked the monk.

'Ned,' said Eddie. 'I . . . I – er – think it's my name.'

'Oh, Ned,' nodded Po. 'Good –'

'Or Neddie,' added Eddie, suddenly feeling less sure of himself.

'Or Neddie.' Abbot Po nodded. 'Well, why don't we call you Neddie until you remember whether it is Neddie, or Ned or something completely different altogether?'

Now it doesn't take a great leap in imagination

to see how Eddie ended up thinking his name was Neddie, what with being called Eddie and having recently read a book about Ned Kelly after whom he'd named the baby in the bulrushes. It's a small step from Eddie to Neddie. If only he or Abbot Po had realised just *how* close it was to his actual name.

'Well, my name is Po. Abbot Po,' said the monk.

'You're a monk?' asked Eddie.

'A monk,' agreed Abbot Po.

'So Brother Hyams is the only one in fancy dress?'

'In costume,' said the monk. 'We're taking part in the annual Lamberley Pageant. Brother Hyams always dresses as a red dragon, it being the national symbol of Wales. Other brothers will be wearing other costumes on the day. It's one of our rare trips into the local community in such numbers.'

Eddie sat up. 'I must go . . . There's something important I should be doing . . . I'm sure of it . . .'

'Where will you go?' asked Abbot Po. 'Do you know where you live?'

'I . . . er . . . I don't remember anything,' said Eddie, which wasn't strictly true. He's just had a rather confusing image of a giant wooden cow – yes, a giant wooden cow – with a chimney toppling off the top of it. He decided not to mention this to the monk.

'Your trap was damaged beyond repair, I'm afraid to say,' said Abbot Po, 'but, I'm pleased to report that your horse seems fine. He has a nasty cut between his eyes, but no broken bones and Brother Felch will take good care of him. We've stabled him with our horses. We didn't find any belongings in the wreckage of your accident and no clue as to your identity.'

'I wonder if I've travelled far?' said Eddie.

'And whether you were travelling in the direction of your home or away from it,' added Abbot Po. 'From the tracks in the mud where your horse and trap left the road, it's clear that you were coming from the direction of Charlington.

'Charlington?' said Eddie. 'The name doesn't sound familiar.' He'd had another strange fleeting image; this time of a stoat in a stovepipe hat, spitting like a cobra. *That can't be right!* Then he had another thought, and burst out laughing. 'I've just remembered something!' he said.

'What?' asked the monk.

'That "po" is another name for a chamber pot!' said Eddie. Then he fainted again. This was becoming a habit.

Episode 5

Getting to Know You

In which we recall a couple of Greats, and
encounter the author dressed as a chicken

After a remarkably good night's sleep in a guest cell – he wasn't a prisoner, all of the single rooms in the monastery were called cells – Eddie (who thought he was a Neddie, remember) was led to the refectory to meet the other monks.

The refectory was a huge dining hall and, when he and Abbot Po entered, Eddie was faced with one long table running almost the entire length of the room, with a row of monks on benches on either side. They were all dressed almost identically: in light brown habits with slightly pointy-looking hoods.

Eddie was amazed by the noise that greeted him; not the talking – there was none – but the

207

clattering of pewter spoons on pewter plates as hundreds of monks guzzled their breakfast porridge.

'Brothers!' said Abbot Po loudly, attracting their attention. The clattering came to a stop and hundreds of pairs of eyes turned to look at him and the newcomer. 'This is Neddie. He suffered an accident yesterday and is currently in our care.'

'GREETINGS, NEDDIE!' said all the monks as one, their faces breaking into a smile. (Don't forget that the order had been founded by Ethelbert the *Funny*. As monks go, they were an outwardly cheerful lot.)

'G-Greetings,' said Eddie, a little weakly. He was quite a sight to behold. As well as all the little puncture marks all over him, from all those gorse bush prickles (which would have looked very unsightly in the illustrations had Mr Roberts bothered to draw any) he was also walking with the aid of a stick, having hurt the knee and ankle of his left leg. The most noticeable result of his accident, however, was the iodine-soaked bandage wrapped around his head. It looked like a yellowish turban. The overall effect was that Eddie resembled a pantomime street beggar: an exotic but sorry sight.

'Have a seat,' said the nearest monk and all the others on his side of the table shunted down the bench to make room for him. Eddie looked to Po who nodded. The monks on the other side shunted down to make room for him opposite Eddie. They both sat.

Two monks on breakfast duty – Eddie was to discover later that every brother took it in turns to do most tasks in Lamberley Monastery – gave them a plate and a spoon each, then doled out great splodges of porridge with a huge ladle. A large earthenware jar of clear honey and a bowl of rich brown sugar were passed down the table to them.

As Eddie sprinkled his porridge with sugar he frowned.

'What is it?' asked Abbot Po.

'I don't see how I can remember how to walk and talk and eat porridge and things like that, but not remember things about me . . . about my past. I know the days of the week, but I don't know who I am!'

'Don't worry,' said Po. 'It'll all come back to you in time.'

'And there's the noise.'

'The noise?'

'I can distinctly remember the noise of a – er – stuffed stoat hitting the knees of a bearded stranger.'

'A stoat?' said Po.

'A bearded stranger?' asked the monk on Eddie's immediate right.

209

'Y-Yes,' said Eddie. 'I know it sounds crazy,' (he'd got that right) 'but I'm sure of it . . . No, hang on, I think the stranger turned out to be the Empress of All China.'

A look passed between the monks within earshot: a look which seemed to say *'The poor boy's rambling. The bonk on the head must have been more serious than you thought'*. Those of you familiar with the events outlined in *Awful End*, however, will probably have realised that he was recalling the noise made when Mad Aunt Maud – for this was back in the days before she'd officially become known as Even Madder Aunt Maud – hit the heavily disguised actor-manager of a group of wandering theatricals named Mr Pumblesnook in the knees with Malcolm (or was it Sally?) her stuffed stoat . . . the self-same actor-manager who later went on to assume the role of a Chinese Empress.

So Eddie wasn't really rambling at all. It was just that he couldn't fill in the blanks to make sense of it. (Not that the events in *Awful End* make a great deal of sense anyway.)

The awful crunching noise of stoat on kneecap was obviously such a remarkable one that it would take more than a serious loss of memory to remove it from young Neddie's – sorry, that should be young *Eddie's* – mind.

210

I did once mention in passing that this was a noise which Eddie would remember right up until his sixteenth birthday, and that his finally forgetting it had something to do with a hypnotist called the Great Gretcha, not to be confused with an escapologist called the Great Zucchini. (Well, you can see how the confusion might arise; they're both '-ists' by profession and both 'Great' by name.) The Great Gretcha, whom Eddie was to meet a number of years *after* this Further Adventure (having met the Great Zucchini a number of years *prior* to this one), was an American stage hypnotist of German extraction.

Unfortunately, by the time she'd picked out Eddie from a number of arm-waving would-be volunteers in the audience, and had called him up on to the New York stage halfway through her act, she was past her prime. In truth, the night of their meeting was the very last of her professional career.

Poor Gretcha suffered from an illness called narcolepsy which meant that she could suddenly fall asleep without warning – even mid-sentence – which she did with increasing regularity. The show in which Eddie was called up on to the stage, and 'put under' (as hypnotists describe it when a volunteer is put under their hypnotic influence) was her last because, having put him under, she fell asleep . . . leaving him hypnotised.

211

It was a deep sleep and, once the curtains had been hurriedly lowered and the angry audience promised their money back by the nervous theatre proprietor (a Mr Dundas), they had to awaken the no-longer-so-Great Gretcha in order for *her* to awaken Eddie. By the time she'd snapped him out of his trance, there were one or two gaps in his memory, and the horrible crunch that greeted his ears the day Malcolm and Mr Pumblesnook had made contact was wiped away.

When I told this tale to a well-known stage hypnotist, he insisted that such a thing wasn't possible; that a hypnotist can neither make people do what they don't want to do, nor forget what they don't want to forget. I'm simply stating the facts as they came to me. And, anyway, after my conversation with this chap, I found that I was dressed as a chicken and had no recollection as to how or *why*.

And, now that you've seen what I look like dressed as

a chicken (or is it more of a speckledy hen?), my work here is done, so let's return to Lamberley Monastery, to the refectory, to this end of the table and to Eddie with a fine sprinkling of rich brown sugar on his porridge. He was deep in conversation with a plump jolly-looking monk who reminded him of a picture of Friar Tuck he'd once seen in a book about the adventures of Robin Hood and his Merry Men. But *when* had he seen it? Why, where and how? Had the book been his or someone else's? Perhaps it belonged to a brother or sister . . . if he had brothers or sisters. If only he could remember. It was so *frustrating*!

The monk introduced himself as Brother Pugh (like Brother Hyams, a Welshman). 'P-U-G-H, but pronounced *pew*, like the benches,' he said (referring to the name for those wooden seats you find in churches). After breakfast, it was he who took Eddie-he-thought-of-as-Neddie outside to get some fresh air.

They started off by walking around the cloisters. When first constructed, the cloisters had been a covered walkway built around a quadrangle; a large square area of grass. Over the years, though, most of the cloisters had sunk into the ground, so the stone floor had long since disappeared under the earth and the high vaulted ceiling of the cloister now seemed very low indeed. In fact, in some places, Brother Pugh had to duck to avoid hitting his head.

There were various doorways off the cloister leading to the abbey, the Chapter House, a private chapel, and the like, but Pugh led Eddie through an open archway into the herb garden.

A very small elderly monk was making his way along a brick path towards them. He had a large well-worn leather-bound book in his hand which Eddie assumed was either a Bible or a book of herbs. When he got nearer, though, Eddie could read the title in faded embossed gold on the cover: The Bertian Bumper Book Of Funnies. These guys obviously took their jokes very seriously indeed.

Now I'm sure the more caring amongst you are concerned as to the fate that befell Eddie's father, Mr Dickens, when Eddie failed to return with a doctor, so let me put your minds at rest. Or, at the very least, furnish you with the facts (which is a little like furnishing a room but, instead of using tables and chairs, using bits of information. And there's no room involved. Or heavy lifting).

The Dickens household waited and waited and waited and, when neither Eddie nor Dr Humple appeared, and Mr Dickens's groans grew louder

and louder and louder, Even Madder Aunt Maud
decided to take matters into her own hands.

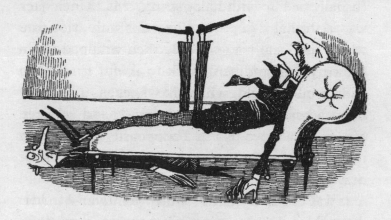

The dear lady knew little about caring for the sick
or injured but remembered having heard or read
somewhere about a boy called Jack who'd gone up
a hill with a girl named Jill in order to fetch a pail
of water. As a result, Jack had received a head injury
(having then fallen down the hill), and he had been
treated with vinegar and brown paper.

Even Madder Aunt Maud instructed Mrs
Dickens to go to the kitchen to find vinegar. (They
rarely used it on food or in cooking, but Mrs
Dickens was a firm believer in using it as a cleaning
agent. She insisted that windows, table-tops and
even MUJ's ex-soldiers were regularly scrubbed
down with the stuff.) Even Madder Aunt Maud,
meanwhile, went in search of brown paper.

Brown paper was the kind of paper used to wrap parcels when sending items through the post (usually tied up with hairy string). Mad Uncle Jack was in the habit of paying for items with dried fish, which the local tradespeople then wrapped up in brown paper and sent back to Awful End along with a bill of sale, where Mr Dickens then sent them actual money for their goods and services. He kept the dried fish in a cupboard (for his uncle to re-use) and the brown paper and string in the drawers of the desk in his study.

It was to Mr Dickens's study that Even Madder Aunt Maud now went. She would sometimes spend time annoying her nephew whilst he was trying to sort out the bills, by a variety of different means. Sometimes she would simply hum loudly or shout out random numbers when he was trying to add up a column of figures in his head. Sometimes she would stand behind the curtains and stick Malcolm's head out with a cheery, 'Peekaboo!'. Occasionally, she'd drink the water from the vases, gargling loudly before each swallow. If this failed to gain Mr Dickens's attention, she'd sometimes end up eating the flowers in the vase, too. (They'd die soon anyway, once she'd drunk the water.)

It was whilst she'd been involved in such activities that she'd spotted where he kept the brown paper, so now she was able to go straight to the relevant desk drawers and to gather it by the armful.

Hurrying back to the *chaise longue* where Mr Dickens lay, she almost collided with Mrs Dickens who was carrying an enormous earthenware jar of home-made chutney.

'I couldn't find the vinegar,' Mrs Dickens explained.

'I'm sure that'll do nicely,' said EMAM.

They proceeded to cover Mr Dickens with the apple-based chutney and then applied the brown paper (the chutney acting as a remarkably effective glue, in much the same way that the marmalade had on the breakfast plate).

Somewhat surprisingly, Mr Dickens found the treatment quite soothing. So much so, that his wife and aunt decided to try the same healing approach on Dawkins, still bent double from his 'locked' back. Unfortunately for the gentleman's gentleman, they only succeeded in attracting a swarm of bees that stung him repeatedly, whilst he was in no fit state to run away.

In all this excitement, Eddie's absence was put to the back of everyone's mind.

Episode 6

The Game's Afoot

*In which Fandango Jones plays detective and
Even Madder Aunt Maud plays the bagpipes*

Whilst the others were concerned with Mr Dickens's injuries, Fandango Jones had been investigating the scene of the crime, for that's what he was sure that it was: a *crime*. He was convinced that the chimney falling on Mr Dickens had been no accident. Perhaps Mr Dickens hadn't been the intended target, but the engineer was sure that the chimney had been deliberately dropped from the roof of Awful End on to the cluster of people below, which was why it was on the roof that Fandango was now standing.

The little man was re-checking the calculations he'd made from the ground and had reached the same conclusion. There was no way that the chimney could have landed, or even been pushed, from its original position and fallen where it had. Someone must have lifted the chimney on to or over the parapet and pushed, dropped or thrown it over the edge! And whoever had done that must have seen the members of the household below, so *must* have intended them harm.

'Most interesting,' said the engineer, for he was one of the very few people in the world who really did speak to himself out loud (unlike characters in books, who seem to do it all the time).

Fandango Jones was used to standing on tall things because he'd built so many of them. He built the Tottering Tower at Totteridge, for example, and the Scarbourne Lighthouse. I wouldn't be surprised if you haven't heard of either of them – unless you live in Totteridge or Scarbourne, and are interested in local history – because neither is still standing. They both fell down a long time ago. Quite a few of Fandango Jones's taller structures did, many in his lifetime; a fact not mentioned in his pamphlet *Bridging the Gap*.

Jones was about to go back through the tiny doorway which led to and from this section of roof – Awful End was a very higgledy-piggledy building with roofs of different heights and designs – when something caught his eye: a flash of colour against the grey of the stone edging. He went to investigate and picked up a piece of faded gold brocade (a rich fabric woven with a raised pattern, like you used to get on military uniforms). It was caught on a peg holding a damaged roof tile in place.

Perhaps the person who'd dropped the chimney over the edge had snagged his clothing on the peg when walking past.

Fandango Jones slipped the brocade into the back of his notebook for safekeeping. This looked very much like a clue to him.

As he walked back down the winding staircase to the top landing, he wondered about the chimney itself. If it had been a statue or a stone urn that had been pushed over, that could have been a spur of the moment thing. It needn't have been planned. Whoever it was could have been looking over the edge and thought, 'I know, I'll flatten one of those Dickenses today,' and then pushed the object over. But not with the chimney. The chimney would have to have been dislodged from its original position on top of the stack – it was one of a cluster of four barley-sugar chimneys sharing a base – and then carried to the edge and over the parapet. Premeditated. That was what they called it in those detective magazines Jones liked to read: 'a premeditated act'. The dropping of the chimney had been pre-planned. Fandango Jones hadn't been this excited since . . . since he'd got all enthusiastic about the suggestion of a bridge made of soup (until he'd come to his senses).

Jones hurried into the nearest room – about two-thirds of the rooms in Awful End were unused, and most without furniture, remember – sat himself on an old hatbox, and immediately started drawing a diagram. Sadly, this no longer exists but, based on a description from the son of someone who actually saw the original, here's David Roberts's reconstruction of what it looked like:

Thanks, David. Not bad.

By the time Jones had finished his diagram and made his way back downstairs to the others, a few of them were beginning to wonder, if not worry exactly, about the whereabouts of Eddie and the doctor.

Unaware of the calamitous events resulting in both Mr Dickens and Dawkins lying flat on their backs in the withdrawing room, Gibbering Jane had emerged from below stairs with a happy baby Ned gurgling in her arms, to ask the whereabouts of Master Edmund. At the mention of his name, it was the general consensus that he should, indeed, have returned by now.

'Perhaps he's been kidnapped by escaped convicts up on the misty moors,' suggested Mad Uncle Jack.

'Unlikely,' snapped Even Madder Aunt Maud.

'Or been mistaken for an escaped orphan and locked in a police cell,' MUJ added.

Even Madder Aunt Maud poo-pooed that suggestion too.

'Or stuck himself to the underside of a circus elephant,' said Mad Uncle Jack, going all misty-eyed at the memory of when his own dear wife had done that very thing many years previously.

Even Madder Aunt Maud threw her arms around him, showering him with slobbery kisses from her prune-like lips. 'You remember, my love pumpkin!' she cried.

Mrs Dickens turned away. Not only was this not a pretty sight, but she'd also been side-swiped, in the face, by Malcolm – or was it Sally? – whom Maud was clutching when she threw her arms around her Jack. She decided to go and find something to lessen the bruising.

Gibbering Jane was now in the withdrawing room, gibbering at the sight of poor Dawkins, covered in bee stings, doing a very good impersonation of a right angle. Baby Ned seemed to find the gibbering amusing, and his face broke into a gummy smile. He dribbled with pleasure.

The not-so-famous engineer, meanwhile, went in search of Mad Uncle Jack and Even Madder Aunt Maud. He found them emerging from a broom cupboard.

'The family chapel is much smaller than I recall,' Eddie's great-aunt was saying.

Mad Uncle Jack grunted in agreement. 'Perhaps the whole house is shrinking.'

Even Madder Aunt Maud nodded. 'It did rain a great deal in the winter,' she said, 'and water does shrink things. Remember your brother George. He shrank in that fish tank, didn't he?'

Even Madder Aunt Maud was referring to George Dickens who took to living in a fish tank in a rented space near what is now the Victoria & Albert Museum in London.

'He didn't shrink, my sweet,' said Mad Uncle Jack. 'He drowned.' Which was also true. Refusing to come up for air one day – a Thursday – he did, indeed, drown. This was the same George Dickens who accidentally burnt down the Houses of Parliament in 1834. (You can read all about it in my book *Terrible Times* . . . if you haven't already done so, that is.)

'But he could have shrunk a bit before he drowned,' EMAM pointed out.

At this stage, Fandango Jones cleared his throat to let the couple know that he was there.

When Even Madder Aunt Maud spotted him, she let out a yelp. 'It's the spitting man!' she cried, leaping behind her husband to use him as a human shield.

'I thought you were the engineer,' said a puzzled Mad Uncle Jack.

'Indeed I am, sir,' said Fandango, 'but it's in the capacity of amateur detective that I must speak with you now.'

'Then spit it out, man!' said Mad Uncle Jack. 'What's troubling you?'

'Be quick about it, mind,' said EMAM. 'This house is shrinking and something must be done!'

'You were in the broom cupboard, madam,' he said.

'I beg your pardon?'

'You weren't in the chapel. That is through the door over there.' He pointed. (Mrs Dickens had given him a tour of Awful End when he'd undertaken to build the bridge in its grounds.) 'You and your husband entered the broom cupboard in error.'

'Are you trying to tell me that I don't know the Dickens family chapel when I see it?' demanded Even Madder Aunt Maud.

'Are you suggesting that we don't know a place for storing brooms from a house of God?' Mad Uncle Jack bellowed, his beakiest of beaky noses quivering with rage.

Fandango Jones squirmed. He'd never seen his employer so angry, and this had been of *his* making. 'I – er –'

'This is outrageous,' Mad Uncle Jack shouted, turning to the broom cupboard and yanking open the door. 'Are you telling me that this doesn't contain some of the finest examples of wood carving since Grinning Gibbons?' (None of them, including Mad Uncle Jack, had any idea who Grinning Gibbons was.)

Fandango Jones didn't know what to say. Certainly the family chapel at Awful End – which was just behind that wall, there – had some very fine wooden carvings . . . but the only wood he could see in this dingy cupboard were the handles of the mops and brooms, and (rather oddly) a small log next to a large piece of rock.

'Er, very nice,' he said lamely.

Mad Uncle Jack looked in the cupboard. 'Great heavens!' he said. 'It's nothing but a broom cupboard.'

'What did you think it was?' Even Madder Aunt Maud snorted. 'A slice of cheese?'

'It's your nephew –' said the engineer, in a desperate bid to steer the conversation back to the fallen chimney.

'My nephew is a broom cupboard?'

'A slice of cheese?'

'Preposterous!'

'Ridiculous!'

'No . . .' protested Fandango Jones. 'It's your

nephew, Mr Dickens, about whom I must speak!'

'Spit, more like,' said Even Madder Aunt Maud.

Jones felt happier to be back on more familiar ground. 'I believe that the accident with the chimney was no accident at all.'

'Then why refer to it as an accident?' asked EMAM.

'Exactly!' said MUJ. 'Are you some kind of an idiot? A buffoon?'

Jones tried again. 'I meant, of course, that which we *took* to be an accident was no accident at all. I believe that the chimney was deliberately dropped upon our party below.'

'Party? I don't recall a party,' protested Even Madder Aunt Maud. 'Where were the jellies? The ices? The most-amusing of party games?'

'Party as in assembled group, madam,' spat Jones. 'I believe that the chimney was deliberately dropped upon us and is, therefore, a case of attempted murder . . . and a matter for the police!'

There always seems to be police involvement in an Eddie Dickens adventure, doesn't there?

Caped Capers

*In which the author makes an apology
and Brother Gault makes a potion*

L et me start by way of an apology. It's not the
first one I've had to make and I doubt it'll
be the last. So here goes: Some of you will have
spotted that the previous chapter begins with the
lead-in: '*In which Fandango Jones plays detective and
Even Madder Aunt Maud plays the bagpipes.*' Well,
we certainly had the Fandango-Jones-playing-
detective part (what with his diagrams and clue-
collecting, and clambering about the roof), but
what about Even Madder Aunt Maud and the
bagpipes? Now if it had said, '*In which Fandango
Jones plays detective and Even Madder Aunt Maud
plays the fool*' or even, '*plays about in a broom*

cupboard' that would have been fine. But *'plays the bagpipes?'* I think not!

You see, the thing is, I was going to get to the part where Maud plays the bagpipes and then I thought, No! HANG ON! THAT'LL HAVE TO WAIT! This book is the second of the Further Adventures of *Eddie Dickens*, so I think we should get back to Eddie – even though he doesn't know that he's Eddie, of course – and we can come back to Even Madder Aunt Maud and her bagpipe-playing later on. OK? OK. Good. Thank you for being so understanding.

So back to Eddie we go. A good few days had passed and the pock marks where the gorse bush prickles had been pulled out were a lot less painful, and the yellowing iodine-soaked bandages had been unwound from his head. He did, however, still have to walk with a stick, and his memory hadn't come back.

That's not to say that certain memories hadn't returned in fleeting flashes, including riding on the back of a turtle . . . removing a large sparkling bauble from a chandelier . . . leading a gang of scruffily dressed, cucumber-wielding children out of a grim building . . . digging up a coffin with his bare hands . . . but none of them seemed to make any sense or give him a clue as to who he was.

Abbot Po had deduced from Eddie's clothing,

accent and horse that 'Neddie' was from the well-to-do classes but, beyond that, nothing.

One of the problems was that, except for rare occurrences, such as taking part in the upcoming Lamberley Pageant (which would require Brother Hyams to dress as a Welsh dragon), the Bertians had little to do with the world around them. They were what's known as a 'slightly ajar order'.

A closed order (of monks or nuns) is one that has no dealings with the outside world. Then there are the open orders that go out in the community (to do good deeds, I suppose). A slightly ajar order is one that is more closed than open, but not completely closed. In other words, Bertian monks in general, including the monks at Lamberley Monastery, usually kept people out and out of people's way, except when it suited them.

This appears to have meant that, in the case of Eddie's accident, it was only right and Christian to rescue the injured boy and his injured horse, when he was spotted by the side of the road, but not necessarily to involve the authorities. So they didn't.

Eddie had quickly adapted to life in the monastery. He didn't go to all the prayers the monks attended throughout the day but sometimes he sat at the back of the chapel and listened to the brothers chant and sink. Sorry, that should be *sing*.

Of course, the building was sinking, but not right before their very eyes. Not then, at least. Everyone was terribly nice to Eddie/Neddie and he was eager to help out around the place as much as possible: in the kitchens, on the land, or wherever he could lend a hand.

Brother Gault, the herbalist, concocted a potion designed to speed Eddie's recovery and he took a spoonful each morning and a spoonful each night. This may not sound a very high dosage until you see the size of the spoon (which you probably have done if you looked at the picture first). It was the biggest wooden spoon Eddie had ever seen in his life, not that he could remember any of the other wooden spoons he'd seen. Fortunately, the medicine tasted rather nice, as medicines go, and this one went in his mouth and down his front.

Another thing you might have noticed from the picture is that Eddie was now wearing a habit. It's not that they were insisting Eddie become a Bertian novice or anything like that. (A novice is a monk in training.) It was just that Eddie had only one set of clothes and they weren't in the best of condition since his accident anyway.

Eddie's habit had been made-to-measure from an old (much larger) garment by Brother Henry, who was very good at sewing. Because Eddie wasn't really a monk it didn't have a proper hood but, apart from that, it was just like the clothes everyone else wore at Lamberley Monastery (except that, unlike the others, Eddie wasn't wearing humorous undergarments). It felt very rough and itchy.

'Do you think I'll ever find out who I am?' he asked Abbot Po in the monastery library, after breakfast one morning.

'I'm sure you'll be home again in no time,' replied Po in his kindly voice. 'When we attend the pageant, I've no doubt someone will come forward and claim you.'

'I do hope so,' said Eddie. 'Please don't misunderstand me, Abbot Po. No one could be kinder to me than you and the other monks, and there's no place I'd rather be with a loss of memory than here, except for home . . .'

'But home is where the heart is,' Abbot Po nodded in understanding. 'Even if you don't know where home is.'

'Or who's in it,' Eddie added.

'Which is why I've given instructions that should any of the brothers have reason to be out in the community, they should make enquires about you.'

'How do you mean?' asked Eddie.

'I mean,' Po explained, 'that it is against the orders of our order to walk into a police station and to report you missing, but if one of my brothers should be out selling our vegetables and happens to ask if anyone had heard reports of a missing boy –'

'Then that is all right.'

'Then that is, indeed, perfectly acceptable,' said Abbot Po.

'You monks have funny rules, don't you?' said Eddie, hurriedly adding: 'No disrespect, Abbot.'

'None taken,' said Po. 'You're forgetting that our order was founded by Ethelbert the Funny.'

A few moments later, Brother Hyams entered the monastery library. 'It's the sheep, Abbot Po!' he said. 'I'm afraid they've got out again.'

★

Just a few miles away, as the crow flies (if the crow is concentrating and hasn't been sidetracked by a juicy worm he's spotted far below, or been blown off course on to the misty moors) a Bertian monk by the name of Brother Guck was trudging his way up the ever-so-long driveway of a very impressive house indeed. He knocked on the door.

No sooner had his knuckles left the wood than the door was flung wide open and the startled Bertian was confronted by an elderly woman playing the bagpipes. (Yup: b-a-g-p-i-p-e-s.)

'What is it?' she demanded, letting the bag deflate with a painful whine.

'Sheep, madam,' said Guck. 'I am here about our sheep.'

'Why would I wish to buy sheep?' demanded Even Madder Aunt Maud – for, as you guessed, it was she – peering around the tall thin monk to see whether he had brought any samples of his wares with him.

'I'm not selling them, madam,' the young monk explained.

'Good!' said EMAM. 'Because I found two perfectly good sheep grazing outside my cow this morning, so I now have more than enough.'

'But those are the very sheep I'm referring to, madam,' said Brother Guck, wondering what she'd meant by *outside her cow*. 'They strayed from monastery land. They belong to the monastery. I am here to –'

'Finders keepers!' Eddie's great-aunt stated with a haughty chuckle.

'Whilst I'm here,' the monk added hurriedly, 'I should also mention a lost boy whom, we believe, is named Ned –'

'Why didn't you say so in the first place?' said the elderly woman, throwing the bagpipes with great force into the fireplace. 'You're here about Ned?'

'You know him?' asked Guck. He and his fellow monks had been visiting various neighbouring properties to round up the sheep, but none of the others knew anything about a missing boy.

'I certainly do! You've come to the right place,' said Even Madder Aunt Maud. 'He was like Moses in the bulrushes. Have you heard of him?'

'I most certainly have, madam,' said the monk.

'He's in the Bible, you know.'

'I know,' nodded the brother.

'Then follow me!' said the strange old lady, picking up what appeared to be a stuffed ferret or weasel or stoat off an occasional table.

Slightly bemused – which is like puzzled but with fewer 'z's in it – Brother Guck followed the old lady through a large hall where he couldn't fail to notice possibly one of the most hideous painted ceilings that he'd ever had the misfortune to clap eyes on: there was something frighteningly *liver-sausagy* about it all.

They finally entered the kitchen where an ex-soldier was standing in a tin bath filled with vinegar, being scrubbed down by Mrs Dickens.

'He's here about young Ned,' said Even Madder Aunt Maud.

'Good morning, madam,' Brother Guck said to Mrs Dickens.

'Good morning,' she replied, dipping a large brush into the iron tub and giving Ex-Private Drabb's back another scrub.

Even Madder Aunt Maud marched over to the drawer in which Baby Ned was peacefully sleeping.

She picked him up and plonked him down in the arms of the startled monk.

'There you go!' she said. 'One missing Ned safely returned to his rightful owner.'

'There must be some mistake –' Guck began.

'You come to my door. You ask about a lost boy named Ned. I give you a found boy named Ned and you say there's some mistake, is that it?' she demanded, her voice rising to a grating pitch.

'I . . . er –'

'You lost a Ned. We found a Ned and you're saying that they're not one and the same? Hmmm? Is that it?'

At that moment, Mad Uncle Jack ambled in through the back door (having slept and abluted in and around his dried-fish treehouse). 'Who the devil are you, sir?' he demanded. 'And what are you doing with that bawling babe?'

'He's come to claim Ned,' said Mrs Dickens above the howls.

'Ned?' asked MUJ.

'That baby we found.'

'Oh, him,' said Mad Uncle Jack. 'Good. Good. Now get off my land before I have you shot.'

It was then that Brother Guck made a decision. He would forget about the two stray sheep that the bagpipe-playing woman had mentioned. He would forget about the other missing boy called

Neddie, back at the monastery. He would try not to think about the poor man being given a vinegar bath and about the horrendous ceiling in the hallway. His number one priority in the whole wide world at that precise moment was to get this poor baby out of the madhouse.

'Th-Thank you and good day,' he said, then, cradling the crying child in his arms, made for the nearest exit . . . and found himself in a broom cupboard.

'I suppose you think that's funny?' snapped Even Madder Aunt Maud.

★

Whilst Guck and a group of fellow monks were off scouring the surrounding countryside for the missing sheep, a visitor came to Lamberley Monastery.

He was a stocky, swarthy man with eyes of such a dark brown that they were almost black. He had a large gold tooth at the front of his mouth and a large gold hooped earring in his right ear. He wore a red neckerchief with white spots around – you guessed it – his neck. If it wasn't for the fact that he smelled strongly of horses, one might have supposed that he was a pirate. In truth, he was a gypsy.

Gypsies used to be called *gipcyans* or *gyptians*

because people thought that these travelling folk had originally come from Egypt. Many gypsies speak Romany, their own special language which is Indo-European (which means that it's spoken across Europe and Asia as far as northern India), which makes things all the more confusing. This gypsy, however, was called Fudd, and had spent his entire life, man and boy, travelling around the British Isles.

'I'm here about the boy who's lost his memory,' he told the monk who finally opened the door to the monastery gatehouse after it became clear that the gypsy wasn't going to stop banging on it with his knobbly walking stick until somebody did something.

The mention of 'the boy' got a speedy reaction, and it wasn't long before Fudd was taken to see Abbot Po in his office.

'By the Lord, you're ugly!' gasped Fudd when he laid eyes on the warty-nosed peg-toothed monk.

'That's no word of a lie,' agreed Po from behind his desk, 'which is fortunate for you, sir, because it means that I don't judge you by appearances alone.'

'Meaning?' demanded Fudd, his eyes narrowing.

'Meaning that there are those who won't give a gypsy so much as the time of day,' said Po.

'But you're a man of God!' said Fudd. 'It is your duty to like all men.'

'And it's because you're in God's house that I ask you to remove your cap, sir,' said Po, quietly.

The gypsy snatched his hat off the top of his head, mumbling an apology. He and the abbot had got off on the wrong foot.

'Do, please, sit down,' said Abbot Po, indicating towards one of the few comfortable chairs in the whole building.

'Thank you,' said the gypsy. 'And I means no harm by my comments. I speaks my mind, that's all.'

'Admirable if you find someone beautiful, Mr –?'

'Fudd,' said Fudd.

'Mr Fudd, but it's probably best to bite your tongue if you meet someone as hideous as me. Not everyone would be so understanding.'

Fudd grinned. 'Speakin' me mind has lost me

a few teeth over the years, but I gives as good as I get.'

'I'm told you're here about a boy?'

'Yes. He went missing from our camp last week sometime.'

Abbot Po leaned forward in his chair. 'And what is the boy's name?' he asked.

''Tis Fabian, sir,' said Fudd. 'His mother's choice.'

'And you are the father?'

'Lord, no,' laughed Fudd. 'I am their chief. Father to 'em all in a way though, I suppose. I also deals with all important business.'

'And what could be more important than a missing child?'

''xactly!' said Fudd. 'When I heard your monks asking around about a child who'd lost his memory, I came straight here.'

'Would you describe Fabian to me, please?' he asked.

Fudd was happy to. He described a boy of Eddie's age, height and appearance. 'He has eyes like saucers,' he finished.

This description of Fabian certainly sounded like the boy he knew as Neddie, but how could he be sure? And then there was the fact that the horse Neddie had been found with appeared to be a *gentleman's* horse, and Eddie spoke like a little gentleman, not at all like Fudd.

'Could you describe his horse?' asked Po.

The gypsy looked down at his lap and wrung his cap in his hands somewhat awkwardly. 'You see, the thing is, sir, that he shouldn't have had no horse with him . . .' he said. 'If you found Fabian with a horse, it weren't his by rights.'

'You're suggesting that he'd stolen it?'

'Now don't get me wrong,' said Fudd. 'We gypsies have a bad reputation as horse thieves and it's mostly unfounded . . . but, if Fabian takes a fancy to a steed, he sometimes feels the need to take it for himself, see?'

'I see,' said Po. He was about to have Neddie brought to his office when something else occurred to him. 'His speech,' he said. 'How does Fabian speak?'

'I'm not sure I follows you,' said Fudd.

'How does he sound? What kind of accent?'

'Aha! I sees where you're heading!' said Fudd. 'I should have said from the outset that the lad speaks real beautifully. He sounds as if he comes from the very best of society.'

'But how did Fabian come to speak this way?' the abbot asked with interest.

'His mother, Hester, weren't born a Romany,' Fudd explained. 'She's an outsider who married into our family. A very well-to-do lady.'

'Unusual,' said Po, but he had no reason to doubt the man. He was now convinced that 'Neddie' was none other than Fabian. 'We must reunite you with Fabian this instant.'

And this is how Eddie, who still thought of himself as Neddie, now came to believe himself to be Fabian. Of course, he didn't recognise Fudd when he was ushered into the office by Brother Pugh but, then again, he wouldn't have recognised Florinda Dickens as his mother nor Laudanum Dickens as his father if they'd been standing there in the gypsy's place.

When Fudd looked up as Eddie entered the room, a flicker of surprise crossed his face, but Abbot Po was too busy looking at Eddie to notice.

'Fabian!' said the gypsy, giving Eddie a hug. 'It's good to see you. Remember me?' he asked.

'I'm afraid not, sir,' said Eddie. 'Are you my father?'

'I'm not, but I'll be taking you back to him,' said Fudd, grinning his golden grin.

On the Case

In which Fandango Jones
helps the police with their enquiries

Fandango Jones had been the one who'd volunteered to bicycle to the police station to report his suspicions about the chimney hitting Eddie's father being a case of attempted murder. He also agreed to report Eddie's own disappearance whilst he was at it. But what everyone had forgotten about in the excitement – what with Gibbering Jane being so good at looking after him – was Baby Ned (or whatever his real name was). Had Fandango mentioned his being found in the bulrushes, the baby would probably have been looked after by some local orphanage and not ended up being taken by Brother Guck. So, as things turned out, it's lucky that what Jones was *really* interested in was playing detective with a real live one.

Those of you familiar with the Eddie Dickens Trilogy will also be familiar with the figure of the detective inspector. In the three previous books in which he's appeared, he's only ever been described as being 'the inspector' or 'the detective inspector'. This was for legal reasons which have been dragging on and on and on and on down the years. Now that these have been resolved, I'm happy to give you his full name: Detective Inspector Humphrey Bunyon.

Now there were two very distinct things about the detective inspector. No, come to think of it, there were *three*: one – in no particular order – was that he was prone to repeat what the previous person had just said but, often in such a way that it made a strange kind of sense; two, he couldn't read (which wasn't uncommon at the time, but was more uncommon amongst detective inspectors); and, three, he had a very large tummy indeed. It was gigantic, and looked even more so because of the loud checked suits he always wore.

Well, amazingly, although one (his repetition) and two (his illiteracy) still applied when Fandango Jones went to spit at him that day, number three was no longer true. Detective Inspector Humphrey

Bunyon had been on the ultimate diet – locked in a trunk by a gang of purse snatchers and cut-throats for nearly a month – so was now remarkably slim. This wouldn't have been a problem if the policeman hadn't intended to put the weight back on – he loved his food – so hadn't bothered to buy himself any new clothes. His old ones hung off him like . . . like . . . Well, he looked like a thin man in fat man's clothing.

When the engineer managed to get past the desk sergeant (who was proudly trying out a set of newfangled handcuffs on himself) he was shocked by the sight of the detective in his extraordinarily baggy clothing.

'Good morning,' said Jones.

'Good morning.'

'Are you the detective inspector?' asked Jones.

'The detective inspector,' nodded Humphrey Bunyon.

'My name is Fandango Jones, the fairly well-known engineer –'

'Fandango Jones, the fairly well-known engineer,' the policeman nodded.

'Perhaps you've heard of me?' said Jones.

'Heard of you,' nodded the detective inspector.

'Excellent!' said Jones, trying not to be distracted by just how strange Bunyon looked with the folds of clothes hanging off him, like the loose skin of a rhinoceros.

'Excellent,' agreed the inspector. 'Why are you here, Mr Jones?' The policeman was seated behind a large desk. In the past, he'd found it difficult to reach for items on his desk because his stomach had kept him more than arm's length away from it. Since he'd escaped from the evil clutches of the Smiley Gang, though, he now found life behind his desk much easier. He picked up a buff-coloured folder, not to read (he didn't know how to, remember) but to use as some form of protection against this *spitting* man.

'I believe that my current employer's nephew has been the victim of an attempted murder!'

'Attempted murder?'

'Attempted murder!' Jones spat.

'Attempted murder? Hmmmm,' said the inspector. 'Please go on.'

Fandango Jones sat on the only chair in the

room (Inspector Bunyon was using a pile of books). 'I am currently constructing a bridge at Awful End,' he said. The policeman said nothing. His face dropped at the very mention of the place. 'My employer's name is Mad Mr Jack Dickens and –'

The detective inspector put up his hand for silence. 'Unfortunately,' he sighed, 'I am familiar with the Dickens household. Do go on.'

So Fandango Jones told him his sorry tale.

Detective Inspector Humphrey Bunyon listened in silence. He was a very good detective inspector and would occasionally interrupt with a question.

When Fandango Jones had finished, the policeman got to his feet, his laughably large clothes making him look like a half-deflated hot-air balloon. 'I do believe you're right,' he said.

'Right?' spat the engineer.

'Right that a person or persons deliberately dropped the chimney on to the gathering below and that Mr Dickens may or may not have been the intended target. And right that Master Edmund Dickens's disappearance may somehow be connected to the affair.'

Fandango Jones glowed with such pride that a piece of his spit which had settled on his chin sizzled in the heat that such a glow can generate.

'So what do you intend to do about it?' he asked.

'Do about it?'

'Do about it.' Jones nodded, his two-tier stovepipe hat wobbling under the strain. Fandango Jones was not a man to take his hat off indoors; especially not one as heavy as this.

'I intend to make immediate enquiries!' said the inspector. He crossed the floor, opened the door to his office and called for his desk sergeant.

'Yes sir?' said the sergeant, entering the room with a somewhat sheepish expression on his face.

'Round up a few constables! I'm going to Awful End.'

'Yes, sir!' said the sergeant but, rather than turning and leaving the room sharpish, he stood with his back to Jones and spoke to the inspector in almost a whisper. 'Only there's something I need to ask you first, sir.'

'What is it?' asked the inspector.

'Keys, sir.'

'Keys?'

'Keys . . . to these handcuffs. You wouldn't happen to have them, would you?'

It was only then, using his police-enhanced powers of observation, that the detective inspector noticed his desk sergeant had managed to lock his wrists together with his own handcuffs.

★

With Fabian . . . I mean Neddie . . . I mean *Eddie* now convinced that he was part of Fudd's band of gypsies, he asked if he could say goodbye to Horsey (whose name he didn't know either), because it was agreed that the animal should stay at the monastery whilst the monks tried to find his 'rightful owner'. Eddie felt strange leaving behind the one link he had with his arrival at the monastery. He went with Abbot Po and the gypsy chief, Fudd, to the stables.

Brother Felch led the horse out into the yard. The nasty cut between Horsey's eyes was healing nicely. 'He'll soon be as fit as a fiddle,' he announced, slipping him a carrot from a bag slung on the rope belt tied around his waist.

Eddie patted him on the muzzle. 'Goodbye, boy,' he said.

It was just as Fudd reached the gatehouse, Eddie hobbling beside him on his stick, that Abbot Po called out after them.

'Just a moment, Mr Fudd!' he said.

Fudd stopped and turned. 'Yes, Abbot?'

'I haven't heard you ask young Fabian about his injuries.'

'Beg pardon?' said the gypsy, an uneasy feeling creeping over him.

'You haven't once asked the boy how he is.'

'S'not true,' said Fudd defensively. 'I asked the lad if he remembered me.'

'You enquired about his memory, yes,' said Po, 'but, despite the puncture holes all over him and his walking with a stick, you've never once asked how he's feeling. You, the chief and father to them all.'

'We're manly men, us gypsies,' said Fudd.

'And if this boy really is Fabian and one of your own, I'm sure you'd have asked him about his wellbeing by now.'

'Are you calling me a liar?' asked Fudd, raising his knobbly stick above Po's head.

'I'm simply saying that, before you leave with the boy, I feel that we need more proof that he is who you say he is.'

Now, before we go any further, I think I'd better do a little explaining here. Ready? When Fudd arrived at Lamberley Monastery, he really *was* hoping to find Fabian. It's not that he'd made Fabian up with a view to kidnapping Eddie for some nefarious purposes (and if you're not altogether sure what nefarious actually means, you could always look it up). Fabian existed and he was exactly whom Fudd had said he was: one of the gypsy children whose mother hadn't been born a gypsy but had fallen in love with one and married him. It was just that when Eddie was led into Abbot Po's office and turned out *not* to be the boy, Fudd saw an interesting opportunity. And Fudd was not one to turn down an opportunity in a hurry.

A plan formed very quickly in his mind. He would claim this Neddie as being Fabian, take him away with him and then track down his real parents. There was bound to be a reward, and Fudd would be far better at tracking them down than a bunch of monks who didn't get out much. And he'd still be on the lookout for the *real* Fabian in the meantime.

Clever, huh?

And if you're sitting there/standing there/squatting there/kneeling there/lying there thinking, 'Poor old gypsies! Here's yet *another* book giving them and travelling people a bad name,' let me say this:

1. Fudd was just Fudd, and was not representative of all gypsies.
2. There are good gypsies and bad gypsies in just the same way that there are good dentists and bad dentists. They're only human. (Bad

example. I'm not sure my dentist is.)

3. Eddie came across a wide variety of unsavoury characters over the years, and Fudd the gypsy was just one of them. So, as a percentage of the not-so-marvellous people Eddie encountered, gypsies probably made up less than one per cent.

4. Fudd wasn't that bad anyway!

Enough said.

Fudd lowered his stick. 'I'm sorry, Abbot,' he said. 'I had no real intention of hitting you.'

'I'm glad to hear it,' said Po.

'Not just because you're a man of God, but because I don't hit no defenceless man with nothing but me fists.'

'Even one as ugly as me?' asked Po.

''specially one as ugly as you,' grinned the gypsy.

'Is this boy really Fabian?' Po asked, staring straight into the man's eyes.

Fudd blinked and looked away. 'How come God made one so kind and clever as you so ugly?'

'Perhaps to remind us that we shouldn't always judge a book by its cover,' said Po, putting his arm around Eddie's shoulders. 'Come on, Neddie,' he said. 'It looks as though you won't be leaving our company just yet after all.'

'You mean, I'm not this Fabian fellow?' asked

Eddie. He turned to Fudd, who shook his head.

'I'm sorry, son. No,' he said. 'Though you are like two peas in a pod. Uncanny it is. Unnatural.'

'Then why –?'

'I'd have found your real folks for you, and no mistake,' he said.

'At a price, I suppose?' said Po.

The gypsy nodded again.

'Good day to you, Mr Fudd,' said Abbot Po briskly.

'You'll be reporting this to the authorities?' asked Fudd, who wasn't on the best of terms with police throughout the country.

It was Po's turn to shake his head. 'I report to the highest authority,' he said, looking skywards. 'If you never return to Lamberley, I have no reason to tell anyone of what happened here.'

'Right . . . Well – er – Good luck with your memory and the like,' said Fudd, then he marched through the gatehouse out into the world.

One of his men was waiting by his horse. 'Was it Fabian, chief?' he asked.

'No,' said Fudd, jumping up on to his animal. 'There's nothing for us here.'

*

By the time Fandango Jones returned to Awful End in the horse-drawn police van (his bicycle slung up

254

on to its roof), Dr Humple had arrived to tend to the wounded.

For someone who'd had a chimney dropped on him from a great height, Mr Dickens was, the doctor declared, in remarkably good condition. Humple had ordered all the chutney and brown paper removed before he could make his initial examination of the patient. Mrs Dickens had managed to get much of the chutney back into the earthenware jar, declaring that it would be 'a shame for it to go to waste', whilst Even Madder Aunt Maud was busy licking what remained stuck to the brown paper.

According to Dr Humple, it was Dawkins who was in need of more immediate attention. 'Time will heal your husband's broken bones, Mrs Dickens,' he said, 'but Dawkins needs those bee stings extracted this instant.'

Feeling a little guilty that it was her applying of the chutney to the gentleman's gentleman that had attracted the swarm of bees in the first place, Mrs Dickens insisted on helping the doctor pull out the stings. Even Madder Aunt Maud, who'd been watching from the sidelines, decided that she wanted a go, too, which is why, on entering the house, Detective Inspector Bunyon found three people attacking Dawkins with tweezers.

Fandango Jones had then taken the policeman

and his constables up on to the roof, shown him where the chimney had originally stood, shown him where it must have been dropped over the edge and, leaning over the parapet, pointed out where they'd all been standing below. He then produced the piece of brocade from the back of his notebook and handed it to the inspector, pointing out the exact spot where he'd found it.

'Remarkable!' said Bunyon. 'If you ever decide to give up being an engineer, Mr Jones, I'm sure there'd be a place for you in the detective branch of the police force!' What he didn't add out loud, but was certainly thinking, was, *if you didn't spit so much.*

When the detective inspector showed the piece of gold brocade to various members of the household, Mad Uncle Jack recognised it at once.

'That's off Private No-Sir's uniform!' he said.

'Private No-Sir, sir?' asked the detective inspector.

'One of my men.'

'Men?'

'One of the four ex-soldiers in my old regiment who now work for me.'

'Aha,' nodded the inspector. 'One of them. Is his name really No-Sir?'

'No.'

'No?'

Mad Uncle Jack shook his head, his beakie nose

cutting through the air like a wire cutter through cheese. 'I can't remember his real name. Called him No-Sir for so long.'

'And why do you call him that?'

'Damned if I can remember!' snorted MUJ.

Only seven people under Mad Uncle Jack survived from his entire regiment, after whatever the final campaign it was that they fought in. It wasn't the biggest of regiments, but that was still a pitifully small number. Soon after, two men died (one in an accident and the other of an extremely rare disease contracted from sponging down cacti in a private botanical garden near Norwich). This left five men, all of whom were in the 'lower ranks' and all of whom chose to go and work for Mad Major Jack Dickens at Awful End. Since then, one (a certain Private Gorey) had died not so very long before the events related in this book. Then there were four.

Private No-Sir's real name was Private Norman Sorrel, but the joke in his ever-decreasing regiment was that his initials, N.S., actually stood for 'No Sir' because he was always refusing to carry out orders. This is probably what saved his life. Officers even more senior that MUJ were forever sending men on terribly dangerous missions from which it was unlikely they'd ever return . . . except, perhaps in small pieces. MUJ, meanwhile, was forever making equally dangerous demands of them, but in a more low-key manner. Instead of ordering them to 'capture an enemy position' or 'hold the line' (whatever that may mean), he was asking them to try to catch cannon balls, or to nip across to the enemy encampment to ask them to keep the noise down.

Private Sorrel should probably have been court-martialled for insubordination in the ranks, or some such thing. Instead, he ended up with the nickname Private No-Sir, ignored all crazy orders – though he was always happy to retreat when told to – and came out of the various conflicts in one piece.

What's interesting is that those five survivors remained very loyal to MUJ and were happy to work for him at Awful End. This was, no doubt, partly to do with the fact that he appeared to know no fear.

Having never had it explained to him that being hit by a cannon ball or a mortar shell or a bullet might not only hurt him but also do some serious damage or even, believe it or not, kill him, Mad Major Jack Dickens pottered about various battlefields as though he was surveying his vegetable patch. He thought nothing of strolling through enemy fire to inspect a particularly interesting specimen of insect, or to heave a wounded soldier on to his back and carry him off to a hospital tent with little more than a 'And what have you managed to do to yourself this time?'

Occasionally he would have lucid moments where he seemed to realise that there were nasty foreigners trying to make life difficult for him; or that a particular bridge, or building or piece of land needed defending, but much of the time was spent asking people not to point that thing at him.

Detective Inspector Bunyon rubbed the gold brocade between his fingers. 'And why does Ex-Private No-Sir still go around in uniform?' he asked.

'I've never really thought about it,' said MUJ. 'He always does, that's all. Perhaps he doesn't own any other clothes. Come to think of it, all four of them pong a bit . . .'

'Couldn't you insist that they spend some of their wages on new clothing?' the inspector suggested.

'Wages?' asked Mad Uncle Jack, as though the word was new to him.

The policeman steered the conversation back on track. 'You suspect that this comes from No-Sir's uniform because he's the only one who still wears a uniform?'

MUJ nodded. 'Of course, Gorey used to as well.'

'Gorey used to as well?'

'That's what I said.'

'And who's Gorey, sir?'

'He's a very ex ex-private,' sighed Eddie's great-uncle. 'Sadly no more.'

The detective inspector asked to see No-Sir and they found him with the others playing cards on an iron girder. (All work had stopped on the bridge following the accident that increasingly looked like it hadn't been an accident.) Mad Uncle Jack asked him to step to one side.

Sure enough, No-Sir was in uniform – albeit a very tatty, worn and faded one – and even had a row of four medals. One, battered and bent, read 'BEST OF BREED' and had originally belonged to Gorey. Another was a campaign medal. The third read 'I'VE BEEN TO BLACKPOOL' and the fourth, on closer inspection, appeared not to be a medal at all but a flattened bottle top.

Detective Inspector Bunyon looked at No-Sir's epaulettes (or what was left of them) and at the piece of brocade in his hand. It would have been clear even to the untrained eye that the material came from the ex-private's left shoulder.

'Perhaps you'd like to explain what you were doing on the roof,' said the policeman.

'When, sir?' asked the ex-soldier.

'When what?' asked the detective inspector.

'What was I doing on the roof *when*?' asked No-Sir.

'You mean to tell me that you regularly go up onto the roof?' asked Bunyon. 'Why?'

Ex-Private Norman No-Sir Sorrel nodded his head in the direction of his ex-commanding officer.

The detective inspector took the hint. He was a good detective inspector. He turned to Mad Uncle Jack. 'I think I'd better talk to this man alone, sir,' he said.

'Very well,' said MUJ, who was rapidly losing interest anyway. 'I shall stride purposefully in this direction!'

The two men watched him go. Detective Inspector Bunyon turned back to Sorrel. 'Why do you go up to the roof sometimes?' he asked.

'To hide,' said No-Sir.

'To hide?'

'Yes, sir.'

'From whom?' asked the inspector.

'From Mad Major Dickens . . . from Even Madder Mrs Dickens . . . their nephew, Mr Dickens . . . his nephew's wife . . .'

'Basically, the entire Dickens family?' asked Bunyon.

'Except for Master Edmund,' said the ex-soldier, referring, of course, to Eddie. 'He seems . . .'

There was a pause. 'Normal?' the policeman suggested.

'That's it, sir,' nodded No-Sir. 'The very word I was looking for.'

'But why hide?'

'They're always wanting us to do things and I don't always want to.'

'And saying "no, sir" doesn't always work?'

'No, sir.'

'And when were you last up on the roof?'

'When Mad Major Dickens wanted us to beat the bounds,' said No-Sir.

'And you had nothing to do with dropping the chimney over the edge?' asked Bunyon.

'Oh, no, sir! I'd never do nothing like that.'

'So you know nothing about it?'

The old soldier looked at the detective inspector long and hard. 'I didn't say that,' he said.

Episode 9

Two Neds

In which some bright spark could point out
that two Neds are better than one

Baby Ned cried all the way back to Lamberley Monastery. Brother Guck only stopped once in his journey, and that was to stick moss in his ears. It didn't do much to block out the sound, but it looked nice.

Brother Guck tried singing. (He was good at chanting.) He tried a few monkish jokes. He tried everything he could think of, but Ned just cried and cried and cried.

Back at the monastery, Abbot Po didn't fare any better. His soothing voice which, given half the chance, could probably have convinced man-eating tigers to become vegetarian, had no effect whatsoever. Ned simply went on crying.

He only stopped crying when Eddie came to the abbot's office to find out what the noise was about. Eddie looked at Ned. Ned looked at Eddie. And smiled. And gurgled. And *coooooed*.

'Neddie, meet Ned,' said the abbot. 'Though I'm still not absolutely clear how he comes to be with us, I think from what Brother Guck here, said, Baby Ned is another lost soul.'

Brother Guck was watching the way the two boys were looking at each other.

'Do you know this baby, Neddie?' he asked.

'He does look familiar,' said Eddie, trying to fight his way through the fog of amnesia. It was no use.

'He was found by the family living over at Awful End,' said the monk.

'Awful End?' said Eddie. The name meant nothing to him.

'It's the biggest house around here after Lamberley Hall,' said Abbot Po.

(Lamberley Hall has since been converted into 'luxury apartments' which, in this instance, is a posh phrase for lots of badly converted flats. It's almost entirely populated by people who like to crunch up the swish driveway imagining that they own the whole house, when they really live in a few awkwardly shaped rooms and pay a huge annual service fee for someone to mow all the lawns and put over-the-top bouquets of flowers on the big round table in the centre of the communal hall.)

'Awful End is a strange name for a house,' said Eddie.

'And a strange family lives there!' said Brother Guck. And maybe if he'd had a chance to describe a few of what were, unbeknownst to all three of them, Eddie's closest relatives, something might have jogged Eddie's befuddled mind.

As it was, Abbot Po interrupted. 'It's not for us to judge who is strange and who is not. Our behaviour may seem strange to some outsiders.'

'You mean the scratchy habits, the humorous undergarments and the nearly-but-not-quite cutting yourself off from everyone?'

Po nodded. 'That and our belief in God,' he added.

Eddie was now holding Baby Ned. There was something familiar about him. The freshly powdered baby smell, perhaps?

'Until I decide what we can do about the child, perhaps you'd be kind enough to look after him, Neddie?' the abbot asked Eddie. 'Know you or not, he's certainly taken a shine to you.'

'I'd be happy to,' said Eddie.

The detective inspector was staring at No-Sir. 'You're claiming that you saw *Master Edmund* push the chimney on to his father?' he asked, struggling to control his professional composure.

'That's exactly what I'm claiming. Yes, sir,' said No-Sir, who had, indeed, made the startling revelation only moments before.

'What about all the eyewitnesses who state that he was right next to his father, down on the driveway, when the chimney flattened him?'

'So you don't believe me, then, sir?' said No-Sir.

'I don't believe you then.'

'Are you calling me a liar?'

'I'm suggesting that you were mistaken, at the very least,' said the detective.

'Like I said, the chimney was already balanced sideways on the parapet when I came out onto the roof and, moments later, I saw Master Edmund give it a shove.'

'And you're sure it was him?'

'As sure as eggs is eggs.'

'As eggs is eggs?' asked the detective inspector.

'As eggs is eggs,' No-Sir nodded.

'Which leaves me with four possibilities. One, you are lying –' The ex-soldier was about to

266

protest, but Inspector Bunyon frowned. Despite looking like a stick insect in comedy clown pants, he still had that indefinable air of authority about him, and No-Sir fell silent. 'Two, you imagined the whole thing. Three, you are mistaken. You genuinely thought you saw Edmund Dickens but, in actuality, you did not.'

'And four?' asked No-Sir.

'I was just coming to that,' said the inspector, 'and four, you were right – it *was* Master Edmund – and everyone else was mistaken.'

'It must be that last one,' said No-Sir, emphatically.

'I'm inclined to give you the benefit of the doubt at this stage,' said the policeman, 'and am willing to rule out options one and, possibly, even option two. You don't drink, do you?'

'Oh, yes, sir!' said No-Sir proudly. 'Gallons of the stuff. That's what they teaches you to do in the army.'

Detective Inspector Bunyon had a fleeting image of men being given their daily grog ration, then decided that that was for sailors in Her Majesty's Navy.

'Stops deforestation,' No-Sir explained.

The inspector looked at him like he was an idiot, which was probably appropriate. 'Do you mean dehydration?' he asked.

'That too,' said No-Sir, his medals jangling.

'So when you say that you drink, you mean water, don't you?'

'The very same, sir,' said the ex-private. 'Adam's Ale.'

'We all drink, man!' said the inspector. 'If we didn't drink, we'd die!'

'My point exactly, sir,' said No-Sir. 'Which is what they teaches us in the army.'

'So when I asked whether you drink, I meant *drink* drink, not drink . . . Don't you see?' asked the now somewhat exasperated policeman.

'No, sir,' said No-Sir.

'Do you drink alcohol?'

'Never touch the stuff.'

'Never?'

'No, sir,' said No-Sir.

'Good,' said the detective inspector. 'Then I'm inclined to rule out the first two options, which leaves three and four. And your being mistaken, rather than everyone else, seems likelier, doesn't it?

Detective Inspector Humphrey Bunyon had steered Ex-Private Sorrel away from his three card-playing companions and they were now some way off. From their vantage point on the lawn, he looked back at the iron skeleton of the treehouse and Fandango Jones's bridge that was beginning to take shape.

'What is the point of this bridge you're building?' he asked the old soldier.

'None whatsoever, sir,' he replied. 'It's a mad idea. Not as dangerous as some of the things we're asked to do, though, and I quite enjoys the riveting.'

'So nothing the Dickenses get up to surprises you any more?'

'Not really, sir,' said No-Sir.

'So Master Edmund pushing that chimney over the edge was just another typical Dickens act then, was it?'

'Yes and no, sir,' said No-Sir.

'Yes *and* no?'

'Yes it would have been another typical Dickens act if it had been any Dickens but Master Edmund doing it.'

'But Master Edmund is – what did you call him? – normal. And dropping a chimney on to one's family is hardly normal, now, is it?'

'That's my point exactly, sir,' said No-Sir. 'Though I can't blame him.'

'You can't blame him?'

'There's many a time I've wanted to strangle Mad Major Dickens, or run him over with a train, or poison him, or stab him repeatedly –'

'Repeatedly?'

'It means again and again, Inspector.'

'I know what it means,' said Bunyon, 'I was simply wondering why you wanted to do these things, and why you're confessing them to a police officer.'

'Oh, you'd want to do the same if you worked here for any length of time, sir,' said No-Sir, with utter conviction. 'We all of us feels this way. They're quite mad, you see . . . Forever changing their minds and wanting the most ridiculous things done.'

'For example?' asked Bunyon.

'Like the time Even Madder Mrs Dickens made Private Drabb stand atop of me, then painted black rings around us at one-foot intervals.'

'Why on earth did she do that?'

'That's what I was wondering at the time. I should have guessed when she insisted on *waterproof* paint.'

'Because?' asked the detective.

'Because she then made us wade into the middle of that there lake,' said No-Sir. 'She were using us to see how deep it was.'

'A human depth gauge!'

'Exactly, sir. A measuring rod. Only we was no good at it because the water was deeper than we were tall.'

'I can appreciate that life here at Awful End might be a little – er – frustrating at times,' said the detective inspector, 'but I do hope that you never resort to physical violence.'

'Oh, no-sir!' said No-Sir, snapping to attention as best a man of his age and health could snap to attention. (There was, in fact, an actual snapping noise as he did so. Bunyon hoped that it wasn't the poor man's bones.) 'We all thinks it, but we'd never do nothing about it, see?'

'I see.'

'Thank you, Private Sorrel. You've been most helpful,' said the inspector. 'Now I'm going to have another look at that roof. In the meantime, my men must start the search for this missing Master Edmund.'

You see. No one mentioned Baby Ned. Not one of them. During Detective Inspector Humphrey Bunyon's brief visit to Awful End (long before Brother Guck came to call, of course), Gibbering

Jane happened to be taking Ned for a walk around the grounds in his pram, which is short for perambulator, from the verb to perambulate, from the Latin *perambulare*, meaning to walk about. Interestingly (or not, as the case may be), in its British historical sense, perambulate meant to walk around in order to assert and record a place's boundaries . . . which is a bit like beating the bounds back in episode whatever.

Even *more* interestingly (or not, *see above*), baby Ned's pram and/or perambulator was a somewhat makeshift, home-made affair. The main body of the pram was another of the old dresser drawers, and the four wheels were made from cross-sections of a large log that Eddie's father, Mr Dickens, had made MUJ's ex-soldiers cut up in order for him to carve from. (I suspect that lump of old wood, next to the chunk of stone, in the broom cupboard that MUJ and EMAM mistook for the private chapel, had something to do with Mr Dickens's attempt at carving, too.)

Anyway, the pram-of-sorts was proudly made for Baby Ned by Dawkins at Gibbering Jane's request. Of course, Gibbering Jane's request had included much gibbering – one would expect no less from her – so it had taken time for the gentleman's gentleman to make head or tail of what she was saying. In fact, he had enough time to rustle up an eggy snack for himself and Jane whilst she was trying to make herself understood. It was whilst he was washing up the frying pan that everything fell into place and he realised that a pram was required of him.

Lacking any suspension, the end result – of the pram-making, not the pan-washing – was a bit of a boneshaker, but Ned seemed to love it. He spent much time laughing as he was wheeled judderingly about the place. He seemed blissfully happy if Eddie or Jane was with him and, with Eddie currently out of the picture, Gibbering Jane was doing a grand job.

Gibbering Jane's favourite walk with Ned was along the edge of Awful Wood. Awful Wood existed long before Awful End although it was now a part of the house's grounds (and still is today). I suspect the house must have got its name from the wood, or *gotten* its name from the *woods* if you're American.

If you're wondering why anyone would name a wood 'awful', especially when it wasn't that bad, I suppose it's my duty to point out that although 'awful' has come to mean bad or unpleasant, it also used to mean 'to fill one with awe'. For those of you who only know 'awe' as the noise the movie star John Wayne used to make when he drawled, let me tell you that it also means a feeling of reverential respect mixed with wonder or, sometimes, fear. So far from being a grotty wood, this was once seen as being pretty amazing.

Walking past it now, wheeling Baby Ned in front of her, gibbering away happily to him, Gibbering Jane caught a glimpse of what looked to her like a Red Indian wigwam nestling between the trees, but which could be more accurately described as a Native American-style tepee (what with Native Americans being neither red nor from India, and the thing Jane saw being tent-like, and a wigwam being more dome-shaped).

When Gibbering Jane finally returned to the house, the police had long gone and all the talk was of attempted murder, Eddie and Horsey's disappearance and what to have for supper. Baby Ned couldn't have been further from their minds.

'Here's Eddie!'

*In which saying too much here
might give the game away*

The fact that the monks at Lamberley Monastery didn't take baby Ned straight to the police made Eddie think about his own situation. Obviously, his primary concern had been to try to get his memory back, and the monks had been very kind to him. Because he didn't know who he was or where he rightfully belonged, he wasn't missing anywhere specific and, anyway, he liked it there. This had meant that, strange though he found some of the rules the Bertian order had about getting involved-but-only-so-far in the outside world, he hadn't been too bothered by them.

In the past few days, however, Eddie was beginning to think that he should visit the police station himself. There was nothing to stop him going out and about, and he should probably take Ned with him.

Eddie decided to speak to Abbot Po about it. As usual, he found him in his office.

'I've decided to go into town,' said Eddie.

'You're leaving us?' asked the abbot.

'No . . . I was thinking more of a day trip,' said Eddie. 'I'd like to carry on living here with you until I'm claimed.' He paused. 'If that's all right?'

Abbot Po looked at Eddie across his big oak desk. 'Of course you can stay with us, Neddie, for as long as you like.'

'Thank you,' said Eddie. 'I wasn't sure you'd say yes.'

Abbot Po looked at his hands. 'I've been waiting for you to ask to visit the town,' he said. 'I knew that you'd come around to it in your own good time, and that would prove you were ready to make the next step. This had to be a decision you came to yourself.'

'I'd like to take Ned with me,' Eddie suggested. 'His parents may be worried.'

'It would probably be better to leave him here for the time being,' said Po. 'He's getting better treatment than he'd get from any nurse or certainly any poor-house or orphanage. But, by all means, tell the authorities of his whereabouts.'

'That's a great idea,' said Eddie.

'As a matter of fact, we have a lad of about your own age visiting the monastery today,' said Po, getting to his feet. 'He's interested in the possibility of taking up religious orders so his father made arrangements for him to come and see us. When he's finished, I'll ask him to accompany you into town. It's a big step you're taking, Neddie. It'd be good for you to have young company.'

'Thank you,' said Eddie, blissfully unaware that things were about to change in a big way.

He spent the rest of the morning helping some of the brothers make a more permanent repair to the break in the fence that had allowed the sheep to escape. It was whilst he was being chased around the field by one of the friskier of the fleecy beasts that he had another one of his flashbacks. This time he had memories of being chased by policemen with sheep on leashes . . . if they *were* memories. It seemed far more likely that his befuddled mind was playing tricks on him again. All these so-called flashbacks he'd had were so *weird*.

A job well done, Eddie, Brother Guck, Brother Pugh and a Brother Klaus were sitting under a tree, sharing a pitcher of water. (That's a pitcher as in jug, rather than something you look at hanging on the wall of a gallery.) Brother Po came striding across the pasture with a boy at his side.

David Thackery, for it was he (and if you can't remember who this particular *he* was, look back at page 191 to refresh your sadly failing memory), was surprised to find Eddie Dickens in a monastery of all places *and* dressed in a habit. The truth be told, he was a little jealous. 'Eddie!' he said.

'Neddie,' Eddie corrected him, because he'd got so used to this being his name.

'No, David,' said David, thinking that Eddie thought that *he* was someone called Neddie, rather than Eddie telling him that his own name was Neddie which, of course, it wasn't anyway. (You get the idea.)

'My name's really David?' asked Eddie in amazement.

'It's Eddie, stupid!' said David impatiently. 'What is this? Some sort of a game?'

'Wait a minute! Wait a minute!' said Abbot Po. 'Are you telling me that you *know* this young man?'

'I most certainly do, Abbot,' said the Thackery boy. 'Has he been playing tricks on you?'

'Please answer the question, child,' said Po. 'Do you know who this boy is?'

'He's Edmund Dickens from Awful End,' said David Thackery.

'Awful End!' gasped Brother Guck. 'I was there only the other day.'

'Do you recognise David Thackery?' Abbot Po asked Eddie, who'd leapt to his feet. He put a hand on the shoulder of each boy.

Eddie shook his head.

'And the name Edmund Dickens – Eddie – doesn't mean anything to you?'

Eddie shook his head again.

Abbot Po turned to David Thackery. 'You're in absolutely no doubt that this is Eddie Dickens?'

'None whatsoever, sir,' said David. 'I promise you, that's who he is.' And David wouldn't break a promise. He wanted to be a saint one day, remember? 'His parents and my parents are best friends.'

'Eddie,' said Abbot Po. 'This is the lad I was telling you about. The one who's interested in taking up religious orders. God certainly works in mysterious ways!'

Now any half-decent storyteller would have put the conversation Eddie and the abbot had regarding the upcoming visit from the (then) unnamed boy much, much earlier in the story. That way, when David turned up, the reader would go, 'Oh, so *that's* who it was!' having pretty much forgotten that anyone was due to turn up at all.

This way (*my* way), one minute you're told the boy's due to come and BAM! – a few paragraphs later – here he is and he turns out to be David Thackery. Not much of a build-up there, is there? No evidence of multi-layered storytelling or planting the seed of an idea. No suspense. No. But, then again, that's how it happened, so that's how I'm telling it. Publish the Truth with a capital 'T' and be damned, I say!

And where does this leave us? With Abbot Po and Brother Guck taking Eddie back to Awful End.

*

And here we are:

It was Even Madder Aunt Maud who opened the door to them.

'Do you know this boy, madam?' asked the abbot, eager to get straight to the point.

'I've never seen him before in my life,' said EMAM.

'You're sure?'

Even Madder Aunt Maud leaned in closer and peered at them all in more detail. 'I tell a lie,' she said. 'He came here the other day asking about sheep, and took away young Ned with him,' she said.

'That's Brother Guck –'

'A ridiculous name, if ever I heard one,' said Eddie's great-aunt.

'I was referring to this boy, here,' said Po, putting his hands on Eddie's shoulders and pushing him forward, his heels skidding on the gravel. The abbot was beginning to suspect that this woman might be a little *unusual*.

'Oh, *him*,' said Even Madder Aunt Maud. 'Of course I know *him*. He's my missing great-nephew, Edmund. Why ask me if I know my own great-nephew?'

'He doesn't know he's your great-nephew, you see,' said the abbot.

'Does that mean I don't have to buy him Christmas or birthday presents any more?' she asked, obviously keen on the idea.

'Well, he's missing no more, madam,' said Abbot Po. 'It's my happy duty to return him to you.'

281

'So you've found him then?'

'He's standing right in front of you.'

'So he is,' said EMAM, adding a 'silly me' with a fluttering-of-the-eyelashes that only her beloved husband Jack would find endearing. To anyone else, it was about as appealing as being in an ascending room/lift/elevator with a flatulent hippo. 'Why's he dressed in a sack?'

'It's a habit,' the abbot explained.

'Well, it's a very silly habit, if you ask me, and one he should grow out of,' snapped Even Madder Aunt Maud.

'Are you really my great-aunt, madam?' Eddie asked politely. The truth be told, there was something more than a little terrifying at the prospect of having this . . . this *lady* as a relative.

'Well, I'm hardly a tucker bag full of jumbucks, now, am I?' she demanded, proud to be able to employ some everyday Australian speech that she'd gleaned from a book entitled *Everyday Australian Speech*.

'Indeed not, no,' said Eddie, beginning to wonder whether life in a monastery wouldn't be such a bad option after all.

'Are the boy's parents at home?' asked Abbot Po. David Thackery had mentioned his mother and father being friends of Eddie's parents.

'Mr Dickens is currently indisposed, a chimney

having been pushed upon him,' said Eddie's great-aunt, unable to suppress a chuckle. 'I'm a great believer in seeing the funny side of things.'

'Not so funny for my father, I suppose,' said Eddie.

'You're behaving very oddly, boy,' said EMAM, fixing a stare on Eddie.

'The child has lost his memory,' the abbot said. 'If we might be allowed in to see his parents – his mother, at least – I can explain everything.'

'No memory, you say?'

'Not of his family, no, madam.'

'Ridiculous!'

'Helping him regain it could be a slow process,' said Abbot Po. 'The mind is a delicate tool and –' He was interrupted by a loud 'THUMP!'

The loud 'THUMP!' was generated by Even Madder Aunt Maud leaning back inside the doorway, lifting Malcolm the stuffed stoat from an occasional table just out of view, and hitting Eddie over the head with him.

Slightly dazed, Eddie blinked, then looked from Malcolm to Even Madder Aunt Maud and back to Malcolm. Suddenly, the world made *sense* again.

'Malcolm!' he said in delight, throwing his arms around the rigid animal. 'Now I remember everything!'

'Cured!' said his great-aunt triumphantly. 'Now there's no time to stand around talking, I need to get on!'

She slammed the front door, leaving Abbot Po, Brother Guck and Eddie out on the driveway.

'That's Even Madder Aunt Maud,' said Eddie.

'Delighted to meet her,' said Abbot Po.

'My great-aunt,' said Eddie.

'Charmed, I'm sure,' said Po.

The front door flew back open. 'And might I just add that you're the ugliest man I've ever seen,' said Maud, before slamming it shut again.

None of them had to guess who she was talking to, or even to whom she was talking.

There was much back-slapping and a few tears when Eddie was welcomed back into the bosom of his family. Gibbering Jane had been so upset when Even Madder Aunt Maud had given Baby Ned to Brother Guck that she'd gone back to the cupboard under the stairs and refused to come out. Now that Eddie was back, she emerged. Eddie was quick to assure her that little Ned was safe and well – and bawling his eyes out – back at Lamberley Monastery. She gibbered with delight at the news.

Mad Uncle Jack shook Eddie's hand solemnly. 'I take it that you told the enemy nothing?' he asked.

'I was in an accident,' Eddie explained for the umpteenth time. 'I lost my memory.'

'So that's what you told the blackguards, huh? And they believed you? Excellent, my boy! I knew that a Dickens would never talk under interrogation. We're part of what makes this country great: chin up . . . stiff upper lip . . . eyes front, and all that!'

In Eddie's absence, his mother (Mrs Dickens, of course) had 'knitted' him a suit using the unravelled material from the sofa. 'It was my way of telling myself that you'd be back,' she said, kissing her son on the forehead. Her breath smelled of mothballs. She'd been sucking on a handful now and then, to calm the nerves.

Eddie changed out of his monk's habit and into the suit. Looking at himself in the wardrobe mirror, he quickly changed back again.

Mr Dickens was delighted to see Eddie, but could still only manage a horizontal position. He'd solved this by asking his wife – Mrs Dickens to you and me – to lash him to the tea trolley he remembered from his youth. Mrs Dickens hadn't been able to find any rope at such short notice (or of such a short length) so had used some bunting last hung out for one of the Queen's jubilees.

It was in this extraordinary state that his father first greeted Eddie on his return. It'd be interesting to know what Eddie would have made of this if he'd met his father in this condition *before* his memory came back to him. As it was, this was just another typical Dickens family scene.

'Fandango Jones – you remember him, I take it?' asked Mr Dickens. Eddie nodded. 'He had a theory that the chimney was deliberately pushed from the roof; a theory which the detective inspector –'

'The same detective inspector?' asked Eddie.

'The very same,' nodded his father, with a wince. 'The fat one with the checked suit. Only now he's very thin, but still has the same suit. Well, he agrees with Jones. He says that this was no accident, not that I was necessarily the target.'

'How dreadful!' said Eddie.

'Nothing a piece of sacking wouldn't fix,' said Even Madder Aunt Maud, passing by with what

286

appeared to be a stuffed moose's head (mounted on a wooden shield) under her arm.

'I beg your pardon?' asked Eddie.

'I assume you were referring to the abbot's ugliness. I was saying it's nothing a piece of sacking wouldn't fix! He could cut out a pair of holes for his eyes.'

'He was referring to someone deliberately pushing that chimney on to me,' said Eddie's father, somewhat indignantly. 'And where are you going with that moose head?'

'What moose head?' asked his aunt.

'*That* moose head,' Mr Dickens managed to point. 'Under your arm.'

EMAM looked down and flinched in surprise as though noticing the moose head for the first time. 'I read somewhere that they make nourishing soup,' she said, somewhat unconvincingly. I'd hazard a guess that she had no idea why she was carrying it either.

'I think she's thinking of carrots,' muttered Laudanum Dickens as she strode out of earshot.

Eddie found that he couldn't sleep that first night back at Awful End. It was a strange feeling getting all his memories back, even though they were rightfully his. It wasn't so much the having-regained-his-identity part that was so odd but the looking-back-at-his-time-in-the-monastery now that he knew who he was. It was difficult to remember what it was like *not* knowing. And if you find my trying to explain that confusing, think how hard it was for Eddie to make sense of it in his head.

After staring at the ceiling for what seemed like an eternity, Eddie got up and went for a wander around the house, to try to stop his brain working overtime. It was a moonlit night and Awful End had more than its fair share of curtainless windows, especially since, some years previously, Mad Uncle Jack had used so many of the curtains to fuel an enormous beacon to warn of the coming of the Armada. (Of course, he'd been confused.

He'd read in his newspaper a report marking the *anniversary* of the coming of the Spanish fleet some three hundred years earlier but had mistaken it for current news.) Still, the local fire brigade – also known as three men and a horse-drawn fire cart – had great fun trying to douse the flames, and the only victims were the local ducks who were homeless because the fire fighters had drawn all the water for their hoses from their pond. The Thackery family (with the notable exception of Master David, of course) had rallied around, travelling up especially, and giving the ducks temporary accommodation whilst their original watery home was restored to its former glory.

Eddie decided to go up on to the roof. He liked doing that some summer evenings. It was usually a haven of peace and quiet in an otherwise frenetic household. Away from the big windows, the enclosed upper stairways were in darkness. Eddie held up his bedside candle before him.

Out on the roof, he placed the candle on the parapet. The air was so still that the flame barely flickered. Eddie looked up at the star-filled night sky, dark blue in the moonlight. Then something caught his eye.

There, over in Awful Wood, was a glimmering light. Someone had lit a campfire on the estate. Eddie was too far away to make out anything more.

Had he been closer, he would have seen the strange tent that Gibbering Jane had passed that day of her afternoon perambulations with Baby Ned. Of course, she'd failed to mention it to anyone or, if she had, they'd probably failed to understand her through all that gibbering.

Eddie wasn't too alarmed by the sight. It was clearly a self-contained campfire and not a danger to property. He guessed that it must be one of his great-uncle's ex-soldiers practising night manoeuvres, or some such thing. He yawned. He'd investigate in the morning.

Falling Into Place

*In which Eddie Dickens makes
a startling discovery and a late breakfast*

To English ears and eyes – well, to mine, at least – the word doppelganger doesn't sound like it means anything, and looks made-up. But, no! Apparently, it's from the German meaning 'double-goer'. Double-goer? Well, a doppelganger is your double. If you come face-to-face with yourself in the high street, then that person is your doppelganger, or you're theirs . . . or both. Unless, of course, you're looking at your own reflection in a shop window, or anywhere else for that matter.

Eddie met his doppelganger when he'd made his way across the lawns and into Awful Wood, the following morning. He saw the tent before he saw the remains of the fire, now long since turned to ashes, that had caught his attention the previous night. The tent was expertly constructed from branches and leaves collected from the wood.

'Is there anyone in there?' he asked, not knowing who to expect. Life at Awful End was full of surprises and, for all Eddie knew, Even Madder Aunt Maud had hired a dwarf to pretend to be a garden ornament by day and live in the wood at night. He wouldn't put it past her.

What he didn't expect was the person who came blinking into the morning sunlight to look how he looked. Eddie blinked. Twice. And then again, for good measure.

He and the boy-emerging-from-the-tent looked remarkably like each other. *Like two peas in a pod.*

The boy-who-had-now-emerged-from-his-tent looked equally startled.

'Good morning,' said Eddie, politely. 'I don't think we've met.'

'No,' said the boy. 'I don't think we have.'

They even sounded similar. The boy was a fraction taller than Eddie and his hair was a lighter shade of brown.

'You're Fabian, aren't you?' said Eddie. 'Hester's boy.'

Fabian, for that was, indeed, who he was, was flabbergasted (and what a brilliant word that is).

'How . . . how on earth did you know that?' asked Fabian. He furtively looked from left to right, as though he was expecting that this was some kind of trap, and that a swarm of peelers might appear from behind the trees and start beating him with their truncheons.

Of course, the reason that Eddie knew that Fabian was Fabian was because he guessed that there couldn't be that many gypsies of about his age and appearance loose in the countryside; and there was no doubting that Fabian was a gypsy, what with the clothes he was wearing and the skills with which he'd made the tent from branches in the wood.

'I keep my ears open,' Eddie grinned. 'And Chief Fudd is out looking for you.'

'Has he been to the house?' asked Fabian, nodding in the direction of Awful End.

Eddie shrugged. 'I've been away,' he said, 'but no one here's mentioned him to me.'

Fabian took a knife out of his pocket and began to whittle a small piece of wood which he took from the other. Eddie was tinged with jealousy. His parents only let him whittle with a carrot, which is another way of saying 'not at all', carrots being one of the blunter vegetables. Whittling was out for Eddie. They were worried he might cut himself. Eddie was pretty sure – which is similar to fairly confident – that Fabian had primarily produced the knife not to whittle but to let Eddie know that he was armed. It was obvious from his manner that he was jumpy about something. He looked decidedly uneasy.

'You went off the day that the chimney landed on that man,' said Fabian.

'That's right,' said Eddie. 'The man is my father. I went to fetch the doctor.'

'Is he all right? Your father, I mean,' asked the gypsy boy.

'He's always having accidents,' said Eddie. 'The doctor says that he'll make a full recovery.'

'That's good,' said Fabian. 'What happened to you? You didn't come back.'

'Until now,' said Eddie. 'I was waylaid.'

There was a period of silence between them. Fabian whittled and Eddie stuck his hands in his pockets.

'Is this a bad place?' asked Fabian, when he next spoke.

'Bad?' said Eddie, in genuine surprise. 'Mad, maybe, but I wouldn't say bad.'

'What about the beatings?' asked Fabian.

'Beatings?' asked Eddie. The only beating he could think of was being beaten over the head with Malcolm, and that had done him the power of good.

'The day you went and didn't come back. The tall beaky man was talking about beating people . . .'

'Oh,' said Eddie. 'You mean beating the bounds! He was only going to hit a well-padded ex-soldier with a stuffed stoat.' The minute the words came out, he realised how odd they'd sound to a stranger. But just how much of a stranger could someone who looked so like Eddie be?

'And what about Oli – about the baby?' asked Fabian. 'What happened to the baby? They let someone take him away!'

'You seem to know an awful lot about what's been going on here,' said Eddie. 'Who exactly are you?'

There was the loud flap of a wood pigeon's wings as it took flight, and Fabian threw himself to the ground as though dodging a bullet.

Eddie put his hand out, which Fabian sheepishly took, pulling himself back to his feet. He stuffed the knife and whittled wood back into a pocket.

'Are you a relation?' Eddie asked.

'A relation?'

'Are you and I related in some way?' asked Eddie. 'You must have noticed how similar we look.'

'I – er –' Fabian stuttered to a halt. 'The baby?'

'The baby's fine. He hasn't been stuck in any poor-house or orphanage. He's staying with some monks for the time being.' Just at that moment, Fabian's tummy rumbled and Eddie seized the opportunity to turn the situation to his advantage. 'Do you want to come up to the house for something to eat? We've had our breakfast, but there's always plenty left over.'

Fabian seemed hesitant. 'I – er – I'm not sure I want the others to see me,' he said at last.

'I'm not sure you wanted *me* to see you,' said Eddie. 'It's probably too late now.'

'So they're not bad people?' asked the gypsy boy.

Eddie put his hands on his hips. 'How many times am I going to have to say this: they're not bad, just eccentric. That's all. Come on.'

Eddie sneaked Fabian into the kitchen, sat him at the table, and then went into the larder to find him some leftovers. No one had invented the fridge yet, though someone of Eddie's slight acquaintance (a Tobias Belch) had been experimenting with a 'steam-powered ice box' in his laboratories in Bristol. So far, with little success and a few big explosions.

Eddie returned with some bacon, kedgeree (a kind of cold fish curry designed specifically to be eaten in the morning) and something called 'devilled kidneys', which are not kidneys with little horns and fork tails but those cooked with hot seasoning.

'I would offer you bread, but my mother's is an acquired taste,' said Eddie. He didn't bother to tell Fabian about her special recipe which included those troublesome watch springs.

Fabian ate hungrily. 'We *are* related,' he said, after he'd eaten his last mouthful.

'I thought so,' said Eddie. 'How?'

Fabian wiped his mouth on his sleeve. 'Have you heard of a man named Doctor Malcontent Dickens?' he asked.

'Yes,' said Eddie. 'He was my great-grandfather. That "tall beaky man", as you called him, is his only remaining son, Jack. He's my great-uncle.'

'If he's Jack, then you'll know that Malcontent had two other sons –'

'My grandfather, Percy Dickens, and my Great-Uncle George –'

'The one who burnt down the Houses of Parliament,' Fabian nodded. Eddie could sense that he was getting excited.

'But what I don't understand is where you fit

in?' said Eddie. 'Out of Grandpa, Mad Uncle Jack and George, only my grandfather had a child . . . That's my father, Laudanum. And he, of course, had me.'

Fabian pulled a piece of paper from inside his shirt and unfolded it on the table, smoothing it flat with a fist. 'That's not strictly true,' he said. 'Look at this.'

Eddie found himself looking at an incomplete branch of the Dickens family tree. Sure enough, his father, Laudanum, was down there as being married to Florinda, but there was no mention of their having a son, Edmund. What really caught Eddie's eye, though, was what appeared under George's name.

'My Great-Uncle George had a daughter?' he said in amazement. 'No one ever mentioned that before. In fact, I'm sure that Mad Uncle Jack told me that his brother George never married –' It's true, you know. That's exactly what MUJ told Eddie. If you don't believe me, you'll find it on page 49 of the UK edition of *Terrible Times*. '– let alone had a daughter.'

'She's my mother,' said Fabian, producing a stubby pencil from a pocket, and adding the next generation to the family tree.

Here's what it looked like after Fabian had finished with it:

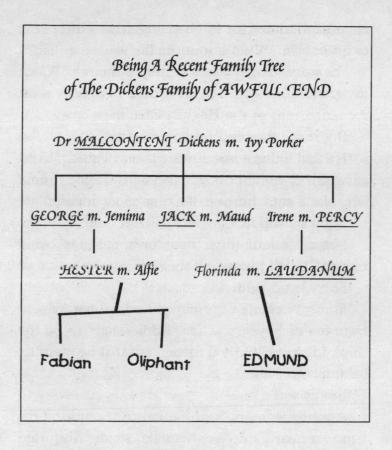

Being A Recent Family Tree
of The Dickens Family of AWFUL END

Dr <u>MALCONTENT</u> Dickens m. Ivy Porker

<u>GEORGE</u> m. Jemima   <u>JACK</u> m. Maud   Irene m. <u>PERCY</u>

<u>HESTER</u> m. Alfie   Florinda m. <u>LAUDANUM</u>

Fabian   Oliphant   <u>EDMUND</u>

'Ned – I mean the baby – is your brother, Oliphant?' gasped Eddie.

'Yes,' said Fabian.

'So it was you who brought him here and put him in amongst the bulrushes!'

'It was my mother's idea,' said Fabian. 'She wants Oliphant to have the life that she never had . . .'

'But what about you?' asked Eddie, pulling out a

chair from under the kitchen table and sitting next to his cousin. 'What about the life *you* never had?'

The story Fabian told was simple enough: 'When my grandfather, your Great-Uncle George, was on a walking tour of the English Channel –'

'But that's the sea!' Eddie protested.

'He had a thing about water,' said Fabian. 'And a big pair of lead boots. He met a boy called Jimmy who was a cook on one of the support vessels.'

'What's a support vessel?' asked Eddie.

'Some kind of large boat or small ship,' said Fabian. 'Can I please tell this?'

'Sorry,' said Eddie.

'Jimmy worked in the galley,' said Fabian (which, from his early years at sea, Eddie knew to be the ship's kitchen). 'Only it turned out that he wasn't a he at all but a she.'

'Jimmy was a girl?'

'A young woman,' said Fabian. 'She couldn't get a job on board ship as a woman, so she disguised herself as a boy. I think this happens quite a lot.'

'Oh,' said Eddie. It was the first he'd heard about it.

'Anyhow,' said his cousin, 'Jimmy – whose real name turned out to be Jemima – and Grandpa George fell in love and, after a whirlwind romance, got married.'

'How romantic!' said Eddie.

'But not popular with his father, Doctor Malcontent, and the other Dickenses.'

'They thought that he was marrying beneath his station?' asked Eddie (which, I'm sure I must have explained in some previous book or other, doesn't mean attending a wedding ceremony under Charing Cross, Grand Central or any such railway terminus, but getting hitched to someone of a 'lower class').

Cousin Fabian shook his head. 'It wasn't that,' he said, 'it's just that the Dickenses had a violent and irrational reaction against anyone whose name began with a "J"!'

'But Mad Uncle Jack's name begins with a "J"!' Eddie protested.

'Except for the name Jack,' Fabian added. 'They had nothing against the name Jack.'

Eddie was about to protest that this made no sense at all, when he remembered that this was his own family he was talking about.

'George was always welcome at Awful End and at family gatherings, so long as he neither brought Jemima with him, nor mentioned her name. Fortunately, this wasn't quite as hard on my grandfather as you might imagine, because he was very absent-minded, and often forgot that he was married.'

'So what happened?'

'Sadly, my grandmother, Jemima, died in childbirth, giving birth to my mother Hester. She was brought up by a kind and loving nanny named Nanny Noonan. What's unusual, is that she was actually christened Nanny Noonan. It wasn't just her title,' Fabian explained. 'Grandpa George never even told his brothers that he'd had a child. When my mother grew up, she felt so rejected by the Dickens family and society that she turned her back on them. When a handsome gypsy turned up at the door of Nanny Nanny Noonan's house one day, offering to sharpen her knives and scissors, my mother ran away with him. They married, and me and Oliphant were the result.'

Eddie was bursting to ask a whole series of questions, when they were rather rudely interrupted.

There was the sound of a stoat-carrying great-aunt in tiny black boots stomping across the stone-flagged kitchen floor.

Even Madder Aunt Maud stopped and stared at the pair of them, seated side-by-side at the long, pine table.

'Edmund!' she snapped. 'I suppose you think it's clever pretending to be two of you! Stop it at once!'

Now she too was interrupted, for into the kitchen walked that fairly well-known engineer Fandango Jones beside the once-fat-now-thin Detective Inspector Humphrey Bunyon.

'I was looking for you, Master Edm –' began the policeman, then he saw that Eddie wasn't alone. Next to him sat a lookalike.

Cogs spun in his brain. Lights flashed. Whistles blew. The detective inspector recalled his conversation with No-Sir: the conversation in which the ex-private had sworn he'd witnessed Eddie pushing the barley-sugar chimney over the parapet . . . whilst everyone else had sworn that Eddie had been down below with them.

Now it made sense: two Eddies. And one was an attempted murderer.

303

A Conclusion of Sorts

In which things fall into place,
and a rock falls on the floor

Fabian could spot a policeman a mile off, even one as strange looking as Humphrey Bunyon. He was up and out of his chair before you could say, 'Hello, hello, hello. What's going on here then?', and dashed out of the kitchen door . . . straight into Mrs Dickens who was carrying what appeared to be a small boulder. She dropped it, narrowly missing both their feet – all four of them/two pairs, I'm not implying that they had one foot each – which was fortunate when you see the dent the rock made in the floor, which is still there to this day (but now covered with a swirly patterned carpet).

The detective inspector seized the opportunity, and Fabian's collar, lifting the boy off the ground. 'I think you've some explaining to do, young man,' he said.

Even Madder Aunt Maud looked from Eddie at the table to Fabian at the door, and then back again. 'So he isn't you?' she demanded.

'No, Aunt Maud,' said Eddie. 'I'm sitting over here . . . and he isn't.'

Even Madder Aunt Maud studied him between half-closed eyes. 'This isn't another one of your tricks, is it?' she demanded. 'Like that time you wore those stilts and tried to frighten me at my bedroom window.'

'Your bedroom doesn't have a window, Aunt Maud,' he sighed, knowing that she'd imagined the whole thing. 'You live in a cow.'

Even Madder Aunt Maud seemed momentarily stumped by this, then added triumphantly: 'But I see you don't deny it!'

'Let me go! Let me go!' shouted Fabian, to which he would probably have added 'I ain't done nuffink' if it weren't for the fact that he'd been so well brought up by his mother Hester Grout, *née* Dickens. So what he actually said was: 'I haven't done anything!'

'Then why run?' spat Fandango Jones, his stovepipe hat quivering with excitement. This was like living out one of those penny dreadful detective stories he so loved to read.

'Because no one has a good word to say for gypsies!' he protested.

'Gypsum?' cried Even Madder Aunt Maud prodding Mrs Dickens's dropped lump of rock with Malcolm. 'This isn't gypsum. It looks more like granite to me.'

Very sensibly, the detective inspector ignored her. 'Now just exactly who are you, my boy?' he asked Fabian. 'There's no denying you have a remarkably strong resemblance to Master Edmund, except, of course, for having different coloured eyes.' (Trust a policeman to spot something like that. Though, of course, Chief Fudd must have spotted the same thing at the monastery to know, at a glance, that Eddie wasn't Fabian.)

'He's the cousin I never knew I had,' said Eddie. He turned to Mrs Dickens. 'Mother, this is Great-Uncle George's grandson Fabian.'

Mrs Dickens, who was busy trying to pick up the chunk of rock, looked up at Fabian who was now wearing the desk sergeant's brand new shiny pair of handcuffs. 'So you're a Dickens?' she asked.

'My mother was, ma'am, before she married,' said Fabian politely, even stopping struggling.

'Well I never!' said Eddie's mum. 'I never even knew George had a daughter. Welcome to Awful

End!' She seemed oblivious to the fact that the poor boy was in handcuffs and in the clutches of the law (in the guise of a very skinny man in very baggy clothes).

'Thank you,' said Fabian.

'Why are you arresting Fabian?' Eddie demanded. 'What's he supposed to have done? Trespassed in the wood?'

'Oh, much worse than that, Master Edmund,' said Humphrey Bunyon. 'An eyewitness saw this lad push the chimney over the parapet onto your father.'

Eddie was stunned. 'Is that true?' he asked Fabian.

'It was an accident!' Fabian protested.

'It was a premeditated act!' spat Fandango Jones. 'Don't tell me that you accidentally got the chimney from the stack, down the roof, up on to the parapet and over the edge by mistake!'

'I know my rights!' said Fabian to the policeman. 'Stop that man spitting all over me!'

'The chimney fell off the stack and rolled down the roof,' said Mrs Dickens, who had now managed to lift the boulder to waist height. 'No one moved it. Things like that often happen. This house is in constant need of repair.'

'I beg your pardon?' asked the detective inspector.

'And how did the chimney get up on to the parapet and over the edge?' asked Fandango Jones.

With a grunt of exertion, Mrs Dickens was now holding the rock in her arms again, pressed against her stomach. 'I put it on the parapet,' she said. 'What's this all about, anyway?'

'What's this all about?' spluttered the policeman in absolute amazement. 'This is about a police investigation. Were you not aware, madam, that I've spent heaven-knows-how-long trying to get to the bottom of how your husband came to be flattened by a chimney, and you neglected to tell me that it was you who put the chimney on the parapet in the first instance!'

Realising that she wouldn't be able to get on

with her current task uninterrupted, Mrs Dickens dropped the chunk of rock on the kitchen table, sending an uneaten bite of devilled kidney flying through the air. As it neared EMAM, the old lady batted it aside with Malcolm, and it came to rest in the rim of the fairly well-known engineer's stovepipe hat. He didn't notice, and there it remained for the rest of the day until his wife Clarissa spotted it that evening.

As for the table, the damage caused by the rock knocked quite a significant amount off the reserve price when it was auctioned in the 1960s.

'All I knew was that poor Laudanum had been squashed by the chimney and that you two gentlemen,' she was referring to Bunyon and Jones, 'were convinced that it had been dropped. You even told me that you had an eyewitness who saw someone push it over. That certainly wasn't me, so what relevance did anything else have?'

The detective inspector sighed. 'Sit!' he commanded Fabian, who did as he was told and sat back down at the kitchen table. 'Mrs Dickens,' the policeman continued. 'Mr Jones calculated that the chimney could not have fallen from the stack, down the roof and over the edge, something that my later inspection of the scene confirmed. This then led me to suspect that someone had deliberately lifted the chimney on to the parapet with the sole intention of pushing it on to the assembled company below.'

'Us lot below?' asked Even Madder Aunt Maud, who was wondering why Fandango Jones was walking around with a bite-sized piece of devilled kidney in the brim of his extraordinary hat. What was he? Some kind of weirdo?

'You lot below,' nodded the detective inspector. 'Only now you're telling me that it was you who placed the chimney on the parapet in the first instance, Mrs Dickens.'

'Yes,' said Eddie's mother.

'May I ask why?' asked the detective inspector.

'Yes, you may,' said Eddie's mother, rinsing her hands under the kitchen tap.

'Why?' asked the detective inspector, obligingly.

'So that I could push it over the edge.'

'Push it over the edge?'

'Push it over the edge,' said Mrs Dickens. 'That's right.'

'But *why*?'

'Because it was too heavy to carry down all those flights of stairs, Inspector. I really don't see where you're going with these questions.'

Detective Inspector Bunyon was doing his very best not to burst into tears. He wanted to be lovely and fat again and as far away from the Dickens family as possible. He hated cases involving the

Dickens family. He'd rather be investigating a grizzly murder in a sewer than spending another minute with these infuriating people ... but he was a good detective inspector, and there was a job to be done.

He tried again. 'Why? Why? Why, Mrs Dickens? *Why* did you want the chimney on the ground when a chimney's rightful place is on a chimney stack? *Why*, once you'd got as far as putting the chimney on the parapet, didn't you then push it? *Why*, Mrs Dickens?' He found it impossible to keep the air of desperation out of his voice.

'You may not be aware of it, Inspector, but my husband is a very fine amateur sculptor,' said Mrs Dickens. 'He mainly carves bottle corks and wood, but I've recently suggested that he try stone. He briefly tried carving in coal, but that proved to be a very messy business and also –' she paused to glare at Even Madder Aunt Maud, '– someone, naming no names, kept on eating it.'

'Even better than charcoal biscuits,' EMAM muttered.

'I've been collecting various different types of stone for him to experiment carving with. I got this piece, for example, from the edge of the ornamental lake where Eddie found Ned.'

'Oliphant,' Eddie corrected her, now that he knew the baby's true name.

'Ned?' asked the detective inspector.

'Oliphant?' asked Mrs Dickens.

'Oliphant?' asked the detective inspector.

'The baby,' said Eddie.

'The baby?' asked the inspector. Everyone had still neglected to mention him.

'We found a baby in the bulrushes.'

'Like Ex-Private Moses in the Bible,' said Even Madder Aunt Maud, a trifle confused. (Surprise. Surprise.)

'My brother,' said Fabian. 'I put him there.'

The policeman's brain was beginning to suffer from what, today, we might call information overload. 'We'll come to the baby in a moment,' he said. 'Would someone please get me a glass of water?'

'Certainly,' said Even Madder Aunt Maud. 'Hold this.' She thrust Malcolm into the startled policeman's hands. 'Milk and sugar?'

'J-Just water, please,' he said. He turned back to Mrs Dickens. 'You collected various different types of stone from the house and grounds for your husband to experiment carving with? Is that correct?'

'Exactly, Inspector!'

'And you thought that the fallen chimney would be useful for such a purpose?'

'Too true.'

'But, it being so heavy, you decided to heave it up on to the parapet and then push it over on to the driveway, from where you would then collect it and give it to your husband?'

'Oh, yes.'

'But, once you'd got it up on to the parapet, you left it there.' Detective Inspector Bunyon paused. 'Why was that, Mrs Dickens?'

Eddie's mother clearly had to think before replying. 'Oh, I remember!' she said. 'It was about a week before it fell on poor Laudanum. I'd just got the chimney on to the parapet when I spied the postman coming up the drive. I have a cousin in Australia who'd written to say that she was sending me a parcel of books. It was obvious that this was what the man was carrying, so I hurried down to meet him. In the excitement of opening the parcel and sharing the books out amongst the family, I completely forgot about the chimney.'

The detective inspector was finding it hard to imagine that anyone in Australia printed books. He was under the impression that they were all convicts sent over from England, or people sent over from England to keep an eye on the convicts.

'So there the chimney rested, until *you*, Master Grout, pushed it on to poor Mrs Dickens's husband!'

'It was an accident, sir,' said Fabian, quietly this time.

'I think you'd better tell your story,' said Bunyon. So he did.

Life as a gypsy wasn't all brightly painted caravans, weaving baskets and wearing bright red spotty neckerchiefs. Sometimes things could get tough, wet and cold. And many people, particularly landowners, weren't always big fans of gypsies turning up on their land.

At first, Fabian's mother Hester had loved the life on the open road. Nanny Nanny Noonan had always been kind and considerate, but had brought her up to be a 'lady', and Hester Dickens was filled with a real sense of freedom and relief when she ran away with Alfie Grout (who'd come knocking at their door to sharpen scissors).

When their son, Fabian, was born, things got better and better, because the little boy loved the gypsy life and soon became a firm favourite amongst the other gypsies, who loved the way that he got up to such mischief, yet talked 'so posh-like'.

Things had got harder for Hester when her husband, Alfie, developed a permanent hacking cough. Medicine was far more primitive in Victorian times and, if you were poor, was pretty much nonexistent except for do-it-yourself herbal remedies.

This particular group of gypsies, led by Fudd, didn't include a wise old woman steeped in the old folklore of plants and their magical properties. The best anyone could suggest was that Alfie regularly eat lucky heather. This hadn't helped his year-round cough, or his indigestion, come to that, but at least it kept his breath smelling nice.

Then along came baby Oliphant. After all these years on the open road, sleeping under the stars, Hester decided that perhaps there was more to life than this, and that Oliphant, at least, should have the opportunity to lead the life that the older generation of the Dickens family had denied her.

When Hester's gypsy band found themselves in the vicinity of the Dickens family seat – no jokes, please, I mean Awful End – Hester made the decision that Oliphant should be left in the care of her uppercrust family.

She'd wrapped Oliphant in the finest blanket she could find and had written a note, enclosing one of her late father George Dickens's silk hankies, which had the Dickens family crest embroidered in one corner: a man biting his own leg. This should be proof enough that the child was one of their own.

Hester didn't tell any of the other gypsies her plan. Certainly not Chief Fudd, who would probably have forbidden it, and certainly not her husband who, despite getting more and more ill, would have insisted that they bring up their son. The only two people she told were Oliphant himself (who didn't understand a word of it, being a baby and all) and Fabian, whom she charged with taking Oliphant to Awful End.

'My instructions were to leave Ollie, with the note and hanky, where one of you would find him,' Fabian explained, 'then to stay close and watch for a few days, to make sure you treated him fairly.'

'And instead you overheard talk of beatings and saw a strange woman brandishing a stuffed ferret,' spat Fandango Jones, forgetting himself for a moment.

Even Madder Aunt Maud, who'd given the detective inspector his milk-free, sugar-free water, was now holding Malcolm again, so was able to hit the fairly well-known engineer over the head with him. (Though not hard enough to dislodge the piece of devilled kidney from his hat's brim.) 'Stoat!' she corrected him.

'But what happened to the note and your grandfather's handkerchief with the Dickens crest on it?' asked Eddie. 'It wasn't in the basket when I fished it out of the water.'

'It wasn't?' asked Fabian, in surprise.

'Do you think they'd have let a monk take him away if they'd known who he was?' asked Eddie, secretly not at all sure that, with this family, the answer would have been 'no'!

'And didn't you think it strange that we were calling the boy Ned, if we'd read your mother's communication which, no doubt, informed us that his name was Oliphant?' added Eddie's father, who'd been wheeled into the kitchen by Gibbering Jane just as Fabian had been about to explain matters.

'I . . . I didn't think,' said a crestfallen Fabian. 'So you never saw the note?'

'No,' said Eddie. 'It must have fallen from the basket into the lake before we found it.'

'But why did you put your baby brother in

the bulrushes in the first place?' asked Detective Inspector Bunyon. Being the only policeman present, he thought that it should be *he* who was asking all the questions. 'Why not leave him at the front door?'

'I didn't want to be spotted,' said Fabian. 'I wanted to leave Oliphant, then slip away to a safe distance and observe. But I didn't want it to take too long for him to be discovered, either. When I saw Eddie and her,' he nodded at EMAM, 'knocking turnips about on the lower lawn, I seized the opportunity and put Ollie within crying distance.'

'The roof,' said the detective inspector. 'How did you come to be on the roof?'

Fabian looked down at his handcuffed hands, resting in his lap. 'I soon discovered that most of the rooms in this vast place are empty and how few of you live here, so it was easy to slip in through the back door and hide myself, listening out and keeping an eye on Ollie the best I could.' He looked at Gibbering Jane. 'He obviously likes you very much,' he said. 'He doesn't coo like that for anyone but me and Mother back at camp.'

Gibbering Jane gibbered with pure pride and pleasure, like an over-excited monkey.

'It was harder to keep watch when everyone was out at the front, so looking down from the roof seemed the obvious solution. The last time I was up there, I was just about to lean over the parapet when an old man dressed as a soldier appeared and gave me a terrible shock, and I accidentally pushed over this piece of stone I was leaning on.'

'Which was the chimney my mother'd left there . . . and it landed on you, Father!' said Eddie.

'I don't believe a word of it!' cried Even Madder Aunt Maud, brandishing Malcolm in the air. 'Feed him to the lions, I say!'

'No, wait,' said a familiar voice, and everyone turned to see Mr and Mrs Dickens's good friend Emily Thackery, the animal lover. Unnoticed, she'd walked into the kitchen through the back door a while since, and had been listening to the Eddie lookalike in rapt silence. 'Look at this,' she said.

Mrs Thackery spread a piece of material on the kitchen table. It was damp and looked sort of chewed, but there's no denying what it was: a handkerchief bearing the Dickens crest.

'Where did you get that?' demanded the detective inspector.

'Out of that duck with a terrible tummy ache which I took with me after my last visit,' Mrs Thackery explained. 'She's made a full recovery.'

Detective Inspector Humphrey Bunyon turned to Mr Dickens, strapped to his tea trolley. 'The decision is yours, sir,' he said. 'Do you believe the boy's story? Or do you wish me to take the matter further? Looking at him, there's not a shadow of a doubt in my mind that the lad has Dickens blood in him, and I'm inclined to believe his version of events.'

Mr Dickens smiled. 'What's a few bumps and bruises when we've just discovered a whole new branch of the family we never even knew existed? *Of course* I believe him, Inspector. I consider this case closed.'

Detective Inspector Humphrey Bunyon fished a small key out of his pocket and unlocked the handcuffs, freeing Fabian's wrists. The policeman couldn't have been more delighted. He could now escape Awful End and go home and have a very large celebratory meal. 'Then my work here is at an end,' he said. 'Let me bid you all good day.' Mad Uncle Jack walked into the kitchen as the policeman walked out. 'Good day to you too, sir,' said Bunyon.

'Balderdash!' said MUJ.

★

So, as with all Eddie Dickens books before it, we come to the stage where I draw the adventure to a close and give an indication as to what happened next to those who took part.

Work soon began again on Fandango Jones's iron bridge but, halfway through the project, Mad Uncle Jack changed his mind and had him pull it down and re-use the material to build a giant something-or-other instead. I've seen pictures of the structure, and I still don't know what it was supposed to be. All I *do* know is that, during the Second World War, it was dismantled and the materials were re-used as a part of the war effort, as a result of a nationwide campaign on the home front headed by someone called Lord Beaverbrook.

There is no mention of Jones's design or work on the bridge in *Bridging the Gap: Being the Life of that Fairly Well-Known Engineer Fandango Jones.*

Detective Inspector Bunyon did manage to regain a great deal of the weight that he lost following his incarceration in a trunk at the hands of the deadly Smiley Gang (all of whom he subsequently managed to arrest, with the exception of its ringleader, Smiley Johnson). He never managed to get quite as fat as he was before. By way of compensation, though, he was promoted to Detective *Chief* Inspector not long after the events in this Further Adventure.

His desk sergeant managed to lock himself in his own handcuffs on three further occasions.

And Fabian and Baby Ollie? Why, they both came to live at Awful End, along with their parents Hester and Alfie, which is how they all come to feature in the third and final of Eddie's Further Adventures, so I won't say any more about them here.

As for the Thackerys, young David did go into the church. Many churches, in fact. And cathedrals. And rich people's houses, usually when the occupants were out or their backs were turned. As he grew older, he became more and more disenchanted with his family being so *nice* to animals and less and less keen on the idea of being a man of the cloth . . . so he became a burglar instead, specialising in stealing candle-sticks, crosses and other 'ecclesiastical furniture'. He was finally caught and, sadly, lost an eye in a prison fight before he came to trial. Apparently it was an argument over whether the correct term is 'a cake of soap' or 'a bar of soap', which was a pity, because the two are entirely different things.

Which just leaves the monks of Lamberley Monastery.

One morning, less than six weeks after the events ending on page 284 occurred, Abbot Po awoke from a dream at about three o'clock in the morning.

Dashing to the bell tower, he tolled its only bell, causing his bemused and bleary-eyed brethren to rise from their beds and assemble in the Chapter House. Once they were all present, he told them that he'd dreamt of a huge plug being pulled out of the ground and of a dreadful gurgling noise.

'I cannot tell whether it was simply something

I ate or whether it was a vision,' Po said in that beautiful voice of his, 'but I cannot take the chance. I must ask you all to evacuate immediately.'

This they did and, as numerous eyewitnesses will testify, no sooner had the last man left the building – which was Po himself, of course – than there was an appalling gulping *SLERCHING* noise, and Lamberley Monastery disappeared into the ground like a sinking ship beneath the waves.

Being monks of the Bertian order, they all saw the funny side of it and were remarkably jolly about being homeless. Not that they were for long.

Where could they find a large building with enough empty rooms to offer them temporary accommodation, and at such short notice?

It was Eddie who answered the knock on the front door of Awful End later that morning. Standing on the doorstep was the ugliest man he'd ever had the privilege to know.

'Good morning Eddie,' said Po. 'Remember how we put you up for a while?'

Eddie nodded.

'I wonder if you could return the favour?'

Eddie nodded. There were monks as far as the eye could see.

THE END
until the final Further Adventure

AUTHOR'S NOTE

This is not a history book, so please don't go
stating any of the information contained within
it as 'fact' without checking it first. I've always
found *Old Roxbee's* books an excellent source of
information but, then again, that could be another
of my lies.

Final
Curtain

Book Three of the Further Adventures of
Eddie Dickens Trilogy

In memory of
Stephen Cartwright.
It was fun.

A Message from the Author

Who's invested in a big box of hankies

Well, this is the end of the road as far as Eddie's Further Adventures are concerned. First, there was the original trilogy which began with *Awful End*, and then this one, which started off with Eddie Dickens in the heathery highlands of Scotland in *Dubious Deeds*. Blimey. Six books. Who would have believed it, especially when Eddie started out life as a character in a series of letters to my nephew Ben? Will there be yet more adventures one day? Come closer and I'll tell you . . . Closer . . . You'd better believe it! Until then, it's curtain up for *Final Curtain*. Quiet at the back there, please.

PHILIP ARDAGH
Ireland, 2006

Contents

Prologue

HARRY: That's the 'ouse.

THUNK: You sure?

HARRY: 'Course I'm sure!

THUNK: How comes you're so sure you're sure?

HARRY: How many other 'ouses d'you reckon have 'ollow cows in their flowerbeds?

THUNK: I was only askin', 'arry . . . Do we do the job tonight?

HARRY: 'Course we don't do the job tonight. Have you been listenin' to a word I've been tellin' you? We waits until the time is right.

THUNK: And 'ow do we know when that is?

HARRY: When our man on the inside says it is.

THUNK: You mean –?

HARRY: Correct. We're about to rob them Dickenses blind with a little 'elp from a viper in their own nest.

THUNK: Ha! Does that mean we can get out of this ditch now, 'arry?

HARRY: It most certainly does, Thunk. Let's be on our way.

Is This a Dagger?

In which Eddie plays himself, and
Even Madder Aunt Maud acts true to form

As the dagger was thrust towards Eddie Dickens a second time, he managed to throw himself clear, crashing down against a pile of barrels that rolled haphazardly across the bare-planked floor.

'There's no escape, my boy!' bellowed the knife-wielding masked man, looming above him, weapon poised and ready to strike.

'Stop that at once!' cried a voice, grating enough to peel the zest off a lemon at one-hundred-and-two paces, and the next thing the masked man knew was that he was being battered about the head with a stuffed stoat.

The actor-manager Mr Pumblesnook (for it was he in the costume of 'villain') had always tried to impress upon those under his tuition that, when performing, it was of the utmost – the *utmost* – importance to stay in character, no matter what.

Over the past few weeks at Awful End, however, he had learned to take this golden rule, hide it in a piece of sacking, slip it into a bottom drawer and forget ALL about it, when dealing with two particular people. Said people were Mad Mr Jack Dickens (*aka* Mad Uncle Jack, MUJ, or Mad Major Dickens) and his lovely wife, Even Madder Aunt Maud.

It was the latter who was beating the poor man about the head at that moment. 'My good lady,' said Mr Pumblesnook (as himself and not the villain). 'Might I remind you for the umpteenth time that I am not actually attacking your great-nephew. He and I are undertaking a dramatic endeavour. We are rehearsing a play –' He used his forearms and elbows to fend off the blows as best he could. '– as we were when you attacked me three times yesterday, twice the day before and on heaven-knows-how-many occasions on heaven-knows-how-many days prior to that.'

'So *you* say,' snapped Even Madder Aunt Maud. 'But how can I be sure that you're not really attacking him *this time*?'

'I'm fine, Aunt Maud,' said Eddie, who'd already got to his feet. 'We're only pretending.'

'PRETENDING?' boomed Mr Pumblesnook, his voice loud enough to deafen a passing earwig. (I have a sworn affidavit from the earwig to that effect, which is a kind of legal statement not commonly used in the insect world.) 'We are not pretending, Master Edmund. We are ACTING.'

Even Madder Aunt Maud thrust Malcolm's nose right up against Mr Pumblesnook's. Stuffed stoat and actor-manager eyed each other suspiciously. 'Don't shout at the boy,' she said.

Pumblesnook produced a flamboyant kerchief from the breast pocket of his purple jacket and mopped perspiration from his brow. (This sentence is now also available in English: He pulled out a hanky and wiped the sweat off his forehead.) 'Forgive me, dear lady, but my two most oft-repeated reminders of these past few weeks are that I am NOT actually intending to harm the boy and, young Edmund, we are acting – thinking ourselves into living a part and being a character – and are not *pretending*.' He said this last word as though it were an unpleasant gas given off by an embarrassing-looking fungus.

'Sorry,' said Eddie.

'Particularly when, in this instance, the character you are playing is yourself.'

'A point well made, Mr Pumblesnook,' said Eddie for, in the play they were currently rehearsing, Eddie Dickens was indeed playing Eddie Dickens, the play being a dramatisation of certain episodes from his life. The dramatisation wasn't simply the telling of true events from Eddie's recent past; the playwright had decided that he should change the odd fact here and there to make it even more dramatic.

The playwright in question was none other than Eddie's own father, Mr Dickens, who had announced that 'writing can't be that difficult if that oaf Ardagh can do it.' The statement had been greeted with a few polite 'mmms', one 'surely' and an 'absolutely' because no one had any idea who this Ardagh fellow he was referring to actually was. It was once he was under way, with several piles of scrumpled paper, sleepless nights and ink-stained fingers later, that Mr Dickens had realised – as many had before him and have since – that one should *never* let the facts get in the way of a good story.

The scene Mr Pumblesnook and Eddie had been rehearsing when they'd been so rudely interrupted by EMAM (again) was one of a number set on board *The Pompous Pig* bound for America, where Eddie came face to face with the escaped convict, Swags (the true version of which is beautifully laid out in my book *Terrible Times*). Mr Pumblesnook was playing the role of Swags.

Those of you familiar with Eddie's earlier adventures may recall that Swags was a very thin man and Mr Pumblesnook a very large one. The reason for such miscasting was simple: as director and producer of the show, Mr Pumblesnook insisted on taking all the best parts for himself. At the initial casting, he had even tried to give himself the title role of Eddie but even he had to eventually admit that Eddie had been born to play the part.

Most of the other roles were played by Mr Pumblesnook's band of players, made up of the original core of actors Eddie had first encountered at the rather unoriginally named *The Coaching Inn* coaching inn plus those escaped orphans from St Horrid's Home for Grateful Orphans who'd chosen to stay with him after their escape.

In fact, the escape was the climax at the end of the first act. The real Marjorie, the hollow cow-shaped carnival float in which they'd escaped, was now Even Madder Aunt Maud's home in the rose garden of Awful End. In the play, it was portrayed by a much smaller two-dimensional painted wooden cow on wheels.

Like most of the working props, these were constructed by one of the wandering theatricals, Mr Blessing. And, like most of the wandering theatricals, he had rather an annoying nickname: Bless Him. I'm sorry, but there it is.

For this play, Bless Him was ably assisted by Eddie's cousin, Fabian. Fabian would have made a fantastic understudy for Eddie because they looked so like each other that, when they weren't mistaken for each other they were mistaken for virtually identical twins. (Their eyes were somewhat different. More on this later.) When asked, however, Fabian had refused, point blank, to act. The conversation went something like this:

'You are aware that I am writing a play?'

'Yes, Uncle Laudanum.'

'Being an account of some of the more exciting moments in my son Edmund's disproportionately action-packed life –'

'Yes, Uncle.'

'– without the distractions and asides of –'

'Yes, Uncle.'

'Well, Fabian, I was wondering whether you would consider being an understudy?'

'A basement?'

'I think you are confusing an understudy with an undercroft.'

'I'm sorry, Uncle.'

'An understudy is someone who learns another person's part so, if that person is taken ill, he can take on the role in his place.'

'His part?'

'His character. His acting role in the play.'

'But I could never do that . . .'

'You would rather have a role all to yourself?'

'No, it's not that. It's just that I couldn't act in front of people.'

'These are not people, Fabian. They are family, and a few close friends. Not *people*. The stage will be built here at Awful End and the play performed in the grounds.'

'Then perhaps I could help with that, Uncle? With building the stage –?'

'And props! What an excellent idea.'

And so it was. As director and producer and manager and player of all the best parts other than Eddie's, Mr Pumblesnook was clearly in charge but he fully understood patronage. As well as his handsome fee, he was being housed and fed at Awful End, along with his acting troupe, and Mr Dickens had written the script himself. So Mr Dickens got listened to. Mr Dickens got respect. And his weird family, who were also his hosts, were reluctantly tolerated.

The member of the household – for want of a better description – with whom the actor-manager was on worst terms was Malcolm (or was it Sally?). Once, when disguised as a highwayman, Mr Pumblesnook had the misfortune of being hit across the knees with Malcolm – something *not* dramatised in the play – and he had never forgiven the stuffed stoat. This was, of course, totally unreasonable as Malcolm had no say in the matter and, in the improbable – nay impossible – situation where he might have had an opinion, he would, I've no doubt, have felt sorely wronged. It was

Even Madder Aunt Maud the man should have been angry with: it being she who'd used Malcolm as a weapon on him.

Mr Pumblesnook was holding Malcolm's nose in his grip right now, EMAM still clutching his tail end, or should that be 'the end of his tail'?

'Madam,' he said firmly, in a voice he'd used to such great effect when playing the Archbishop in *Steeple Chase*, 'if you would be so kind as to put that stoat away and go about your normal business, young Eddie and I shall do likewise.'

'But you don't have stoats to put away!' she snorted.

'The normal business, ma'am!' Mr Pumblesnook sighed. 'We shall likewise go about our normal business!'

343

Even Madder Aunt Maud went up on tiptoe and glared straight into the actor-manager's eyes. 'There's nothing normal about you, sir!' she declared, then turned and stomped off, waving Malcolm before her, like a commander leading his troops into battle, sword raised.

Mr Pumblesnook watched her go. 'Your great-aunt certainly knows how to make a grand exit, Eddie,' he said, almost grudgingly. There had been a time when he'd greatly admired her, but living in prolonged proximity to her had soon cured him of that. 'Now where were we?'

'You were about to take another stab at me with that dagger,' Eddie reminded him.

'Not I!' declared Pumblesnook, his voice rising. 'That villain Swags!' and, with that, he was back in character and chasing Eddie between the scattered barrels.

Goodbyes, Hellos & Tallyhos!

*In which we say goodbye to a bunch of monks
and get to know a bunch of relatives better*

Eddie had been sorry to see the monks go
when they finally left Awful End. He felt good
at having been able to return the favour and put
them up when they were monastery-less, and now
the place seemed very empty without them. Awful
End was a vast house (and, following the success
of these books, I've heard rumours that the current
generation of the Dickens family are considering
opening it to the public during the summer
months, and then that way you'll be able to see for
yourselves), so it could easily accommodate a few
hundred monks. He would miss their company,
their conversations, their chanting and singing.

With them gone, it was back to 'normal' – as if that term could be applied to Awful End – but with a few noticeable differences. Now there were also Eddie's newly discovered Aunt Hester (whom everyone called Hetty), a newly discovered uncle, called Alfie (who had a permanent hacking cough), and Eddie's newly discovered cousins, Fabian and baby Oliphant, living with them.

As I touched upon in Episode One, Eddie and Fabian looked very similar indeed. In truth, *so* similar that when David Roberts came to illustrate this book he could have cheated and simply drawn Eddie twice – which, my American friends, is how we say 'two times' on this side of the Atlantic – then pointed at one at random and said, 'That one there is Fabian!' (Even professional illustrators employ tricks like that sometimes, you know.)

Despite their eyes being different colours, that wasn't the way most people told them apart (because, generally, people couldn't remember who had the brown ones and who had the greeny-blue ones). It was the fact that Eddie's looked more saucery that was the trick.

The reason why Eddie had such saucer-like eyes is a pretty safe bet. Few people, Fabian included, had experienced as many eye-opening events in his life as Eddie had. Everywhere Eddie turned, he seemed to find himself in extraordinary situation after extraordinary situation (rather like those characters in TV murder mysteries who, wherever they go, always seem to stumble upon a dead body, week after week after week). It probably didn't help living with such an extraordinary family. And, oh yes, whilst I remember, Fabian wore a gold hoop earring in one ear.

Baby Oliphant looked pretty much like any other baby boy, which meant that Aunt Hetty thought that he was the most handsome baby ever born, and the others thought of him as being generally quite nice, apart from the dribbling. He seemed to love Fabian and Eddie in equal measure and cooed when they were around. Apart from his mother, though, Oliphant's favourite person in the whole wide world seemed to be ex-chambermaid (and now 'maid of all works') Gibbering Jane, which made her gibber with pleasure on pleasure-gibbering levels one would never have imagined possible. This is why I've drawn this graph:

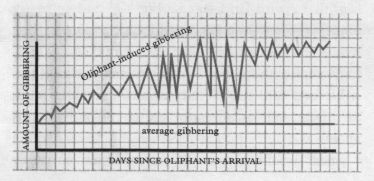

At every available opportunity, she would proudly wheel little Ollie around the grounds in a home-made pram (even though he was now a pretty fast crawler in his own right). As well as being able to say 'Mamma', 'Dadda' and 'narna' the last of which – I think – meant food, he could also do some impressive gibbering noises of his own, which Jane took as a real compliment.

And another noticeable difference at Awful End? Why, the arrival of Mr Pumblesnook's wandering theatricals, of course. Mad Uncle Jack hadn't initially liked the idea of the actors and actresses – female actors weren't called plain actors back then – staying in the house itself. In those days, in the great scheme of things, actors (and actresses) were seen to be below woodlice and earwigs in the hierarchy of living things . . . which might explain why he suggested that they each be issued with a large piece of tree bark to sleep under in the gardens. Mr Dickens had managed to persuade him that Awful End was so big and had so many empty rooms that he would hardly know they were there. When he pointed out that the monks had caused them very little inconvenience, and MUJ had replied, 'What monks?' he knew that he'd won. Mr Pumblesnook's troupe arrived and all was well.

Eddie was very pleased to see again so many

of the orphans he'd helped to escape, and to see how much better fed and happier they looked nowadays. And they were pleased to see him. Eddie Dickens would always be held in special regard by the former occupants of St Horrid's Home for Grateful Orphans.

Surprisingly, it was EMAM who seemed to miss the monks most of all, and this was expressed by the fact that she often mentioned how little she missed them. Or thought about them. Hardly ever.

'I won't miss the one with a face like a gargoyle,' said Even Madder Aunt Maud one sunny afternoon.

'Abbot Po was a very nice man,' said Eddie in his defence.

'Never said he wasn't, but he was ugly enough to stop all the clocks, and Ethel wouldn't lay,' snapped his great-aunt.

'Ethel?' asked Fabian.

It took Eddie a moment to remember about whom EMAM was talking. 'She means her favourite chicken . . . only it's no wonder she didn't lay any eggs while Abbot Po was here. She was dead and buried years ago.' (In fact, Ethel the chicken was buried long before a single Bertian monk set foot in Awful End.)

'That doesn't make my statement any less true!" snorted Even Madder Aunt Maud, bringing an axe crashing down over her head. Not on Eddie or Fabian, I hasten to add. I suppose I should have explained that they were in the woodshed, shouldn't I?

Though called a shed, it was more of a lean-to with the outer wall missing: a covered area where the logs for the fires were cut and stacked.

It used to be the ex-soldiers' job to cut the wood, but they were getting a bit past it now and had had rather too many accidents and near misses over more recent years. Dawkins had a bad back, so wood-chopping couldn't be included in his endless list of duties. The younger monks had loved chopping wood but now, of course, they'd gone.

Even Madder Aunt Maud had announced that it would now be one of her responsibilities. No sooner had the words passed her lips than an involuntary shudder had passed through Eddie's entire body. The thought of his great-aunt wielding a large axe seemed about as safe and sensible as appointing a piranha fish to be a lifeguard or asking a cat-burglar to clean your gutters. That's why Eddie and Fabian were out in the woodshed-that-wasn't-really-a-shed with her, at a safe distance. They wanted to make sure that she didn't do herself a serious injury.

Both boys were impressed how strong their great-aunt was. She wasn't a very tall lady but she was fit and healthy (which was probably why she would go on to live to the ripe old age that she did).

It was as Even Madder Aunt Maud was just about to narrowly miss chopping off the toes of her right foot by the narrowest of narrow margins for the third time that a bugle sounded.

Those of you with an army background might think of the sounding of a bugle as a call to get up in the morning, or to go to the cookhouse, or to fight, or to remember the dead – a bugle has a surprising number of uses in army life doesn't it? – and, if you're a lover of boogie (as in music), the sound of the bugle may remind you of the *Boogie-Woogie Bugle Boy of Company B*, a song made famous by the singing group The Andrews Sisters, not to be confused with the Andrews sisters (small 's') who lived in Lamberley Hall (not too far from Awful End) and owned one of the finest collections of reject china in the British Empire at the time, which included three-handled two-handled mugs (if you see what I mean), some of the finest sets of chipped or incomplete dinner and tea services, and soup bowls so warped that they couldn't hold soup.

The sisters, Kitty and Amelia Andrews, had inherited the Hall from their father, the Honourable Douglas 'Duff' Andrews, (who was 'new money', having made his fortune from coconuts), and neither had ever married.

They had little to do with the outside world and spent so much of the time just speaking to each other that they'd fallen into the habit of knowing exactly what the other was going to say, so rarely needed to speak complete sentences. A typical Andrews sisters' (with a small 's') conversation might go along the lines of:

'Do you know where –?'

'Under the –'

'How on earth –?'

'I hid them from –'

'Wise move!' which, once translated, would read:

KITTY: Do you know where I put the scissors?
AMELIA: Under the sofa.
KITTY: How on earth did they get there?
AMELIA: I hid them from Cleptomania Claire.
KITTY: Wise move!
JULIE: *The hills are alive with the sound of –*

I'm *so* sorry. I've no idea how Julie Andrews ended up in the mix. That's certainly one Andrews too many . . . and do please remind me: how did I get on to the Andrews sisters (with a small 's') in the first place?

Let me work backwards: Andrews sisters (with a small 's') > Andrews Sisters (with a big 'S') > *The Boogie-Woogie Bugle Boy from Company B* > bugles > Even Madder Aunt Maud, Fabian and Eddie in the woodshed, hearing a bugle sounding. Aha! Here we are:

Though the sound of a bugle may mean different things to different people, a bugle sounding here at Awful End meant one thing: the local fox hunt.

Mad Uncle Jack had banned fox hunting on his land, though it had little to do with the fox. A man who paid for everything with dried (dead) fish probably wasn't overly concerned with the foxes' wellbeing. The reason why Mad Uncle Jack (or Mad Mr Jack Dickens or Mad Major Jack Dickens, as he was known locally) had banned it was because he was in dispute with the Master of the Hounds (who was the chap in charge of the local hunt).

This chap was another retired major but, unlike MUJ, who'd reverted to plain 'Mr' now that his fighting days were over, Stinky Hoarebacker still used his military title. Of course, he wasn't christened 'Stinky'. His first name was actually Cheshire, which is also the name of a type of cheese and, if you share your name with a type of cheese and you go to an English public school – which, dear American readers, is what we English call our *private* schools for some unknown reason – there is a 98.6% chance that you're going to end up being called 'Stinky' for the rest of your natural born days.

He and Mad Uncle Jack had fallen out over a bet. A few years prior to the events I'm now relating – sometime between those outlined in *Terrible Times* and *Dubious Deeds*, I think – Mad Uncle Jack and Stinky Hoarebacker had been discussing hats. Mad Uncle Jack had insisted that the deerstalker was the finest hat of its generation. Stinky had insisted that it was the mullion.

'What *are* you talking about?' MUJ had demanded, tightening the strap under his saddle. I'm sure such straps have special names and, being the horsey type, my editor might even point it out to me and suggest we add it here. In other words, if you read this paragraph *without* the technical name for such a piece of tackle added, then it's probably because she's not doing her job properly. 'The mullion is a cap, not a hat!'

'It is most certainly not,' Stinky had insisted.

At this moment, Mad Uncle Jack snorted. 'The

finest of hats is the deerstalker, the mullion is a cap and not a hat, and there's an end to it,' he whinnied.

'It most certainly is a hat, sir!' replied Stinky.

'It most certainly is *not*, sir!' MUJ retorted, which isn't as painful as it sounds.

''Tis, sir!'

'*Not*, sir!'

''Tis! 'Tis! 'Tis!'

''Tisn't! 'Tisn't! 'Tisn't!'

'A wager?' which is a bet, suggested Stinky.

'A wager!' which is still a bet, agreed Mad Uncle Jack. 'What will it be?'

'A shilling!' which is an amount of money, suggested Stinky.

'Done, sir!' said MUJ. 'I'll wager you one shilling, sir, that the mullion is not, was not, and never shall be a hat. It's a *cap*.'

The two retired majors shook hands. Mad Uncle Jack then instructed that the local hunt not be permitted in the grounds of Awful End, and the two men had not spoken to each other since . . . yet the bugle had sounded and here came the hunt. And Even Madder Aunt Maud was ready for them!

Episode 3

A Cracking Time

*In which an enemy is vanquished
and we welcome a new arrival*

'Battle stations!' cried Mad Aunt Maud, not to be confused with Battle Station which is a railway station between Crowhurst and Robertsbridge on the Hastings to London line. (It was at Battle and not Hastings that the Battle of Hastings took place, but it wasn't called Battle – the place, not the fighting – until after the event, of course.) She threw the axe to the ground, snatching her stuffed stoat off the pile of stacked logs where she'd positioned him to 'watch' what she was doing.

The huntsmen didn't stand a chance. I won't go into details as to how she got them off the Dickens estate, but I will say that some of Even Madder Aunt Maud's victims smelled of bats' urine for a good few days after that (despite regular bathing) and, of those who fell down the freshly dug pits, only three had broken bones.

As for the fox, it's far from clear as to whether they were actually chasing one. There was some talk in the local villages about Stinky Hoare-backer setting the dogs on a foreign brush salesman – both the salesman and the brushes being foreign – who, unfamiliar with British ways, had made the unforgivable error of knocking on the retired major's *front* door, rather than trying his luck at the tradesmen's entrance around the back.

Either way, the huntsmen were repelled, and the senior members of the Dickens family felt triumphant in victory. (Even the younger actors had been enlisted to help. The ex-St Horrid's orphans particularly enjoyed themselves, some even wielding cucumbers, evoking memories of the old days.) Fabian was a little overwhelmed by it all. He still found it difficult to adjust to life at Awful End. It wasn't just that, having been brought up amongst travelling gypsies, he was used to forever being on the move, but also had to do with the fact that he found his recently discovered relatives – er – a little eccentric. Oh, all right: he found them CRAZY.

I'm not sure of the derivation of the word 'crazy', and I don't have an ordinary dictionary to hand, because I'm living out of boxes at the moment. (More on this later, no doubt.) What I *do* have is *Old Roxbee's Dictionary of Architecture & Landscape Architecture* (in the revised edition of 1972, long after *Old Roxbee* had become *So-Old-He's-Long-Since-Dead Roxbee*). According to this, 'crazy paving' – the nearest thing I can get to the word 'crazy' on its own – is so called because it's made up of cracked paving stones seemingly laid without order . . . which is a pretty good description of the majority of the members of the Dickens family at the time: cracked and orderless. By comparison, Fabian's family was very normal. His mother behaved like a loving mother, glad to be recognised by her blood relatives at long last. Baby Oliphant behaved like a baby Oliphant, rather than, say, a baby elephant.* His father, Alfie, behaved like anyone with a bad cough: coughing badly, a great deal.

* For those of you've who've been waiting for an elephant joke ever since we discovered that the baby's real name was Oliphant, your wait is over.

Poor Alfie Grout had one of those coughs that sounded so rough you could imagine it sand-papering his innards every time it started, but it also had a strange rattle that suggested he was far from well. One minute he'd be having a pleasant conversation about the annual gypsy horse fair over in Garlington Wake, and the next minute he'd be bent double coughing and rattling with a pained expression on his face.

This caused different reactions from different members of the Dickens household. Fabian would politely ignore it, because his father had told him to. Oliphant would dribble and coo. (That was his job, being a baby.) Fabian's mother would put a sympathetic arm around her husband and offer words of encouragement. Eddie would offer to get him a glass of water. Gibbering Jane would gibber. Dawkins, the gentleman's gentleman, would await instructions. Mrs Dickens would urge him to try stuffing his mouth with something . . . *anything*. Mr Dickens would hurriedly hold a handkerchief up to his *own* face for fear of catching something (usually muttering 'If Ardagh gives this hacking cough to anyone else, it's bound to be me!', whatever that meant). Which leaves Mad Uncle Jack and his lovely wife Even Madder Aunt Maud. Mad Uncle Jack would usually give Alfie a hearty slap on the back with a cheery, 'That's the spirit!',

359

whilst EMAM was more likely to beat him with Malcolm with an 'Oh, do be quiet!'. Interestingly, it was these last two approaches that seemed to have the best effect on poor Alfie, short-term at least. Which only goes to show something, but I'm not exactly sure what.

Hang on? What's this? I've just noticed an old dictionary up on that shelf there, by the battered box of *Scrabble* and something called *Kerplunk*. This isn't my house so I had no way of knowing that there'd be one so readily to hand. Excuse me a moment. I can look up 'crazy' after all. *Craggy* . . . *cram* . . . *crambo* . . . *CRAMBO?* . . . apparently that's a game in which a player says a word for which the others must find a rhyme . . . *craw* . . . *crayfish* . . . *crazy*. Here we are! 'Unbalanced . . . absurdly out of place . . .' And, chiefly in North America – as opposed to a North American chief – *crazies* with an 'i' are crazy people. Not to be confused with *crazes*, without the 'i', which refers to widespread but short-lived enthusiasms for collecting brightly coloured plastic things, or wearing weird clothes which look very silly and outdated in next to no time.

So, there you are. How did I get onto this? I'm not sure, so let's pause for a picture of me in my current surroundings, then return to the main action.

Lovely. (Do you think my new glasses suit me?)

★

The family were gathered in the library. Eddie loved this room. There were books here, there and everywhere, and in places where there weren't books, there were things made to *look* like books. For example, when the doors were closed it was difficult to see them at first glance because they too were built to look like shelves of books. In Eddie's day, books in a such a fine library were leather-bound with the title (and sometimes author) embossed on the brown leather spines with gold lettering. Even the fake wooden book spines on the doors were embossed in this way to create the illusion of uninterrupted shelving all the way around the walls. The only spaces

361

were for the windows but, when it was dark out, wooden shutters could be folded across them and on these were painted yet more book spines.

Though there has been a library, of sorts, for as long as Awful End has stood on that spot, it was Eddie's great-grandfather – in other words, Mr Dickens's grandfather and Mad Uncle Jack's father – Dr Malcontent Dickens who had turned the library into this splendid room. Malcontent Dickens (whose full name was Malcontent Arthur Rigmarole Dickens) was a great lover of knowledge, or 'nolidge' as he called it, spelling not being his greatest forte, and believed (rightly) that much knowledge could be gleaned from books.

The Dickens family had expected great things of Malcontent and he had achieved great things but, sadly, not longevity. He was untimely killed by a human cannonball. It was an accident, and need not distract us here. Eddie's grandfather, Percy Dickens, had inherited the love of books from his father, but not Awful End, which eventually ended up in Mad Uncle Jack's hands. Jack had little time for books but, fortunately, didn't decide to flood the library to make a fish tank (which the eldest brother, George, had considered doing), or to use the books to build his treehouse.

So here they all were, in the library, on the evening that Stinky Hoarebacker's fox hunt had been repelled from the estate in shambolic retreat.

'Congratulations are in order!' said Mad Uncle Jack, raising a glass of sherry high above his head. It hit a light fitting and shattered.

'In order of what?' demanded Even Madder Aunt Maud. She was still wearing a camouflage hat made of laurel leaves which she'd used to sneak up close on her targets. Her original plan had been to bite the horses' legs so that they'd rear up and throw their riders. Then, she'd reasoned that it wasn't the horses' fault – they were just doing what they were supposed to do – so she'd bitten the riders instead. 'In order of age? Size?'

'In whatever order you like, my fountain of love!' said Mad Uncle Jack, in a voice he reserved for speaking to his beloved wife. He was dusting the tiny sticky shards of broken sherry schooner (glass) from what little hair he had. 'You choose!' said Even Madder Aunt Maud.

'Then I choose congratulations in any old order!' announced MUJ.

The others raised their glasses and drank, but not until they'd lowered them and put them to their lips. You try drinking with a glass raised above your head. It's not easy.

Their celebration was interrupted by a sudden outbreak of gibbering which, as the brighter sparks amongst you will have guessed, was caused by

Gibbering Jane. She ran into the library, the singed piece of knitted tea-cosy she always wore on a string around her neck, trailing out behind her, like a scarf on a windy day. She was clutching an enormous egg with both hands. It appeared to be cracking.

'It's hatching!' she yelped, before resuming her more usual senseless gibbering. The room was galvanised, which is a strange phrase when you come to think about it. A galvanised bucket is a bucket coated in a protective layer of zinc using electricity (named after the Italian psychologist Luigi Galvani, who's probably better known for using electricity to make dead frogs' legs twitch . . . perhaps having nothing better to do.) A galvanised room is – in this case, at least – when the people in the room were excited – yippee! – into action.

Everyone put their drinks down, except for Even Madder Aunt Maud who simply let hers fall to the floor, narrowly avoiding a library chair, (which could be folded out to form a ladder to reach some of the books on the shelves at mid-height). The glass bounced on a rug woven into the shape of the Baltic States by a distant cousin of Eddie's mother, spilling its contents without breaking.

Maud snatched the egg. 'Mine, I believe,' she said, which was true enough. The egg had been a gift from the Head of Aviaries at The Royal

Zoological Institute in Kemphill Park (not to be confused with the Royal Zoological Gardens in Regent's Park, which later became better known as Regent's Park Zoo and then, even more recently, as plain old London Zoo.)

The Head of Aviaries at The Royal Zoological Institute, a certain Dr Marcus Loach, wasn't in the habit of giving away eggs to almost total strangers, but it was by way of an apology for what had happened to EMAM during a recent visit to the zoo.

Dr Loach had been under the impression that Even Madder Aunt Maud was a member of a group of visiting foreign dignitaries with a particular interest in zoology, who had suffered an unfortunate accident whilst under his care. Little did he realise that the woman clutching the stuffed stoat was simply tagging along. (The foreign dignitaries assumed that she was a member of staff – possibly in charge of small mammals, by the looks of the rather strange creature she was holding.) She had, in truth, forced her way through a hole in the hedge to the wilderbeast enclosure whilst on what we today might call 'a fungus foray' (in other words, looking for mushrooms).

As for the accident, she hadn't fallen into the crocodile enclosure (as Loach had assumed) but had deliberately climbed over the railings and into the water to get nearer to the single croc occupying it which, she later told her doting husband, 'gave me a warm feeling as it reminded me of one of my dear late mother's handbags'.

She was just about to introduce Malcolm to said crocodile, which was observing her movements with a seemingly indifferent gaze through a half-closed eye (whilst, in all probability, actually sizing her up as a potential pre-lunchtime snack), when she was spotted by what, today, we'd call a zoo keeper. Without a moment's thought for his own safety the man, a Mr Johnson, dived into the pea-soup coloured water and dragged a protesting Even Madder Aunt Maud to safety, receiving a mouthful of algae and several blows from a stuffed stoat for his trouble.

Dr Marcus Loach, whose job it had been to escort the dignitaries throughout the day, though birds were his area of expertise, was mortified (which may sound as if it has something to do with the lime, cement, sand and water mix used to bond bricks together, but, in the case of Dr Loach, meant embarrassed and humiliated). The whole reason he'd been entrusted with the task of showing these important folk about the place was because the Director of The Royal Zoological Institute in Kemphill Park was grooming him as his successor.

When monkeys groom each other, it usually involves carefully going through each other's hair, removing ticks and bugs and eating them. This was certainly not the way that Sir Trevor Hartley-Poole behaved towards Dr Loach. He was simply preparing the younger – though not young – man for the role. This was excellent news for Dr Loach for he knew that, on Hartley-Poole's recommendation, he would become the new director unopposed. A visiting VIP being almost eaten by a crocodile would *not* be the kind of thing to impress Sir Trevor, hence Loach's feeling of mortification.

Dr Loach had to think quickly. He sent the

heroic Mr Johnson to change out of his wet clothes and to have the afternoon off, on the strict understanding that he say nothing to anyone about the incident, hinting that his silence may well result in his promotion to Keeper of the Queen's Giraffe (which was one of the most sought-after jobs in the institute). He gave the crocodile an extra-large lunch (to make up for not having eaten EMAM). And, as for Even Madder Aunt Maud, he took the unusual step of offering her a little something for her collection. (All the dignitaries had animal collections of varying sorts. That's why Sir Trevor Hartley-Poole had instructed Dr Loach to show them around the zoo in the first place.)

'Perhaps an egg?' Dr Loach had suggested, as they entered the aviary, his stoat-carrying guest having refused the offer of dry clothes. She simply squelched after the others, seemingly unconcerned by her terrible ordeal.

'Any egg?' she asked.

'Indeed, madam,' said Dr Loach.

Even Madder Aunt Maud hurried off and, ten minutes or so later, returned – somehow looking even damper than before, if that were possible – with an egg which, despite his vast knowledge of birds, the Head of Aviaries failed to identify.

'How about this one?' she asked.

'Consider it yours,' he said.

368

And now, after Gibbering Jane had lavished all the attention on it that she'd lavished on baby Oliphant when Eddie had found him in the bulrushes and named him Ned, the egg was hatching in the library of Awful End. Out popped a crocodile.

Doctor! Doctor!

In which Annabelle snaps,
and Dawkins almost does

It soon became a common sight for Even Madder Aunt Maud to be followed around the house and gardens of Awful End by a tiny crocodile on a silver chain. She had removed the steps which led up into Marjorie (her hollow-cow home in the rose garden, as I've already mentioned) and replaced them with a ramp that Annabelle – the name she'd given the baby croc – could easily climb up and down. The work was carried out by Mad Uncle Jack's band of loyal ex-soldiers, so took up a ridiculous amount of time and wood.

At the centre of the rose garden lay a shallow rectangular pond, which was ideal for Annabelle to splash about in.

Although Even Madder Aunt Maud was even more eccentric than your average Victorian lady of the well-to-do classes, I should point out that the keeping of exotic pets was not unheard of. There was a chap called the Marquis of Queensberry who came up with the rules for boxing (which must be why they're called the Marquis of Queensberry Rules), and he had a sister whose married name was Lady Florence Dixie. Lady Florence had a pet puma, which she used to take for walks in Windsor Great Park. So perhaps EMAM's crocodile on a chain wasn't quite so utterly ridiculous as you at first imagined, hmmm, clever-clogs?!

Eddie and Fabian were fascinated by their great-aunt's new pet and offered to take her for walks between the endless play rehearsals. EMAM was reluctant to let anyone else but Gibbering Jane (who'd kept the egg warm, remember) look after her new special friend.

For a failed chambermaid who'd spent her life under the stairs at Eddie's previous home, before it was burnt to the ground, Jane was now very much in demand. Oliphant really loved her, and EMAM was regularly entrusting Annabelle to her care. Eddie had never seen her so happy.

Even Madder Aunt Maud took to having a crocodile around in her stride. Though obviously still fond of him, it did seem that living, breathing Annabelle had rather taken over from tatty, stuffed Malcolm as her Number One companion. Shocking, I know, but true.

Mad Uncle Jack hardly seemed to register that his wife now had a croc in tow. He slept in his treehouse at night, and she slept in her hollow cow, with Annabelle at the foot of her bed, so that wasn't a problem.

Eddie's father, Mr Dickens, seemed a little concerned about there being a little crocodile about the place, pointing out that it would soon grow to be a *big* crocodile about the place, and possibly less friendly. But his complaints were half-hearted. His mind was on his *magnum opus* which, in this instance, meant his play.

The person who was the least happy about there now being a many-toothed reptile in their lives was the member of the household who got bitten the most often, and that was Dawkins.

The first time the animal had bitten him was when Even Madder Aunt Maud had instructed him to pick Annabelle up and place her in the sink. This Dawkins had done without protest, and had received a little nip for his trouble. Thereafter, Annabelle would bite him at every available

372

opportunity, which was why the gentleman's gentleman would often try to hide if he saw Even Madder Aunt Maud and Annabelle heading his way.

Once, Mr Pumblesnook's wife (the truly dreadful Mrs Pumblesnook) came upon Dawkins cowering in a very large silver-plated soup tureen. He claimed that he was cleaning it, but he could see that the actor-manager's wife was far from convinced.

Another time, he hid from Annabelle the baby croc in a large wicker basket in the laundry room. Unfortunately, his bad back seized up and it was two days before he was discovered by Bless Him, who'd been looking for some old shirts and longjohns to turn into sails for the stage representation of *The Pompous Pig*.

Like a goat, Annabelle seemed to eat anything and everything. Fabian took great delight in tossing her a whole lettuce or a cabbage and watching her snap it up. Once, he kicked a cabbage to her like a ball. The cabbage veered off in completely the wrong direction, but his shoe came flying off his foot and landed in the pond next to her, with a satisfying splash. Annabelle had eaten it before Gibbering Jane, who was sitting at the water's edge, could stop her.

'Ooops!' said Fabian, who thereafter hobbled around with just one shoe until he 'borrowed' a spare pair of Eddie's just before bed.

He and Eddie got on surprisingly well, in fact, and it was obvious that Eddie was delighted to have someone his own age – and *normal* – in his life! Eddie wasn't used to a child taking his stuff without asking but that was a small price to pay for having an ally in a household full of odd adults. And he was really enjoying this acting lark too. All in all, life was good.

Then Uncle Alfie's health took on a turn for the worse. As well as his appalling cough, his whole chest now felt tight and it was painful to lie down. He had to sleep in a sitting position with plenty of pillows packed around him.

'I think we need the doctor,' said Aunt Hetty at breakfast.

'Muffin or Humple?' asked Mr Dickens.

'A doctor,' repeated a puzzled Hetty, thinking she was being offered something to eat.

'They are both doctors, Aunt Hetty,' Eddie explained. 'Dr Humple is the family doctor and Dr Muffin a specialist.'

'He cured us when we became crinkly around the edges and smelled of old hot-water bottles,' said Mrs Dickens.

'What do old hot-water bottles smell like?' asked Hetty, thinking of her own hot-water bottle, an earthenware cylinder with a cork stopper in it.

'Like we did when we were ill,' said Mr Dickens.

'Then perhaps Dr Humple would be the better choice. Your Dr Muffin sounds very specialised,' Aunt Hetty reasoned.

'If I might interject, madam?' said Dawkins, who usually left the Dickenses and Grouts to serve themselves from the side table (on which he'd place various dishes under silver domes, in order to keep the food warm).

'What is it, Daphne?' asked Eddie's father.

'It's just that Mrs Grout –' he was referring to Hetty, of course '– might make a more informed decision if she was aware of the fact that Dr Humple is no more.'

'No more, what?' demanded Even Madder Aunt Maud, surfacing from her hiding place under the breakfast table. She'd been tying the men's shoe laces together whilst eavesdropping on the conversation. 'No more than a man with a funny hat and a stethoscope? No more than ninety-eight per cent water?'

'Dead, madam,' said Dawkins. 'He is alive no more.'

'He seemed perfectly alive the last time I saw him!' Even Madder Aunt Maud snorted.

'That's because he *was* indeed alive on that occasion, madam,' said Dawkins. 'He has died since.'

'I'm very sorry to hear that,' said Mr Dickens.

'How did he die? Do you know, Daphne?'

'Peacefully in his sleep, apparently, sir,' said Dawkins. 'He was seventy-two.'

'Er, has he a replacement, do you know?' asked Hetty, feeling it slightly indelicate to be discussing someone taking over the doctor's practice, but she needed someone to see her poor Alfie as soon as possible.

'I believe a Dr Moot has stepped in to care for his patients, and intends to take over his medical practice, madam,' said Dawkins, pleased to be the fount of all knowledge.

'Moot?' said Mad Aunt Maud, pulling herself upright with the aid of the tablecloth, causing it to slip across the table top and various items – such as knives and forks – to clatter to the floor. 'Not Moo-Cow Moot?'

'Madam?' asked Dawkins, with a what-on-Earth-are-you-on-about expression on his face.

'Old Mooty, huh?' Mad Uncle Jack joined in. 'It must be the same fella. There can't be that many Dr Moots knocking about the place.'

'I believe that his first name is Samuel, sir,' said Dawkins.

'That's him!' said MUJ, folding his paper and tossing it onto the table.

'The very same!' said EMAM. 'Samuel Moo-Cow Moot!'

'Will that be all?' Dawkins asked the assembled company. He had been summoned to the breakfast room by the bell, and was eager to get back to his sheets of tissue paper, which he was busy sorting in the pantry.

'Yes, thank you, Daphne, just bring those extra sausages we asked for,' said Mr Dickens. Dawkins bowed and backed out of the room.

By now, Even Madder Aunt Maud had found an empty chair at the table. She sat between Fabian and Eddie. 'Which one are you?' she asked Eddie.

'I'm Eddie, Mad Aunt Maud,' he said.

'I do wish you'd stop it!' she said.

Eddie had no idea what she was talking about.

'Is Dr Moot a good doctor?' Hetty interjected.

'Strange fellow,' said Mad Uncle Jack. 'He shot me once.'

'He shot you?' gasped Eddie.

'Yes. When I say once, he actually shot me twice, but on the one single occasion.'

'But why, Uncle?' asked Hetty.

'He deserved it!' said Even Madder Aunt Maud. She had somehow managed to get Malcolm's snout stuck in a pot of marmalade shaped like an orange.

'Absolutely,' agreed MUJ. 'I mean to say, I'd have shot old Moo-Cow if he hadn't shot me first!'

'Was it a duel?' said Eddie, in growing wonder.

'It most certainly was, young Edmund!'

378

'What were you fighting about?' asked Fabian.

'It was before I was married to your lovely great-aunt,' said Mad Uncle Jack looking across the table to his beloved Maud. The expression on his face was so soppy that it would have put a big-eyed puppy dog to shame. 'Moo-Cow was as in love with her as I was and thought that I had insulted her good name.'

Eddie found it hard to imagine anyone being in love with his great-aunt – except for Mad Uncle Jack, of course – and her ever having had a good name which anyone could insult.

'He accused my love pumpkin of having called me ridiculous –' began Even Madder Aunt Maud.

'Which, of course, you are!' said Mad Uncle Jack.

'Precisely!' agreed Maud. Having successfully freed Malcolm's snout from the pot, she was busy licking the marmalade from his matted fur.

'So why did you fight the duel, Mad Uncle Jack?' Eddie asked.

'Because Moot had challenged me to one. It would not have been gentlemanly to decline!'

'I thought duels were illegal?' said Eddie's mother, who'd been silent until now because her mouth had been filled with buttons. (She later admitted that she'd cut them from Eddie's father's clothes, when his trousers fell down.) She would have preferred button mushrooms but, in her opinion, these were the next best thing.

'The law was different back then ... or less rigorously followed, anyhow,' said MUJ.

'Where were you shot?' asked Mr Dickens, who'd never heard this particular family anecdote before, nor noticed any scars.

'Near *The Eel.*'

'The eel?' said Mr Dickens, imagining a place near the spleen.

'The coaching inn near Little Gattling,' said Mad Uncle Jack. He might have said more, but Dawkins burst into the room and burst into tears.

'I'm not sure how much more of this I can take, madam!' he sobbed, facing Even Madder Aunt Maud. One of the sausages he was carrying, piled high on a serving dish, fell to the floor with a dull thud.

'What *are* you on about?' she demanded.

The gentleman's gentleman turned to reveal that Annabelle the baby crocodile had attached herself to his bottom with her teeth.

Surprising News

In which Mad Uncle Jack
receives an offer he can't refuse

Back in Eddie's era, there were numerous postal deliveries in a day. At my home, there's one delivery and it's sometime in the morning. That sometime is usually when I'm in the bath, or changing a nappy or in the middle of an important phone call or jotting down a brilliant idea . . . and the postman invariably knocks because someone has invariably sent me something too large to fit through my letterbox: a rolled-up poster, a big book, or a fan letter wrapped around a bar of gold bullion (*hint hint*). He never seems to come when I'm eagerly waiting for mail or *not* in the middle of something else.

At Awful End, at the time that the events I'm recounting in this third and final Further Adventure occurred, there was definitely an early morning post, a late morning post, a midday post, and an early afternoon post. There may also possibly have been a late afternoon post, but I'm not prepared to swear to it on a stack of Bibles. (I might fall off.) On this particular morning, when Eddie's Aunt Hetty was trying to find a doctor for his poor Uncle Alfie, the morning post brought an innocent enough sounding letter which was, eventually, to throw the house into utter turmoil (not to be confused with Upper Turnall which was a small hamlet not a stone's throw from Awful End, if one was extremely good at throwing stones*).

The letter, when it arrived, lay on the oval table in the centre of the hall, directly beneath the truly dreadful ceiling painted by Eddie's father, Mr

---

* Not that you should throw stones, whether you live in a glass house or not.**

** My editor has pointed out that there are already a great many footnotes in this adventure, which is nice because I thought she'd dozed off. I pointed out that in the UK editions of all the previous Eddie Dickens books, the only one to contain a footnote was *Awful End*, and that was only one, single note . . . which means that I've got a lot of catching up to do.

Dickens, which – though supposedly depicting a biblical scene – left the vast majority of onlookers with a queasy liver-sausagey feeling (though it wasn't quite as dreadful as Mrs Pumblesnook).

Fortunately, said letter had been picked up by Hetty who, suddenly remembering that it was in her pocket, produced it at the breakfast table and handed it to Mad Uncle Jack. I say 'fortunately' because, had EMAM picked it up, she might have absent-mindedly fed it to Annabelle, or posted it through a crack in the plasterwork in the wall by a piece of furniture referred to as the hall stand.

Mad Uncle Jack took the letter and tore open the envelope. In his younger days, there had been no such thing as envelopes, people simply used to fold over their letters when finishing them, write a name and address on the blank side and seal them shut with sealing wax. Some men wore signet rings which they pressed into the wax when it was hot to leave an impression of their family crest, or monogram, so that the person receiving the letter would know who it was from before they'd even opened it.

A cygnet – same pronunciation, different spelling – is the name for a baby swan but, I'm delighted to report that, as mad as the pair of them were, neither Mad Uncle Jack nor Even Madder Aunt Maud ever tried to use a swan (baby or adult) to leave an impression on sealing wax, either accidentally or on purpose (or accidentally on purpose); though they did once try to make an impression on the local bishop with a Christmas goose, but that's quite a different matter.

This letter, however, came in an envelope and hadn't required sealing wax to keep it shut. Mad Uncle Jack scanned the page with his eyes. 'Ridiculous!' he said.

'How so, Uncle?' asked Mr Dickens.

'The buffoon who composed this confounded letter has written the entire thing upside down.'

Immediately to his right, Even Madder Aunt Maud emerged from under the table. She'd grown tired of sitting between the two boys and had resumed her position on the floor.

She snatched the letter from Mad Uncle Jack's

hand, turned it the right way up and handed it back to him.

Eddie was stunned. To him it was like a dog suddenly speaking the Queen's English, or a weeping willow tree stepping out of its bark and running, naked and giggling, into a lake for a swim. Even Madder Aunt Maud doing something *sensible*? That made no sense at all.

'You are a triumph!' said MUJ, kissing his wife on the back of her head with his thinnest of thin lips. In truth, they were his *only* lips – his only lips being thinnest of thin. (I don't wish to imply that he had a *fat* pair nestling alongside the dried swordfish he was inclined to carry around in his inside jacket pocket.) The thinnest comparison is with other people-with-thin-lips' lips, not with any other lips MUJ might himself have had.

'Sloppy characterisation,' muttered Eddie's father, to no one in particular.

'I'm sorry, dear?' asked Eddie's mother.

'One of us suddenly acting out of character, simply to move events along. This –' He stopped. Everyone was looking at him blankly. 'Never mind,' he sighed.

'Ha!' said MUJ, and it was such a *Ha!* that he had everyone's attention, including Annabelle's, who was now back on her silver chain behind EMAM, Dawkins's posterior having been successfully extricated from her pincer-like grip.

'What is it, Uncle?' asked Fabian's mother. 'Not bad news, I hope?'

'My portrait,' said Mad Uncle Jack. 'The War Office wish to commission an oil painting of me, in full military regalia, to hang in Whitehall!'

'–' said Mr Dickens (which meant 'I'm at a loss for words').

'–' said Eddie (which meant, 'I don't know what to say').

'–' said Mrs Dickens (which meant she'd just bitten her tongue). Distressed by Alfie's turn for the worse in the coughing department, she had now filled her mouth with cleaning crystals from the sideboard.★

Mad Uncle Jack's news was quite extraordinary: *extraordinarily* extraordinary, in fact. Mad Major Jack Dickens's final military campaign had been an utter disaster. He would probably have ended up shooting some of his own men by mistake – or doing himself a personal injury – if his quick-witted batman (not a caped crusading superhero, gentleman) hadn't removed all ammunition from but a soldier from the lower ranks whose job it was to act as a kind of gentleman's not-so-gentlemanly

★ If I knew what cleaning crystals were, I'd explain in a footnote right here.

MUJ's vicinity, and stuffed his rifle full of blotting paper.

Mad Uncle Jack's appalling record as a soldier was no great secret, hence the stunned silence. Why on Earth – or any other planet, come to that – would the War Office want someone to paint a portrait of Mad Uncle Jack and hang it at their headquarters in Whitehall?

'Marvellous!' cried Even Madder Aunt Maud. 'They probably need it to cover a damp patch.'

'It is, indeed, a great honour!' said MUJ.

'Congratulations, Uncle,' said Mr Dickens.

'I wonder who they'll commission to paint it?' said Eddie.

'They mention the chap's name here,' said Mad Uncle Jack, referring back to the letter. 'Someone called A. C. Pryden. I can never abide a fellow who uses initials instead of a name –'

'He's very famous, Uncle,' said Mr Dickens, who still fancied himself as a bit of an artist. 'I believe he painted General Gordon.'

'What colour?' snorted Even Madder Aunt Maud. 'Purple, I hope?' Eddie's great-aunt had recently developed an abiding passion for purple having seen a chromolithograph plate of a Roman emperor sporting a purple toga.

'I think he also painted Lord Bulberry,' said Eddie.

'Lazy n'er do well!' said EMAM waving Malcolm dangerously above her head.

'Lord Bulberry?' asked Hetty.

'This painter man . . . too lazy to use his full name!'

Today – I don't mean Tuesday (the day I'm writing this particular paragraph) but nowadays – Lord Bulberry is best-remembered (by those few who remember him at all) for having written *Surviving Three Years Down A Hole* and having invented a pocket knife with a particularly powerful spring. Back at the time of these events, though, he was known as the 'Hero of Guldoon', Guldoon being a place under siege. He defended Guldoon in some far-off war against some far-off enemy until the British cavalry both physically and metaphorically arrived. It was the big news event of the year in Britain, and there were even celebrations in the street. To be painted by the same artist who captured Lord Bulberry on canvas was, indeed, an honour (if totally undeserved in MUJ's case).*

With Mad Uncle Jack and Even Madder Aunt Maud spending much of their time, and every night,

---

* It was later in life that his lordship began to miss the isolation of a besieged town, and so took to living down a hole for three years, only coming out to eat four square meals a day or to have a wash and a shave, and to sleep, of course.

in their treehouse made from creosoted dried fish and hollow wooden cow carnival float respectively, Eddie's mother had assumed the role as (almost) lady of the house, and was suddenly concerned where Pryden the painter would sleep if he came to stay at Awful End whilst painting his subject. It wasn't that there was a shortage of rooms – Mr Pumblesnook's wandering theatricals didn't take up *that* much room when you consider the house could accommodate a whole host of homeless monks remember – it's just that she was one of nature's worriers. And when she worried she was in the habit of stuffing even more things into her mouth. *Anything.* Which was why she now had a mouth full of dried pine cones she'd removed from a small dish on the mantelpiece, when Dawkins entered the breakfast room once more. (What happened to the buttons and cleaning crystals in the meantime, I've no idea.)

Dawkins addressed himself to Eddie's Aunt Hetty. 'I have the pony and trap ready, ma'am, and will be riding into town to ask Dr Moot to attend Mr Grout at his earliest convenience,' he said.

'Thank you, Dawkins,' said Hetty. 'Please do stress the urgency of my husband's health. I fear for him most dreadfully.'

Dawkins bowed and left.

'Who the devil was that?' asked Mad Uncle Jack.

'Dawkins,' said Mrs Dickens.

'Daphne,' said Mr Dickens.

Eddie sighed and looked at the pattern running around the rim of his empty breakfast plate.

Episode 6

Making a Splash

*In which a doctor pays two visits
and later pays the price*

It transpired – which is a posh word for 'turned out' – that the Dr Moot who came to attend poor Alfie Grout and his terrible cough was *indeed* the same Dr Moot who'd challenged Mad Uncle Jack to a duel all those years before and had shot him twice, but on the one occasion. On the surface, there appeared to be no hard feelings between the two men, though it was obvious in a moment that, to use old-fashioned parlance, he still held a torch for EMAM despite her change of circumstance and the passing years (or, to put it in slightly more modern English: he still fancied Maud something

391

rotten, despite her being married and having aged like a prune).

There was nothing he'd like more than to sit with Even Madder Aunt Maud in a secluded spot in the garden, holding her tiny hand in his and reading her poems about larks and dewy leaves and sublimely beautiful sunsets tinged with pink. (I know this for a fact because I was given exclusive access to his diary written at the time.) But, in much the same way that the detective inspector, who more often than not turns up in these books, was a good policeman, Dr Moot was a good doctor. At that precise moment, his interests lay first and foremost with his new patient, Alfie Grout, who was married to the niece of the lovely Mad Maud MacMuckle.

It didn't take Dr Moot long to realise what was wrong with Alfie. As a gypsy, he'd never had access to conventional medicine and, as I've explained elsewhere, the particular band of gypsies he was part of, did not include a healer familiar with the old ways and folklore of nature's medicine. Instead, he'd had to make do with chewing lucky heather and that, no pun intended, was the root of the problem. He was full of the stuff. He was a giant version of one of those little pillows stuffed with sweet-smelling lavender that you give your grandmother for Christmas, and she puts it away in a drawer to give to someone else the following year.

'To use a purely non-medical term, Mrs Grout,' said Dr Moot in muted tones, in the corner of the bedroom out of Alfie's earshot, 'he is packed to the gills with the stuff. Once he's free from the heather, I'm sure you'll find him improved beyond recognition.'

'I'll have him stop eating it at once,' said Hetty. 'How long before it – er – passes through the system?'

Dr Moot, who had no humorous characteristics in appearance or character (except for a remarkably droopy moustache and the extraordinary matter of his being besotted by Even Madder Aunt Maud), flipped open his bag and produced a small dark-brown bottle of pills with a handwritten label gummed to one side. 'Give him one of these every morning at the same time,' he instructed. 'No more than one, and it must be swallowed without food or drink.'

'Thank you, Doctor,' she said. It was such a relief that Alfie was going to be fine, and to speak to a sane adult once in a while.

There was a problem, though. It lay with the 'swallowed without food or drink' part. Swallowing the pills without food wasn't a problem because one of the last things Uncle Alfie felt like doing in his current condition – hacking cough and being full of not-so-lucky heather – was eating. What he felt like doing was pretty much what he *was* doing, which was being propped up in bed groaning (and he did it very well). The problem was not being allowed to wash down the pills with a drink; not even a glass of water.

The pills weren't enormous. They certainly weren't nearly as large as the ones the vet had insisted on giving Edgar, the horse Eddie had 'acquired' from Mr and Mrs Cruel-Streak when he'd hitched him up to the cow-shaped carnival float – yup, we're talking Marjorie – jam-packed full of children escaping from St Horrid's Home for Grateful Orphans. Edgar had needed the pills when he was being weaned off the diet of rich food the Cruel-Streaks had fed him – which included cheese and biscuits at the end of every meal, washed down with some fine vintage port – and put back onto more ordinary horse fare, of the bag-of-oats variety.

These pills had been impressively large. Once, after a particularly fretful game of bridge – not the card game, but a party game of the Dickenses' own invention which involved two teams trying to build a structure long enough and strong enough to support two 'team' members (one on the shoulders of the other) running across the lake at Awful End – Eddie's mother (*aka* Mrs Dickens, *aka* Florinda) had somehow found one of Edgar's horse pills, and had stuffed it in her mouth for comfort. She had no intention of swallowing it and probably couldn't have even if she'd tried. But she did suck it, and suffered the consequences of its medicinal effects.

No one is absolutely clear what followed, least of all Mrs Dickens herself. It was Dawkins who discovered her the following morning in the orangery,* dressed in nothing but a pair of frilly drawers and a bearskin rug, brandishing a poker in one hand and an out-of-date copy of *Bradshaw's* railway timetable in the other. The rather startled gentleman's gentleman later told Ex-Private Gorey – this was before he died, of course, there'd have been little point in talking to him otherwise – that the lady had been screaming at the top of her voice that someone should hurry up and invent the telephone (which, of course, someone already had).

* An orangery is like a lemonery, but for oranges.

Whoa! That illustration came as a bit of a surprise, didn't it? I mean, you'd have thought it would have gone somewhere on the previous page next to the part where I first mentioned Eddie's mother in frilly drawers and bearskin rug . . . but, no, just when you are lulled into thinking that such a vivid scene will be left to your own imaginations, you turn the page and: POW, this massive image hits you fair and square – well fair and *oblong*, actually, which is a friendlier word for a rectangle – right between the eyes.

As well as being an *Eddie Dickens* first – it being the first time we've had a full-page David Roberts drawing in the middle of the text – it also gives us an opportunity to take in more of the scene. If you look closely at the bearskin rug, for example, you'll see that it's not – I repeat NOT – the same bearskin rug as the one Mad Uncle Jack collapsed next to on his study floor when he was pronged in the bottom with a toasting fork that time by Even Madder Aunt Maud. It has a very different expression on its face.

Then there's the strange carving on that rather nice stand by the big potted fern. That's one of Eddie's father's sculptures. Research suggests that it depicts 'Jason with the Golden Fleece from Classical Mythology' though, to me, it looks more like 'Tree Man with a Clump of Moss from the Car Boot Sale'.

You'll also have noticed – and, if not, you'll now have to flip back a page to have a look – that there's a pane of broken glass in the orangery. This was probably caused by Mad Uncle Jack's beakiest of beaky noses on the occasion (not previously recounted) when he wanted to prove that he knew every inch of his own home so well that he could walk around it equally well in the dark as in daylight. That was the same occasion that he broke his foot, a pile of 'best' china, and fell out of an upstairs window. This occurred in the days before Eddie and his parents lived at Awful End, so Jack had had to be aided by the then Bishop of Durham, the dinner guest to whom he had made the original (ridiculous) claim.

This only leaves one or two more items of interest to point out in the splendid illustration, before returning to the main action of this final Further Adventure. Firstly, there's the floor which, at first glance, appears to be made of traditional black and white floor tiles, laid out in the traditional checked pattern. Look again, and you'll see that although the white tiles are indeed white tiles, the black 'tiles' are, in truth, very large slices of dried pressed meat.

These had been intended as supplies for an expedition Mad Uncle Jack had been planning to lead in an attempt to discover the Northwest Passage, whether or not it had been discovered already. Not the northwest passage at Awful End (which led from the boot room to the tack room, or from the tack room to the boot room, depending upon which direction you were going) but the fabled Northwest Passage, a possible route between Europe and the Orient which would make sailing times so much shorter.

Mad Uncle Jack had given up on the expedition when he remembered that he didn't like cold places. The crew he'd assembled got on so well together (without MUJ) that, when the expedition was abandoned, rather than disbanding, they remained friends and opened a seafood restaurant with a nautical theme that became so successful that they opened another one and then another one. Today, there's a whole chain of these restaurants. (You can read about them in an out-of-print paperback entitled *Recipe For Success*.) Never one to waste perfectly good dried pressed meat, Mad Uncle Jack had had the black tiles of the orangery floor pulled up, and the meat trimmed to fit and laid in their place. As to what he did with the black tiles, everyone forgot.

And finally? See that little picture in the oval frame, next to the stuffed heron in the domed glass case? Even Madder Aunt Maud drew that when she was a little girl in Scotland. It's of a butterfly drinking a tankard of foaming ale.

'I can't swallow the pill without water,' said Uncle Alfie, between splutters, the first time he tried.

Aunt Hetty urged him to try again, but it was no good. 'Try chewing it,' she suggested. That was no good either. It was rock hard, and his teeth weren't in the best of condition. 'I'll see if I can grind it into a powder,' she said. 'I'll be back soon, darling.'

Aunt Hetty hurried downstairs into the kitchen and looked for the pestle and mortar. She found the mortar – the bowl part – soon enough, but the pestle – the mini-club part – was nowhere to be seen, which was hardly surprising. Even Madder Aunt Maud had drawn a fish face on it and thrown it into the little formal ornamental pond in the rose garden, for Annabelle to play with.

Rummaging in a drawer by the sink, Aunt Hetty found a steakbeater: an enormous square-headed wooden hammer with some nasty spikes on its head, designed for tenderising meat.

Eddie's Aunt Hetty placed the pill on a cutting block on the kitchen table, raised the steakbeater and brought it down with a resounding crash. The pill didn't break, but the huge wooden hammer did, its head flying loose and hitting –

Now, I must pause here because I want you

to appreciate the problems of being an author. Someone is about to get hit by the head of the steakbeater.

In previous books, in this self-same kitchen, we've had a stray diamond ring (used to grade the size of broad beans) hit Malcolm and subsequently swallowed, in error, by Even Madder Aunt Maud. We've had a piece of devilled kidney fly through the air which, once again deflected by Malcolm, became lodged in the brim of the stovepipe hat of that fairly well-known engineer, Fandango Jones.

Elsewhere, we've had Eddie's father, Mr Dickens, hit by a falling chimney, fall from a tree (following an explosion), *and* fall from a scaffolding rig onto Dawkins, plus Eddie himself falling from a horse and trap into a gorse bush . . .

. . . and here we go again. Accidents aren't unusual around the place, and yet another one might be seen as 'old hat'. But don't blame the messenger. Another accident there was, and I'm here to tell it like it is.

The flying chunk of wood hit none other than Dr Moot who'd returned to the house that following morning on the pretext of seeing his patient, Alfie Grout, but amongst other things, really in the hope of seeing his beloved Maud again. Instead, he saw stars, or blue birds tweeting around his head, or whatever it is one sees on being knocked unconscious. There was a lot of blood.

Mad Uncle Jack was one of the first on the scene. He'd woken up in his treehouse, washed and shaved at the foot of the ladder with the aid of a mirror – one shard to look into and one particularly sharp piece to use as a razor – and had wandered through the back door in search of a piece of string. Instead, he was confronted by a bloodied Dr Moot lying next to a sack of potatoes.

'Shot him did you?' he asked Hetty. 'Not on my account, I hope? Let bygones be bygones, I always say.'

Aunt Hetty was dumbfounded. Speechless and still brandishing the wooden handle of the steakbeater, she stared down at her unintended victim, shaking in shock at what she'd done.

'Suppose we'd better dispose of the body before that confounded Chief Inspector Bunyon comes sniffing about the place,' said MUJ, matter of factly. Hetty wasn't sure whether her uncle was joking or not. (Bunyon was the detective inspector I referred to a while back. He'd been recently promoted.)

MUJ took charge. He bent down and took Dr Moot's pulse. 'Still alive, I'm afraid,' he said. 'Assuming, that is, that you wanted him dead.'

'I – I –' Hetty spluttered. Mad Uncle Jack already had his hands under the doctor's arms and was dragging him out of the room. Hetty feared that he might be about to bury him or something. She dashed out of the back door after him.

As Mad Uncle Jack dragged the unconscious Moot across a brick courtyard, Eddic appeared around the corner, hands in pockets, humming to himself. He stopped in his tracks. Eddie thought nothing Mad Uncle Jack did could surprise him any more. Here was a man who lived up a tree and paid for everything with dried fish . . . yet, here he now was heaving the blood covered body of Moo-Cow Moot out of the kitchen: Moo-Cow Moot who'd once shot Jack twice (but on the one occasion) and who'd obviously still been in love with his wife.

Did Eddie think, even for a fleeting moment, that MUJ had murdered his rival? We have no way of knowing for sure. What we *can* be sure of, though, is that Eddie wondered what on Earth was going on.

'Tap!' MUJ shouted over to him.

'Tap?' asked Eddie.

'Tap!' MUJ repeated, making the conversation sound like one involving Detective Chief Inspector Bunyon, who was the past master at repeating what the previous person had just said. Mad Uncle Jack jerked his head in the direction of an outside tap – that's a faucet, my American chums – set into a wall.

Eddie ran over and switched it on. There was a spluttering belch followed by an icy jet of water cascading to the ground. With one final heave, his great-uncle unceremoniously dumped Dr Moot in its path. The water had its desired effect. Dr Moot spluttered almost as much as the tap and sat up. The blood momentarily washed from the wound on his forehead, Eddie could make out a strange pattern on his skin. It was almost as if someone had hit him with a steakb-e-a-t-e-r . . .

Eddie gasped. What was that *thing* mild-mannered Aunt Hetty was holding in her hand?

Remembrance of Things Past

*In which readers are given a short account of the
death of Malcontent, and meet a very short man*

Once upon a time, not *that* long ago, there lived
a man named Squire Dickens and he owned
all the land as far as the eye could see (and he had
very good eyesight). The squire had a number of
children, but his son-and-heir was Malcontent
Dickens, whom the less cloth-eared of you may
remember my having mentioned before. The first
thing Malcontent did on inheriting Awful End
when his father died, was to have it pulled down,
and the Awful End that Eddie knew built in its
place.

Today, it's one of the finest examples of a
Victorian manor house in Britain, in either private

or public hands. The only slight shame is that some of the building materials Malcontent used were substandard to say the least: downright shoddy would be more accurate, which is why parts of it were crumbling just a few years after Malcontent's death (and partly to blame for the chimney landing on Eddie's father that time). Such materials included bits of the old house, bits found lying around, and even bits stolen from nearby walls and other houses. The story goes that the vicarage over at Stourgate disappeared overnight, with the vicar and his favourite cat, Hook, still in it.

Possibly the finest room in the entire house was the private chapel, with richly carved woodwork throughout. Malcontent was not a particularly religious man but, just to be on the safe side, prayed seven or eight times a day, and more on Sundays, and had an effigy of God on a cloud in his bedroom. The woodwork in the chapel and the effigy in the bedroom were carved by a master-craftsman by the name of Geo Gibbons. I assume that Geo was shot for George – very short, in fact – but this hardly matters because, ever since he first picked up an awl – which may sound like a sea-bird but is, apparently, some form of woodworking tool – he was known as Grinning Gibbons. Why? Because carving wood made him grin like an idiot. Here's a diagram to prove it:

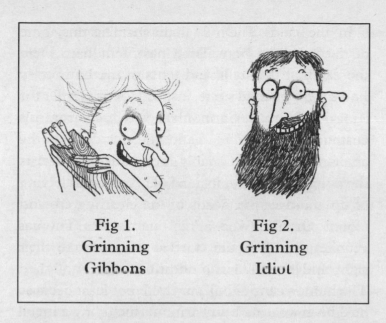

Fig 1.
Grinning
Gibbons

Fig 2.
Grinning
Idiot

Hmmm. The idiot that David Roberts drew reminds me of someone . . . Now, where was I? Yes, Malcontent Dickens, son of Squire Dickens. He lived into his fifties but had had every intention of living far longer. Sadly, Fate had had other ideas (which is also why we're left with two 'had had's together in a few short lines). Fate is often spelled with a capital 'F' – and not just at the beginning of sentences – because it's such an important thing. It's Fate which decides whether you're the one who wins the outsized cuddly polar bear in the raffle, or whether it's you or the person next to you who gets soaked in muddy water when the passing buffalo stampede the water hole.

In the case of Dr Malcontent Dickens, Fate decreed that he be walking past Wyndham Field the day that the stalls and tents of the Lamberley Fayre were pitched on it, just as Count Orville the Amazing Human Cannonball was fired from his custom-built cannon . . . and Fate decided that the cannon would inexplicably lurch and tilt down at the point of firing so, instead of his usual trajectory of up-and-over the heads of the cheering crowds, Count Orville (whose real name was Thomas Plunke) flew past the startled onlookers to their right, and ploughed into Eddie's great-grandfather. The human cannonball survived, not least because he'd been wearing body armour, including a metal helmet of his own design. Malcontent Dickens didn't, not least because the human cannonball had been wearing body armour, including a metal helmet of his own design.

Malcontent's funeral was an impressive affair. As well as the black horses with plumes on their heads – rather like those pulling the hearse containing the coffin containing the very-much-alive Great Zucchini, in one of Eddie's previous adventures – there were many official mourners who'd never known Dr Malcontent Dickens in life, but were paid to weep and wail and generally moan in sadness at his untimely passing. One such official mourner was Gherkin the dwarf.

Because there weren't funerals every day and not every funeral required his services anyway, Gherkin was only a part-time mourner. Amongst other things – make a note of that – he was also a part-time freak in a freakshow, a mummer (not to be confused with a mamma), and an occasional tumbler – one who tumbles, not the drinking tumbler variety – in a touring group of undersized acrobats called 'The Remarkably Small Garfields' which wasn't the catchiest of names, even in the nineteenth century. The pretence was that the troupe was made up of members of the Garfield family who were all, for some unexplained reason, remarkably small. This conceit was wholly unconvincing, not least because some of the 'Garfields' were, like Gherkin, dwarfs whilst others were what they called midgets. Also, all of them were Chinese except for Gherkin and the midget Ebony, who was a black African.

At funerals, Gherkin was by far the best blubberer. He would fight back tears, sob uncontrollably and blow his nose on a white silk handkerchief almost as big as he was. At Malcontent's funeral, Malcontent's widow, Ivy Dickens (*née* Porker) was so impressed by Gherkin's grief that, though she'd already paid extra to have him as a part of her husband's funeral cortège, she pressed a gold sovereign into the hand of Mr Gagstaff of the

funeral directors *Gagstaff, Wagg and Homily* and, between whimpers, asked that it be given to 'the little man'. As it was, Mr Gagstaff put the money on a horse – not literally, he placed a bet – which, to his considerable surprise, won its race. Out of the winnings, he passed half-a-crown to Gherkin which, though not as much as a sovereign, was not to be sniffed at.

Also at the funeral that day were Malcontent and Ivy's three sons, George, Jack (MUJ) and Percy. Jack had been fascinated by Gherkin at the funeral and couldn't take his eyes off him. Whilst he should have been lamenting the untimely passing of his father, he found himself wondering whether he'd be able to lift the dwarf with one hand, or to wear him in a gold cage around his neck. He was wondering where he might be able to buy such a cage, or whether he'd have to have one specially made.

'Excuse me,' said MUJ sidling up beside Gherkin once the door to the Dickens family vault had been closed on his father's coffin. 'Might I have a word with you?'

'Surely, sir,' said Gherkin, looking up at this thinnest of thin young gentlemen.

'I was wondering whether you could fit inside this box?'

The dwarf looked at the empty wooden crate stamped **EAST INDIA COMPANY**, which the beakiest-of-beaky-nosed young men seemed to have pulled out from behind a bush to the side of the mausoleum. He thought it rather an odd thing for a son of the deceased to be dragging around at a funeral. 'I suspect I might be able to, sir,' he said, a little hesitantly, 'should the need arise.'

'Would you mind stepping inside it, just to be sure?'

'I'm afraid that won't be possible at present,' said Gherkin, looking across to Mr Gagstaff, who was deep in conversation with the widow. 'I'm still on duty.'

'I see, I see,' said Jack. 'Perhaps you would be kind enough to call on me at your earliest convenience and to try the box for size then?' He put his hand in his pocket and handed Gherkin something. 'My card,' he said.

Gherkin looked in his palm. He was holding what appeared to be a very small, very dried, fish.

★

Now I expect that one or two of you – if there's more than one person reading this – are thinking, *That's all very well, but why is that nice Mr Ardagh suddenly telling us all of this? What does this have to do with Mad Uncle Jack pouring water on Moo-Cow Moot – with the bloody imprint of a steakbeater on his forehead – whilst being watched by a mortified Aunt Hetty and a flabbergasted Eddie?* Well, you're about to find out. I'm not sure who it was who said 'Patience is a virtue/Virtue is a Grace/And Grace is a little girl/Who wouldn't wash her face' but I do hope:

1. That it's out of copyright; and
2. They'll be quiet and leave me alone ... because Fate is about to play a big hand again.

★

412

Eddie and Mad Uncle Jack helped the groaning Dr Moot to his feet. Blood was still pouring from the poor doctor's head wound and he was now soaked through with cold water from the outside tap.

At least he's alive, thought Eddie, looking across at his Aunt Hetty, who still looked mortified.

Moot lost his footing and staggered to the left, nearly knocking Eddie off his feet. The height difference between Eddie and his extraordinarily thin, tall great-uncle didn't make them an ideal partnership for supporting a semiconscious man under each arm.

'Steady on, boy!' MUJ ordered then, suddenly completely distracted by something or *someone*, he let go of Moot altogether, causing Eddie and the doctor to land, unceremoniously, on the ground in a heap of writhing arms and legs.

The distraction was, indeed, a someone and that someone was an elderly dwarf striding as fast as his little legs would carry him.

Lurkin' with Gherkin

*In which Eddie befriends an extraordinary man and
enjoys a hearty breakfast*

Now, dear reader, *you* know that the man
was Gherkin and *I* know that the man was
Gherkin and there's absolutely no doubt in my
mind that Mad Uncle Jack knew that the man was
Gherkin – not least because he gasped, 'Gherkin!'
in amazement – but, at this stage of the proceedings,
Eddie had never even heard of the man, nor knew
of his role in great-grandfather's funeral.

When Eddie heard the word 'Gherkin!' pass
MUJ's lips he, quite understandably, assumed that
it was an oath – a swear word of sorts – that his
great-uncle was muttering as a result of an apparent
stranger stumbling upon the unfortunate scene

of the family trying to revive an innocent doctor who had been beaten over the head with a meat tenderiser by one Aunt Hetty. He was even more surprised, therefore, when the elderly dwarf thrust a very grubby dog-eared calling card into Mad Uncle Jack's hand. Eddie could see that it read:

MAD JACK DICKENS, Esq.
Awful End

'I came at my earliest convenience,' said Gherkin, his voice deep. He must have been busy. A great many years had passed since MUJ gave him that card (after that fish) at Malcontent's funeral.

Despite the dwarf probably being the oldest person present and, undoubtedly, the smallest, he was also immensely strong – and not just for his size. Having assessed the situation, and waiting for neither instruction nor invitation, he hoisted the dazed Dr Moot up onto his back, in a position known today as 'the fireman's lift', and carried him back into the house, jogging across the brick courtyard with a bouncing gait that even the butcher's young delivery boy couldn't achieve with a far lesser weight of meat on his shoulders.

Before anyone else knew quite what was going on, Gherkin had positioned Dr Moot in a semi-upright position on a Knole sofa, and rustled him up two fingers of Irish whiskey in a crystal-cut glass. Moments later, he was applying a linen napkin to the doctor's wound. He then lifted the doctor's own hand to it. 'If you'd be good enough to hold this here, sir,' he said.

The befuddled doctor nodded appreciatively. He felt in safe hands. They *all* felt in safe hands. For the first time since the head of the steakbeater had come flying off and hit Dr Moot, Aunt Hetty felt that things might turn out right after all. Eddie also felt that, despite their saviour's unusual appearance (as in looks) and unexplained appearance (as in arrival-on-the-scene), an air of authority and *sanity* had descended on the proceedings.

Mad Uncle Jack, who'd had the initiative to revive old Moo-Cow Moot by sticking his head under the tap, was simply rather pleased that the little fellow from his father's funeral had been true to his word and shown up, even if a little later than he'd hoped.

It was soon after Dr Moot had found himself able to speak, and to accept Aunt Hetty's profound apologies for what had happened – particularly when it transpired that she'd been trying to crush one of the pills that he'd supplied for her husband, Alfie – that Dawkins entered the room. He was horrified to see Dr Moot drinking whiskey. It was

416

his job to hand out drinkies as and when required. It would be bad enough if Mad Mister Dickens (MUJ) or Mr Dickens (Eddie's father) or Mr Grout (Uncle Alfie) started pouring their own drinks, and unheard of for the ladies to do so, but for a complete stranger to come into the house and pour out a whiskey for another – a mighty small, complete stranger, at that – well, it was unheard of! An outrage! It was *his* job and no one else's. It wasn't that Dawkins actually liked pouring their drinks, far from it, in fact. Many was the occasion, in truth, when he'd thought, '*Why don't they pour their own stupid drinks? They're not babies!*' but, at this precise moment, that wasn't the point.

How did he know that it was the dwarf who'd poured the drink? Because none of the others would have. That's how.

Dawkins cleared his throat and was about to try to convey how hurt he felt (without overstepping the mark in the servant/master relationship, of course) when he felt something sinking its teeth into his bottom. He spun around with a yelp, to come face to face not with the young crocodile, as expected, but Even Madder Aunt Maud. She was smirking.

'I don't see why Annabelle should have all the fun,' she said, scrambling to her feet, Malcolm tucked under one arm.

417

'Indeed not, madam,' said Dawkins, all thoughts of whiskey now forgotten.

'Ah, there you are, er –'

'Dawkins, sir.'

'Dawkins,' said Mad Uncle Jack. 'Would you be good enough to lay an extra place for breakfast and then take Dr Moot home in his horse and trap? I don't want him bleeding all over the place here.'

'Very good, sir,' said Dawkins.

'Don't you think he should at least stay here until he's –' began Hetty.

'Nonsense! Nonsense!' said MUJ, with a dismissive wave of one of his thinnest of thin arms.

'Shouldn't he at least see a doctor?' Hetty protested.

'Perhaps he could look in a mirror!' snorted Even Madder Aunt Maud.

'I shall be fine, Mrs Grout,' Dr Moot assured her. 'Please think nothing of it. Accidents do happen.' His voice sounded rather weak and wobbly.

'Good, that's settled then,' said Mad Uncle Jack. 'Get him off my property as soon as possible, er –'

'Dawkins, sir,' said Dawkins.

'Yes,' said Mad Uncle Jack. 'Exactly.'

Gherkin strode over to the gentleman's gentleman, went up on tiptoe, and whispered something in his ear. Dawkins nodded.

Eddie realised what the whispering must have been about when he was the first to enter the breakfast room for – you guessed it, the clue being in the name and all – breakfast.

Not only had an extra place been laid at the table but the chair at that place had a footstool next to it and a pile of books* on it, topped by a comfy cushion. When Gherkin came into the room some five minutes or so after Eddie (who was tucking into a pile of bacon) he stepped up onto the footstool and positioned himself on the chair.

*These were a selection of books about Australia, which played a small but vital part in the second of these Further Adventures, *Horrendous Habits*. The books that is, not Australia.

'My name is Gherkin,' he said.

'I'm Edmund – Eddie – Dickens,' said Eddie. 'My parents and I moved here when our own home was destroyed by fire. Mad Uncle – Mad *Mister* Dickens is my great-uncle.'

'I see,' said Gherkin. 'It is very good of your great-uncle to receive me in this manner.'

'I'm not sure I understand, sir,' said Eddie.

'I am not a gentleman,' the dwarf explained. 'I was a humble showman and a professional mourner, retired now, of course.'

'Mourner?' asked Eddie.

By way of an answer, Gherkin burst into (very convincing) tears and picked up a napkin, using it like a hanky to dab his eyes. A moment later, he stopped, as though nothing had happened. 'At funerals,' he said.

'Aha!' said Eddie, clearly fascinated.

'It was at a funeral that I met your great-uncle on the one and only occasion until now.'

'Really?' said Eddie.

'Really,' nodded Gherkin. 'He took an instant interest in me. Some people find it awkward to discuss my height with me, as though being small might somehow be embarrassing, but not him.'

Eddie took another mouthful of bacon.

'He wanted to know whether I was able to fit in a box of a particular size, and, having presented me with his card, seemed to be entertaining the idea of wearing me in a cage around his neck.'

'You're not that small!' Eddie blurted, instantly hoping that he hadn't overstepped the mark.

'No,' said Gherkin. 'I'm not. Your great-uncle would need extremely strong neck muscles to achieve such a feat.'

'Whose funeral was it, if you don't mind my asking?' said Eddie.

The dwarf thought for a moment. 'If Mad Mr Jack Dickens is your great-uncle, then the deceased must have been your great-grandfather.'

'Dr Malcontent Dickens?' said Eddie in surprise, 'Then you can't have seen Mad Uncle Jack in a very long time indeed!'

'Indeed,' agreed Gherkin. He eyed Eddie's plate.

'You have to help yourself at breakfast,' Eddie explained, nodding in the direction of the silver-domed warmers laid out on the side table keeping the various dishes hot.

'Thank you,' said Gherkin. 'I'm not really used to the ways of life in such a grand house.' He was about to climb down via the footstool, when Fabian came into the room (wearing a pair of slippers that Eddie's mother, Mrs Dickens, had given Eddie the previous Christmas). Gherkin looked from Fabian to Eddie and then back again. 'Twins?' he asked.

'Cousins,' said Eddie. 'This is Mister Gherkin. Mr Gherkin, this is Fabian.'

'Ah,' nodded the dwarf. 'The son of the poor lady who inadvertently injured the doctor.'

Fabian's eyes narrowed. 'Haven't we met before, Mr Gherkin?' he asked.

'It's possible, I suppose,' said Gherkin, 'but, in all honesty, I don't recall, Master Fabian. And, please, it's not *Mister* Gherkin, just plain Gherkin.'

'Isn't it your real name, then?' asked Fabian. He was already at the side table shovelling scrambled eggs onto a plate.

'I never knew my real name if I had one, nor my parents,' explained Gherkin. 'According to the very long and badly spelled note that was written on a luggage label and tied around my neck when I was left outside Bramworth's Stern But Fair Home For Foundlings, my mother – whoever she was – had wanted to keep me, but my father – whoever he was – had taken one look at me and decided not to.'

'How awful!' said Eddie.

'Kind of you to say so, Master Edmund,' said the dwarf, 'but at least my mother left me on the steps of the foundlings' home. Many babies suffer far worse.'

Eddie was about to tell Gherkin about the St Horrid's Home for Grateful Orphans escapees

422

. . . when Even Madder Aunt Maud entered the breakfast room.

She took one look at Gherkin teetering on the top of his pile of books and gave one of her most indignant-sounding indignant snorts. 'Ridiculous!' she said. 'A grown man trying to read so many books at once, and with his *bottom*!'

Episode 9

Warts and All

In which a famous painter arrives at
Awful End and probably wishes that he hadn't

No one was thrilled at the prospect of the arrival of A. C. Pryden, to paint the official portrait of Mad Major Jack Dickens for the War Office. Under normal circumstances, Mr Dickens might have been delighted at the prospect of the arrival of a 'fellow artist' . . . but he was currently going through his play-writing phase, and felt MUJ having his picture painted was an intrusion. The performance of his as-yet untitled play in the grounds of Awful End was supposed to be the highlight of the Dickenses' artistic calendar for that year and he didn't want some world-famous professional portrait painter getting all the attention.

Eddie was more concerned that some serious harm might come to the great painter. If Even Madder Aunt Maud's stuffed stoat didn't get him, perhaps her baby croc would? And the crumbling chimney stack falling on his own dear father hadn't happened *that* long ago, though now he was almost fully recovered. (The one lasting side effect was that Mr Dickens could now rotate his head on his neck through almost 360 degrees, in much the same way that an owl can).

For the reputation of the family, Eddie thought it best if *he* was to meet Mr Pryden (who had insisted on travelling by train). Excusing himself from that morning's rehearsal (in which Mr Pumblesnook was playing just about everyone except for the bush over which the character of Mad Aunt Maud first lays eyes on Fabian's wheel-on version of Marjorie the hollow cow), he arrived at the railway station a matter of minutes before the train pulled into the platform.

Eddie was standing by the pony and trap just outside when the great painter emerged, handing his pasteboard ticket to a smartly dressed ticket collector, brass buttons glinting in the sun.

Following Pryden was a railway porter, wheeling

Pryden's luggage (including a large artist's easel) on a trolley similar to the one that Eddie's father, Mr Dickens, had once been lashed to when he needed to get around with his bad back.

'Mr Pryden?' asked Eddie politely.

'Yes,' said A. C. Pryden with a curt nod. Much has been written about Pryden's paintings (and you'll find reproductions of his pictures in most books on nineteenth-century portraiture), but almost as much has been written about his voice.

The general consensus is that he spoke like a penguin would speak if penguins could speak. Apparently, it had an extraordinary quality to it. You could hear the penguin waddle in it. You could imagine his words being spoken by a beak rather than a mouth. Here he was, a man and a very successful one at that, sounding as if he was rather hoping that he could go diving off ice-floes.

'I'm Eddie Dickens. Edmund. Major Jack Dickens is my great-uncle, and I'm to take you to Awful End.'

'Very good,' said Pryden.

The railway porter heaved the painter's luggage up into the back of the trap. Pryden fumbled in his pocket and produced a tartan purse with a large clasp. He undid the clasp and took out a silver thrupenny bit which he handed to the man.

'Thank you kindly, sir,' said the porter, putting

his finger to the peak of his cap in the manner of a form of salute. He whistled as he wheeled the empty trolley back towards the station entrance.

Pryden climbed up onto the slatted board seat on one side, then Eddie climbed up the other side and sat next to him, taking the reins in his hand.

The journey was uneventful. A local greengrocer shouted abuse on recognising the horse, having been in dispute with MUJ for many years over the matter of his squeezing the fruit but never buying any; the ironmonger ran alongside the trap at one stage, long enough to thrust a parcel of dried fish (addressed to Eddie's father) into his hand – fish with which MUJ had paid for various items in the recent past, for which Mr Dickens would substitute real money by return of post – and a few members of the local hunt (some still in bandages) raised a fist as Eddie and his passenger passed *The Pickled Trout* (a local ale house). A. C. Pryden looked more puzzled than put out, and was too polite to say anything.

The ride up the gravel drive was a long one and, every once in a while, through gaps in the foliage, or across the lawn, Pryden would catch a glimpse of children beating each other with what appeared to be cucumbers.

'They're actors,' Eddie explained hurriedly. 'They're rehearsing the role of orphans escaping from a truly horrible orphanage.'

'I see,' said Pryden. What Eddie didn't add was that – as both you know and I know – most of the actors playing the escaping orphans really were escaped orphans. He wasn't sure what the law's opinion on the matter would be, or what Mr Pryden's opinion of the law was. 'And what play, pray, is that?'

'It doesn't have a title as yet,' Eddie explained. 'My father wrote it.'

'Most interesting,' said the painter, in just the way that a penguin would, no doubt, have said 'most interesting' if penguins could say 'most interesting'.

For those of you who find such details add flavour, I should say that the 'cucumbers' were, in reality, another fine example of Fabian's recently discovered prop-making skills. They were made from painted rolled-up newspaper. As for why the children were hitting each other when, during their actual escape they were hitting – or intending to hit – their captors, this was down to youthful exuberance and the fact that Mr and Mrs Pumblesnook were off somewhere doing whatever it was she did with the blotches she peeled from her visage (*aka* her face). Whilst their backs were turned, the young actors and actresses were letting off steam.

Mrs Dickens was standing at the entrance to the house, there to greet the well-known painter on his arrival. 'Welcome to Awful End,' she said. What A. C. Pryden heard was '*Wcowm oo Awwel En*' because Eddie's mother had stuffed her mouth with gravel from the drive, pieces of which were now falling from her lips. At that moment, Dawkins, Mr Dickens's gentleman's gentleman, arrived with a silver salver, in the middle of which rested a schooner of sherry.

'Some refreshment after your long journey, sir?' he asked, proffering Pryden the drink.

'Thank you,' said Even Madder Aunt Maud, snatching the glass as she appeared around the corner. She downed the sherry in one, then tossed the empty glass over her shoulder. Eddie could have sworn he'd heard a muffled 'Ouch'.

A. C. Pryden may well have wished that he could have clambered back onto the trap and caught the next train out of there, but the commission was an important one. If the War Office wanted him to paint a war hero, then a war hero he would paint . . . at least he thought he would. He had no idea of Mad Uncle Jack's appalling military record.

Two of MUJ's ex-privates helped unload Pryden's luggage, carrying most of it to the room which had been set aside as his studio. The rest was taken to his bedroom (except for one small case which never made it to either, and was found years later with the single addition of a mummified mouse which, in its pre-mummified state, had somehow found its way inside it but, sadly, not its way out again). Eddie's mother hurried off to the kitchen to prepare lunch.

'I should like to see my subject as soon as possible,' Mr Pryden told Eddie, 'even if only to watch him from afar . . . to get the measure of the man.'

'Subject?' snorted Even Madder Aunt Maud, who was now leading Annabelle on her silver chain up the porch steps. The baby crocodile had short legs so more slithered forward on her belly than climbed each individual step. 'You're not a king are you?'

'Mr Pryden means the subject of his painting, Mad Aunt Maud,' Eddie quickly explained. 'Not a royal subject.'

'Aha! My beloved Jack, you mean?' she asked,

stopping in the open doorway.

'If you are the wife of Major Jack Dickens, madam, then yes,' said the painter. Then, after a pause, he added. 'Is that a – er – crocodile?'

Even Madder Aunt Maud looked at Malcolm, tucked neatly under one arm. 'Don't be so utterly ridiculous!' she exclaimed. 'He's a stoat. A stuffed stoat! Call yourself a painter, and you can't even tell a mammal from a reptile.'

'He was referring to Annabelle, EMAM!' said Eddie, who was still at an age when he felt he had to compensate for his relatives if not actually apologise for them. Annabelle was busy pulling on her silver lead. She wanted to get inside the house.

'Oh *her*,' said his great-aunt. 'Yes, Mr Pringle, she is most definitely a crocodile. How observant.'

'Pryden.'

'I beg your pardon?'

'Pryden.'

'Pardon me?'

'You said Pringle.'

'I said pardon,' frowned Even Madder Aunt Maud.

'Prior to pardon you said Pringle.'

'What of it, Mr Pringle?'

'My name is Pryden.'

'Mine is Maud. Maud Dickens, Mr Pryden Pringle.'

431

Anyone who knew Even Madder Aunt Maud would have given up at this stage. Sadly, A. C. Pryden did not (know her, nor give up).

'Mrs Dickens, it is plain Pryden!' he said, as emphatically as someone who sounded like a penguin could be emphatic.

'Plain Pryden Pringle? Is there a hyphen in there, somewhere, sir? And why do you want to measure my husband? If his height's so important, can't you simply draw around him?'

At that precise moment, Dawkins reappeared wearing a striped apron and brandishing a dustpan and brush. He began sweeping up the tiny shards of broken sherry glass in the hall.

Eddie seized the opportunity to grab the grateful Mr Pryden by the hand and through the front door into the house.

'Let me show you to your room, sir,' he said.

'Th-thank you,' said the great portrait painter, still recovering from the shock of his first encounter with Even Madder Aunt Maud.

Most (normal) people who met EMAM went through a variety of different overlapping stages. Stage One was Confusion. Believing themselves to be speaking to someone quite sane, they would try to understand what was being said and wondered whether it was *they*, not she, who wasn't making sense. Stage Two was Realisation. This was the stage when people began to realise that Even Madder Aunt Maud didn't have all her marbles/was more than one sandwich short of a picnic/that the lights may be on but that there was no one at home/that she was battier than a belfry . . . and so on and so on. Stage Three was Exasperation. This was the period when people thought, somewhat foolishly in my opinion, that if only they spoke firmly enough and clearly enough, they might somehow 'get through' to Even Madder Aunt Maud and make her see sense. (I feel that this might be better known as the 'Pull The Other One' Stage or even the 'You've Got To Be Kidding' Stage.) Stage Four was Denial: this can't really be happening to me. Surely no one's really as crazy as this old bat seems to be?!?

Of course, not everyone went through all these different stages when dealing with EMAM, nor necessarily in the same order, but that was certainly the common pattern and, nine times out of ten, the final stage – Stage Five, in this instance – was Attempted Flight. In other words, trying to put as much distance between themselves and Even Madder Aunt Maud as possible.

I've no doubt that, despite his excellent upbringing, A. C. Pryden would have found a way of separating himself from EMAM sooner or later, but the fact that Master Eddie Dickens had rescued him, gave him a respect and liking for the boy; a respect which was to grow as he found out just how bonkers the rest of the Dickens family were, even the very subject of his painting, Major Jack Dickens.

A. C. Pryden and MUJ met for the first time that evening. Somewhat unusually, Mad Uncle Jack was brandishing a home-made spear, or harpoon, made from a two-tined (pronged) carving fork bound to the end of a broom handle. He wore no clothes except for a loin cloth made from old copies of *The Times* newspaper, and had smeared his face, arms and torso with lines of soot.

'Good evening, Major,' said Pryden, leaping up from his chair and extending his hand in greeting. 'It is a pleasure to meet you.' He hoped that he hadn't looked too startled when he'd first caught sight of Jack Dickens walking through the door. 'Are you fresh from rehearsals?'

'Rehearsals?'

'The play. Your great-nephew Edmund informed me that his father had written a play and –'

'What on Earth gave you the idea that I might be a party to such theatricals?' Mad Uncle Jack demanded.

Silent alarm bells rang in Pryden's mind. It had suddenly dawned on him that Major Dickens was probably as barmy as his good lady wife but, despite this, he thought he should explain. 'Your costume, sir. Your –'

'Costume? What costume?' asked a genuinely confused MUJ.

Oh, Lord! thought the painter. What if he dresses like this all the time? He cleared his throat, making a sound not at all dissimilar to how a penguin might sound clearing *his* throat. 'I was referring to the – er – body painting and the – er – home-made spear, Major,' he explained. 'It's not often one sees someone dressed in such a manner. A once in a lifetime experience, I should say.' He smiled weakly (which doesn't mean once every seven days, but in a weak fashion).

At that precise moment, as if on cue, a very small man entered the room. He was brandishing a home-made spear, or harpoon, made from a two-tined (pronged) carving fork bound to the end of a broom handle. He wore no clothes except for a loin cloth made from old copies of *The Times* newspaper, and had smeared his face, arms and torso with lines of soot. It was Gherkin. Polite or not, A. C. Pryden, RA,* sat back down again, gripping the arms of his chair.

* RA means Royal Academician (a member of the Royal Academy), though some painters unlucky enough not to achieve such an honour have claimed that it actually stands for Rotten Artist.

'Aha!' said Mad Uncle Jack. 'See what you mean. Should explain. This fine chap here –' He slapped the dwarf on the back '– is Gherkin. Want him in the picture with me.'

'Is he a Pygmy?' asked Pryden politely, having read about tribes of small people. 'Is this his – er – traditional dress?'

'No, Mr Pryden,' Gherkin replied, perfectly able to speak for himself. 'I am, first and foremost, an Englishman.'

'And a dwarf,' MUJ added.

'Apologies,' said Pryden. 'And you want him in the – er – painting with you, you say, Major?'

'I thought it might liven things up a little. I imagine that the walls of the War Office are lined with row after row of portraits of chaps in uniform, so why not wear something different?'

'And what exactly are you dressed *as*, if you don't mind my asking?'

'An abory-jine,' said MUJ. 'Saw a picture of one in a book sent over from Australia. They're the native people. Apparently the place is crawling with them –'

'Ah. An aborigine!' nodded Pryden, trying to find the words to tell Major Dickens what he'd have to tell him next.

'That's the fellow. I should add that, believe it or not, these aren't actually authentic aborigine clothing or weapons.' He pointed to his newspaper loin cloth and broom-handle-and-carving-fork spear. 'But close approximations, made by our own fair hands.'

'Precisely,' said Gherkin. 'We don't for one minute believe a genuine aborigine would wear *The Times*.'

'Probably can't get it over there,' nodded MUJ. 'Must use the Australian equivalent.'

A. C. Pryden wanted to cry.

Intermission

There now follows a brief intermission[*] *

Hello, again. How embarrassing. I was about to make myself a cup of tea in this strange kitchen, when it suddenly occurred to me that some of you may have been wondering whatever happened to Harry and Thunk.

* PLEASE NOTE: This picture of the author dressed as a chicken bears no relation to the text. Because this is an unauthorised intermission – neither sanctioned by the publishers, nor appearing in the index – no money has been allocated for an accompanying illustration. It was half-inched** by the author from *Horrendous Habits*, when somebody's back was turned.

** Half-inched = pinched = stolen

There they were right at the start of things, so early on in the book, in fact, that the page they're on isn't even numbered – it was the piece entitled 'Prologue', if you skipped it – and we haven't had so much as a peep out of them since.

Well, I can soon put that right. (I'm the author, which in Eddie's world is a bit like being a god, only the hours are shorter and you still have to worry about a pension for your old age.)

Before I do that, and before anyone decides to write and ask me about it, I should explain what I mean by 'strange kitchen'. Firstly, it is simply strange as in *unfamiliar* because this isn't my house and I don't know where everything is. Preparing every beverage, snack, or meal is a learning curve. Secondly, it's strange as in *peculiar* because if you lift one of the work surfaces it reveals a bath. *The* bath. And I just can't get my head around the idea of bathing in the kitchen, whether my wife is standing next to me peeling sprouts or not.

And so to Messrs Harry and Thunk.

HARRY: You're late.
THUNK: Sorry, 'arry. I ran into a spot of bother at the *'orse and 'ounds*. Nuffink I couldn't 'andle.
HARRY: I've 'eard from our informant.
THUNK: Our whats, 'arry?

HARRY: Our eyes and ears what was inside the Dickens 'ousehold.

THUNK: Your man inside Awful End?

HARRY: Sssh! Keep your voice down. Yes. That's who I mean. He says that them Dickenses are a bunch of lunatics sittin' on some very valuable items indeed . . . and he's told me the best time to strike.

THUNK: An' will that be soon, 'arry?

HARRY: Real soon, Thunk.

THUNK: So we can stop standing in this ditch?

HARRY: That we can, Thunk.

Now, back to the main action. Enjoy.

Episode 10

State of Play

*In which the portrait is completed
and preparations for the play are well under way*

The news which A. C. Pryden hadn't been looking forward to imparting to Mad Uncle Jack was twofold: firstly, that the War Office had insisted he be painted wearing his full dress (posh occasion) uniform and, secondly, that he – and he alone – would appear in the painting. There was no room for anyone else: even someone as small as Gherkin.

When the artist finally got around to telling MUJ, Eddie's great-uncle seemed decidedly unbothered. His mind had moved on to other things. He was puzzled, for example, by his almost uncontrollable urge to throw Mr Pryden one of his dried fish, even expecting him to swallow it whole. 'It was the damnedest thing,' he later commented to Eddie's mother.

Much to everyone's amazement, the actual sittings – when MUJ sat and Pryden sketched or painted – went surprisingly well. Mad Uncle Jack didn't need to be in front of the portrait all the time whilst the artist was painting. Pryden would carry on working on it between sittings, making any tiny alterations and corrections with the stroke of a brush or the scrape of a palette knife at the following sitting. He even grew to rather like the old fellow, but he wouldn't let him see the oil painting before it was completed. No one could. (It rested on his easel, hidden by a curtain.) No one except Eddie, that is.

You will recall that A. C. Pryden believed that he'd found an ally in Eddie – a lifeboat of sanity in a sea of madness – and didn't want to lose him. Eddie's Aunt Hetty seemed pleasant enough, but she had a sick husband to tend to, and seemed racked with guilt about something. As for the rest of them – the mad major and his even madder wife aside – they seemed to be wrapped up in putting on this play of theirs, apart from Eddie's mother who was forever filling her mouth with

442

whatever was to hand, which, on her one and only visit to Pryden's makeshift studio, included little tubes of oil paint. Fortunately, he always carried spares.

Then the day came when, much sooner than most of them had expected, the picture was completed.

'Why don't you unveil it on Monday, before the first-night opening of the play, sir?' Eddie suggested when he heard the news. 'You'll have a ready-made audience.'

'Of course, the official unveiling will be at a small ceremony at the War Office itself,' A. C. Pryden reminded him, 'but it would be an excellent opportunity to show it to the Major, his family and friends. A capital idea, Edmund!'

Eddie's father was less than pleased. 'That's supposed to be *my* night, Eddie,' he said. '*Our* night. Mine because I wrote it. Yours because the play is all about your life –'

'Well, a version of it, father –'

'*And* you play the leading role on stage. Having A. C. Pryden unveil his picture of your great-uncle would . . . well, would steal your limelight.' (The especially bright light at the front of stages used to be created by burning lime, which is where the phrase comes from, if you were wondering.)

'It makes perfect sense, father,' said Eddie. 'After all, Mad Uncle Jack has been a big part of my life since I first headed for Awful End.'

The orphan girl playing Even Madder Aunt Maud happened to be waddling by at that moment. She hit Eddie over the head with her papier-mâché Malcolm. 'Drink more milk!' she snapped, stomping off. This particular aspect of acting is called 'staying in character'.

'She's very good, isn't she?' said Mr Dickens.

'Very,' agreed Eddie, rubbing the top of his head. If the truth be told, one of Eddie's greatest fears regarding the whole play was how MUJ and EMAM would react. Would they be outraged? It wasn't that his father had written anything particularly outrageous about them, it was just that they were inclined to take offence at the slightest thing . . .

. . . and if they *were* outraged, how would they express it? He wasn't worried about shouts from the audience, or one of them stomping off in disgust, though he'd far rather they loved every minute of it, of course, and showered him with accolades.* No, what bothered him was that they might storm the stage and take matters into their own hands.

* a type of champagne**
** a terrible lie

When Eddie raised the matter with the actor-manager-director-cum-just-about-everything-else, Mr Pumblesnook, he simply chuckled and said, 'The whole *raison d'être* behind acting is to stimulate an emotional response from your audience, me boy! Joy . . . sadness . . . anger . . . rage. All is fuel for the actor's craft!'

'I'm thinking more about actors getting hurt. Being hit with Malcolm is no joke –'

Mr Pumblesnook grinned, to reveal a chipped tooth. 'You're forgetting that I too have been a victim of the stoat's scorn,' he boomed. 'But when in character, a good actor must simply overcome such distractions.'

'But –'

'I remember being horse-whipped by an agent of the Shah of Persia who leapt up onto the stage during *Turban Trysts* in Greenwich back in '56. If anything, it made my performance all the more riveting. As he was dragged from the stage, rest assured that all eyes remained on me. I had that audience under my spell, and it would take more than a few tattered clothes and a few dozen, painful lashes to put me off my stride!' he said. 'It was only a matter of weeks before the welts stopped bleeding and the pain subsided.'

If Mr Pumblesnook was trying to reassure Eddie, he probably wasn't going the best way about it.

Eddie now had the image of Even Madder Aunt
Maud with a horse whip in her hand, and it wasn't
a pretty sight.

'Then there was the time that a minor member
of royalty attempted to drown me during my cameo
performance in the second act of *Storm in a Teacup*.
I had just –'

Eddie stopped listening after that. He was
beginning to wonder whether he could get away
with wearing cushion padding under his clothes
on the night, without anyone noticing. (Ex-Private
Drabb had done much the same when he was most
recently 'volunteered' by his colleagues to take
part in the beating of the bounds of the Awful End
estate. In Drabb's case, it made the wizened old
man look impressively muscly.)

As it was, it would turn out that his great-aunt's and uncle's reaction was one of the least of his worries on the play's opening night.

*

See that last sentence? I suspect there's a technical term for such sentences in creative-writing course circles. If not, there jolly well should be. It's one of those sentences hinting at what's to come. It's also a way of saying to the reader, 'I know that there ain't much happening at the moment and it might be more fun spending a few minutes going through your old toenail clippings collection, but trust me: things really are going to liven up eventually'. . . which means that such sentences might be seen as being a bit of a cheat.

Rather than saying 'hang on in there', wouldn't it be better for an author to make every page so interesting that they don't have to resort to whetting the appetite with promises? (Whetting – with an 'h' – refers to sharpening the appetite, here, and has nothing to do with slobbering.)

On the other hand, such sentences can make you, the reader, reassess what you've just read. Take the shopping list currently attached to the fridge door (by a magnet shaped like a sticking plaster) in this house. It must have been left here by the owner.

Here's what it says:

447

Milk (full fat)
Doughnuts (chocolate)
Carrots (large sack)
Baked Beans (4-pack)
Chocolate biscuits (plain)

Now, what if I was to tell you that what makes this *particular* shopping list so interesting is that one of these items has been poisoned . . ?

Aha! Not such a boring list after all now, is it? Well, it is, the truth be told, but at least you might be wondering which the poisonous item is . . . and whether it was deliberately poisoned . . . and, if so, who the intended victim was.

Or what if I told you the person who wrote it was supposed to be on a diet? Now all that chocolate is telling a different story . . . or if the person who wrote it was having a rabbit to stay, or conducting experiments about trying to see in the dark which might – in both instances – explain the carrots . . . and how come the list is still here?

So maybe my *As-it-was-it-would-turn-out-that-his-great-aunt's-and-uncle's-reaction-was-one-of-the-least-of-his-worries-on-the-play's-opening-night* line is part of a worthy tradition and doesn't deserve such contempt after all. I'll let you decide.

It's just that I didn't want to try to sneak it in under the radar.

My conscience is clear.

★

In the weeks that Eddie had been rehearsing, rehearsing, rehearsing, and watching A. C. Pryden's portrait of Mad Uncle Jack turn from a few lines on an otherwise blank canvas into a startlingly lifelike representation of his great uncle, his cousin Fabian had become a very skilled props assistant. Bless Him – sorry, it's that nickname again, of course his real name was Mr Blessing – had never really had a title before but, now that he had an assistant, things changed. He became 'Props Master'.

It wasn't only Fabian's job to make some of the props – which included coming up with ideas on what to use and how to construct them – but he also had to help source props that didn't need making. For example, one day Bless Him gave him the job of trying to create the impression that there was a hot-air balloon on stage. (Mr Pumblesnook was to play the role of Woolf Tablet, the famous photographer, in whose balloon various members of the Dickens family, accompanied by a private detective – also played by Pumblesnook – had chased Eddie's kidnapper, driving a stolen hearse across the moors below.) Creating the basket of the balloon had been straightforward enough. Fabian 'borrowed' the self-same laundry basket that Dawkins had previously been trapped in. The envelope – the actual balloony part of the balloon – was a lot harder to solve and it was whilst Fabian was searching the warren of rooms in Awful End for inspiration that he saw a chandelier and realised that he could use one of the crystal baubles as a prop for the Dog's Bone Diamond.

As Fabian was crossing the driveway to the stable block, which housed the props' store, he encountered EMAM and Mad Uncle Jack walking hand in hand. Annabelle was trotting behind them – or, at least, doing as passable an attempt at trotting as a little crocodile could – delicately holding poor Malcolm between her jaws. (Think of a faithful dog carrying a newspaper.)

'What's that you've got there, Edmund?' demanded Even Madder Aunt Maud, looking at the bauble in his hand.

'Fabian,' he corrected her.

'Don't lie to your great-aunt,' snapped Mad Uncle Jack. 'That's far too small to be Fabian.'

'Oh, this? This is from one of the chandeliers, Mad Aunt Maud –' began Fabian, breaking off as he saw an extraordinary glint appear in EMAM's eye.

'Shiny,' she said, elongating the word so that it came out as: 'Shiiiiiiiiiiiiiiiiineeeeeeeeeeeeeeee!' She reached out to try to touch the cut crystal.

Mad Uncle Jack grabbed her wrist. 'Go and put that thing away at once! You know full well that your great-aunt suffers from picanosis.'

Of course, Fabian *didn't* know full well that Even Madder Aunt Maud suffered from picanosis because he was Fabian, not Eddie . . . and, equally importantly, he had no idea what picanosis was either.

Because I've been unable to find any contemporary medical reference to such an ailment, I can only guess at what it was supposed to be. It's a pretty educated guess, though. Firstly, as any reader of *Terrible Times* will know, Even Madder Aunt Maud had a strange attraction to shiny things (a polished shell case and a fabulously expensive diamond, to name but two). Secondly, there are a few birds with reputations for collecting shiny things, too, including jackdaws and magpies. And the Latin name for magpie is *Pica pica*. And, thirdly, the word-ending nosis comes from the Greek *nosos*, meaning disease. See where I'm heading? I think it's a pretty safe bet that – whether made up or not by the doctor who originally diagnosed her with it – picanosis must be a form of magpie-disease or shiny-nosis.

Fabian slipped the bauble in his pocket, wished his great-aunt and great-uncle a pleasant day and hurried on his way.

Inside the stable, he expected to find Bless Him hard at work with a pot of glue or a hammer and nails turning something into something else that would look good from where the audience was sitting. Instead, he found him wrestling with a chimney-sweep.

An Old Acquaintance

*In which Eddie dodges punches
and low-flying vegetables*

Traditionally, chimney-sweeps are considered good luck, though I'm not sure why that should be. It can't have been much fun being a chimney sweep in Victorian England, particularly if you were a child, seeing as how you were often sent up the actual chimney. The description 'sooty' doesn't do justice to the state these poor boys ended up in. But lucky they were considered to be, if you followed certain rituals. According to *Old Roxbee's Book of Etiquette & Folklore*, if you came across a sweep – and he had to be in his working clothes and good 'n' dirty, or it didn't count – you had to raise your hat, or bow, or call out a cheery greeting, or (if you were of the female persuasion) curtsey.

Eddie Dickens didn't feel inclined to do any of these when he caught sight of this particular sweep, who tumbled out of the stable block, in a mass of tangled arms and legs which seemed to include his cousin Fabian and the props man.

There was much shouting and grunting, and the occasional punch was thrown by all three parties. Eddie quickly deduced that Fabian and Bless Him were on the same side, in a united front against the sweep – not that all the blows reached their intended target – so decided he should go to their aid. Three against one is always better than two against one, as the old saying goes. (Not *fairer*, just better if you're trying to win.)

Eddie launched into the melee and somehow managed to grab the sweep's collar which came off in his hand. It wasn't that he'd ripped the shirt, it was just that many more people wore detachable collars back then.

With Eddie now having entered the fray, the chimney-sweep admitted defeat. He simply stopped struggling and slumped, dead-weight, to the ground. 'I surrender,' he groaned.

'What did he do?' Eddie asked Fabian, helping his cousin to his feet.

Fabian shrugged. 'To tell you the truth, I don't know,' he admitted.

'Then why were you fighting him?'

'Why were *you* fighting him?' Fabian asked Eddie in return.

'Well – er – because you were. I thought you could do with some help!'

'Well, I was helping him,' said Fabian, indicating Mr Blessing, who was yanking the chimney-sweep to his feet.

I don't want you to be under the impression that the sweep was a boy. Far from it. (Look at the picture on page 453). Though younger than the white-haired Props Master, he was old enough to be Eddie's father and then some. He was also very large. Not large in the same way that the detective (now chief-) inspector was large before his unintended diet, which was on the fat side of fat. Nor large in the sense that an escaped convict by the name of Bonecrusher – whom Eddie had once had the misfortune to meet – was large, which was on the great-big-wall-of-muscle side of large. The sweep was large-framed and stocky. Which is why it had taken three of them to calm him.

It also meant that if he didn't want to be yanked to his feet he could probably have made sure that he wasn't, but he didn't put up any resistance.

'What's going on, Mister B?' Eddie asked Bless Him.

'I found him tampering with some of the equipment,' said the Props Master, 'and when I confronted him, he came at me.'

'I did nuffink of the sort,' the sweep protested. 'I was lookin' that's all, an' you startled me.'

'A likely story!' said Bless Him who, like Eddie and Fabian, had become smeared with soot following their brief skirmish.

'Look,' said the hulk of a man. 'If I 'ave something to 'ide, why haven't I legged it outa 'ere? It ain't likes you three could stop me.'

'True,' said Eddie and Fabian, not only simultaneously but also at the same time.

'So what are you doing here, Mister –?'

'Scarple,' said Mr Scarple.

The name sounded very familiar to Eddie, though he couldn't quite place it. 'So what brings you to Awful End, Mr Scarple? I know it's not to clean chimneys. My great-uncle has his ex-privates to do that for him.'

'I'm 'ere to meet an old acquaintance, and to send greetin's from my daughter to another,' said the sweep. 'One of you lads ain't by any chance Master Edmund? Daniella never said there was two of yous.'

'Daniella!' said Eddie in amazement. Of course! That's where Eddie had heard the name Scarple before. The lovely Daniella Scarple had been the assistant to the escapologist the Great Zucchini! Despite bearing more than a passing resemblance to a horse and treating Eddie as though he were an idiot – not surprisingly, because at the outset he had become a mumbling, dribbling buffoon in her presence – Eddie had taken quite a shine to her. 'You're Daniella's father?'

The sweep put out his hand. 'I most certainly am. So you're Edmund. My daughter laughs about you still, and sends 'er best regards.'

'Is she nearby?'

Scarple shook his head. ''Er an' that man Zucchini is currently in Paris, entertainin' the crowned 'eads of Europe, or so she'd 'ave us believe.'

'A pity,' said Eddie. 'It'd have been good to see her again . . . What were you, in fact, doing when Mr Blessing came in on you?'

'Daniella 'ad told me 'ows you'd first met Zucchini in a coffin in this 'ere stable block, so I took the liberty of 'aving a quick look round before presentin' meself at the 'ouse –'

'If that's true,' said Bless Him, 'why were you tampering with the mechanism of that dagger?' One of the props which had been in the possession of Mr Pumblesnook's band of wandering theatricals for many a year was a spring-loaded dagger. When pressed against an actor, the blade retracted into the handle, giving the impression that it was sinking into the victim's flesh. If anyone was to cause the blade to jam, it could give someone a nasty injury.

'I weren't tamperin',' Scarple protested. 'Just lookin', I assures you.'

'And who's the old acquaintance?' asked Fabian, who'd been busy trying to brush the soot off his clothes.

'Beg pardon?'

'You said that you were here to see an old acquaintance.'

'Oh, 'im. I'm 'ere to see a certain Gherkin. I'm sure you knows who I mean, if you've met 'im.'

'You know Gherkin!' Eddie smiled. 'It certainly is a small world.'

'It's just that I do weddin's and 'e used to do funerals. Our paths would sometimes cross in churchyards.'

'Weddings?' frowned Eddie.

'Most certainly, Master Edmund. It's considered good luck to 'ave a sweep outside the church at ya weddin'. I not only gets an 'andshake from the groom 'an a kiss from the bride but, most important of all, some money for me troubles. It's what Gherkin would describe as a lucrative sideline.'

'Do we believe him, Master Eddie?' asked Bless Him, who would defer to a Dickens on the matter, but didn't want to ask Fabian because Fabian was supposed to be working under him.

'If Gherkin can vouch for Mr Scarple, then everything's fine by me . . . Forgive our less than friendly welcome, Mr Scarple.'

'A misundertandin', that's all,' said the sweep. He limped back into the stable block to retrieve his battered top hat from the floor of the props room, where it had fallen at the outbreak of the scuffle. The condition of the hat didn't bother him in the slightest. It had been second- or third-hand when he'd first acquired it, and had been battered even then.

Fabian went back to work on the props with Bless Him, whilst Eddie led the limping chimney-sweep to the summerhouse which had become Gherkin's home since the day he'd arrived. Back in the days of Dr Malcontent Dickens, the summerhouse had been furnished with kiddie-sized tables and chairs for his three young sons. Even the shelving and door handles were at a lower height, which made it the ideal bedroom and sitting room for the dwarf, who still took his meals and bathed in the main house (though not at the same time).

Eddie and Scarple found Gherkin reading a book.

'Harry!' said Gherkin, obviously delighted to see him.

STOP. Wait a minute. Before I type another line, I should make it absolutely clear that Harry Scarple was not – I repeat NOT – the Harry (aka 'arry) in the Prologue and the (illegal) intermission on pages 438, 439 and 440. In books and films it's quite rare for characters to have the same name – probably to avoid confusion – but in real life, it's quite a different matter. Glad to be of service.

Gherkin shook Scarple's hand warmly. 'What brings you to this neck of the woods?' he asked.

'I've been cleaning them chimneys over at Lamberley 'all. Old Jim Langham who used to do them is now Jim long-gone, an' the job's been passed on to me.'

'Old Jim's loss is your gain,' said Gherkin.

'I raised a pint of thrupenny gargle* to his memory,' said the sweep. 'It's good to see you, Gherkin. I 'eard you was workin' for Mad Mr Dickens now, and Master Eddie is an ol' friend of me daughter, Daniella, so I thought I'd kill two birds with one stone by payin' a visit to Awful End.'

Gherkin turned to Eddie, eyebrow raised. 'You know Daniella?'

Eddie nodded. 'It's a long story,' he said.

'I would very much like to hear it sometime,' said Gherkin.

'I'd be delighted to tell you,' said Eddie.

'By all accounts, it were quite an adventure,' said Daniella's father.

'Where are my manners? Sit down! Sit down!' urged Gherkin.

There was only one adult-sized chair, and Scarple lowered himself into it, left leg stuck out stiffly.

* a particularly strong and unpleasant-tasting drink

Eddie perched himself on the edge of a small table. 'Were you injured during our fight?' he asked with concern.

'Fight?' asked the dwarf.

'A misunderstanding, is all,' Scarple explained quickly. 'No, Eddie. I've been a chimney-sweep man and boy and 'ave sustained more injuries than is good for any of God's creatures.'

Once again, Eddie was reminded what a sheltered life he led as a child of the upper classes ... or *would* have led if he hadn't kept on finding himself the centre of some extraordinary events. Things had been remarkably peaceful these past few months.

His thoughts were interrupted by a distant dull thud, followed by a dreadful 'CRASH!' as something the size of a cannonball came hurtling through the closed door of the summerhouse, glass shattering and wood splintering in its wake.

Eddie and Gherkin threw themselves to the ground in an instant. Scarple was less speedy but fortunately the projectile missed him by a stoat's whisker and hit the back wall of the summerhouse with enough force to cause the pictures to shake on all the walls.

'We're under attack!' said Scarple in amazement. He struggled to his feet and joined the other two on the floor.

'What on Earth –?' said Gherkin.

'It could be nothing to worry about,' said Eddie.

'Nuffink to worry about? I coulda been killed!' protested Scarple.

'I mean that we may not be under attack, Mr Scarple,' said Eddie. 'It could simply be another of my great-uncle or great-aunt's harebrained schemes. There could be a perfectly – er – simple explanation.'

A second or so later, there was another distant thud, and another projectile came into view, heading in the direction of the summerhouse.

'Heads down!' shouted the dwarf, putting his head in his hands and rolling himself into a ball.

This time, the object landed on the grass just short of the summerhouse.

Eddie got into a crouching position and made it over to the shattered door. He peered outside. 'It appears to be a cabbage.'

'A cabbage?'

'A cabbage,' said Eddie.

'Someone is firing cabbages at us?' asked Harry Scarple.

'It would appear so,' said Eddie.

The chimney-sweep stood up and retrieved the projectile which had caused so much damage. 'Yup, this one is certainly a cabbage too.'

'Keep down, Scarple!' said Gherkin. 'A cabbage

fired at this speed could still take your head off.'
Gherkin wasn't wrong. A candle fired from a
shotgun can pass through a wooden door, so why
not fire a cabbage from a cannon or a giant catapult
. . . apart from the fact that it would be a ridiculous
thing to do, of course.

'I suggest we retreat!' says Gherkin, 'But keep
low!'

Gingerly trying to avoid the shards of broken
glass scattered across the floor, the three of them
pushed open one of the tattered doors and dashed,
still crouching, across a stretch of lawn into the
cover of a nearby shrubbery. The third cabbage
came smashing into the summerhouse moments
later.

Episode 12

A Blast from the Past

*In which matters turn from worse
to even worse, which can't be good*

Eddie didn't waste any time. Whilst Scarple and Gherkin were still recovering from the shock of it all, he was skirting through the undergrowth, heading in the direction from which the cabbages had been fired, as fast as his legs could carry him. He tripped once, having caught his foot in a tree root, and scraped his skin against some particularly spiky leaves of some foreign specimen, but this barely slowed him down.

When Eddie broke his cover, bursting from the undergrowth onto the upper lawn, he didn't know what to find. He could be forgiven for thinking that MUJ or EMAM might have been behind the firing of cabbages at the summerhouse. If any of the household were going to undertake such an action, it was more than likely to be them; or some of the ex-privates following their instructions. But it wasn't.

With preparations for the play under way, it had also crossed Eddie's mind that the sudden onslaught of low-flying cabbages might be the testing of a prop which had somehow gone wrong. Eddie's father, Mr Dickens, had, as you may recall, included a few scenes set aboard *The Pompous Pig*. You may also recall my telling you that he embellished the truth in places (which is another way of saying he made things up). Although there were no cannons aboard the vessel, Laudanum Dickens had the character of first mate, Mr Briggs, firing one at the fleeing Swags. So, again, it might be reasonable to suppose that it was Bless Him or Fabian or someone testing such a cannon, either real or home-made. But it wasn't.

There before him was indeed the props cannon – which had been delivered *after* the Dickenses had repelled Stinky Hoarebacker's hunt, or it might well have been pressed into service by the defending army – but the person busy loading another cabbage into the menacing barrel was a stranger to Eddie.

Eddie had hoped the commotion might have brought others to the scene because he wasn't yet

466

sure whether he was about to deal with someone who was firing vegetables for a bit of fun, unaware of the damage and endangerment to human life . . . or whether this small round man was intent on serious harm.

'STOP!' shouted Eddie running towards the man.

The man did nothing of the sort. Cabbage now loaded, he began fiddling with what Eddie knew to be the fuse. The man tried unsuccessfully to suppress a worrying giggle. The resulting sound was even more worrying.

'There are people down there!' shouted Eddie, pointing in the direction he'd just come. 'You might kill someone!'

'HA!' shouted the man. 'HA! I say. HA! to you and HA! to them. HA! I say!'

'Help!' shouted Eddie. 'Somebody! Anybody!' He had once been told that the best way to attract people's attention when you needed help was to shout 'Fire!'. But he wasn't about to risk this when standing by a man with a cannon. 'Help!' shouted Eddie. 'Father! Dawkins! Uncle Jack! Anyone!' He waved his arms around frantically.

As well as genuinely seeking assistance, Eddie was also trying to let the rotund stranger know that there were plenty of people about, and to disorient him with noise and movement.

What should I do? What should I do? thought Eddie. So long as I'm not standing in front of the cannon, I should be safe. Should I jump on him? Tackle him? Although Eddie was as sure as he could be that he'd never met the man before, there was something strangely familiar about this stranger. He reminded Eddie of someone . . . or something. That was it! Of course!

'Peevance!' shouted Eddie. 'Is that you?'

The man was clearly startled. He hesitated and, in that moment, skinny saucer-eyed Eddie bravely launched himself at the man –

– and let's leave him there in mid-air for a moment whilst I remind those who've read *Dubious Deeds* and tell those who haven't, who and what Peevance was. Lance Peevance was originally the name of a man (a hard-working schoolteacher, in fact) whom Mad Uncle Jack had spotted in town on a number of occasions. Mr Peevance was rather round and knobbly and, to most eyes, an unfortunately ugly man. Later, Lance Peevance also became the name of a hybrid vegetable which looked like a very large, knobbly pea. Mad Uncle Jack had been the creator of said vegetable and had also been the one to name it. The instant it grew, it reminded MUJ so strongly of the teacher, that he went to the trouble of finding out the man's identity, and named his creation after him. Mr Peevance was far from happy about this and, very foolishly, took Mad Uncle Jack to court over the matter. I say foolishly because not only was MUJ a gentleman and Peevance was not, but MUJ also lived up at the big house, which meant that no local court would dare find him guilty of anything. Technically, of course, Lamberley Hall was the really big house in those parts, but it was built with 'new money' and its occupants were a couple of sisters*, and women really didn't count in the same way.

The outcome was that the human Lance Peevance was crippled by costs and fled to the Continent.** He was eventually caught in France and brought back to England, a debtor and a ruined man.

The vegetables retained his name and Mad Uncle Jack still grew them once in a while. Eddie had heard the story and seen the vegetables many times, which was how he finally recognised the man, at whom he now launched himself –

– and, sadly, missed, landing winded on the grass beside him. The cannon fired for a fourth time and, what had been a distant thud to him on the three previous occasions was much more of a loud 'WUMPH!' close to, though certainly not a bang.

---

* the Andrews sisters with a small 's', of course
** disguised as a bag of coal, somewhat surprisingly

The man started kicking Eddie as he lay there which is as horrible as it sounds. Eddie had always felt rather sorry for the schoolteacher whenever he had heard the story. He knew how exasperating his family could be and, on top of that, the poor man had lost his job and home and everything . . . but being kicked by someone can rather change your opinion of them.

As Eddie tried to grab Peevance's leg the next time it took a swing at him, four other pairs of legs came into view. Two of them were decidedly short and green and belonged to Annabelle. The other two pairs belonged to Mad Uncle Jack and Even Madder Aunt Maud.

'Help me!' shouted Eddie. 'It's Lance Peevance!'

'You're mistaken, Edmund,' said Mad Uncle Jack, picking up one of the cabbages stacked next to the cannon. 'It's a common or garden cabbage.'

'No, *him!*' shouted Eddie, who now had the ex-schoolteacher standing on top of him.

'No, I don't know him,' said MUJ. 'And I'm not sure I want to.'

Lance Peevance was eyeing his arch nemesis with such hatred that it looked as if his eyes might actually burst into flames.

Eddie tried to get to his feet, but – without taking his eyes off MUJ for one moment – Peevance trod on him. Hard. 'Help me, Aunt Maud,' Eddie managed.

EMAM slapped Peevance on the back. 'Excellent costume, Mr Pumblesnook,' she said. 'Wonderful make-up!'

'Help me!' rasped Eddie a second time.

'Keeping in character? Good boy, Edmund,' said his great-aunt. 'Mr Pumblesnook has taught you well.'

Eddie felt like throttling her.

It seemed Peevance had similar thoughts regarding Mad Uncle Jack. 'I'm going to kill you, Dickens!' said Peevance, using Eddie as a launch pad to land on MUJ's back, hands around his throat.

MUJ fell to the ground in an angular tangle of jutting-out elbows and knees. He looked like a daddy-long-legs in distress.

Even Madder Aunt Maud was outraged. 'My Jack

471

isn't in your stupid play!' she snapped. She went to beat the man she took to be Mr Pumblesnook with Malcolm . . . but she wasn't carrying him. She looked to Annabelle, and she wasn't carrying him either. Now she wasn't sure what to do. It was obvious from his sticking out tongue and bulging eyes that her dear, sweet Jack didn't particularly like being strangled. And the sudden discovery of the absence of her stuffed stoat caused EMAM such anguish that it completely knocked the wind out of her sails.

Battered and bruised, Eddie struggled to his feet and was about to throw himself on Peevance a second time, when help arrived.

It arrived in the form of Scarple and Gherkin. In next to no time, Scarple was sitting on Mr Peevance, pinning down his arms and legs, whilst Gherkin was tying him up with some bunting.

'Are you all right, Eddie?' asked the chimney-sweep.

'I'll be fine,' said Eddie.

'Who is this madman?' asked Gherkin as he tied another knot.

'My husband, Jack,' said Even Madder Aunt Maud. 'I believe you've already met.'

Gherkin did his eyebrow raising thing again.

'I think you'll find he's a Mr Lance Peevance,' said Eddie. 'He has a grudge against the family.'

'By Jove!' said MUJ. 'You're right! It is that rascal Peevance.' He turned to their captive. 'Aren't you supposed to be in jail?'

Suddenly, there was a cry of 'CHARGE!' and the small gathering found themselves surrounded by members of Mr Pumblesnook's ragtag group of wandering theatricals – including Mr Pumblesnook and his good lady wife, but with the exception of Bless Him and Fabian – each brandishing a weapon of sorts, ranging from newspaper cucumbers to a genuine sword, a table leg and a garden rake. Dawkins was there too, brandishing a rolling pin. Gibbering Jane was also on the scene, brandishing baby Oliphant, who was brandishing his silver rattle. The ex-privates were also in attendance. They all formed a tight circle around the cannon.

Dressed in resplendent uniform, and waving a sabre, Mr Pumblesnook pushed himself to the fore. 'It would seem that you gentlemen have everything under control,' he said.

Better late than never, thought Eddie.

'Apologies for the delay,' said Pumblesnook, 'but I thought it best to be correctly dressed for a rescue of such great importance.'

Eddie had to admit that he did look splendid.

Whilst everyone fussed over Mad Uncle Jack (*I'm fine! Fine! Had worse happen every day when*

I was fighting the Hoolers*'), helped the distraught Even Madder Aunt Maud in her search for Malcolm (*'If anyone's so much as harmed a hair on his beautiful head, they'll have me to answer to!'*) or assisted with the hauling off of poor old Lance Peevance (*'HA! You've not heard the last of me, you Dickenses! No jail cell can hold me!'*), Eddie slipped away. He wanted to nurse his wounds in private.

As he mounted the first few steps of Awful End's main staircase, A. C. Pryden came hurrying down. 'Eddie!' he said. 'Terrible, terrible news. Please follow me,' and he turned and ran up again, two or three stairs at a time.

Eddie followed the artist into his bedroom. In the corner stood a canvas covered by the familiar curtain on the easel. Now that MUJ's portrait had been completed, Pryden kept it in here rather than his makeshift studio downstairs.

'Lift the curtain,' said Pryden.

Eddie obeyed. Underneath was a blank canvas.

'Stolen,' said A. C. Pryden. 'The painting's been stolen!'

* Not some foreign tribe, but former neighbours

474

Eddie on the Case!

*In which Eddie sees some familiar faces
in some unfamiliar places*

'Stolen?' gasped Mr Dickens. 'Are you sure?'

'You didn't – er – hide the painting by any chance, Father, did you?' asked Eddie.

'Surely you're not accusing your father of being a thief?' demanded Mrs Dickens.

'Not at all, mother,' said Eddie hurriedly. 'It's just that I thought you might have – er – put the painting aside until after Monday night's first performance of the play, so that the unveiling of Mad Uncle Jack's portrait didn't –' He tried to remember his father's exact words '– steal our thunder.'

'No, I did not,' said his father indignantly.

'You don't think Jack or Maud could have taken it, do you, Laudanum?' asked Mrs Dickens.

'I do not!' snapped Mr Dickens, in a tone of voice which suggested that he couldn't imagine MUJ or EMAM ever doing something strange like that.

'And they both have an alibi,' said Eddie.

'A laundry basket?' said his mother.

Eddie thought for a moment. 'I think you're thinking of an ali baba, mother,' he said. 'I said alibi. I mean that a number of people can vouch for where they were when Mad Uncle Jack's portrait was swapped for the blank canvas. Including me.'

According to A. C. Pryden, he had knocked the easel when opening the flap in the desk in his room in order to write a letter, and the curtain had fallen from it, revealing the picture beneath. He had replaced the curtain and, finding that he'd run out of writing paper, went downstairs to get some which he'd seen on a writing table in the drawing room. Whilst in the drawing room, he'd looked through the window and witnessed the antics at the bottom of the top lawn, involving Eddie, Peevance and the others. His short time at Awful End had taught him one thing: DON'T GET INVOLVED. He went back upstairs to write his letter. He'd been gone from his room for less than ten minutes.

Just as he was about to sit down at his desk, he noticed something strange – he had an artist's eye for things, remember. The curtain over the painting was the wrong way up. Technically, of course, there was no right way or wrong way. There was no pattern on the curtain, and the hem was the same on all four sides. It was just that the thick material had a pile: brush it in one direction and it lay beautifully flat. Brush against the pile and it stuck up. Pryden always hung the curtain so that the pile could be smoothed downwards. Puzzled, he lifted the curtain. The painting had gone, and the thief's only window of opportunity had been the ten minutes or so that he'd been away from the room.

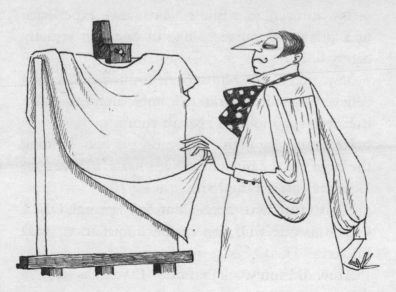

'Has he sent for the police?' asked Eddie's father.

'No,' said Eddie. 'He doesn't want anyone to know yet, father. Not even the police. You must promise not to tell anybody. No one. Both of you, please.'

'My lips are sealed,' Mr Dickens reassured him.

'*Fow aw moy*,' said his mother, which was mouth-full-of-ball bearings for 'so are mine'.

'Thank you,' said Eddie. 'It's just that it's a little – er – embarrassing for him. He doesn't want the War Office to get wind of it until he's exhausted all other avenues. Those were his very words.'

'What does he plan to do, hire a private investigator?' Mr Dickens asked.

'No, not yet,' said Eddie, whose own experience of a private investigator hadn't been an entirely happy one.

Now that Eddie had spoken to his parents, and believed that they genuinely knew nothing about it, he returned to Mr Pryden's room.

He found the artist sitting on his bed, holding the large blank canvas across his lap. He looked up as Eddie entered the room.

'This must have been a carefully planned theft with someone who had inside information,' said Eddie.

'How did you work that out?' Pryden asked.

'The canvas,' said Eddie. 'It's exactly the same size as the painting they replaced under the curtain.'

'Which means that someone must have seen and measured the original and had it made especially!' said the painter, in that penguiny way of his. 'This was no spur of the moment thing. It was carefully plotted –'

'Which means that the whole Mr Peevance firing the cabbages from the cannon could have been *a diversion!*'

'I suppose he could have been a decoy,' said Pryden. He didn't sound convinced.

'But how could they have got him to play his part?' said Eddie. 'I'm afraid Mr Peevance appears to have – er – lost control . . . I seriously doubt he could have been following orders.'

'An unwitting accomplice?' said the painter.

'Does anyone know how he got out of jail, and from the jail to here?' asked Eddie. 'Where did he get those cabbages from? How did he know that there was a cannon here in the first place?'

'We'll never know,' said Pryden.

'You could try asking him,' Eddie suggested.

'How?' asked the painter. 'I thought the peelers had carted him off to the local police station whilst they decide what to do with him next.'

'Exactly,' said Eddie. 'You can speak to him there.'

'The peelers will want to know why, and I really want to keep this our secret –'

'Then we won't ask them,' said Eddie.

★

Eddie was familiar with the cells in the basement of the local constabulary, and knew that each had a little barred window which was at ankle-height with the pavement outside (not that pavements have ankles). Eddie crouched down and looked into the first cell. There was an extremely large woman, smelling of grog – even from where Eddie was – and snoring loudly. He moved on to the next window. This revealed a man dressed as a cleric, playing a game of patience on a rickety table, with home-made cards. (Based on information gleaned from local papers of the time, it seems likely that this was Barnaby Hawthorne, the notorious con artist whose speciality was tricking ladies of a certain age to part with their money. His *modus operandi* was to dress as a clergyman of some description or other, in order to gain their trust more quickly.)

The third cell housed two men, both in handcuffs, sitting glaring at each other from opposite sides of the room. Through the fourth barred window, Eddie saw the back view of the unmistakeable figure of Lance Peevance.

'He's in there,' said Eddie, straightening up.

480

'Good luck.' He and A. C. Pryden had agreed that there was no point in him trying to talk to Peevance. Not only because of their confrontation by the cannon but also because it would now be obvious to the ex-schoolteacher that Eddie was one of the dreaded Dickenses. Pryden would have a far better chance of getting information from the man. 'I'll walk the streets and keep an eye out for peelers.'

'I'm still not sure about this,' said Pryden.

'There's nothing to lose,' Eddie reminded him.

The artist crouched by the window. He stuck his head up against the bars. 'Psssst! Peevance!' he whispered.

Eddie wandered to the corner of the building and looked both ways down the street. He tried to look as casual as possible when the desk sergeant strode purposefully down the steps of the police station and across the road. The policeman entered a small bow-fronted shop named TRUMBLES, emerging soon after with a large paper bag.

When the sergeant recrossed the street, Eddie turned away and pretended to be interested in a horse-drawn open-topped omnibus which was approaching from the opposite direction. His interest became genuine when he saw a familiar face sitting on the top deck: it was Daniella's chimney-sweep father. Then he recognised the man he was talking to.

The bandaged head should have been a clue. It was Doctor 'Moo-Cow' Moot. How curious, thought Eddie. What are Scarple and Moot doing travelling on a bus together? Doctors and chimney sweeps didn't mix in ordinary society except perhaps, as Eddie had so recently learnt, at weddings.

Eddie put his hand in his pocket and pulled out a handful of pennies, ha'pennies and a farthing, which was more than enough for a bus fare. He was tempted to jump on the vehicle as it came to a halt a few yards away, and passengers hopped on and off. The only thing which stopped him was that he was on lookout duty for Mr Pryden.

The desk sergeant now back inside the station – probably behind his beloved desk – and the omnibus now moving off down the street, Eddie went back around the corner to check up on Pryden. There was no sign of him. Eddie hurried down the pavement and glanced through the tiny barred window into the ex-schoolteacher's cell. Peevance was lying face down on the large wooden bench set into the wall below, which was used as a bed. He appeared to be chewing his pillow, or more tearing at it with his teeth. Eddie could hear ripping sounds between Lance Peevance's anguished mutterings, and the odd stray feather fluttered about the cell.

Eddie guessed that A. C. Pryden's conversation

with him hadn't gone too well . . . but where was the artist now? Eddie straightened up and went in search of him, wanting to tell him about the strange sight of a well-to-do doctor in an exclusive practice talking with Scarple, as thick as thieves . . . *Thieves*. Were they somehow involved in the theft of the painting? If so – and if Peevance really had been some kind of a diversion – it can't all have gone to plan. The possibility of Scarple's head being blown off by a cabbage cannonball had been a very real one.

Eddie had been so deep in thought that he almost walked slap-bang into a lamppost and, in avoiding it at the last moment, stepped on the foot of a child hurrying past him.

'I beg your pardon,' said Eddie. The child said nothing, just kept on moving. Eddie turned to watch him go, realising that this was no child after all. Sure, the figure was dressed in a sailor suit and carrying a lollipop almost as big as his head, but Eddie would have recognised the distinctive body shape and spritely walk anywhere. It was Gherkin the dwarf!

Eddie almost called out his name, but stopped himself just in time. It was obvious that the man hadn't wanted to be recognised. With A. C. Pryden nowhere in sight, there was nothing to stop Eddie following someone this time.

Gherkin, outsized lollipop in hand, was now skipping down the street. Despite his ridiculous outfit, Eddie thought it unlikely that anyone looking at his face would be fooled into thinking that he was a child for one minute. It wasn't only a man's face but a fairly *old* man's face at that. Then again, he was way below most adults' eye level, and people didn't generally pay much attention to children. *And* he's probably using that lollipop to hide behind, thought Eddie.

Gherkin passed the police station, the post office and a shop selling everything you ever needed for riding and looking after horses (except, perhaps for stables, which would have been difficult to store out at the back). Taking a quick look from left to right – not noticing Eddie who had positioned himself behind two conveniently large women who were deep in conversation about the merits of a certain type of hat ribbon – he darted down a narrow alley. Eddie waited a moment, then nipped over to the entrance, peered around it and, seeing that the coast was clear, hurried down the alley himself, just in time to see Gherkin disappear through a large door. When Eddie reached it, he could make out faded lettering on the wood. What did it say?

I ATE PROPER Y

'I ate proper y'. *Who* ate proper y? What was proper y anyway? And was there such a thing as *im*proper y, Eddie wondered. Then it occurred to him that it might originally have read 'I ATE PROPERLY', like someone was announcing that they'd eaten a decent meal.

It was then, and only then, that Eddie realised that what the writing must have originally said was: PRIVATE PROPERTY. Feeling the tiniest bit foolish, Eddie gave the door a push. It wouldn't budge. Now what? he wondered.

He would've liked to have dragged an old packing crate under a window and have climbed up on it to take a look inside. The problem was twofold, though: there was neither a packing crate nor a window. The handleless door was set into a blank brick wall. The wall was only blank in the sense that there were no windows in it. It wasn't blank like the canvas that had been switched for A. C. Pryden's portrait of Mad Uncle Jack. There was an advertisement painted directly onto the brickwork which read:

ALWAYS USE
OLD ROXBEE'S
SAFETY MATCHES.

It looked like it had been there a long time, but that – unlike the writing on the door – the black lettering had been regularly touched up with paint to keep it looking fresh.

Eddie was no expert on the subtleties of advertising but, the more he looked at it, the more puzzled he was by this advertisement. Firstly, most advertisements painted on the side of buildings were painted high up for all to see, not at chest and head height. Secondly, such adverts were usually painted on main roads or at least where lots of passers-by would pass by ... not down some narrow little alleyway.

Eddie was beginning to wonder whether he was seeing mysteries where none existed. Maybe there was a perfectly good reason for Dr Moot to have been on a bus, rather than in his pony and trap, speaking to Scarple. And what business of Eddie's was it if Gherkin dressed as a child? He'd worked in a team of tumblers hadn't he? And they must have worn costumes ... Maybe he'd always played the role of a youngster in 'The Remarkably Small Garfields', and wore the outfit occasionally, whilst hankering after the good old days?

Eddie heard a sound, and managed to duck into another doorway, just as the door by the Old Roxbee's safety match advert swung open. Gherkin emerged, clutching a brown paper parcel under his left arm. He nipped back down the alley the way he'd come. Once the dwarf had reached the street and turned left, in the opposite direction to the police station, Eddie broke his cover and ran up the alley after him.

Eddie found that he was very good at not being noticed. The moment he sensed or suspected that Gherkin might be about to look around, Eddie would duck into a doorway, or look into a shop window, or obscure himself behind an object or person and, on one occasion, a sheep on a lead, which tried to bite him. Its owner – a smartly dressed haughty woman whose expression seemed to dare him to ask her what on Earth she was doing taking a sheep for a walk – scowled at him, which seemed to suggest that he shouldn't tempt Isobel (her name was engraved on a tag on her collar) by putting his biteable human body so close to the animal's teeth. Remembering some Scottish police sheep of yesteryear, Eddie wondered why no one reminded sheep the world over that they were supposed to be herbivores, but his mind was soon back on his task.

Eddie suspected that Gherkin might have recognised him when he'd stepped on the dwarf's foot by the side of the police station, but didn't think that he knew that he was following him. Gherkin – whatever he was up to – was being

487

generally cautious, rather than watching out for Eddie in particular.

They were nearing the eastern outskirts of the town now, where there were far fewer pedestrians on the pavements, more trees and less traffic on the roads. Gherkin, who'd been moving at a pace which had left Eddie a little breathless, now came to a halt at the corner of Corncrake Avenue and the Lamberley Road. Eddie looked at the house on the corner. He recognised it immediately. It had been the home and medical practice of the late Dr Humple, but the brand-new brass plaque screwed onto the brick and plaster gatepost read: DR SAMUEL MOOT.

All roads lead to Moo-Cow Moot, thought Eddie, wondering what would happen next.

Gherkin had been busy unwrapping the brown-paper parcel. From it he produced what appeared to be a very large stick of dynamite.

Episode 14

Den of Thieves

*In which Eddie sees various acquaintances
in a different light*

I expect many of you have heard of the Nobel
Prize for Peace, and some of you may also have
heard of other Nobel Prizes, including the Nobel
Prize for Literature. (I wonder how long before
I have to go to Stockholm and accept that little
award? Perhaps I should start on my acceptance
speech just as soon as I've finished this book.) I
expect far fewer of you knew that the prizes are
named after Alfred Nobel, the Swedish inventor of
dynamite. (I know YOU knew, I was talking about
the others.)

The story goes that, feeling guilty about the
death and destruction his explosive invention
caused – which had many peaceful applications,

including mining – he decided to give large sums of money to recognise the higher achievements of Mankind with a capital M (which, in Swedish is Mänskligheten with a capital M). Which would all be very interesting if what Eddie could see Gherkin holding was the stick of dynamite it appeared to be.

Eddie's first thought was to go straight back to the police station to get help. By the time he'd run all the way back there, managed to convince someone to take him seriously – some of the peelers Eddie had met over the years weren't the most shining examples of the human race – and had then run all the way back *here* again, however, it would be far too late. Gherkin would have done whatever it was he was going to do. Eddie should have known that there was something odd about an official mourner who'd been given a card by Mad Uncle Jack forty or fifty (or however many years) ago it had been, suddenly turning up out of the blue like that. The trouble was, living with such a potty family, it was easy to forget what *normal* behaviour was. A dwarf dressed as a child with what appeared to be a huge lollipop in one hand and a stick of dynamite in the other could only be classed as normal by Dickens family standards.

With the remarkable agility of an ex-acrobat, Gherkin leapt over the side wall into Dr Moot's front garden. There was a rustling through the laurel bushes, like ripples on the surface of water hinting at hidden activity below, then he appeared beneath a large bay window. The only difference was that he was now holding a match in his right hand instead of the lolly. He lit the fuse.

'NO!!!' shouted Eddie, running through the gate. 'STOP!'

This didn't have the desired effect. The opposite, in fact. An angry-looking man threw open the bottom sash window in the middle of the bay, and demanded. 'What's the meanin' of this?'

And Gherkin took the opportunity to throw the stick into the house, fuse burning. Eddie, meanwhile, threw himself to the pavement, waiting for the bang . . .

. . . that never came. The room, however, began to fill with smoke. It billowed from the window in great clouds. The front door flew open and the angry man, the bandaged Doctor Moot and Harry Scarple ran down the stairs. Before the first man's foot touched the garden path, Gherkin had jumped up, caught the windowsill and back-flipped up and in through the open window.

To say that Eddie's head was in a spin would be like saying that an ostrich is slightly larger than the average chicken. He didn't know who to trust or what to think, so he decided the best thing to do was to hide. He dived into a bush in the garden next door, just before the three men dashed out onto the pavement; which was when he got his next surprise.

'Sssssh!' said a voice, with great authority.

Eddie turned in amazement to find that Detective Chief Inspector Bunyon had claimed the hiding place before him. (Weren't you wondering if he might turn up? I certainly was.)

Eddie ssssh-ed.

'Who threw the bomb, did you see?' spluttered Scarple.

'Na,' said the angry man. 'There was a saucer-eyed kid out 'ere shoutin', but 'e didn't throw nuffink.' He coughed a bit.

'That'll be Eddie – young Edmund Dickens,' said the chimney-sweep.

'You don't think he –?'

'He don't know nothing, Moot, calm down . . . and that weren't no bomb, Thunk.'

Thunk? thought Eddie. Who's Thunk? Has a fourth man come out of the house?

'Then what was it 'arry? 'Cos I'd say old Moot's 'ouse 'as gone up in smoke!' said Scarple.

Just a minute, thought Eddie. I thought Scarple's name was Harry, and why is this other Harry calling him Thunk?

'It's an hincendiary device, that's what that is,' said Harry, the angry man.

492

'An hincendiary device?'

'An incendiary device,' said Doctor Moot. 'Something which starts fires.'

'Well, it's certainly done that,' said Scarple.

''Ere, 'old on! I ain't so sure, Thunk. 'Ave you actually seen any flames?'

'Well, I've seen plenty of smoke, 'arry, and there's ain't no smoke without fire!'

'Harry's right!' gasped Moot. 'We've been tricked! Come on!'

'Where?'

'Back inside, of course!'

'Are you mad, Moot? You're supposed to run outa burnin' buildin's. Not into 'em!'

There was a sound of footsteps as the three men ran back up the black-and-white tiled garden path.

'Stay put,' Detective Chief Inspector Bunyon whispered in Eddie's ear. Eddie repositioned himself so that a particularly spiky branch stopped jabbing him so painfully in the ribs but, apart from that, stayed right where he was. So did the policeman. Even from his cramped position, Eddie could tell that the detective chief inspector had gained an impressive amount of weight since he'd last seen him, but was still nowhere as large as he'd been during their first encounter. Still, it was fortunate that it was such a large bush.

They sat in silence for a while. No one appeared

to come in or out again but, through the leaves, Eddie could see Harry Scarple opening some of the ground floor windows to let the smoke escape.

Eventually, Bunyon spoke. 'Time we made our exit,' he said. 'Follow me.' He crawled out of the bush on his hands and knees, and – still in this position, crawled out through the gate of Dr Moot's neighbour, and onto the pavement. Eddie did the same. A revolver fell from the detective's pocket.

Without a word, he picked it up and slipped it back inside his checked jacket. 'This way,' he said. They crawled along the pavement, further from the medical practice. When Bunyon deemed that they were a safe enough distance, he stood up, dusting down his trousers. Eddie removed a twig from his hair. A passing group of philosophers eyed them suspiciously.

'Good afternoon,' they said as one.

'Good afternoon,' said the detective chief inspector. He led Eddie to the corner of Wisteria Road where a covered carriage was waiting. 'Get in,' he said.

No sooner had Eddie shut the door than the horse trotted off. He – Eddie, not the horse (which was a *she* called Moonlight, anyway) – had a whole host of questions to ask the policeman.

Bunyon obviously guessed as much, and put up his hand for silence. 'I don't know what you thought you saw back there, Master Dickens, but one thing you can be sure of is that nothing is what it seems.'

'What I do know I saw was a dwarf calling himself Gherkin, dressed as a child, throw what looked like a stick of dynamite – which he got from a building a stone's throw from your own police station, sir – but which may have been some kind of smoke bomb, and –'

'It was a modified plumber's mate,' said Bunyon, as the carriage went over a bump.

Now, you might be forgiven for thinking that a plumber's mate was someone who held the plumber's bag of plumbery tools for him, or went for a drink with him after a hard day of strangling pipes, but you'd be wrong. What Bunyon was refering to was a plumber's smoke rocket. Those of you familiar with Victorian plumbing methods and readers of the first Sherlock Holmes short story, *A Scandal in Bohemia*, will know that a plumber's smoke rocket was a kind of smoke bomb fired up pipes to reveal holes (the smoke coming out of them). In the aforementioned story, Sherlock Holmes sets one off to trick a woman into thinking her house is on fire so that she'll rescue an important photograph, thus revealing its hidden whereabouts.

'They make very effective smoke bombs,' said the detective.

'But why?' asked Eddie. 'And –' He stopped. The detective had obviously positioned himself in the bush before Gherkin had arrived. He knew exactly what Gherkin had thrown through the window. He'd been *expecting* him. 'How did you know this was going to happen?'

'How did I know this was going to happen?' asked Bunyon.

'How did you know this was going to happen?' repeated Eddie.

'A good policeman has plenty of underworld informants,' said Bunyon, 'People who'll sell their own mothers for the price of a drink.'

Eddie thought for a moment. 'I don't think any underworld informant told you about Gherkin. I think he's working for you!'

Detective Chief Inspector Bunyon glared at Eddie. 'Think he's working for me? We do have height requirements in the police force, Master Dickens, and I can assure you that your Mr Gherkin wouldn't reach them.'

'Maybe he's not exactly a policeman,' Eddie suggested, 'simply someone you can use when you need an acrobat who can get through small spaces.'

The chief inspector smiled. 'An acrobat who can get through small spaces . . .'

'I really think you owe it to me to tell me, sir. I've already been in a fight with Mr Scarple, or Thunk, or whatever his name is . . . I've been fired on in a summerhouse, with cabbages. I've been kicked and jumped on by Mr Peevance –'

Eddie was interrupted by a cry of, 'There he is, sir,' by the driver, and the cab slowed to a halt.

The door opened and Gherkin scrambled in. He looked at Eddie. 'I thought that was you outside the house. You could have ruined everything. What were you –?'

'He followed you,' said Bunyon.

'He can't have!'

'I did,' said Eddie.

The dwarf didn't know whether to be annoyed, or embarrassed or impressed, so he was all three.

'Dr Moot, Harry Scarple and that other man called Harry all have something to do with Mr Pryden's stolen painting, don't they?' said Eddie.

The detective chief inspector looked at Gherkin. Gherkin looked at the detective chief inspector. They both turned to Eddie. 'What stolen painting?' they asked.

The Final Act

In which the curtain rises and the plot is revealed

That had been Friday. It was now Monday evening and, after over a month of preparation and rehearsal, Mr Dickens's play was ready for its opening-night performance. After much deliberation, and a last-minute change of mind, he had entitled it *That's My Boy*. Dawkins had been sent to the local printer to give him the change of title. Unfortunately, Eddie's father hadn't written it down, and Dawkins delivered the message verbally. Unfortunate because, after years of working amongst the clatter of printing presses, Mr Sodkin was a little hard of hearing. The posters and programme came back with the title *That's*

Mabel, and there was nothing much anyone could do about it.

Mr Pumblesnook had suggested that they might make a few last-minute changes to the script, making one of the orphans Mabel, but Eddie's father had argued that this would simply confuse matters, giving the character undue importance. Fabian had come up with the idea that they could write a whole new scene at the beginning in which Eddie's parents – played by Mr and Mrs Pumblesnook – decide that if they have a girl they'll call her Mabel, and if it's a boy they'll call him Edmund. 'But when Eddie's born they still mistakenly call him Mabel once in a while.' Laudanum Dickens hadn't been keen on that idea either. In the end, they left the play unaltered and had Mad Uncle Jack's Ex-Privates Dabble, No-Sir, Babcock and Glee cross out the word '*Mabel*' on the programmes and replace it with '*My Boy*'.

The stage itself, however, was most impressive, in the beautiful setting of the lower lawn with the lake beyond.

As Mr Dickens had promised his nephew, Fabian, the audience was made up of family members, both immediate and distant, and friends, including those members of the Thackery family not in prison. What Eddie knew and most others did not was that there were plain-clothed policemen in both the audience and 'mingling' backstage. They were plain clothed in that they were uniformed policemen out of uniform, not from a special division, and Eddie's fear had been that they might have stuck out like sore thumbs. He was impressed, however, by how well they blended in with the other misfits around them.

Mad Uncle Jack and Even Madder Aunt Maud sat in the front row. Dawkins sat next to EMAM with Annabelle on his lap. He just knew that she was going to bite him. It was only a matter of *when*. Even Madder Aunt Maud looked incomplete. It's the only way to describe it; rather like encountering someone you've only ever known with a beard after they've shaved it off. She was without Malcolm. She was Malcolmless. She hadn't seen him since Friday, when she'd been out walking with MUJ before Peevance had started firing those cabbages. She felt heartbroken. Guilty. Forlorn. How could she have put a baby crocodile – anyone or anything – above her beloved Malcolm? Now she was paying the price. She picked up her programme (which had somehow remained uncorrected). '*That's Mabel*: Being The Dramatic Early Years Of My Only Son Edmund,' she read. 'Excellent title!'

'Ridiculous!' snorted Mad Uncle Jack.

Backstage, Eddie was jiggling from one foot to

the other. Mr Pumblesnook gave him such a hearty slap on the back that Eddie could have sworn his teeth rattled.

'Nervous, me boy?' he asked.

'Very,' said Eddie. What he didn't say was that, quite apart from the play, he was nervous about what Dr Moot and others had in store, and what the detective chief inspector had in store for *them*.

'Stagefright is what fuels some of the great actors of our generation,' Mr Pumblesnook tried to reassure him. 'Frockle swears that his performances would be a mere shadow of what they are without the benefit of stagefright.'

Eddie wondered whether the actor-manager had made up Frockle on the spot. Frockle certainly sounded like a made-up name.

'Five minutes to curtain, Mr Pumblesnook,' said a boy a year or two younger than Eddie. A former inmate of St Horrid's, he'd only just been promoted to assistant stage manager since the boy who'd been *supposed* to be doing the job had disappeared.

'Thank you, Fishy!' said Mr Pumblesnook, the boy's name being Turbot. 'Nothing beats the excitement of a first night,' he said with the same enthusiasm that he'd said that nothing beat the excitement of the first read-through of a new play, or the first dress rehearsal, or a hundred-

and-one other things theatrical.

'Don't forget the announcement,' said Eddie.

'Your father's speech? How could I?'

'I mean the announcement of the reward for anyone who finds Malcolm. Mad Aunt Maud insisted that it be done before the curtain goes up, and by you. She's a great admirer of your performing skills, as you know.'

'She first saw me as Pompom in *All About Alex* if memory serves,' said the actor-manager, warming to EMAM once again now that rehearsals were over. 'She came up to me afterwards and presented me with a pair of opera glasses she'd stolen from the seat in front of her. Most generous.' He meant it.

'Positions, please!' said Fishy Turbot. The curtain was ready to rise.

Mr Pumblesnook walked onto the stage amid cheers from those he'd ordered to cheer, and ripples of polite applause from the others.

His speech was incredibly long and remarkably boring so let me give you the edited highlights, which are quite enough, I promise you.

'Ladies and gentlemen. Firstly, let me welcome you to the beautiful grounds of Awful End, as the guest of . . . *blah, blah, blah* . . . Secondly, let me introduce myself . . . *blah, blah, blah* . . . Tonight is a very special night. It's special, because the play you are about to see was written by Mr Laudanum Dickens about his own son, Edmund. And, if that weren't enough, not only will Edmund be playing the part of himself, but also, other members of the cast shall also be reliving events in which they too participated . . . *blah, blah, blah* . . . and so to one correction, and one announcement. The first concerns the title of the play as it is printed upon the programmes you have before you . . . *blah, blah, blah* . . . The second concerns a missing stuffed stoat –'

'My Malcolm!' shouted EMAM, leaping to her feet. 'There's a substantial reward –'

'– and no questions will be asked of the one returning it,' said Mr Pumblesnook, attempting to seize back control of the moment.

'*Him*,' said EMAM.

'Him,' said the actor-manager, finally winding up his speech, with an all-that-it-remains-for-me-to-do section that lasted another eight-and-a-half minutes. Then it was curtains up.

Bunyon and Gherkin may not have known about the theft of A. C. Pryden's portrait of MUJ, but they certainly knew plenty about Harry 'Thunk' Scarple, Harry 'The Fingers' Morton and Doctor Samuel 'Moo-Cow' Moot.

'Scarple's called Thunk for two reasons,' Bunyon had told Eddie in the back of the carriage. 'First off, he got the nickname from falling down chimneys so often. It's the sound he makes when he hits the hearth. Secondly, as far as Harry Morton is concerned, he wants to be the only Harry in their little gang, and what he says goes.'

'What about the doctor?' Eddie had asked.

'No criminal record. We thought at first that Scarple and Morton might have been blackmailing him, then Gherkin discovered that it was revenge.'

'He's going to help them strip Awful End of all its finery,' the dwarf had explained.

'But revenge for what?' Eddie had said. 'He was the one who shot Mad Uncle Jack twice –'

'But on the one occasion,' Bunyon and Gherkin had said, together.

'Don't forget that your great-uncle won the ultimate prize, though, Master Edmund.'

'Even Madder Aunt Maud?'

'Even Madder Aunt Maud.'

Eddie found it hard to imagine his great-aunt as a prize. 'But, surely, if Dr Moot is as in love with Mad Aunt Maud as he claims to be, he wouldn't want to upset her by robbing her home?'

'Years of jealousy can do terrible things to a person,' said Gherkin. 'Dr Moot stopped seeing things straight long before your Aunt Hester hit him over the head with the end of the steakbeater. He has grown so jealous of Mad Major Dickens that it was easy for Thunk and Morton to get him to be their "inside man" on the job.'

Eddie had frowned at this. 'But if my Uncle Alfie hadn't been so ill, we'd never have called Dr Moot to Awful End.'

'It didn't matter. If Moot hadn't had the good fortune of being asked to attend your poor uncle, he'd have simply turned up on your front doorstep one day. He would have claimed it was a courtesy call: an old acquaintance taking over the medical practice and that. Once he had his foot in the door, he'd be able to return.'

The carriage had pulled up beside what turned out to be the other end of the alley that Eddie had followed Gherkin down. The three of them had stepped out, and Eddie had followed them through the door (almost) marked 'PRIVATE PROPERTY' (which was opened from the inside after Bunyon knocked on it with a series of *rat-a-*

tat-tats). He found himself in the back of the police station.

'Saves me being seen walking through the front entrance,' Gherkin had explained. 'I don't want everyone knowing my business now, do I?'

This had led Eddie to ask the question he'd been dying to ask: why Gherkin had thrown the makeshift smoke bomb through the window. He'd guessed that it was to get them out of the house, but *why* exactly?

'We've had our eye on those three for a while,' the detective inspector – sorry, the detective *chief* inspector – had said, leading them into his office. 'It soon became obvious that their latest target was your home, but we want to catch them red-handed, so they can't deny it –'

'Which is why we did nothing to stop them getting that poor deranged Mr Peevance out of debtors' prison,' Gherkin had added.

'Precisely. But then Larkin disappeared.'

'Larkin?'

'Larkin. Larry Larkin. A member of Mr Pumblesnook's group of wandering theatricals.'

'Oh, I know who you mean,' Eddie had nodded. 'He's – he *was* – the assistant stage manager. I remember Mrs Pumblesnook saying that he'd gone missing. She didn't seem too concerned. She said he'd wandered off for a few days once before.'

'That's as maybe,' Gherkin had said.

'Maybe,' Bunyon had added, 'but we wanted to make sure that the boy hadn't overheard something he shouldn't, and been kidnapped by the gang. Morton, Scarple and Moot aren't murderers, but they may not be averse to locking some poor child up in a back room, so we had to be sure.' The detective chief inspector had personal experience of being locked in a trunk (against his will, obviously).

'But you couldn't send a bunch of peelers bursting in on them, because they'd know the game is up . . . so you did the smoke trick?'

'And in I went, only to find absolutely nothing. Which means they're either holding Larkin elsewhere, or he really has just wandered off for a few days.'

This had been a lot of information for Eddie to take in, but it all seemed to make a certain kind of sense. 'But won't the smoke trick make them suspicious that *something*'s going on?' he'd asked, just as the detective inspector had gone to sit on a large pile of books, which began to topple. The policeman grabbed the nearest thing, which was a bust of Queen Victoria, and both he and Her Majesty would have hit the floorboards if the acrobatic dwarf hadn't sprung to their rescue.

'A point well made, Master Edmund,' Bunyon had continued, completely unruffled as though nothing had happened. 'Which is why we had the foresight to attach a note to the plumber's mate.'

The next obvious question was: 'What did it say?', so Eddie had asked it.

'MOOT GO HOME. WE DON'T WANT YOUR KIND HERE,' Gherkin had replied, with a mischievous grin.

'What kind is he?'

'That's the beauty of it, young Edmund. He can be any kind you like. The note could be from someone who doesn't like doctors, or droopy moustaches, or the way he pronounces his "r"s . . . He'll be racking his brains trying to work out who's got it in for him and why.'

'That's very clever,' Eddie had said.

'Ingenious,' Gherkin had agreed. 'It was the detective chief inspector's idea.'

See, dear readers? I told you he was a good policeman.

'We've also been surprisingly successful at eavesdropping on some of their conversations,' Bunyon had added. He'd straightened up the pile of books – gazetteers – and was gently lowering himself into a sitting position. 'And we know that they plan to steal whatever they plan to steal – in addition to the painting you tell us that they have already stolen – tomorrow evening during the first performance of *That's Mabel*.'

'*That's My Boy*,' Eddie had corrected him.

'That's not what it says on the posters and programmes,' Gherkin had told him.

Oh dear, Eddie had thought. Oh dear.

★

And now the curtain was up and the play had begun. Eddie was still wondering what 'valuables' the gang of three were after. It wasn't as though Awful End was one of those country houses stuffed with treasures and family heirlooms. MUJ and EMAM had rather a different approach to things. They liked what they liked and valued what they valued, regardless of its so-called value in the wider world. When Even Madder Aunt Maud was to die, many, many, many years after the events in this book, she was buried with her most treasured possession: a tatty old stuffed stoat. One of Mad Uncle Jack's most prized objects was a prune stone: the first thing his beloved Maud ever spat at him. If you're a sentimental old thing like me, you might be moved to tears by such things and mutter 'a price beyond rubies' into the nearest beard. If you're a thief, however, you might be annoyed and demand, 'Where's the good stuff?'

Mad Uncle Jack did have a safe – made by Dullard & Fisk of Birmingham in 1863 (according to the big metal badge-like thingumy on the front of it) –

but he'd long since forgotten what was in it and lost the key. But there were also some valuable – in the money-money-money sense – pieces of silver and oil paintings to be had. And to have them, Harry Morton intended.

Episode 16

The Grand Finale

*In which the final curtain falls on
Eddie's Further Adventures*

Now, the more eagle-eyed amongst you might just have spotted that the illustration above is not a David Roberts original. In truth, some of you might not consider it an illustration at all. I confess: I drew it myself. Why? I'll tell you why, because David is a very busy man – he must have a cleaning job on the side, or something – so he agreed to do a certain number of pictures for this book, and no more. Then, because there was *so* much to fit into this final adventure, I had to make the book a little longer than I thought I would . . . and there aren't enough pictures to go round. But will I let a small thing such as that defeat me? No way. Let the story continue.

Whilst all eyes were (apparently) on the stage, the lovely Daniella's father and Harry Morton were studying the safe in what had once been MUJ's study. Dr Moot had told them exactly where he'd found it and they went straight there. They weren't even going to attempt to open the safe in the study. The plan was to take it elsewhere and then to blow the door off with dynamite. The whole point of a safe was that it was designed to be difficult to move. This particular one wasn't bolted to the floor or set in concrete, but it was incredibly heavy. The two Harrys had come armed with some special kind of hoist (or lifting device) and a very tough-looking metal trolley to wheel it away on.

Whilst Eddie was performing on the stage in the grounds in an early scene (where he learns that his parents have gone yellow, crinkly around the edges and smell of old hot-water bottles), Scarple and Morton managed to ease the safe onto the trolley. It was hard work, and they'd worked up a good sweat.

'Now what?' asked Scarple.

'We sticks to the plan, that's what, Thunk.'

'Remind me.'

'The solid silver stuff in the back of them cupboards Moo-Cow told us about.' Morton unfolded a rough plan of some of the rooms that Dr Moot had sketched out for them. 'Our very own treasure map,' he grinned.

They hurried from room to room, putting their booty into the large sack that they'd initially used to carry the hoist into the house.

'Beats workin' for a livin',' said the chimney-sweep with a smile. Next, they started taking the oil paintings off the walls.

Now came the tricky part. With everyone outside and them inside, knowing exactly where the 'good stuff' was, they could work quickly and efficiently, but now they had to get the stuff out of the house and off the grounds.

Fortunately for this pair of thieves, there was an ancient path crossing the Dickens estate, which anyone and everyone had a right to walk along (or ride a horse along, though not a mule or a donkey, apparently) without permission. At one point, it passed surprisingly close to the house itself, and – to give the Dickenses some privacy – hedges had been planted either side of it for this stretch. What's more, it was on the opposite side of the house to the stage.

Part of the plan was simply to tie off the end of the silver-filled sack and to toss it over the hedge onto the Way (as the path was called locally). The path was rarely used and they could simply collect their booty later.

Wheeling the trolley off the grounds with the safe and a pile of pictures on top would be a little harder. Morton unfolded the sheet he'd brought with him especially for the occasion and threw it over the trolley. On it was printed:

PUMBLESNOOK'S

If stopped or challenged, they'd claim to be a part of the night's proceedings, moving props and scenery for *That's My Boy*.

Harry Morton admired his own handiwork, straightening the sheet at one corner. 'A very professional job though I says so meself, Thu–'

There was a crash from the next room, as though someone had kicked a vase or something. Scarple dashed over to the door, as nimbly and as silently as his limp allowed. There was no point in hiding and hoping that whoever it might be would go away. They'd left the sack in there, and they weren't about to give it up without a fight.

Scarple looked left and right; under the table and behind the door; and even in a cupboard or two. No one. He tied off the top of the sack, and headed for the back door. 'I'll just toss this onto the Way, an' be right back,' he told Morton. The sack was good and heavy, and Daniella's father was thinking of all the lovely things this silver would buy.

It was some twenty-five minutes later, when the two thieves were pushing the heavily-laden trolley across a stretch of grass, that Even Madder Aunt Maud went and spoiled everything. The play had reached the stage where Malcolm appeared, and the sight of a pretend Malcolm made her pine for the real one even more keenly. She'd got up from her seat and gone for a walk.

Morton – who was, most definitely, the brains of the outfit – hadn't taken into consideration the effect the weight of the safe on the trolley might have when moving it. The plan had been to wheel it boldly down the gravel drive, but you try wheeling something that heavy down gravel. It sank like a stubborn elephant digging its heels in (if elephants have heels). They were lucky that they even managed to get it off the drive and back into the house. This change of plan meant that they'd have to push it across grass, including a small stretch that would be in full view of anyone in the audience who chose to glance to their left . . .

. . . and now here was Mad Aunt Maud.

'Beautiful evenin', ma'am,' said Morton, raising his cap.

'Drop dead,' she said.

'I beg your pardon?' said Morton, with righteous indignation.

'Not you, nincompoop,' she muttered. 'I was talking to myself.'

The two Harrys dared not stop pushing the

trolley, for fear of it sinking into the lawn and becoming lodged. The upper lawn was on a slight slope, sweeping down to the lower lawn and the ornamental lake. Their rather one-sided conversation with EMAM caused a momentary lapse in concentration. Morton let go of the trolley just as it started to roll down the slope, Scarple running to keep up with it, his hands still on the handle. Morton reached out and grabbed it too, but the laws of physics dictate that something feels a lot heavier if it's rolling down hill gathering speed. (But don't put that in an answer to an exam question, just in case I'm wrong.) Soon both men were forced to let go of the trolley as it gathered nuts in May.* They chased after it and so did Eddie's great-aunt.

'This is fun!' she screeched.

It was her shout which made a member of the audience look up and see a large trolley hurtling towards the rows of people watching the first-night performance. The man in question, Johnny Bluff, had been a big game hunter. He'd loved endangering species in Africa and India, until one day his rifle jammed and he was charged by a very angry bull elephant indeed. He'd escaped with his life, and a few squashed toes, but had become

* I'm sorry, that should, of course, read momentum.

a bag of nerves ... and now something else was charging his way.

'Elephant attack!' he shouted, leaping to his feet.

Even Mr Pumblesnook would have been hard-pressed keeping all eyes on the stage with that interruption. In fact, this was one of the rare moments when the actor-manager was in the wings.

The audience jumped up and scattered, knocking chairs hither and thither (which is not dissimilar to here, there and everywhere).

Logically, this would have been the moment for Harry 'The Fingers' Morton and Harry 'Thunk' Scarple to turn and run. They must have known in their heart of hearts that the safe and its contents were never going to be theirs after all. But human nature's not like that. You let go of something and it runs away, and you chase after it, so on they went, through the small crowd and beyond.

The own-clothed policemen dropped all pretence of being friends, relatives or theatre-lovers and gave chase, but – jumping from the edge of the stage – Eddie had a head start . . . which is how he came to be only seconds behind Morton when the thief tripped over something, and fell.

The something in question was the tail of some kind of stuffed stoat, which had been buried in the mud, nose-first, by a young crocodile, perhaps intent on removing a rival to her mistress's affections. (Who knows what goes on in the mind of a young female crocodile? Not I.)

'Malcolm!' screeched Even Madder Aunt Maud, redder-faced from all that running than any beetroot's face could ever be. She pulled him out of the ground like a gardener plucks out a carrot, and there followed a reunion to rival any scene – romantic or sentimental – in any film/movie/flick/ motion picture ever made.

Eddie's father, meanwhile, had nabbed Morton before he'd fully struggled to his feet. The rage at his play being interrupted was so great that it seemed to give him super-human strength. If someone had been in a position to hand him a baby grand piano there and then, he felt that he could have ripped it in two. With his teeth. Holding on to a snarling villain was a piece of cake/a stroll in the park/a walk in the rain.

Which left the chimney-sweep Scarple who, true to his nickname Thunk, was the victim of yet another little accident. The trolley must also have hit Malcolm and the safe had lurched off it, landing on him with a loud 'thunk!', of all things. The force of the jolt had also made the door fly open. I'll write that again, just to make sure you got it: *made the door fly open*. The safe had been unlocked all the time. Its contents were now littered across the grass.

520

A puzzled Eddie picked up a square black object, the size of a floor tile. It *was* a black floor tile, and the safe had been full of them. Now where in heavens could they have come from? Your guess is as good as mine. As to why Mad Uncle Jack had put them in the safe in the first place, I doubt even he knew. Anyone who's journeyed through all six Eddie Dickens books with me will know that M-a-d at the start of his name is there for a reason.

'You're both under arrest,' said Detective Chief Inspector Bunyon, arriving on the scene at last, a little out of breath.

'What for?' sneered Morton. 'Wheelin' a bunch of floor tiles around a garden? What will we get for that, then? A slap on the wrist?'

'What about this, then?' said Bunyon, stepping aside to let two officers bring forward a large sack between them. 'Once you threw that sack over the hedge into the Way, you'd taken it off Major Dickens's property without permission. There's a word for that: theft.'

'Prove it was us what threw it,' said Morton.

'Yeah,' said Scarple trying to sound defiant, but they could tell that he had no fight in him.

Bunyon opened the sack, then, looking into it, opened his eyes wide with surprise. The sack started to *move*.

'You!' gasped Scarple, as Gherkin stepped out of the sack and into the evening air, as though it was the most natural thing in the world.

The dwarf was nursing a nasty bump on his head. 'Not the best place to hide under the circumstances, I'll admit,' he said. 'But the one place you didn't look ... *and* I was able to hear everything you two villains said, whilst, at the same time, keeping the stolen silver in sight.'

Detective Chief Inspector Bunyon gave the two Harrys the benefit of one of his withering stares. 'So now all you have to do is tell us what you did with the painting, and –'

'They don't have the painting,' said Eddie.

'Wh–?' said Gherkin.

'–at?' said Bunyon.

Eddie walked over to A. C. Pryden who was standing amongst the semicircle of onlookers who had gathered round. 'I only realised it this afternoon, Mr Pryden, but there was something wrong with your story about leaving the picture while you went to get some more writing paper downstairs. You wanted the picture to *appear* to have been stolen, without any of us in the household being under suspicion. That's why you seized the opportunity to say it had been stolen at a time when we all had alibis, as we gathered together on the lawn. That's why you didn't want the police involved. That's why you were reluctant to speak to Mr Peevance in his police cell. You knew he had nothing to do with it.'

'Is this true, sir?' demanded Bunyon, whose men had now freed Scarple from beneath the safe and were putting him in handcuffs.

'Yes,' said the painter, sounding like the most guilty penguin anyone of us is ever likely to meet.

'But why? That's what I don't understand,' said Eddie.

By way of an answer, A. C. Pryden stuck his hand in a pocket and pulled out a crumpled letter. He handed it to the detective chief inspector.

'Can't read,' he said, handing it to the desk sergeant, who thought that it was jolly unfair of him to have been called away from his desk. (And he didn't like not wearing his uniform with the lovely shiny buttons either.) 'Won't read,' he said, passing it to Eddie. So Eddie read it. Aloud.

'*Dear Mr Pryden, I regret to inform you that, due to a simple clerical error, you have been commissioned to paint a portrait of the wrong Major Dickens.*' Eddie gulped. '*Whilst it was the War Office's intention that you paint Major* Jock *Dickens, a fine soldier who has distinguished himself in a series of campaigns during an illustrious career spanning many decades –*' Eddie paused at this point. He wasn't sure that he wanted to read any more out loud.

'A typing error meant that you ended up painting my uncle instead?' said his father.

'That's the gist of it,' the portrait painter nodded. 'And I felt it would be shabby and disrespectful to simply pack up and leave, but neither did I want a public unveiling. If I could convince you in the family that the painting had gone, then those at the War Office could inform the Major themselves, at a more appropriate time and in a more respectful manner.'

'Very noble sentiments indeed, but you could have wasted valuable police time,' said Bunyon. 'However, seeing as how things have worked out . . .'

'Thank you,' said Pryden.

When Malcolm had been washed, Harry 'The Fingers' Morton and Harry 'Thunk' Scarple taken off to the police station (and Moot arrested in Harborough Wensley, trying to pretend that he was someone else, simply by having shaved off his moustache), Fabian asked Eddie the all-important question: 'What was it that Mr Pryden said that made you realise that he'd made up the whole thing about the painting having been stolen?'

And here's the sad part. I've no idea what Eddie's reply was.

A shame that. There's no record of his explanation anywhere that I could find.

Still, this isn't a detective novel with all the suspects gathered in the library for the grand unmasking. This is an Eddie Dickens adventure. We're here for . . . for . . . What are we here for? Now, that would be a profound question to end on.

★

But I can't leave it there, of course. There are plenty of other questions I *can* answer. I can, for example tell you that, though the first night's performance of *That's Mabel* was abandoned, despite Mr and Mrs Pumblesnook's chorus of 'The show must go on!', it was performed two nights later (on the Wednesday). It was, by all accounts, appalling. The writing was patchy to say the least, and Mr Pumblesnook performing so many of the meaty roles led to terrible confusion as to who he was supposed to be when, especially during the scenes where he was playing three or more characters on stage at the same time. Eddie managed to remember all of his lines and put in a creditable performance.

Mad Uncle Jack said to him afterwards, 'You made a very believable Edmund Dickens, young man. Please call upon me one day at your convenience.' He handed Eddie a dried sea horse.

The missing boy, Larkin, turned up a few days after the abandoned first-night performance, smelling of mothballs. He'd somehow managed to lock himself in an old laundry cupboard in one of the many disused parts of the house.

A week or so later, Gherkin left to work with an Inspector Ryman up north. His working for the police in 'an undercover capacity' meant that, once people knew what he was up to, he had to move elsewhere. The reason why Fabian had thought he'd recognised him that first morning was because their paths had, indeed, crossed fleetingly before. Gherkin had been working for a Sergeant Kelpitt in a part of Hampshire when Fabian's gypsy family had been passing through.

Lance Peevance had, indeed, been unaware of his role in the plan; to cause a distraction whilst Moo-Cow Moot had one last good look around before his accomplices paid a visit. When he was eventually released from prison, he moved to the distant village of Lower Upton (or Upper Lowton) where he led a quiet life, building a little chapel with his own hands, over an eleven-year period. This greatly impressed the other inhabitants, until the building fell down one blustery November morning, injuring the village mascot (a goose called Tawny).

Once Fabian's father stopped eating any more lucky heather, let the rest pass through his system, and (finally) took his medication (in liquid rather than tablet form), he made a splendid recovery. The original cough was cured with some syrup or other. Discovering that Dr Moot had been a no-good scoundrel, Aunt Hetty soon got over the guilt at having nearly brained him.

As for the older Dickenses, they went on doing what the older Dickenses did best. And Eddie? For him, the best was yet to come.

THE END
of the Further Adventures . . .

AUTHOR'S NOTE

You've been a wonderful audience.
Thank you, and goodnight.